*continued . . .*

"Ms. Singh's world-building is as fascinating as the characters with whom she populates it."  —*The Eternal Night*

"Nalini Singh has done it again . . . [A] must read!"
—*Fallen Angel Reviews* (Recommended Read)

## Caressed by Ice

"A sensual, dangerous adventure not to be missed."
—Lora Leigh, *New York Times* bestselling author

"A compelling read with wonderfully developed characters and the strong world-building that has made Singh a star."
—*All About Romance*

"With a truly inspired mix of passion and danger, this story will keep you on the edge of your seat. [It] will surely earn itself a place among your favorites."
—*Romance Reviews Today*

## Visions of Heat

"Breathtaking blend of passion, adventure, and the paranormal. I wished I lived in the world Singh has created. This is a keeper!"
—Gena Showalter, *New York Times* bestselling author

"This author just moved to the top of my auto-buy list."
—*All About Romance*

"Brace yourselves because . . . [it] will set all your senses ablaze and leave your fingers singed with each turn of the page. *Visions of Heat* is that intense!"  —*Romance Junkies*

*continued . . .*

"I don't think there is a single paranormal series as well planned, well written, and downright fantabulous as Ms. Singh's Psy-Changeling series."   —*All About Romance*

# Slave to Sensation

"I LOVE this book! It's a must read for all of my fans. Nalini Singh is a major new talent."
                —Christine Feehan, *New York Times* bestselling author

"An electrifying collision of logic and emotion . . . A volcanic start to a new series that'll leave you craving for more."
                —*Romance Junkies*

"Make room for [*Slave to Sensation*] on your keeper shelf."
                —*Romance Reviews Today*

"A sensual romance set in an alternate reality America with just a bit of mystery to keep readers flipping pages."
                —*Fresh Fiction*

## Berkley Titles by Nalini Singh

### Psy-Changeling Series

SLAVE TO SENSATION
VISIONS OF HEAT
CARESSED BY ICE
MINE TO POSSESS
HOSTAGE TO PLEASURE
BRANDED BY FIRE
BLAZE OF MEMORY
BONDS OF JUSTICE
PLAY OF PASSION

### Guild Hunter Series

ANGELS' BLOOD
ANGELS' PAWN
*(A Berkley Sensation eSpecial)*
ARCHANGEL'S KISS

### Anthologies

AN ENCHANTED SEASON
*(with Maggie Shayne, Erin McCarthy, and Jean Johnson)*
THE MAGICAL CHRISTMAS CAT
*(with Lora Leigh, Erin McCarthy, and Linda Winstead Jones)*
MUST LOVE HELLHOUNDS
*(with Charlaine Harris, Ilona Andrews, and Meljean Brook)*
BURNING UP
*(with Angela Knight, Virginia Kantra, and Meljean Brook)*

# Play of
# Passion

## NALINI SINGH

BERKLEY SENSATION, NEW YORK

**THE BERKLEY PUBLISHING GROUP**
**Published by the Penguin Group**
**Penguin Group (USA) Inc.**
**375 Hudson Street, New York, New York 10014, USA**

Penguin Group (Canada), 90 Eglinton Avenue East, Suite 700, Toronto, Ontario M4P 2Y3, Canada
(a division of Pearson Penguin Canada Inc.)
Penguin Books Ltd., 80 Strand, London WC2R 0RL, England
Penguin Group Ireland, 25 St. Stephen's Green, Dublin 2, Ireland (a division of Penguin Books Ltd.)
Penguin Group (Australia), 250 Camberwell Road, Camberwell, Victoria 3124, Australia
(a division of Pearson Australia Group Pty. Ltd.)
Penguin Books India Pvt. Ltd., 11 Community Centre, Panchsheel Park, New Delhi—110 017, India
Penguin Group (NZ), 67 Apollo Drive, Rosedale, North Shore 0632, New Zealand
(a division of Pearson New Zealand Ltd.)
Penguin Books (South Africa) (Pty.) Ltd., 24 Sturdee Avenue, Rosebank, Johannesburg 2196,
South Africa

Penguin Books Ltd., Registered Offices: 80 Strand, London WC2R 0RL, England

This is a work of fiction. Names, characters, places, and incidents either are the product of the author's imagination or are used fictitiously, and any resemblance to actual persons, living or dead, business establishments, events, or locales is entirely coincidental. The publisher does not have any control over and does not assume any responsibility for author or third-party websites or their content.

PLAY OF PASSION

A Berkley Sensation Book / published by arrangement with the author

PRINTING HISTORY
Berkley Sensation mass-market edition / November 2010

ISBN: 978-0-425-23779-3

BERKLEY® SENSATION
Berkley Sensation Books are published by The Berkley Publishing Group,
a division of Penguin Group (USA) Inc.,
375 Hudson Street, New York, New York 10014.
BERKLEY® SENSATION and the "B" design are trademarks of Penguin Group (USA) Inc.

PRINTED IN THE UNITED STATES OF AMERICA

10  9  8  7  6  5  4  3  2  1

*To two wonderful friends in different corners of the world:*
*Junko, who made sure I wasn't lost in translation;*
*and Cora, who has both courage and heart;*
*with a special shout-out to Cian and Calisto from Roman*
*and Julian*

# CAST OF CHARACTERS

In alphabetical order by first name
*Key: SD = SnowDancer wolves     DR = DarkRiver leopards*

**Abel Riviere** SD soldier, father of Indigo and Evangeline
**Andrew Kincaid** SD tracker, brother of Riley and Brenna
**Anthony Kyriakus** Psy Councilor, father of Faith
**Ashaya Aleine** Psy member of DR, former Council scientist, mated to Dorian
**Ben** SD pup
**Brace** SD juvenile
**Brenna Kincaid** SD tech, mated to Judd, sister of Andrew and Riley
**Devraj Santos** Director of the Shine Foundation, one of the Forgotten (Psy who dropped out of the PsyNet over a hundred years ago and intermarried with the changeling and human populations)
**Dorian Christensen** DR sentinel, mated to Ashaya
**Elias** SD soldier, mated to Yuki, father of Sakura
**Evangeline (Evie) Riviere** SD, sister of Indigo
**Faith NightStar** Psy member of DR, cardinal F-Psy (foreseer), mated to Vaughn, daughter of Anthony
**Ghost** Psy rebel
**Hawke** SD alpha
**Henry Scott** Psy Councilor, husband of Shoshanna
**Indigo Riviere** SD lieutenant, daughter of Abel and Tarah, sister of Evangeline
**Joshua** SD juvenile

**Judd Lauren** Psy member of SD, lieutenant, mated to Brenna, uncle of Sienna, Toby, and Marlee

**Kaleb Krychek** Psy Councilor

**Lara** SD healer

**Lucas Hunter** DR alpha, mated to Sascha

**Lucy** SD, trainee nurse, assistant to Lara

**Matthias** SD lieutenant

**Max Shannon** Human, Nikita's security chief, married to Sophia

**Mercy Smith** DR sentinel, mated to Riley

**Ming LeBon** Psy Councilor

**Nikita Duncan** Psy Councilor, mother of Sascha

**Riaz** SD lieutenant

**Riley Kincaid** SD lieutenant, mated to Mercy, brother of Andrew and Brenna

**Sascha Duncan** Psy member of DR, cardinal empath, mated to Lucas, daughter of Nikita

**Shoshanna Scott** Psy Councilor, wife of Henry

**Sienna Lauren** Psy member of SD, sister of Toby, niece of Judd and Walker

**Silvia** SD juvenile

**Sophia Russo** J-Psy, works for Nikita, married to Max

**Tai** SD, novice soldier

**Tarah Riviere** SD, mother of Indigo and Evangeline

**Tatiana Rika-Smythe** Psy Councilor

**Teijan** Rat alpha

**Walker Lauren** Psy member of SD, father of Marlee, uncle of Sienna and Toby

**Xavier Perez** Human priest

# PURITY

**The Psy have** been pure, have been Silent for over a hundred years, their emotions conditioned out of them until a wall of ice separates them from the world. Passion and love, hate and sorrow are no longer things they know, except as weaknesses of the emotional human and changeling races.

But as winter thaws into spring in the year 2081, change is more than a whisper on the horizon. Too many powerful Psy have defected, too many are breaking conditioning, and too many fractures riddle the Net.

Some say it is inevitable that Silence will fall.

And some will kill to hold it.

# CHAPTER 1

**Indigo wiped the** rain off her face, clearing it for a split second, if that. The torrential downpour continued with relentless fury, slamming ice-cold bullets against her skin and turning the night-dark of the forest impenetrable. Ducking her head, she spoke into the waterproof microphone attached to the sodden collar of her black T-shirt. "Do you have him in your sights?"

The voice that came back was deep, familiar, and, at that instant, lethally focused. "Northwest, half a mile. I'm coming your way."

"Northwest, half a mile," she repeated to ensure they were both on the same page. Changeling hearing was incredibly acute, but the rain was savage, drumming against her skull until even the high-tech receiver she'd tucked into her ear buzzed with noise.

"Indy, be careful. He's functioning on the level of a feral wolf."

Under normal circumstances, she'd have snarled at him for

using that ridiculous nickname. Tonight, she was too worried. "That goes double for you. He hurt you in that first tangle."

"It's only a flesh wound. I'm going quiet now."

Slicking back her hair, she took a deep breath of the watery air and began to stalk toward their prey. Her fellow hunter was right—a pincer maneuver was their best bet of taking Joshua down without damage. Indigo's gut clenched, pain blooming in her heart. She didn't want to have to hurt him. Neither did the tracker on the boy's trail—the reason why the bigger, stronger wolf had been injured in the earlier clash.

But he'd have to if they couldn't bring Joshua back from the edge; the boy was so lost in anguish and torment that he'd given in to his wolf. And the wolf, young and out of control, had taken those emotions and turned them into rage. Joshua was now a threat to the pack. But he was also their own. They'd bleed, they'd drown in this endless rain, but they would not execute him until they'd exhausted every other option.

A branch raked across her cheek when she didn't move fast enough in the stormy weather.

*Sharp. Iron. Blood.*

Indigo swore low under her breath. Joshua would catch her scent if she wasn't careful. Turning her face up to the rain, she let it wash away the blood from the cut. But it was still too bright, too unmistakable a scent. Wincing—their healer would strip her hide for this—she went to the earth and slathered mud over the superficial injury. The scent dulled, became sodden with earth.

It would do. Joshua was so far gone that he wouldn't detect the subtle undertone that remained.

"Where are you?" It was a soundless whisper as she stalked through the rain-lashed night. Joshua hadn't taken a life yet, hadn't killed or maimed. He could be brought back—if his pain, the vivid, overwhelming pain of a young male on the cusp of adulthood, allowed him to return.

A slashing wind . . . bringing with it the scent of her prey. Indigo stepped up her pace, trusting the eyes of the wolf that was her other half, its vision stronger in the dark. She was gaining on the scent when a wolf's enraged howl split the air.

Growls, the sickening clash of teeth, more iron in the air.

"No!" Pushing her speed to dangerous levels, she jumped over fallen logs and new-made streams of mud and water without really seeing them, heading toward the scene of the fight. It took her maybe twenty seconds and a lifetime.

Lightning flashed the instant she reached the small clearing where they fought, and she saw them framed against the electric-dark sky, two changelings in full wolf form, locked in combat. They fell to earth as the lightning died, but she could still see them, her eyes tracking with lethal purpose.

The tracker, the hunter, was bigger, his normally stunning silver-colored fur sodden almost black, but it was the smaller wolf, his pelt a reddish hue, who was winning—because the hunter was holding back, trying not to kill. Aware her drenched clothing would make stripping difficult, Indigo shifted as she was. It was a searing pain and an agonizing joy, her clothes disintegrating off her, her body turning into a shower of light before forming into a sleek wolf with a body built for running.

She jumped into the fight just as the red wolf—Joshua—slashed a line into his opponent's side. The bigger wolf gripped the teenager's neck. He could've killed then, as he could have earlier, but he was attempting only to subdue. Joshua was too far gone to listen; he reached out, trying to go for the hunter's belly. Teeth bared, Indigo leaped. Her paws came down on the smaller wolf, holding his struggling, snarling body to the earth.

She didn't know how long they stood there, holding the violent wolf down, refusing to let him go over that final destructive edge. The hunter's eyes met hers. A brilliant copper in his wolf form, they were so unusual she'd never seen the like in any other wolf, changeling or feral. She glimpsed a piercing intelligence in that gaze, one that many people missed because he laughed so easily, charmed with such open wickedness.

Most in the SnowDancer pack didn't even realize he was their tracker, able to trace rogue wolves through snow, wind, and, tonight, endless rain. And though it was not their practice to call him Hunter, he was that, too, charged with executing those they could not save. But Joshua understood who it was he faced. Because he went silent at long last, his body limp beneath theirs.

Indigo released her grip with care, but he didn't spring up, even when the larger wolf let go. Worried, she shifted back into human form, her hair plastered to her naked back between one instant and the next. The tracker stood guard next to her, his fur rubbing wet against her skin.

"Joshua," she said, leaning down to speak to the boy, determined to bring him back from his wolf. "Your sister is alive. We got her to the infirmary in time."

No recognition in those dark yellow eyes, but Indigo wasn't a SnowDancer lieutenant because she gave up easily. "She's asking for you, so you better snap out of it and get up." She put every ounce of her dominance in her next command. *"Right now."*

A blink from the wolf, a cocked head. As Indigo watched, he rose shakily to his feet. When she reached for him, he lowered his head, whimpering. "Shh," she said, gripping his muzzle and staring straight into those wolf-bright eyes. His gaze slid away. Joshua was too young, too submissive in comparison to her strength, to challenge her in that way.

"I'm not angry," Indigo said, ensuring he heard the truth in her words, in the way she held him—firm, but not in a grip that would cause pain. "But I need you to become human."

Still no eye contact. But he heard her. Because the next instant, the air filled with sparks of light, and a split second after that, a young male barely past his fourteenth birthday was kneeling naked on the earth, his face drawn. "Is she really okay?" It was a rasp, the wolf in his voice.

"Have I ever lied to you?"

"I was meant to be watching her, except I—"

"You weren't at fault." She put her fingers on his jaw, anchoring him with touch, with Pack. "It was a rockfall—*nothing* you could've done. She's got a broken arm, two broken ribs, and a pretty cool scar on her eyebrow that she's already showing off like a peacock."

The recital of injuries seemed to stabilize Joshua. "That sounds like her." A wavering smile, a quick, wary glimpse up at her before he dropped his gaze.

Smiling—because if he was scared about the conse-quences of his actions, he was back—Indigo gave in to her relief and nipped the pup sharply on the ear. He cried out. Then buried his face in her neck. "I'm sorry."

She ran her hand down his back. "It's okay. But if you ever do this again, I'll strip your hide and use it to make new sofa cushions. Got it?"

Another shaky smile, a quick nod. "I want to go home." He swallowed, turned to look at the tracker. "Thanks for not kill-ing me. I'm sorry I made you come out in the rain."

The huge wolf beside Indigo, its tail raised in a gesture of dominance, closed its very dangerous teeth around the boy's throat. Joshua stayed immobile, quiescent, until the tracker let go. Apology accepted.

Making a futile effort to shake the rain from her hair, Indigo looked at the boy. "I don't want you turning wolf for one week." When he looked shattered, she touched his shoulder. "It's not punishment. You went too close to the edge tonight. No use taking chances."

"Okay, yeah." A pause, a whisper of shame in his eyes. "The wolf's getting hard to control. Like I'm a kid again."

That, Indigo thought, explained his irrational response to his sister's accident. She made a mental note to kick some ass on the heels of that thought. Adolescents and young teens did occasionally have control issues—Joshua's teachers should've picked up the signs. "It happens sometimes," she said to him, keeping her tone calm and matter-of-fact. "Did to me when I was around your age, so it's nothing to be ashamed of. You come directly to me if you feel the wolf taking over again." She shifted into her other form as he nodded, his relief obvious.

The journey home to the den—a huge network of tunnels hidden deep underground in California's Sierra Nevada, out of sight of enemy eyes—was quiet, the rain letting up about ten minutes after they began. A human might've slipped and fallen a hundred times on the slippery terrain, but the wolf was sure-footed, its paws designed for increased stability—and it found the easiest route for Joshua.

Indigo, with the tracker taking position behind the boy,

herded Joshua all the way to the wide-open door in the side of
what would otherwise appear to be a sheer rock face—where
his shaken mother was waiting with another wolf, a silver-gold
one with eyes of such pale, pale blue, they were almost ice.

The boy fell to his knees in front of the SnowDancer alpha.

Indigo and the tracker backed away, their task complete.
The pup was safe—and would be taken care of. Now they
needed to run off some of the strain of tonight. She'd really
thought they'd have to kill Joshua. The boy had been all but
insane when they'd managed to corner him earlier. Glancing
toward her companion at the memory—the larger wolf having
kept pace with ease—she realized he was bleeding.

She came to a halt with a snarl. He stopped only a step
later, circling back to nudge her nose with his. Shifting into
human form, she bent over him, pushing back her rain-wet
hair. "You need to see Lara." Their healer would be better
able to check his wounds, ensure they weren't serious.

The wolf nipped at her jaw, growling low in his throat.
She pushed him away. "Don't make me pull rank on you."
Though to be honest, she wasn't sure she could—and that
disturbed both woman and wolf. He occupied an odd space
in their hierarchy. Younger than her, he wasn't a lieutenant,
but he reported directly and only to their alpha. And as their
tracker, his skills were critical to the safety and well-being of
the pack.

Another growl, another nip—this one on her shoulder.

She narrowed her eyes. "Watch it or I'll nip that nose
right off."

He made a growling sound of disagreement, his canines
flashing.

Reaching out, she tapped him sharply on the muzzle.
"We're heading back right now."

Color under her hands, the wolf with fur the distinctive
color of silver-birch bark shifting into a human with lake blue
eyes and rain-slick hair. "I don't think so." He was on her
before she knew it, cupping her face in his hands, his mouth
on hers.

The caress was hot, hard, a slamming fist that held her
motionless. And then . . . an inferno punching through her

body, making her tangle her hand in that thick brown hair, tug back his head. "What," she said on a gasping breath, "are you doing?"

"I thought it'd be obvious." Laughter in his eyes, the lake seared by sunshine as his thumbs stroked over her cheekbones. "I want to lick you up right now."

She didn't take it personally. "You're high on adrenaline from the hunt." Pushing off his hands, she angled her head. "And loss of blood." It ran in a clean, water-diluted line down his side. "You definitely need stitches."

"No, I don't." He kissed her again, pushing her down to the earth.

This time, she didn't back away at once. And got the full impact of the kiss . . . and of the rigid arousal nudging at the sensitive dip of her abdomen. Her heartbeat accelerated, startling her enough that she bit hard at his lip. "It's cold down here." Though the snow had melted away in this part of the range, the Sierra Nevada retained the chill kiss of winter even in the blush of spring.

A repentant look. She found herself on top an instant later. Still being kissed. Groaning at the stubborn wolf—who could kiss so insanely well that she was tempted to let him have at it—she pushed at his shoulders. "Get up before you die of blood loss, you lunatic."

A scowl. And then Drew kissed her *again*.

# CHAPTER 2

**Andrew heard Indigo** moan, felt her body soften a delicious fraction before the lieutenant got herself under control. Pushing off his shoulders, she rolled away to crouch beside him on the forest floor, her namesake eyes bright with the wolf's night-glow gaze. "I'll forgive you for slobbering over me that one time. But do it again and I'll put you on your ass."

"I'm already there." He sat up. "And I seem to recall you slobbering back." Her tongue had been a sleek, fast dart in his mouth before that damn self-discipline of hers had kicked in. "Want to do it some more?"

She pushed back her hair. "I give up. Stay here. Die of blood loss. I'm going to go slip into a nice warm bath and eat the slice of New York cheesecake I bribed Lucy to sneak up to me past the ravaging hordes."

"You have cheesecake?" He prowled over to crouch by her. It was hard, so fucking hard, to pretend this was only a game, to play with her, when all he wanted to do was bury his face in her neck and just . . . be. "Will you share if I come back?"

A low feminine growl that probably would've sent most men packing. "Are you trying to blackmail me?"

"Would I do that?" *Needing* to touch her, he pressed his lips to the skin of her shoulder.

She didn't push him away—a high-ranking female allowing skin privileges to a male she thought needed the anchor. He didn't want to be just another male, just another wolf. But if it would get him near her, then he'd take it . . . for now.

"Indy." Shifting so that he was behind her, he buried his nose in her neck, drawing deep and smiling in savage satisfaction when he scented her alone. No male. She didn't have a lover she'd accepted to that level. He'd already known that, but it was good to have the confirmation. Because he'd made his decision—to stop circling and fight for what he wanted.

And he wanted Indigo.

Smart, dangerous, fascinating Indigo.

Reaching back, she tugged at his hair. "No cheesecake unless you stop using that stupid nickname."

He nipped at her fingers. Got a sigh. "Come on. Let's go home." She shifted under his hands, a beautiful deep gray wolf with eyes that were a startling burnished gold.

Taking a deep breath, he shifted beside her and let her lead them back. Once in the den, she bullied him to the healer and stood there snarling low in her throat until he shifted into human form and let Lara poke and prod at him. Only when Indigo was certain he was behaving did she leave.

His joy dimmed.

He could still feel her skin, silky and wet against his, still taste the wild heat of her mouth. God, but he craved the right to have her. Except that she was a dominant female, the highest-ranking woman in the pack, and he was a male whose dominance level was ambiguous—an unusual situation in a wolf pack, but his work for their alpha depended on him being seen as outside the hierarchy. However, no matter how you cut it, she outranked him; she'd been lieutenant for years. Added to that, she was four years older.

Frustrated at his thoughts, he moped his way back to his rooms when Lara released him, barely noticing the flesh-colored thin-skin bandage the healer had slapped on his side.

He was just getting out of the shower when he heard the door to his room open. Indigo's scent followed a moment later. Rubbing haphazardly at his hair, he wrapped the towel around his waist and walked out to find her sitting cross-legged on his bed, her back to the wall, a huge slice of cheesecake on the saucer she had in her hand.

She was here. In his territory.

Leaning against the bathroom doorway, he just watched her. Her skin was flushed with heat, so she'd taken that bath. And the hair she usually tied up in a ponytail lay sleek and damp down the back of her white T-shirt. Her soft black pajama pants hid the long length of her legs, but Andrew had memorized every lithely muscled inch of her.

"Do you want some or not?" She lifted the fork.

Not stupid enough to refuse, he shot her a smile deliberately laced with pure wickedness. "Let me put on some clothes. Unless you want me naked?"

A feminine snort. "Seen it, felt it, don't want to buy the T-shirt."

The insult cut. He was male, and he wanted her until he could hardly see straight. But he couldn't let her know that, not when she already held all the cards, so he shrugged. "Fine." And dropped the towel.

**Indigo almost choked** on her cheesecake as Drew walked over to the bureau on the other side of the room. Oh . . . *my*. Her eyes couldn't seem to move off his butt. Hard and muscled and bitable. Definitely bitable.

It was all she could do not to moan when he pulled a pair of sweats over that beautiful golden skin, those taut muscles. About to ask him to take the thing off, she realized exactly who it was she was ogling. *What was* wrong *with her?* Horrified, she stabbed the fork into the cheesecake and stuffed a big gob into her mouth just as Drew turned.

There was no longer any humor on his face, and suddenly, she saw not Riley's younger brother, not the laughing, teasing male who could charm every female in the den to get what he wanted, but the tracker who'd hunted down his prey in a storm so harsh even the feral wolves had taken shelter. And he'd never lost the scent—a task she'd have thought impossible given the mix of torrential rain and driving wind.

Shoving his hands through his hair, he walked over to the bed. The muscles at the front of his body, she thought, were as impressive as the ones in the back. But her eyes, right then, were on his face. She couldn't read him, she realized with gut-wrenching shock, not like she could the other young males. But she knew she'd insulted him. Predatory male changelings could be very touchy about that kind of a statement from a female—but that was usually within the confines of a relationship or courtship.

Still . . .

He sprawled beside her, bracing his back against the wall. Turning a little, she scooped up a bite of cheesecake on her fork and lifted it to his mouth. He took it, holding her gaze as she drew the tines out from between his lips. Her body warmed with a slow burn of heat as she remembered those lips on her mouth, strong and confident . . . and tempting.

He flicked out his tongue to lick up a bit of the cream, his eyes never leaving hers. When he sat up and took the fork from her hand, she let him. And when he raised the cheesecake to her lips, she almost let him put the tines to her mouth. Except that the intimacy of the act suddenly hit her with blinding force.

"Drew, we're not—" The cheesecake was in her mouth, the flavors lush and rich, the tines warm as he drew them through her lips oh-so-slowly.

Drew took a long, deep breath. "I can scent your hunger," he murmured, his voice dropping until it scraped over her skin, raw and arousing. "I want to taste it."

Thrown off center by the unexpected, shocking shift in atmosphere, she shook her head even as her muscles seemed to melt, her body aching in a way that had nothing to do with the hunt they'd just completed. "I don't sleep with my subordinates."

"And I don't report to you." Another bite of cheesecake lifted to her lips in teasing promise. "I'm independent of the lieutenant hierarchy."

Her skin tingled, her palms itching to trace the sculptured beauty of his pectorals. It had been so long since she'd had a lover. The pickings weren't exactly plentiful for a dominant changeling female in this region—though since Drew's brother, Riley, had mated with a cat, she'd checked out the leopards, too, even gone on a date or two. None of the men had made her body spark. Not even a little.

But that body was making up for lost time now, her skin seeming to stretch as a voluptuous warmth invaded her very cells, curling through her veins to pulse beneath flesh turned unbearably sensitive. Too long, she thought, shocked at the spread of need, it had simply been too long. "Drew . . ."

His mouth so close, his tongue licking over the seam of her lips to steal a tiny bit of the creamy treat she'd bought into the room. "Let me in, Indy." The heat of him was wild, fresh, young, and it stroked over her like a physical caress.

Groaning, she nudged the next bite to his mouth. "I can't sleep with Riley's baby brother." She wouldn't be able to face her fellow lieutenant when he came back from his trip to South America.

A hard glance out of blue eyes gone a turbulent cobalt. "I'm not a child, Indigo."

She was so startled at his use of her full name that she blinked. "You're too young for me—and I was your trainer, for God's sake."

He snorted. "Next excuse."

The tone of his voice made her hackles rise. "Careful, Drew. I'm not one of your little playmates." He had a harem that tumbled into his bed at the crook of a finger. And they all apparently left happy—none of his former lovers had ever bad-mouthed him. In fact, as far as she knew, they continued to adore him.

"Did I say I wanted a playmate?" Putting the cheesecake carelessly on the mattress on his other side, he reached for her. His fingers were on her jaw and his mouth on hers while she was still forming a response to his snapped question.

The punch of sensation went straight to her gut, but so did the wolf's confusion at the sudden change in this relationship. She pushed against his chest. Of course, since he *was* a predatory changeling male, he kept on kissing her. She could've gotten away, but unwilling to reject him so roughly, she chose to push at him again. He broke off only long enough to say, "You want me. I can scent it." His tongue licked against hers in blunt demand, his free hand closing over the back of her neck as he pressed her to the wall, the heat of his skin burning her through and through.

*A red haze of anger, powerful enough that she had to fight to keep her claws sheathed.*

Wrenching away using the skill and strength that made her one of SnowDancer's most senior lieutenants, she swept off the bed, fury pulsing in every inch of her. The kiss she would have forgiven. Even the pushiness—she understood what he was, wouldn't have penalized him for it. But the hand around her neck, the way he'd tried to use his body to pin hers to the wall, and most of all the arrogance with which he'd taken it as a given that her touch-hunger made her his for the taking? No.

"I," she said, in a tone so calm it took all of her control to maintain it, "haven't given you the right to touch me as you please." There was play . . . and then there were lines you didn't cross. "Next time you try to touch me like that"—in possession, in *ownership*—"be prepared to get that pretty face shredded."

So infuriated she couldn't hear anything but the surge of her own blood, she turned on her heel and left. The worst of it was that she'd trusted Drew, thought he was a friend who accepted and appreciated her for the dominant female she was—but clearly, he was just another cocky young male who thought the lieutenant could be brought to heel by sex. And where she might've easily forgiven everything else, she could not forgive that betrayal.

# CHAPTER 3

**Enclosed within the** privacy of a secure London apartment, Councilor Henry Scott looked across the desk at his "wife," Councilor Shoshanna Scott, and considered the pros and cons of their relationship. They were Psy—unlike with the other races, emotion didn't come into the mix when undertaking that evaluation. Their marriage had been—was—a piece of political strategy, a way to placate the human and changeling media by giving them an easily relatable image.

However, of late that plus was being canceled out by the questions people were asking about the exact nature of their relationship—there had been too many leaks and the emotional races now had information they should have never had. It had led to several probing inquiries at the most recent press conference, inquiries that wouldn't have been made even two years ago.

But, though problematic, that issue could wait.

"It is still possible to close the Net to outside influences," he said, focusing on the more important concern. "Nikita is incorrect to say that things have reached a critical mass, that Silence is close to falling." Councilor Duncan had been tainted by her constant and prolonged contact with the changelings in her territory and, as such, was a threat to the purity of Silence, the Protocol that erased their race's madnesses as it erased their emotions.

Henry intended to reinitiate that purity at all costs, and he had a significant amount of support. Membership in Pure Psy, the group formed to ensure Silence didn't fall, was rising day by day. "Our race neither wants nor needs any change in the Protocol."

Swiveling in her chair, Shoshanna picked up a remote and switched on a screen to her right. "These are the key players we need to eliminate in order to initiate a full closure of the Net."

The first image on the left was that of Sascha Duncan, Nikita's flawed daughter. It was followed by those of Faith NightStar and Ashaya Aleine. "All high-level defectors from the Net," he murmured, watching as Shoshanna brought up more images.

"The males they've bonded with in the DarkRiver leopard pack will also need to be executed," Shoshanna added. "Changelings are proprietary about their women."

"They're also relentless," Henry said, staring at the row of images. "We need to eliminate the entire pack, or at least the strongest part of it, if we're to ensure success."

"Correct." She flicked up another image, that of a man with ice blue eyes and hair of an unusual silver-gold. "The alpha of the SnowDancer pack needs to go, along with his lieutenants." Nine new images appeared on-screen. "The wolves are too tightly allied with the leopards to risk leaving them untouched."

"I thought our data stated that SnowDancer had ten lieutenants."

"It appears they've lost one, or we had the wrong information in the first place."

That, Henry knew, was quite possible. Their spy in the SnowDancer ranks had been executed over a year ago. Since then, any information they had was sketchy at best. "Any assassination attempt on a changeling stands a high chance of failure. Their natural shields give them enough of a warning that they have an opportunity to retaliate." And while he considered the animal races far less intelligent than his own, he respected their physical strength against weaker Psy bodies.

"Agreed, but we can finalize the logistics later. However," she continued, "in light of the close alliance between Snow-Dancer and DarkRiver, it may be a good strategic move to remove the wolf alpha from the equation before we target the leopards. Their emotional natures will mean they'll be weakened by the damaging psychological impact of such a loss."

Since Shoshanna had proven skilled in predicting such responses in humans and changelings, Henry had no argument with that. "Focusing our resources on the San Francisco area first," he said, "makes sense. The majority of the problems have been spawned by a relatively small group."

Two more images appeared on the screen—Nikita's human security chief and the fractured Justice Psy who was likely in a relationship with the man. The J-Psy's shields were inexplicable and impenetrable, but the fact that she was still in the Net in spite of her broken Silence was so unacceptable that it needed no discussion.

Another three images. All fellow Councilors.

"Nikita needs to go." Shoshanna's tone was flat, with no room for compromise. "Ming has access to significant military resources. If we can't co-opt him, he must be eliminated."

"Agreed," Henry said. "But he is not a primary target." He nodded at the third image. "What are your thoughts on Anthony?" He didn't trust his wife an inch, but he respected her political acumen. Just as he respected the fact that one day soon he'd have to kill her—to ensure she didn't kill him first.

"Uncertain," she said now. "Anthony has supported Nikita in the Council on the issue of Silence, but he has also supported our interests at times and could therefore be turned. He has no connections outside the Net except for his subcontracting arrangement with his daughter, and that decision is one I may have made myself in the same situation."

Since Faith NightStar was the strongest F-Psy in the world, able to predict futures other foreseers couldn't even glimpse, her services worth millions if not billions, Anthony's decision was one Henry understood as well. "He is, however, protective of his investment. We'll have to think carefully before we eliminate Faith."

"Yes, we can consider her toward the end." A pause. "F-Psy are, after all, often fractured and kept under psychic guard. She could be reassimilated into the Net."

"A possibility." Henry made a note to investigate whether Shoshanna had a "pet" F-Psy of her own. Her telepathic reach was more than powerful enough to direct the unstable mind of a broken foreseer. "These two," he said, picking up the remote to highlight the images, "are the primary targets. Kill them and we bring the city to its knees."

And he already had the operation in place to ensure it.

# CHAPTER 4

**Andrew knew he'd** messed up—badly.

Standing under the cold spray of his morning shower, he pressed his forehead to the tile, his hand fisted against the cool white surface. He didn't blame Indy for thinking he was only interested in sex, in the physical. Yes, he *was* sexually hungry. Very, very hungry. But not just for sex. For sex with Indigo—he'd wanted her for what seemed like forever, but these past few months, his needs had turned highly specific in every way.

The sole thing that had kept him from imploding was the fact that he knew she hadn't been with anyone those months, either.

And now he'd gone and mucked his chances up but good. Not only that, he'd reinforced her opinion of him as a young male led by nothing but his cock, not worth taking seriously in the personal arena. "Damn it." Wanting to strike out at something—preferably his own stupidity—he wrenched off the shower and stepped out to rub himself dry. He was thrusting a hand through his damp hair when his phone beeped. It was his alpha.

"My office, five minutes."

Adrenaline pumped through his veins at the summons. Better, far better, to be given some task that would mean racing through the cold climes of the Sierra than trapped in this room, this *den,* saturated with Indigo's unique scent.

Rainstorms and fire, ice and steel, that was what Indigo was to him.

And it was a scent that was waiting for him in Hawke's office. Sucking in a breath as he entered, he reined in the lunge his wolf wanted to make. Indigo glanced at him from where she stood in front of their alpha's desk, but her eyes told him nothing.

However, the straight line of her spine, the angle of her jaw, it all said "keep your distance" loud and clear. Though it kicked him in the guts that he'd broken the trust between them, Andrew wasn't about to listen to the silent order. And if Indigo thought he'd give up that easily, she had no idea who she was dealing with.

"Grab a seat, both of you," Hawke said, sitting down in his own chair. "Have you heard from Riley, Drew?"

Andrew slid into a seat beside Indigo, stretching his legs out in front. "Got a text saying they're planning to visit Rio de Janeiro today. Oh, and that he's already in love with Mercy's grandmother. Since she hasn't clawed his guts open yet, he thinks she might like him back."

Hawke grinned. "Poor Riley. I hope he survives."

"He knew what he was getting into when he mated with a dominant female," Indigo said, tapping a finger on the arm of her chair. "If he has the sense to continue to treat Mercy as exactly what she is, I'm sure her family will have no problem with him."

Andrew knew the words were directed at him. Yeah, they cut. But they also shored up his determination. Because no way in hell was last night going to be the final word on their relationship. "You know the two cats who came up here?" he said out loud, mentally vowing to melt that icy control, and more, to make her *see* him. "The ones who thought they might have a shot with Mercy?"

"Eduardo and Joaquin?" Hawke said, his hair catching the light as he leaned back in his chair and folded his arms behind his head. "What about them?"

"They took Riley out drinking last night."

The three of them digested that for a second . . . before grins appeared on all their faces, segueing slowly into chuckles, then outright laughter—including from the lieutenant sitting so straight and stiff next to him. His wolf bared its teeth in a feral smile. Indy might think she could freeze him out like she could everyone else, but just wait.

After they'd gotten the amusement out of their system, Hawke picked up a notepad. "Okay, with Riley and Mercy both away, we've got to move some things around. I need you"—glancing at Andrew—"to do a few extra security shifts."

"No problem." While his position as Hawke's eyes and ears in the wider pack had him on the road much of the time, he also functioned as a senior-level soldier during the times he was in the den.

Hawke made a note. "Indigo, you good with continuing to coordinate our resources?"

"Yes." Indigo's tone was calm, practical, with not the slightest hint of the passionate nature he'd glimpsed for a brief moment last night. "Are you handling the liaison with the leopards?"

Hawke's scowl had Andrew fighting a grin. "Yeah. Do you know how many juveniles I had to spring from cat territory yesterday? *Five,*" he said without waiting for an answer. "They'd gotten the bright idea to catch a leopard juvenile in animal form and cover him in blue and silver paint."

Andrew snorted. "At least they chose the pack's colors."

"Yeah, too bad for them that the 'juvenile' they caught was actually a full-fledged female soldier who just happens to be slightly smaller in size."

Indigo's wince was a hiss of air. "How bad did she slice them up?"

"They'll live." Hawke's wolf was in his eyes, clearly amused. "My punishment was probably worse. I doused the idiots in their own paint and told them they're not allowed to shift to get rid of it. It washes off in the shower, or it doesn't come off."

That, Andrew thought, explained the sheepish-looking teenager he'd seen on the way here, his hair sticking up in stiff blue spikes. "You want me to handle any of that?"

"No." Hawke shook his head. "Indigo or I will move you around as we see a gap. Riaz will be arriving later today, so we'll have another lieutenant soon, but he'll need a few days to rest and get himself up to speed."

Indigo leaned forward a bare fraction. "I didn't know he was coming home."

Andrew's wolf growled a warning inside his mind at the sign of her interest in the other man. Riaz, he knew, was around Indigo's age and ranked just below her in the hierarchy. The male had spent most of the past couple of years away from SnowDancer territory, roaming through various parts of the country and the world to gather information; to function as the pack's business representative when necessary; and more recently, to initiate contact and/or informal alliances with other changeling groups.

But none of that was important to his wolf. What made its fur bristle was one simple, inescapable fact: Riaz and Indigo had once been lovers. His hand clenched on the arm of his chair, his claws slicing out to dig into the leather-synth. He retracted the physical evidence of his emotions before anyone could notice, but there was nothing he could do about the claws slicing at the insides of his skin as the wolf paced, a low growl humming at the back of its throat.

The intensity of his response surprised even him.

"When'd Riaz get back into the country?" While he continued to fight the wolf's primal urges, Andrew knew without conceit that no one would guess he was having trouble maintaining an even keel—that ability to slide under the radar was a skill he'd had all his life. But he'd truly honed it to perfection in the months following his sister Brenna's abduction and torture. Riley had had nightmares. Andrew . . . Andrew had run himself into exhaustion every night for weeks. Alone. "Last I heard, he was in Europe."

"He was," Hawke said, interrupting the dark wash of

memory. "Landed in New York only a few hours ago. Should be in San Francisco by this afternoon."

"I'll pick him up," Indigo volunteered.

Andrew flexed his hand on the side of his chair hidden from Indigo's view, his claws slicing in and out. "Is that everything?" He needed to escape the intoxication and provocation of Indigo's scent, get a handle on himself before he did something else stupid.

Hawke shook his head. "I've got something I want you two to do." Settling back, he blew out a breath. "The thing with Joshua? Shouldn't have happened. And it's a pack issue, not a case of one or two individuals dropping the ball."

Andrew relaxed a fraction as his wolf's protective drive toward the pack overcame its more primitive instincts. "We've been so busy with protecting SnowDancer against the Council that we haven't paid enough attention to the young ones."

"Drew is right." Indigo braced her forearms on her thighs, her scowl apparent in the tone of her voice. "We've been focusing on training up the older soldiers, the dominants, to the detriment of the other ranks, and that's not how a healthy pack, how *our* pack, is supposed to work." She sounded both angry and frustrated—with herself, Andrew knew. "Why the hell didn't we notice the problem earlier?"

"Someone did. I told him it wasn't a priority."

Startled, Indigo followed Hawke's gaze to Drew, who shrugged in that fluid way he had. "I should've pushed you harder on the point," he said to their alpha, "but it *didn't* seem necessary at the time—and Joshua was shoved over the edge by a highly volatile situation. None of the others are anywhere near that stage. I would've made you pay attention if it was that bad."

Indigo wasn't used to finding herself out of the loop. It irritated her, but more, it made her wonder exactly how much more she didn't know about the things Drew did for the pack, for Hawke. Sitting up straight, she folded her arms and pinned him with her gaze. "How is it that you're so on top of what's happening with the juveniles?"

"People talk to me." Easy words, but there was an edge to them, his wolf baring its teeth in response to her aggressive tone. "It's not just the den kids," he continued. "There are a few out in the wider territory who are struggling in various ways."

"Get them up here by the weekend," Hawke said, pale eyes dangerously intent.

Indigo wondered what he saw, but she didn't ask. Because she wasn't sure she wanted to know. Drew had changed the status quo last night, changed it in a way that left only confusion and a restless fury in its wake. It wasn't a feeling she appreciated. "What're you planning?" she asked Hawke, determined to find her balance again. Other wolves might enjoy chaos, but Indigo, wolf and woman both, preferred order. Hierarchy was the solid core of that order. No wolf pack as strong as Snow-Dancer could survive without it.

Now Hawke, the man at the top of that chain of command, said, "I want you two to take the affected juveniles up into the mountains for a couple of days, give them some intense one-on-one attention, find out if there are more serious issues below the surface that we need to be handling." He pushed across a piece of paper. "These are the names Drew gave me last time. Add any others you think might benefit. If we have too many, we can split them into two groups."

Indigo's wolf saw the sense in what he was suggesting—bonding was at the heart of a healthy pack. And at present, things were relaxed enough that they could take time out to nurture those in danger of faltering. But the idea of spending that much time alone with the young male sitting to her left rubbed her fur the wrong way. Before last night, she'd have gone with him without a blink, trusting him to do what was necessary—and not act the ass.

However, below all that—the frustrated anger, the inability to understand why he'd done what he had—she was still a SnowDancer lieutenant. "They'll want to see you, too," she said to Hawke.

"I'm clearing the decks so I can join you for at least one of the days." His facial muscles tensed without warning.

A second later, Indigo caught a familiar scent on the air currents. Not long after that, a pretty girl with brown eyes, her hair tamed into a long braid, poked her head around the corner. "Oh, I'll come ba—" she began at seeing the three of them.

"No. We're just finishing up." Drew rose to his feet with a muscular grace Indigo had always known about, having sparred with him more than once. They'd also done any number of climbs together, both of them enjoying the thrill that came with pitting themselves against the peaks of the Sierra Nevada. But she'd never truly *seen* that grace until this moment.

The sudden awareness of him as a male, and not only that, but as a strong, handsome male, unsettled what balance she'd managed to regain. For the first time, she found herself seriously worried that things would never return to the way they'd once been—that their friendship had died in his room last night. The thought shook her enough that she had to make a conscious effort to catch Drew's next words.

"We'll finalize the list today," he said to Hawke. "We can decide the details, time of departure, et cetera, once we've contacted everyone. That work, Indy?"

Her concern was swept away under a surge of annoyance as she wondered if the damn copper-eyed wolf thought he could smooth things over with so little effort. "Fine. You take care of contacting the out-of-towners; I'll do the juveniles in the den."

Andrew nodded and headed toward the door, sentient to the rising tension level in the room—and it wasn't all his and Indigo's fault. Sienna gave him a small smile as he came close to where she waited in the doorway. Even after all these months, it was strange to see her with those eyes and that brown hair that was nothing close to her spectacular true shade. But no matter the shell she'd had to don to allow her to move safely in the outside world, her personality shone through. Quiet, determined . . . and with a little bit of hellion thrown in for spice.

Leaning down, he cupped her jaw in his hand and kissed her on the cheek. "How are you doing, little sister?" The question wasn't a simple courtesy. She'd been in trouble, her psychic abilities starting to spiral out of control before she'd moved away from the den to spend time in the care of the DarkRiver leopards.

"Good."

"That's all I get after I sent you a whole box of premium chocolate-cherry cookies?" he said, feigning extreme disappointment. "Just 'good'?"

Furrows appeared between her brows, dark little lines that marred the beauty of her sun-dipped skin. "Drew."

But when he grinned and took her into his arms, she not only allowed the affection, she slid her own arms around him. It had taken him months of patient care to get her to trust him with her body in that way. "Is that leopard boy . . . what's his name"—Andrew pretended to think—"that's right, Kit. Is Kit treating you right?" He murmured the question at a volume Hawke was certain to overhear, knowing full well he was throwing the cat among the pigeons.

"*Drew.*" Sienna pulled back, fisting a hand on his chest. Her eyes sparked fire at him, and for an instant he could almost see through the dark brown of her contact lenses and to the night-sky eyes beyond. White stars on a spread of black velvet, it was said that the eyes of a cardinal Psy reflected the stark, sprawling beauty of the PsyNet.

Leaning down, he kissed her other cheek and—dropping his voice low enough that it would skate under even his alpha's acute hearing—said, "Give him hell, sweetheart. Then come tell me about it." Ruffling her hair, he finally let her pass and exited the office.

Indigo fell into step beside him a second later. "The famous Andrew Kincaid charm in action?" Her question was sharp . . . but held an undertone of amusement. Because she'd been close enough to hear what he'd said to Sienna at the end.

His wolf wasn't fooled—the ice hadn't melted. It had simply been eclipsed momentarily by the wolf's curious nature. "Sienna could do with some charming." The Psy girl—young woman now—had been through things that would've broken far older and stronger men, been scarred by them. "If Hawke would figure that out, he'd be much happier."

Indigo snorted. "Yeah, I can just see him pulling charm out of a hat."

Andrew angled his body toward her. He'd planned to apologize for his behavior last night as soon as they had privacy, but as he went to open his mouth, he glimpsed a fleeting expectation in her eyes. The lieutenant was waiting for him to say it. When he did, she'd forgive him—both because she wasn't the kind of woman to hold a grudge and because it would shove them firmly back into the roles she'd decided were the only acceptable ones.

His wolf went quiet, thinking.

Better, he thought, feeling sneaky and downright delighted with himself, far better to keep her angry and thinking about him. Oh, there was no question he'd been a dick and needed to apologize, but he'd do so in a time and place of his own choosing—and in a way that would further his cause, not hers. "See you later, Indy."

He was almost sure he heard a low feminine snarl as he strolled off down the corridor.

His wolf peeled back its lips in a feral grin.

# CHAPTER 5

**Sienna ran her** hands self-consciously over her hair, wondering how badly Drew had messed it up. "I didn't mean to interrupt." The words came out stiff, jerky. No matter how composed she was around everyone else—until more than one wolf in the den had called her an "old soul"—she got to Hawke and it all fell apart.

He rose to his feet, his desk between them. "We were done." Ice blue eyes swept over her face . . . her cheeks—which she knew were ridiculously freckled after all the time she'd been spending out of doors.

"I didn't know you and Drew were close." It was a question phrased as a statement.

She fought the urge to cover up the cheeks he continued to stare at and shrugged—a very human or changeling motion, something she'd picked up after spending almost three years outside the PsyNet. Once, she wouldn't have answered Hawke's implied question, awaiting a direct query. But once, she'd been Silent, her emotions chilled like so much ice . . . not full of so much fire that it terrified her.

"Drew figures that since his sister is mated to my uncle," she said, focusing on a spot beyond Hawke's shoulder in an effort to regain her equilibrium, "that gives him the right to claim me as family." She was a cardinal Psy, her psychic power blinding, but she still couldn't figure out how Drew had snuck in under her defenses and made room for himself in her life. She just knew she'd miss him horribly if he ever left. "But," she said, her voice stupidly breathy, "he says he's not old enough to be an uncle, so he's decided to treat me like another younger sister."

Most people would've rolled their eyes at the convoluted reasoning, but Hawke simply nodded, as if it made perfect sense. Of course, to him, it probably did. The predatory changelings she knew were all big on family—and she had to admit, it was . . . nice to be treated with such easy affection by those she trusted. Drew understood that she was powerful, that she could cause incredible damage, and yet he continued to tease her as mercilessly as he did his real sister, Brenna.

Sometimes, Sienna even teased him back. Self-defense, she called it.

"Do you want permission to return to DarkRiver land?" Hawke asked, and his voice was as cool as Drew's had been warm, shattering what stability she'd managed to recapture. But no, she thought, remembering what Sascha had told her the last time she'd spent the night in the home of the woman who was a fellow defector from the PsyNet—and an empath able to sense and heal emotional hurts.

*No one can take from you what you don't want to give. It is your choice.*

And, she thought, steeling her spine, she chose not to let this strange compulsion toward a man who wasn't interested, who would never be interested, break her. "I wanted to say thank you," she said, controlling her volatile emotions by reciting a calming mantra she'd learned during her conditioning in the PsyNet, "for letting me spend so much time with the cats."

Hawke finally walked out from behind that desk he always

kept as an impassable wall between them. And that quickly, everything shifted, her shields trembling under the impact of him.

"Has it helped?" he asked.

"Yes." She would not give in, not today. "My control over my abilities is far better." Because he wasn't constantly *there*, wasn't breaking through her defenses with nothing but his presence. "Sascha and Faith have been helping me refine and strengthen my shields."

"Faith?"

"F-Psy," she said, referring to Faith's ability to see the future, "have incredibly tough shields. And Faith's recalibrated hers for maximum effectiveness." For now, those same shields were giving Sienna a measure of peace.

Though now, today, her heart beat like that of a trapped rabbit against her ribs, her skin suddenly too tight over heated flesh.

Reaching out, Hawke touched the top of her right cheekbone. It was the barest graze . . . but it was the first time he'd touched her in over a year. Fractures cracked across her shields, sudden and vicious and threatening to shove her into the black abyss of her power.

Trembling, she stepped back. "Please don't touch me." Choked-out words.

Hawke curled his hand into a fist at Sienna's near-silent command, his wolf snarling to get out, to teach this slender girl that he would not be rejected. "You have a cut there."

Her fingers lifted to that cheek, a cheek that also bore a scattered spray of sun golden freckles she hadn't had the last time they'd spoken. "Oh," she said after a moment, "that must've been from when I was with Kit yesterday."

His wolf pulled back its lips, baring the lethal sharpness of its canines. Kit was young, extremely dominant, and very close to Sienna in age. That didn't mean he was right for her. "He hurt you?" It came out a cold question, his wolf gone predator-still.

Sienna's eyes widened. "No. I wasn't looking where I was going on the run back from a sparring session and I tripped." An embarrassed look. "I'm never going to be as graceful as a changeling."

Hawke said nothing, could say nothing, his mind filling with images of the young leopard male touching her, laughing with her as he helped her up from the earth. "How much longer are you planning to stay in the den?" He'd fought against her going to DarkRiver, but there was no arguing that she was far more stable now than she'd been before.

"A while longer. I miss Toby so much when I'm with the cats," she said, referring to the little brother she loved with an intensity that was almost wolf in nature. "I also want to talk with Judd about some things to do with my abilities. But later this month, I'm going on a small hiking trip with Kit and a few other novice soldiers in DarkRiver."

"Make sure you speak to Indigo so she can adjust your duties." Hawke's wolf was scraping at the insides of his skin now, his vision starting to blur. "And stay out of my way while you're here." The order came out harsh as the edge of a rusted blade.

Sienna's face went white even as fury tightened the corners of her mouth. "Don't worry. I didn't come back to see you."

**Indigo stood with** her back to the airport wall, waiting for Riaz to exit his gate. She'd already tracked down and spoken to all the teenagers on her half of the list, informing them they needed to be packed and ready to head out into the cold but spectacular beauty of the mountains in a couple of days' time. The responses had ranged from gulps to outright glee.

She'd also had a message from Drew saying he was almost through his half of the list, too, but hadn't actually seen him since the meeting with Hawke. That only fired up the burner on her anger—because if nothing else, she'd expected an apology for his behavior. Instead, he'd acted like nothing had happened. Idiot.

Scowling, she lifted her head just as Riaz appeared in the stream of passengers disembarking from the New York flight. At six feet two, he was taller than her by four inches and built along the lines of his solid grace in wolf form. It was all pure muscle—and Riaz knew how to use it well.

He scented her from the gate, teeth flashing white against

his dusky skin as their eyes connected. *"Hola, bella,"* he said, dropping his bags on the floor and lifting her up in a powerful hug as she met him halfway.

Laughing, she kissed him on the jaw, feeling the rasp of stubble against her lips. "Hello, stranger. You back for good?"

"Depends who's asking." A lazy smile in those eyes that were such a pale brown as to be beaten gold. Unusual. And for most females, fascinating. He raised an eyebrow when she continued to stare. "Did I grow a second nose or something?"

Stepping out of the soap-and-earth-and-warmth of his embrace, she watched him pick up his bags. "No, but you've put on some more muscle." It was a dodge. Because in truth, she'd been thinking something far different—that Riaz, with his jet-black hair and eyes of Spanish gold, was gorgeous and sexy and—very importantly—a dominant only just below her in the hierarchy. The difference wasn't enough to bother her wolf. And they'd never had a problem with physical chemistry.

All facts to consider.

Riaz's lips curved into a deeper smile as he hefted one duffel over his shoulder while gripping the other in his free hand. "So you noticed. Want to feel?"

"Sexy you might be; Don Juan you're not." Laughing at his affronted look, she led him to the vehicle, and they clambered inside after dumping his bags in the trunk. "How was Europe?"

"It was all pretty girls, flash hotels, five-star food," he moaned, pushing back his seat as far as possible so he could stretch out those long, powerfully muscled legs. "I thought I'd go mad."

Smile tugging at her lips, she waved her debit card at the parking gates, and they opened with a quiet swish. "Poor baby."

Riaz said nothing for several minutes, putting down the window to let the wind ruffle his hair. "God, it's good to be home, Indigo." Heartfelt words, the homesickness of his wolf evident in every syllable. "I can't wait to run through the forests, to walk in the den, to shoot the bull with the rest of you."

"You've been back now and then."

"I always knew I'd be leaving again," the other lieutenant said, "so I never really gave myself a chance to settle. But now . . ." He exhaled, long and slow. "Anything I should know?"

"Riley's gone to meet his mate's grandparents."

Riaz shook his head, that black-as-night hair whipping off his face as she accelerated. "I couldn't believe he'd mated with a cat when I heard, but having met Mercy on my last trip home, I can say the man has excellent taste." Another comfortable silence, then, "So, what was that at the airport about me being tall, dark, and irresistible?"

"I don't recall using those words."

Eyes of beaten gold met hers full-on for a single instant before she returned her gaze to the road, and he moved his hand to the back of her neck, massaging gently. It was a familiar and intimate touch. Unlike with Drew, her wolf allowed this one. Because Riaz had earned the wolf's trust on that level, been given that right. He hadn't simply tried to claim it the way Drew had—as if a few kisses gave him the prerogative to demand everything. Her hands clenched on the manual steering wheel.

"I'm not attached, Indigo," Riaz said with a solemnity that struck her as somehow "wrong," though she couldn't put her finger on why. "So if you're thinking you need someone with whom to work off the tension, I'm more than happy to oblige."

Shoving away the memory of Drew's kisses, the infuriating arrogance of his attempt to use her touch-hunger against her, she nodded slowly. "I'm thinking about it."


**It gutted Andrew,** fucking eviscerated him, to see Indigo laughing with another man, a man who had no concept of the true value of the woman beside him. No, that was unfair. Riaz's remarkable eyes sparked with intelligence, with respect, when he looked at Indigo. The male lieutenant understood exactly who she was.

Staying in his shadowed spot—in the back of the room where all the senior members of the pack had gathered to throw Riaz an impromptu welcome-home party—Andrew sucked on his beer and forced his attention off the couple on the other side—to something, anything, else.

He saw Hawke speaking with Elias and Yuki, glimpsed Sing-Liu playfully grabbing her mate's ass, and—He blinked. Walker Lauren was here. That wasn't a huge surprise, because though quiet, the Psy male had turned out to be a genius when it came to dealing with young hotheads, to the extent that Hawke had assigned him as the go-to man for the ten-to-thirteen-year-old crowd.

What held Andrew's attention was the fact that Walker was standing very close to Lara, and from the expression on the healer's fine-boned face, the way she was all but poking the much taller man in the chest, she was well and truly pissed. Walker's own expression was more difficult to read, but—

Low female laughter. Intimate. Painfully familiar.

Clenching his jaw, he refused to turn, to watch.

"You look like you've been gut-punched." Quiet words from a man who'd once been the shadow in the dark, the assassin you'd never see, never know about, until it was far too late.

Andrew glanced at his sister's mate as Judd came to stand against the wall beside him. "I feel worse."

Judd's eyes were on the other side of the room—on the curious tableau presented by his older brother and Lara—but he spoke to Andrew. "Do you want me to leave you alone?"

And that was why—in spite of the fact that the other male dared get into bed with Andrew's beloved sister on a regular basis—Andrew liked Judd. "No, but I need to get the fuck out of here."

Judd didn't say anything, just put down his own drink and melted away in the direction of the door. Andrew followed, leaving his unfinished beer on a table in the corner as he walked out, refusing to torture himself any further. It had always been bad, seeing her interact with other men in a way she simply didn't interact with him, but never like this— because he knew just how dangerous Riaz was to his own goals.

His senses told him there was nothing sexual between Indigo and Riaz . . . now. That last word was the operative one. Because the way Riaz looked at Indigo, the way she looked at him—they were considering it on some level. And if Andrew wasn't careful, proximity alone might push them into making a decision that would rip Andrew's heart into a thousand pieces.

"This way." Judd nodded at a corridor that led eventually to one of the less utilized exits. Leaving through it, they walked out past the White Zone—the area closest to the den, where their young were free to play—and into the more densely forested area beyond. Sandwiched between the heavily guarded perimeter and the equally well-guarded entrance to the White Zone, it provided a massive range for adult and juvenile wolves to run in, play in, and come to find solitude.

Like now.

Silence was something Judd was good at, but after almost ten minutes of it, the Psy male glanced at Andrew. "If it was me," he said, "I'd understand the need to walk alone. But you're a social individual, one of the most popular people in SnowDancer."

The unspoken question hung in the air between them.

# CHAPTER 6

**Andrew hadn't spoken** of his attraction to Indigo to anyone, ever. Because though he loved his pack with every breath
in him, he didn't want them peering over his shoulder while
he fought for his right to court her. "God, if Riley could see
me now." He'd hassled his brother endlessly about Mercy.

Judd continued to walk, his stride elegant even along the
soaked earth. It was an explicable grace, given that the man
most thought a telepath was actually also a viciously powerful
telekinetic. Judd had already been in the pack for well over a
year before any of them discovered that truth. So Andrew had
no doubts about the fact the man could keep secrets—at least
from the pack. "You'll tell Brenna, won't you?"

The Psy lieutenant turned and simply looked at him.

"Yeah." Andrew blew out a breath. "Not like that's a question." Neither was it reason enough to keep his silence—his
sister was loyal to the bone. She might mess with him in private, but she'd keep it close to her chest if he asked.

"You don't have to say anything." Judd's voice was calm

and clear in the snow-laced chill of the night. "I've seen the way you look at the lieutenant. So has Brenna."

"Fuck." The pack, with its loving teasing, could do more harm than good right now, when Indigo was so determined to draw a line in the sand between them. "Is it that bloody obvious?"

"No." Judd waited until Andrew began to walk again to continue. "However, we are . . . family." Emotion—being open with it—was still difficult for Judd. But not only had Drew once stood in the path of a bullet that had been aimed at the woman who was Judd's heart, the wolf male had used his considerable charm to bring a smile to Sienna's face.

For those two things alone, Judd would've owed him. But even before Drew started interacting with Sienna and the other Lauren children, he and Judd had also forged a cautious kind of friendship—built on their shared love for Brenna. "Brenna worries about you."

Drew gave a startled laugh. "What? I'm not Riley. I don't take responsibility for the world's ills." It was said with open affection for the brother Judd knew had all but raised both Drew and Brenna.

Using a slight amount of Tk, Judd absently braced a water-logged branch that had been about to break off right above their heads. "I think Mercy might be trying to cure him of that."

A minute . . . two, of silence. Except it wasn't silent. He'd been an assassin, knew how to move without sending a ripple through the air currents, thought he'd been familiar with the quiet dark of night. But Brenna, his mate, had shown him *her* night, *her* silence, and it was an amazing, beautiful world.

The rustle of a rabbit as it caught their scent and froze.

The dull thud of that branch falling to the earth.

The soft touch of rain-heavy air against his face.

Small things that filled the silence, the dark, until it wasn't bleak, but a serene wonderland.

"Indigo thinks Riaz—or someone like Riaz," Drew said at last, his voice taut, strained, "will be right for her. I can see it clear as day."

"You disagree."

"None of them know her, not like I do."

Judd angled his body left, taking them down a slight slope that would lead eventually to one of the lakes that dotted the Sierra. Most in the higher altitudes, especially in the central and southern areas, remained locked in ice, but this one was liquid, its waters rippling under moonlight as the clouds parted. "But do you truly know her, Drew?"

Andrew felt his shoulders go stiff, his wolf baring its teeth in instinctive response, but he respected Judd's intelligence enough to rein it back. "Are you saying I don't?"

"I'm saying that from what Brenna's noted, you've had a crush on Indigo since you were a very young man." Judd held up a hand when Andrew would've interrupted. "I'm not questioning what you feel; I'm not telling you that you're wrong. I'm simply asking you to examine your own emotions," he said with implacable logic. "Ask yourself if it's Indigo you want, or a mirage of her you've built up in your mind."

With that, Judd jogged down the final steep part of the incline to the pebbled edge of the lake. Andrew followed with far less grace, for all that he was changeling. His mind was misfiring, his body not quite under his control. It felt as if his world had just been skewed on its axis.

A few feet away, the lake lapped with placid regularity over the smooth water-shaped pebbles, in stark contrast to his own disordered state. Swearing under his breath, he ripped off his sweatshirt and went for his boots.

Judd walked away without a word, taking a path along the curving edge of the dark spread of water.

Stripping down to his skin, Andrew looked up at the moon, his wolf confused, floundering. The bright sphere, its face covered by clouds an instant later, could give him no answers, and the more he thought, the more he tangled himself up in the sticky confusion of a thousand cobwebs. Shrugging off the cutting bite of the wind, he strode in through the shallows and dived.

*Ice.*

The shock of it tore the air from his lungs, froze the blood in his veins . . . and returned clarity to his mind.

*Indigo snapping at him because he'd been messing around during training.*

*Indigo allowing him to cuddle into her because she thought he needed the touch of Pack.*

*Indigo pissy on a short trip they'd taken to Los Angeles.*

*Indigo laughing with Mercy as the two of them teased Riley.*

*Indigo calm and smart as she advised Hawke against a planned maneuver.*

*Indigo whooping with glee as they finished scaling one of the tougher climbs they'd attempted.*

*Indigo teeth-grittingly obstinate as she arrowed toward the man she* thought *was right for her.*

Wiping the water from his face, he sucked in a breath of the bracing air and yelled out to the night, "I know every part of her, warts and all! And I still adore her!" He began to head back to shore without waiting for an answer. Even his tough changeling body couldn't handle water this icy for long.

A towel was waiting for him by his discarded clothes. He grinned. Having a telekinetic as a friend did come in handy sometimes. Wiping himself off with rough strokes that got his blood pumping, he rubbed at his hair then pulled on his clothes. He was sitting on the rocky shore, the towel around his neck, when Judd returned to his side. The other man took a seat beside him, his movements so quiet that if Andrew hadn't scented him, he'd never have known there was anyone beside him.

"So," Judd said, "what're you going to do?"

"What I have been doing," Andrew said, his wolf growling in feral agreement. "I'm not about to let her ignore me just because I don't fit neatly into the box she has marked out for the man she'll take as her own." He wanted to use the word *mate*, but that had a very specific meaning for changelings.

And though it hurt him to admit it, there was no mating dance between him and Indigo, no compulsion from the wild heart of their natures that would—if nothing else—tug her inexorably to him, make her pay attention. No, all he had was his stubborn determination . . . and his heart.

Judd sighed. "That's not your strength."

"*You're* giving *me* dating advice?" Andrew was dumbfounded.

"I'm mated," Judd pointed out with a cool arrogance that almost hid the laughter in his voice. "You can't even get the woman you want into bed. I'd listen if I were you."

Andrew gave him the finger, but his wolf pricked up its ears. "Yeah, so?"

"Sienna," Judd said in an abrupt change of subject, "is slow to take to people, suspicious of everyone's motives. She's had to become that way to protect herself, but she lets you hold her. Do you understand how big a deal that is for her?"

Judd had almost intervened the first time he'd seen Drew pull Sienna into a hug. He'd thought his niece was being forced. But then, right before he'd turned Drew's bones into so much shrapnel, he'd seen Sienna's arms go around the wolf male's waist, her face lift up to his with a tiny smile of welcome.

The sight had literally stopped him in his tracks.

"Yeah," Drew now said, a tenderness in his voice that was most usually apparent when he spoke to his sister. "I knew she was hurting. Hell, I probably understand what she's going through in one particular area of her life better than anyone."

Judd didn't pursue that avenue of thought—trouble was brewing there, but they had time yet. Tonight, he'd focus on Drew. "How did you get Sienna to trust you?"

"How?" A shrug Judd sensed more than saw, the moon eclipsed by the rain-heavy clouds. "I talked to her."

"And bribed her with a dozen deluxe cupcakes, each with its own weight in frosting." Judd could still remember how the three cousins—Sienna, Toby, and Walker's daughter, Marlee—had sat around and gobbled up the sweet concoctions. "There wasn't even a crumb left by the end of the day, and I'm pretty sure Sienna and the kids were in sugar comas."

Drew's laughter was warmth in the darkness. "I saw her eyeing a photo of them in a magazine. It was just a way to get into her good graces."

"Same with painting pink daisies on the door of the vehicle she most often uses to drive to DarkRiver territory?"

"It was water paint," Drew said, clearly unrepentant, "barely took her a minute to wipe it away." A grin. "She only got mad when she found out I'd painted her rucksack, too."

Judd couldn't help it. He laughed. It was still new to him, that sound, the feel of it. But he liked laughing, liked the bubbles of joy in his bloodstream, the feel of his chest muscles flexing in a way that had once been wholly unfamiliar. "You're an idiot, Drew."

A low growl colored the air. "My sister might be a sucker for your face, but that doesn't mean I'll hold my punches."

"I'll ask the question again—how did you get Sienna to trust you?"

Obviously irritated at the repetition, Drew threw a pebble into the water, picked up another. "Indigo would say I charmed her into—Oh." Still holding the pebble, he stared at Judd. "I *am* an idiot."

**Having left Drew** to plot the next step in his courtship of Indigo, Judd went home to kiss his mate and promise her he'd be home in a couple of hours. Brenna tugged down his head, rubbed her nose affectionately against his. "You'll be careful." It was an order.

"Nothing dangerous tonight," he murmured, stroking his hands down her back, stunned as always by the delicate strength of her—such power in so small a frame. "Are you planning to wear one of those lacy things to sleep in?"

"I don't know why I bother." A smile against his lips, her wolf dancing in her eyes. "They never stay on long."

"I like them." He most especially liked peeling them off her inch by slow inch.

A husky laugh. "Then don't be too late."

Properly motivated to complete his errand and return to her arms, he made his way down into the night-cloaked streets of San Francisco, and from there, to the peaceful hush of the place Father Xavier Perez called both his vocation and his home. Xavier was waiting for him in the otherwise empty confines of the simple Second Reformation church, and Judd's light mood transformed into concern as he came close enough to see the lines of strain on the other man's normally serene countenance.

"Xavier," he said, meeting the man of God in the center of the aisle, right below the peak of the roof, "what is it?"

"What I tell you now, you cannot share with our mutual friend." Xavier's eyes were troubled but resolute. "It's not that I don't trust him . . ."

"But the Ghost has his own agenda." Judd, too, was worried about the powerful Psy rebel who was the third part of their triumvirate. The Ghost was connected to, and loyal to, the PsyNet. But the growing darkness in that very Net seemed to be in danger of corroding what remained of the other man's soul. And if the Ghost snapped . . . A chill snaked its way up Judd's spine. "I will not tell him."

Xavier dipped his head in voiceless acknowledgment before saying, "I've never spoken of it, but there are a number of Psy among my congregation."

Judd bit back his surprise. Religion was nonexistent in the PsyNet. Silence did not allow for it. "Do they come to you for guidance?"

A faint smile that did nothing to ease the tension around Xavier's mouth. "No, they hide in the shadows. But I know they are there, and some have been coming for long enough that I feel they are mine to watch over."

Judd waited as the priest opened his Bible and withdrew a folded piece of paper.

"A few of them have, over time, trusted me with their contact details." He passed the paper to Judd. "This woman, Gloria, has attended the service every Thursday night without fail for two years."

Judd had been an assassin, an Arrow the Council used as a weapon. He connected the dots before Xavier drew them. "She has stopped coming."

"Just once, tonight," Xavier said. "But she *always* contacts me if there's even a chance she might miss a service. I received no message today, and no one answers when I attempt to call."

Memorizing the information on the slip of paper—a simple telephone number—Judd passed it back to Xavier. "I'll see what I can find out."

Xavier slid the paper back into the Bible, his dark eyes

drenched with worry. "Her soul was so lost when she first began coming—she was cold to the point of lifelessness. This past year, though, I could see her coming to life."

Judd didn't say anything, but he had a feeling that Gloria's awakening had brought her the wrong kind of attention—the kind that led to rehabilitation. No one came back from rehabilitation. It erased the personality, wiped the mind, and left only the shambling husk of an empty shell behind.

# CHAPTER 7

**Indigo didn't see** Drew the next morning as she strode through the corridors, her destination the small office that was her own near the training rooms. She'd glimpsed him leaving Riaz's party early with Judd the previous night. Now she found herself wondering if he'd stayed with the Psy lieutenant, or hunted up one of his little playmates and gone horizontal.

Gritting her teeth against her mind's obliging slide show of images that displayed Drew tangled up with some faceless female, she told herself she should've taken up one of the offers that had come her way last night as the senior members of the pack let down their hair. A good sweaty workout between the sheets would certainly have wrung the tension out of her body. But she hadn't—for reasons she couldn't quite understand—and now she was paying for it, her skin too sensitive, her wolf irritated and out of sorts.

Ordering herself to focus, she switched on her datapad as she walked, bringing up the day's schedule. She'd been in charge of training the novice soldiers for eight years, four of them as assistant to her father, Abel, the last four on her own, with Abel taking over another role. However, over the past couple of years, she'd also started handling more personal issues related to the young dominants in the pack. They came to her with questions, for advice, to vent, and sometimes just to hang out—because her wolf calmed theirs. "Which you will not be able to do unless you get yourself under control," she muttered, annoyed with herself for allowing Drew to rattle her in this way.

That was when she ran into the one person who could take one look at her and read her like an open book.

"Baby," her mother said, her smile so full of love it made Indigo's heart ache, "give me a hug."

Indigo was already leaning across to do exactly that, every part of her adoring this woman who was the template from which she'd been cast. Tarah Riviere had the same jet-black hair, though hers bore a few—very few—glimmers of silver now, the same vivid blue eyes shot with streaks that were almost purple, the same long-legged height.

But that was where the similarities ended. Where Indigo's frame was all supple muscle, her mother was fit but sweetly curved. Where Indigo was a dominant and had been from soon after birth, Tarah was a true submissive, one of the gentlest people in the pack. And where Indigo would never surrender everything to any man—even one she loved—Tarah found incomparable joy in leaning on her mate.

"Morning, Mama."

Cupping Indigo's face in her hands, her mother examined her with those wise eyes. "What's troubling you, my big girl?"

With every other person in the den, Indigo would've stood firm and frozen off any inquiries. In front of her mother's tender concern, she folded like a leaky balloon. "I'm fighting with Drew," she said, hoping Tarah would take that at face value. She really didn't want to explain the genesis of the fight.

Tarah laughed and, dropping her hands from Indigo's face, slipped her arm through her daughter's and began to walk toward one of the large common areas in the den. "Have you got time for a morning coffee with your mother?"

"Always." It was a ritual they had—though it had no rules, no set dates. But at least a couple of times a week, Indigo found herself alone with Tarah. Sometimes they chatted over coffee, sometimes they walked in the forest, and sometimes they made a bowl of popcorn and watched some movie that made them both bawl like babies.

Her father tended to avoid being in those nights.

Grinning, Indigo found herself thinking back over the years. "We've been doing this in one form or another since I was, what, ten?" It was, she knew, because of Evangeline.

Her much younger sister had been frighteningly weak as a child, though no one could diagnose the reason behind it. Indigo would catch a cold and be up and running the next day. Evie would catch a cold and need to be hooked up to machines so she could breathe, her little body wracked by shivers. It used to terrify Indigo that she might lose the sister she loved so much—and to something Indigo couldn't fight, couldn't defend against.

Her mother squeezed her arm. "You're my baby, too."

Indigo shifted closer to her mother, the wolf wanting to brush up against her as they walked. "How is Evie? I haven't spoken to her for a few days." Her sister had finally thrown off the inexplicable—especially for a changeling—sickliness in her teens. Now in her second year of college, she was a sweet-tempered, submissive wolf chased by more than one young wolf in the den—and humans outside of it.

"She's coming for a visit in three weeks' time."

Indigo's wolf stretched out its paws and arched its back in pleasure.

"And," Tarah continued, "she told me to tell you not to scare off all the men beforehand—she wants to date the wild and dangerous types, thank you very much." Laughing at the look on Indigo's face, she said, "Grab us a good seat. I'll get the coffees."

Still scowling at the idea of her willow-slender sister with some of the rougher young males, Indigo wandered through the room filled with furniture in bright citrus tones until she found two armchairs facing each other in a quiet corner. They were both a funky orange, the table between them a dark, varnished wood that bore the nicks and scratches of constant use.

"Hey, Indigo."

Waving a casual hello at Tai as the young soldier passed by, she settled in to wait for her mom. That was part of the ritual, too. It was always Tarah who got the coffee, mixing the ingredients in a way that made it taste incredible.

*It's love,* Tarah had once laughingly said. *That's the secret ingredient.*

"Indigo?" Tai had circled back.

She looked up into his pretty, pretty face, all silky hair and those wild green eyes with a slight upward tilt that spoke of the Balinese ancestry on his mother's side. "Yes, she's coming home for a visit. No, I will not give you a free pass. You put one finger on her, I'll beat you to a pulp."

Tai snarled low in his throat, his wide shoulders going stiff as he fisted his hands. "Yeah, well, maybe I'll beat you back." Face thunderous, he stalked off as she fought her smile. Hmm, perhaps Judd's young protégé had potential. None of the others had dared stand up to her. And Indigo wasn't handing over her vulnerable younger sister to a wolf who couldn't protect her from all comers.

Tarah placed a tray between them as Tai left the common room. It held two steaming mugs of coffee and a couple of large blueberry muffins. "They were the last ones there," Tarah said, shaking her head. "And it's only nine."

"Pack's got a young population," Indigo said, taking a sip of her coffee before putting down the mug and picking up a muffin. "You should see how much some of my trainees go through in a day."

"Speaking of the young population"—Tarah eyed Indigo over the top of her own mug—"I told you not to scare off Evie's dates."

Indigo wasn't the least cowed by her mother's mock scowl, well able to see the amusement behind it. "She's mine to look after."

"You always were possessive about her." Shaking her head, Tarah sipped her coffee.

"Mama?" Indigo asked after several minutes of companionable silence.

"Yes, baby."

Indigo felt her lips curve. Tarah alone could call her that and make it sound perfectly acceptable. Of course, her father tended to call her "pumpkin" and ruffle her hair like she was five years old. No respect, she thought with an inward smile, she got no respect from her parents. "Do you ever get angry at Dad?"

Tarah's eyes sparkled. "Sure I do. You know that."

"No, I don't mean the little spats." Though you couldn't really call them that, either. Her parents were so in sync it was scary. "But at his dominance . . . don't you sometimes wish he'd let you take control?" She'd never before asked her mother that question, had always felt it would cross some line, but today, she *needed* to know.

Putting her mug on the table, Tarah leaned forward and picked a blueberry from her muffin. She chewed thoughtfully before answering. "No," she said at last, her response free of ambiguity. "My wolf needs to feel protected, feel safe." Angling her head when Indigo remained silent, Tarah said, "I know you've never understood that, baby, for all that you love me."

"Mama, I didn't mean—"

"Hush." A gentle command that had Indigo swallowing her apology. "The fact is, you're a dominant—that's why you and your father always butted heads."

"Was I that bad?"

"A terror." It was a cheerful reply. "But because of the hierarchy, we could deal with you without too many problems. Your father outranked you—so when push came to shove, you had to listen."

Now Indigo outranked Abel—though she would never in a million years actually bring that up. Ever. Some relationships were sacred, and when she was with her father, Indigo treated him as the dominant. "That used to make me crazy—that he could shut me down by pulling rank," she said in answer to her mother's statement, "but at the same time, it was calming."

"There, you see, you do understand." Tarah plucked out another blueberry. "Strict adherence to the hierarchy helps maintain the balance of the pack. Our wolves are happiest when they know their place in the scheme of things. For my wolf, that place is in the shelter of Abel's arms."

Indigo gave a slow nod, seeing a deeper truth in her mother's words. "I would never be happy," she said, the words spilling out before she realized how much they might betray, "either with a man who treated me as a submissive or with a man my wolf saw as weaker."

Tarah gave her a penetrating look and Indigo knew her mother saw too much, but all she said was, "Yes, that's true. Your place is not the same as mine. For you to be happy, you must accept and respect your partner to the very core of your soul—or your wolf will make both your lives a misery."

**Having come down** to the city to talk to one of his contacts in the human population, Andrew decided to say hi to Teijan as well, figuring he might as well use the time in a productive fashion. Because if he went back to the den, he'd undoubtedly end up tracking Indigo. And he couldn't tip his hand, not yet, not before he was prepared.

So he was waiting for the Rat alpha at Fisherman's Wharf as the sun rose high enough to chase off the whispers of fog that still licked over the bay. Teijan turned up as slick and neatly attired as if he'd stepped out of some sophisticated men's magazine.

"Shucks," Andrew said, leaning his arms on the metal fence that lined this section of the wharf, "you didn't have to get all dolled up on my behalf."

"You should be so lucky." Teijan aligned his cuffs with the sleeves of his jacket. "I'm going for a job interview."

Andrew narrowed his eyes. "Since when does the Rat alpha need to find a job?" Teijan operated what was effectively the biggest information network in the city, and probably the state. And there was serious money in information—especially since SnowDancer and DarkRiver had both decided to share the profits from any deals that came about because of intel the Rats passed on.

Brutal fact was, they could've demanded that data as a condition of allowing the weaker changeling group to remain in the city, but Lucas and Hawke were highly intelligent men. They understood that the Rats would be far more invested in the protection of the city if they not only had the right to call it home but were treated as an integral part of its functioning. Which they were most assuredly becoming.

Now Teijan shot him a sharp little smile, full of teeth. "Funny how easy it is to get into some buildings if you carry a résumé and look 'respectable.'"

"Do I want to know?"

"No. Nothing to tell yet." The dark-haired male looked out over the glittering sun-struck water of the bay. "My animal knows it can swim," he murmured, "but just the same, neither it nor the human part of me is too fond of the water."

"Then why San Francisco?"

A shrug. "We'd been scraping by, trying to find a home for a long time, and the old subway tunnels were unclaimed." A whisper of wind ruffled his *GQ*-perfect hair. "Good thing it was the cats who found us out. You wolves would've probably decided we tasted good spit-roasted over an open fire."

"No self-respecting wolf would eat a rodent—though we might've been able to use your teeth as decorations," Andrew said with a straight face.

Teijan hissed out a very unratlike snarl. "Why the hell do I bother to talk to you?"

"Hawke thinks I give you cheese." He pulled a small, foil-wrapped wedge out of his pocket. "Here you go."

"Fuck you." But the Rat alpha was laughing. "Why'd you want to meet?"

Putting both hands in the pockets of his jacket, Andrew let the salt-laced wind sweep across his face. "Wanted to see if you had any news to share." DarkRiver always copied Snow-Dancer in on any reports as per their alliance, but Teijan quite often had little tidbits in progress that he didn't put into the reports until he'd confirmed everything.

"Something weird going on with the Psy," the Rat alpha now said. "Can't quite put my finger on it, but if I didn't know better, I'd say they were jumpy."

Since Psy didn't feel, that kind of apprehension was more than curious. "Anything to back up that feeling?" he asked, knowing Teijan had finely developed antennae for trouble after keeping his people safe and protected for years in spite of their lack of numbers and physical strength.

Teijan made a clicking noise with his tongue. "I've heard whispers of two or three Psy dead in suspicious circumstances, but no confirmations yet. Could just be a bad rehabilitation or two."

Andrew felt his skin creep at the thought of the Psy punishment of choice—a total psychic brainwipe that destroyed the individual and left a drooling shell behind. "Maybe they suicided." At Teijan's glance, he shrugged. "If that was me . . ."

"Yeah." Teijan blew out a breath. "But word is there's nobody home after rehab, and there would have to be for them to understand what they'd become." He glanced at his watch. "I better get going. I'll send the intel through the grapevine if I hear anything else."

As Andrew watched the other man leave, he wondered what face this world would've worn if the Psy Council had been successful in seizing total power as it had been trying to do for decades.

The vision was chilling.

"Drew?"

Shaking off the brutal images, he shifted on his heel to find himself facing Lara. "You must've come down before the shops opened," he said, looking at the bags she had in hand.

"I'm in a bad mood," she said. "I decided to work it off by spending money, but I hate everything I've bought. Who needs a stupid yellow dress anyway? Not someone with my skin tone." That skin, a natural dark tan stroked with gold in this light, scrunched up as she made a face.

"I think you'll look gorgeous in yellow." He wrapped an arm around her shoulders, cuddling her smaller body to his. Like most people in the den, he tended to forget she wasn't that much older than he was, she was so competent. But today she looked unbearably young. "This bad mood have anything to do with—"

"Don't go there," she warned, even as she slid her own arm around his waist, the soft black of her corkscrew curls glinting with sparks of red. "And I won't hassle you about Indigo."

He froze. "How the hell do you healers pull that shit?"

"Trade secret." A hint of a smile, those high cheekbones giving her eyes an almost feline appearance as she glanced up. "How come she's so mad at you?" she asked with a blunt honesty that reminded him of Ben, the pup the healer often babysat for her friend Ava.

"Not telling."

She scrunched her nose at him. "You going to do anything about it?"

Andrew thought of the plan he'd hatched late last night. "Oh, yeah, I'm going to do something about it." And the lieutenant would never see it coming.

# CHAPTER 8

Having said good-bye to her mother a few minutes earlier, Indigo found Hawke and they sat down to coordinate the pack's resources. "We have a lieutenant meeting later today," she said toward the end.

"I remember." Rising from his desk, he folded his arms, unfolded them, then shoved his hands through his hair, hair that echoed the stunning color of his pelt in wolf form. Right now, that wolf was riding him hard.

"Want to go for a run?" she asked, feeling more than a little twitchy herself. "We could both use it."

The fact that Hawke didn't even bother to pretend he didn't need to let the wolf roam told her more than anything else. "Wolf or human?" he asked, his voice shifting in a way that made it clear the wolf was already in charge. His eyes, too, shimmered in the most subtle of ways—the wolf watching her from a human face.

"Human wolf," she said, "it's harder to maintain."

"Let's go."

By the time they cleared the den, her wolf was at the forefront of her mind. She was still physically human, but her thought processes were no longer those of the cool, collected lieutenant. They were of the wolf who lived in her soul—of her body, only her eyes would've reflected the change. Though as they began to run, she felt her claws pricking at the insides of her skin and decided to let them slice through.

They ran side by side, getting out of the White Zone and into the thick darkness of the forest beyond, the trees whipping by in a blur of rich green and—as they began to climb higher—the occasional splash of snowy white. She was damn fast, but she knew Hawke could've outstripped her. It wasn't simply that he was alpha—though that played a part in it. Her own wolf didn't *want* to outstrip him, would've been confused if it could. But a larger part of it was that he was naturally faster.

But she was making him work for it, and that was what was important. It was a lieutenant's job to challenge her alpha when necessary—as it was an alpha's job to look after his pack. So Indigo ran them both to the edge of exhaustion, flying over fallen rocks and old trees, branches grazing her arms and threatening to slap her face, the wind a crisp knife across her skin.

Her wolf gloried in the rush of speed, the pump of blood, the wild pleasure of running with a packmate. It was only when they reached the top of a ridge, when there was only silence around them, the pack lands spread out below in a sea of white, green, and lake blue, that the wolf sighed and halted. Hawke stood with his hands on his knees beside her, chest heaving and face gleaming with sweat.

Glancing at him, she saw his wolf grinning back at her, the shimmering ice of his eyes filled with fierce joy. She grinned back, allowing herself to collapse onto her back on the snow-dusted grass, the chill a welcome kiss against her heated skin. The sky was a gorgeous crystalline blue overhead, Hawke's eyes a curious and much paler hue as he looked down at her, his head angled in a way that was simply not human.

She snapped her teeth at him.

It made him laugh, relax, and lie down beside her, their

arms companionably tangled. "So," he said, his voice holding the edge of a growl.

"So," she replied, her own wolf prowling contentedly inside her skin.

Shifting, Hawke raised himself on his elbow before leaning down to nip at her lower lip in a quick, sharp bite.

With those amazing eyes, and that gorgeous mane of silver-gold, many women would've taken what he'd done as a sensual invitation. She was wolf. She knew that coming from her alpha, it was very much the opposite.

Rubbing at her lip, she scowled. "What did I do?" Because it had been a rebuke. A playful one, sure, but a rebuke nonetheless.

Hawke tapped her on the nose with his index finger. "My wolf can sense that yours is in trouble. Why didn't you come to me?"

"It's nothing," she said, pushing him away with a growl when he would've used his teeth on her a second time. Yes, he was alpha, but she was a dominant female. "Correction—it is something, but it's not anything I need your help to manage." Drew was her problem, and she *would* get a handle on the situation.

Bracing himself on his elbow again, Hawke watched her for several more minutes, the eye contact searing. His wolf was far closer to the surface than that of any other male in the pack, and she was one of the few people who probably knew why. Reaching up, she clenched a hand in his hair and tugged him down until their noses almost touched. "I'm not the only one who's got a problem."

He growled at her. She let him feel her claws against his face. Ice blue eyes locked with her own. "You know what it is," he finally said, his voice so deep it was difficult to understand. Rolling away from her, he lay on his back with one arm under his head.

Yeah, Indigo knew what it was. "She's far older now than she was when she first entered the den."

Hawke said nothing. He didn't need to—she could all but feel his thrumming tension.

"No one's going to stop you if you decide to—"

Hawke was suddenly leaning over her in one of those electric snaps of movement, his wolf very much in charge. "Riley made it clear she was off-limits."

Indigo knew her fellow lieutenant had issued that warning not simply because Sienna was family and thus his to protect, but because the girl had needed time to come into her own before she had to pit the strength of her personality against Hawke's.

"Then, she was." She stroked her fingers through his hair because he needed the touch of Pack. "Now . . . she's stronger. I'm not saying she's ready for the full Hawke assault"—her wolf bared its teeth when he growled—"but she can take a little bit." That said more about Indigo's judgment of Sienna Lauren than anything else—because there were very few women on the planet who she thought might be able to handle Hawke.

The fact that the top contender was an eighteen-heading-for-nineteen-year-old Psy defector was one hell of a surprise, but that didn't mean they should just ignore the subject and hope it went away. Especially not when the girl seemed to reach parts of Hawke no one else could even see.

Indigo knew what Hawke had said to Riley when the subject came up last time, waited to see if he would reject the idea out of hand again. As she watched, he flowed to his feet and went to crouch at the edge of the cliff, his back and hair dusted with ice crystals that glittered in the sunlight. "We should get back," he said after several long minutes, his voice human once more.

Indigo didn't push. This was a decision Hawke would have to make on his own. Because once made, she knew that decision would be final and absolute. If he decided to pursue Sienna . . . Sucking in a breath, Indigo promised herself she'd warn the girl if and when the time came—because no woman should have to face that kind of a campaign unprepared.

**In spite of** his determination to keep his distance, Andrew found himself following the compulsion to track down Indigo as soon as he returned to the den—only to be told that she'd gone running with Hawke.

Images of what they might be doing at that moment slammed into him without warning. Indigo was the highest-ranking female in the den. Only two people outranked her. Riley, who was happily mated to Mercy. And Hawke.

Who was very definitely not mated.

Claws digging into his palms, he shut himself inside his room and tried to fight the buzzing in his head, to think. That proved close to impossible. No matter all his plans, all his instructions to himself, he might've gone off half-cocked and made a fool of himself if his cell phone hadn't rung at that moment.

He answered without looking at the caller ID. "Andrew speaking."

"How's everything in the den?" came Riley's familiar voice.

"Relax, big brother." Andrew tried for a breezy tone. "We're managing to limp along without you."

A small pause. "What's wrong?"

Ah, hell. His oldest sibling knew him better than anyone else—there was no way he'd buy a bullshit answer. "I have a question. Have Indigo and Hawke ever . . ." Acid burned in his gut as he gave voice to a possibility he'd never even considered before.

Another, longer pause. "No. Never."

Andrew collapsed into a sitting position on the bed. "Now you have to forget I ever asked you that question."

Other wolves might have teased, but Riley handled it in his own way. "Piece of advice—don't ever let Indigo catch even a hint that you had that particular thought. The asinine stupidity of it will outweigh any gains you make."

Andrew winced. "I'm not making many gains right now."

"When you were a kid," Riley said, "it was impossible to make you let go of a toy once you'd clamped your teeth on it."

"Indigo's hardly a toy." No, what she was, was a tough, intelligent woman who would fall easily into no man's arms—least of all one she was determined to think of as off-limits.

"The point," Riley said dryly, "is that you're even more stubborn than I am—just takes people a hell of a lot longer to figure it out."

That suddenly, Andrew's brain started functioning again. Smiling at the thought of sinking his teeth into Indigo—not to hurt, just to mark a little—he said, "How's the vacation going?"

"Mercy's grandparents want cubs or pups to spoil—they're not fussy which. Tomorrow would be nice, but they're willing to give us a whole entire year to 'get down to the business.'" Riley's tone was deadpan, but Andrew didn't miss the way his voice softened when he spoke of children.

Mercy's grandparents, he thought, might just get their wish sooner rather than later. "Brenna's out with Judd," he said aloud, "but you should be able to get her on her cell. I know she wants to catch up with you." Having effectively raised both Andrew and Brenna, Riley was, for want of a better word, the patriarch of the Kincaid family. Even Brenna's assassin of a mate treated Riley with quiet respect. They all missed him—and his rock-solid advice—when he wasn't in the den.

"I'll give her a quick call." A rustle. "Mercy says to tell you she hopes you're behaving."

Smiling at the thought of Riley's fiery mate, Andrew said, "Not a bit."

Mercy came on the line an instant later. "Did I hear you say something about Indigo?"

"Mercy," Andrew began.

"No, no, I'm not going to meddle. But I am going to give you a little advice in return for something important you said to me once, so listen up."

Not having been born stupid, no matter his recent actions, Andrew did just that.

"Don't be anyone but who you are," the leopard sentinel told him. "It'll give you the element of surprise when you pounce."

On the surface, it was a lighthearted comment, but Andrew saw it for the truth it was. How had Mercy known? he thought. How had she guessed that his confidence had been badly dented by the knowledge that he was so much not what Indigo had in mind for her mate? However she'd known, he was grateful for the boost. "Thanks, Mercy."

"What can I say—you remind me of the fiends I call brothers." An affectionate comment. "'Bye, Drew."

Hanging up after replying in kind, he took a deep breath and fired off a quick e-mail to Hawke with his notes on what Teijan had shared. And though the temptation to track down Indigo was a fever in his gut, he set his jaw and went to the weight room, funneling his need into the physical. Because when he, as Mercy had put it, "pounced," he wanted Indy all to himself, no avenues of escape, no buffer of pack.

# CHAPTER 9

**In spite of** her earlier run with Hawke, Indigo couldn't quite find her balance at that afternoon's lieutenant meeting. She told herself it had nothing to do with the fact that she'd seen Drew only minutes ago, his hair damp with sweat and his arm around Lucy as the sunny-natured young female hugged him affectionately.

Women loved Drew. No wonder he'd thought he could get Indigo into bed with so little trouble—and then pick up right where they'd left off, as if he hadn't fundamentally altered the nature of the relationship between them. Her wolf bared its fangs at the idea of being lumped in with his little playmates until she had to consciously fight for control. It was as well that she was sitting in a special comm room surrounded by SnowDancer lieutenants.

Because of the breadth of SnowDancer territory, it was rare for all the lieutenants to meet in person. However, they had monthly meetings by comm-conference and each lieutenant passed through the den at least once every two months, which ensured the pack continued to function as a cohesive unit. Hawke, too, made trips to each part of their territory on a regular basis. Then there was Drew, who, with the support of his small and tight-knit team, roamed across the state on an as-needed basis.

Gritting her teeth as the damn wolf intruded into her thoughts once again, she looked up and focused on the screens set up in a semicircle around the room. The computronic setup allowed all of them to interact with each other at such an effective level that they often forgot they weren't actually in the same physical location.

Jem—real name Garnet—had logged in from Los Angeles and was currently trading barbs with the startlingly green-eyed Kenji, something the two of them did so often, there was a running pool on exactly when they'd rip each other's clothes off and just get it over with.

Alexei and Matthias were watching, quiet as always. Those two only moved when necessary, and they spoke even less most of the time. Of the two, Alexei, with his sun gold hair and movie star looks, was probably the more talkative— which meant he spoke maybe two words an hour instead of one.

Cooper, as one of the more senior sentinels—his place in the hierarchy similar to Riaz's—looked on with open amusement, his skin gleaming a rich dark bronze in the sunlight pouring in through what Indigo knew to be a huge window to the left of his office, the jagged scar along his left cheek adding a rough accent to his features.

Women tended to look at him and shiver in a mix of fear and anticipation.

That was the closest they'd ever come to him, because Coop was crazy in love with—and courting—a woman so sweet, it had the whole pack abuzz. No one had expected mad, bad, and dangerous Coop to fall head over heels for the submissive wolf, least of all the wolf herself. Indigo bit back a grin as she thought of how bewildered Coop's beloved had looked when it had dawned on her that she was being pursued by one of the most lethal men in the pack. That hadn't lasted long. Because she might've been sweet, might've been submissive, but as Coop was learning, that didn't mean she didn't have a mind—and a will—of her own.

Then there was Tomás, who happened to be one of Drew's closest friends—and consequently, seemed to take nothing seriously and had a way of smiling with those chocolate-dark eyes that made most women melt into puddles of goo.

Indigo gave Tomás a quelling stare when he glanced at Jem and Kenji and winked. But she couldn't help her wolf's answering grin. Because seriously . . . "You two need to get a room."

Jem didn't even stop arguing to give Indigo a highly specific nonverbal gesture with one deceptively delicate-looking hand. Kenji echoed the move with such unerring accuracy, it was as if they'd synchronized it across two different parts of the state. Next to Indigo, Riaz mouthed, "Kenji" to Tomás, who shook his head and mouthed, "Jem." Riaz held up a hand, fingers spread. Tomás nodded, accepting the bet.

Judd said nothing from where he sat two seats to Indigo's left, but he was relaxed to an extent he'd never have been a year ago, his chair tilted back to lean against the wall and his legs stretched out in front. But no matter his apparently lazy pose, Indigo had no doubts that he'd seen and logged every word that had passed since he entered the room.

Pushing back her own chair, Indigo put her legs up on the table in front of her and raised a hand in a casual wave as Hawke arrived to grab the empty seat on her right. "Now that we're *all* here, we can begin."

"Cut me a break, *Indy*." Hawke grinned at the look she shot him, but his next words were pure growl. "I just spent ten minutes explaining to the juveniles why they can't go around sniffing after the leopard girls without expecting to get their asses kicked by the leopard boys at least once. When the hell is Riley coming back?"

Alexei and Matthias both smiled, slowly and with the wolf in their eyes, while Tomás rocked back and laughed with open amusement, the lean male dimples that creased his cheeks turning his handsome face even more gorgeous. Shaking her head, Indigo reached over to tap Hawke lightly on the cheek with her pen. "You'll live." Turning back to the others, she said, "Kenji, cut the foreplay. Report."

Kenji switched into lieutenant mode so fast, Indigo would've gotten whiplash if she hadn't seen him do the exact same thing before. "Nothing significant to report. We've had a few extra Psy move into the region, but our intel says they're no threat—looks like most came in for a job at a new Psy computronics factory."

"Any indication the factory is a front for something else?" Hawke asked. "We've seen that before."

"I've got my eye on it." Kenji thrust back strands of his stick-straight black hair. "But everything checks out so far. And it's one of Nikita Duncan's—she tends to like to keep her profits separate from her politics."

Indigo agreed with that assessment, but made a note to have the den's resident hackers dig deeper into the factory's files nonetheless. "Tomás, how's your patch?"

"No change."

Jem went next. "We've had a spike in the murder rate, but it looks to be human-on-human gang violence."

"You on it?" Hawke tapped a finger restlessly on the arm of his chair.

"We've already had a talk with the gangs. They want to make trouble, they don't do it in our territory." What was left unsaid was that if they continued, they'd soon find themselves hunted down like so much prey. The pack didn't hold the largest territory in the country because it played nice. One warning was all you got.

Matthias spoke for the first time, and his deep voice was a pleasure to listen to, resonant and with an almost impossible clarity. "I sent you that note about some weird ship movements. We haven't been able to pin anything down yet, but I'll keep you updated."

Indigo looked at Cooper. "Anything new?"

"I've got two female novices who're showing signs of skill at sharpshooting."

"Send me their details," Judd said. "I'll evaluate them and set up a training schedule."

"Hey, Coop," Tomás called out, the devil in his eye. "How's it going with your pretty little wolf?"

Cooper glanced over, unruffled. "You'll be the last to know. But the next time you send her flowers, I'm going to come over for a nice friendly visit and shove them where the sun don't shine."

Ignoring the suspicious cough that seemed to have affected everyone in the meeting, Indigo pointed at Alexei.

"This sector's stable," the young lieutenant said, making a valiant effort to fight a laugh, "though I think we need to organize one of the packwide parties again. I've got too many unmated adults in my area and they're starting to irritate each other."

The last thing Indigo needed to be thinking about was the sexual hunger of their animals, but she set her jaw and got to it—because fact was, touch-hungry changelings, especially wolves as aggressive as those in SnowDancer, needed an outlet—and if they couldn't have sex, they'd choose violence. Add in the lack of choice in Alexei's comparatively small sector and you had a recipe for trouble.

"May," she said, checking her calendar. "We can have a week-long event in den territory. That'll give us the flexibility to ensure security doesn't slip."

No one had any issues with that, so they moved on.

"The falcons are making use of the flight treaty," Matthias said toward the end, his thickly lashed eyes dark and intense. "I've seen them flying over my sector."

"Me, too." Alexei leaned forward, bracing his arms on a glowing cherrywood desk. "Where are we on a possible alliance?"

"I think it's a real possibility," Hawke said. "I sent Drew to spend some time with them on the ground a month ago, and his report backs up my instincts."

"He in the den?" Cooper asked. "It'd be good to hear what he has to say."

When Hawke nodded, Indigo said, "Ten-minute break," in

a tone she hoped sounded practical and nothing else, "then we reconvene. I'll hunt down Drew."

That proved to be child's play. He opened the door to his room with a towel wrapped around his waist, his hair wet. "Indy." Blinking water from his eyes, he stepped back and angled his head. "Come in. I was just about to throw some clothes on."

Heat uncurled in her abdomen—because no matter how pissed she was at him, Andrew Kincaid made her fingers itch to touch. Smooth, gleaming skin, toned muscle, and those eyes that never lost the edge of wickedness. "You're needed in the main conference room, five minutes."

Heading back inside when she remained on the doorstep, he disappeared behind the door. "What about?"

"Falcons." Her mind insisted on providing her with all sorts of salacious images as she heard the soft rasp of the towel leaving his body to pool on the floor, the rougher sound of him pulling on jeans—"Don't be late," she bit out and swiveled on her heel.

**Andrew's fingers clenched** convulsively on the T-shirt in his grasp. She was still mad; that much was clear. And no matter that keeping her angry was part of his ultimate strategy, he had the violent urge to tug her close and kiss the anger right off her lips.

Of course, he thought, in her current mood the only thing that would get him was a nicely eviscerated chest. "Charm," he muttered under his breath. "Don't forget that—it's all about charm. Stick to the plan."

Pulling on the T-shirt, he laced up his sneakers and made his way to the conference room. "Nice to see everyone hard at work," he said when he walked in to find them playing virtual poker.

There were a slew of responses to that, some rude, some friendly, but the game was cleared away in under a minute, with Alexei declared the winner. After the golden-haired lieutenant took a mock bow, Andrew—viscerally aware of Indigo's silent presence on Hawke's other side—laid out his impressions of the falcon wing.

"Good, strong unit," he said. "Well drilled and trained to work together. The ancestors of the core group formed the wing prior to the Territorial Wars, so they've been around several hundred years."

"Why aren't they bigger in numbers by now?" Judd asked from his position at the far end of the table.

Hawke was the one who answered. "Birds tend to keep their wings small. I think it has to do with ensuring enough open sky, though I've heard they stay in close contact with other wings across the country."

"Hawke's right," Andrew said, even as his wolf picked out Indigo's scent from all the other threads in the room and rolled around in it like a pup. "I asked Adam, their wing leader, about that. He says their flight paths often overlap, so it makes sense to keep things pleasant. But the end result is that while WindHaven might not be huge, we ally with them, we gain access to a network of wings across the country."

Cooper raised an eyebrow. "Nothing to sneeze at. So long as they can handle us." A blunt truth. "Otherwise, the dominance issues will make a mess of things."

Hawke rocked back in his chair, linking his hands behind his head. "Having dealt with Adam, and Jacques, his second, I don't think that's going to be a problem."

"So we're going to start the ball rolling?" Indigo's voice, slicing through Andrew's concentration with the ease of a razor.

"I'll talk to DarkRiver," Hawke said, "see if they have any further information, but yeah, I think we should take advantage of the opportunity."

Andrew listened as Indigo went through a couple of other matters before ending the meeting. Her words were crisp, her commands clear, and her intelligence as sharp as a blade—there was no way in hell she was going to make this easy for him.

His wolf sat up in anticipation—he'd never wanted easy. He'd always wanted Indigo. And tomorrow, he'd have her all to himself, far from the den and the hierarchy . . . and the rules that she used to keep her own explosive response to him under vicious control. But he knew. He'd tasted it.

And he was going to make Indy admit it—even if he had to sneak in under her defenses using every dirty trick in the book. This was war. Who the hell cared about playing fair?

# CHAPTER 10

**Councilor Nikita Duncan** met Councilor Anthony Kyriakus outside a small house situated on the heavily forested edges of Tahoe, having driven herself there in a bland gray sedan with tinted windows. "Was this where your daughter lived while she was in the Net?" she asked Anthony when he pushed open the door.

Anthony's black hair, silvered at the temples, lifted a fraction in the forest breeze as he answered. "Yes." He nodded at the door. "Please."

"Thank you." As she entered, she took in everything about the place. The room immediately to her right may once have functioned as a living area, but was now an office/meeting room with a small table featuring a built-in computer panel and four chairs. "Does the F ability make an appearance every generation?" The NightStar Group's grip on the market for foreseers was all but airtight.

"There are sporadic skips, but overall, yes," he said, as

they took their seats opposite each other. "It is the same in your family, is it not?"

Nikita answered because it was no secret—the "flawed" E designation was the Duncan family's genetic millstone. "It tends to skip a generation." Not quite the truth, but close enough that it would pass. "You know why I contacted you." And why she'd done it away from the dark skies of the PsyNet.

Anthony's eyes were penetrating as they met hers across the table. "Something is happening with the Arrow Squad."

"Yes." Ming was the official leader of the assassins who were the Council's most lethal army, but Nikita's spies had caught ripples that said things might well be changing. "If the leadership shifts, there are only two possible successors."

"Kaleb and Vasic," Anthony said. "But while Vasic is an Arrow and the single true teleporter in the Net, my information is that he doesn't consider himself a candidate for the position."

"However, with his support, someone else could take the leadership." The squad was incredibly secretive, but Nikita wasn't a Councilor because she gave up at the first hurdle. She'd unearthed enough data that she felt confident in saying, "There are rumors of another Arrow the squad may accept as a leader."

Anthony took a moment to reply. "His name is Aden. I'm keeping an eye on affairs as they develop."

It was, Nikita understood, a very deliberate sharing of information. "Good. But that situation, while important, isn't the critical one as far as we are concerned." Neither of them was in the fight to lead the Arrows.

Anthony made no pretense of not understanding her meaning. "Henry and Shoshanna," he said. "They support the idea of Purity to the exclusion of all else, though it is clear that Silence is failing."

"Divided, we have a high chance of falling to their stratagems," she said, having made her decision the first time she called Anthony, "but together, we are a force to be reckoned with." Then she asked the most important question. "Where do you stand, Anthony?"

Anthony took a drink from the glass of water at his elbow,

answering only after almost ten seconds of thought. "I do not support any group or system that would erase my individuality, and the Scotts are determined to create a true hive mind in one form or another." He put the glass on the table. "More importantly, they have interfered once too often in this territory—and in my business interests."

Nikita wondered if the Scotts had attempted to meddle in Anthony's subcontracting agreement with his daughter. Not that the details mattered; whatever they had done, it was to Nikita's benefit. "If we are to work effectively together," she said, "there is something else we need to discuss." And then she spoke of death.

# CHAPTER 11

**It had taken** Judd more time than he'd expected to track down Xavier's missing parishioner, Gloria. His mate, with her brilliant mind, had done most of the cyber-detective work, backtracking the phone number and digging through layers of security to unearth the address that went with it.

"No activity on her charge cards for the past four days," Brenna had said, worry a dark shadow in her eyes when she gave him the information. "And it appears she's given up her lease. She might not even be there."

Now, in the chill quiet of the midnight hours, Judd picked the low-security lock on Gloria's former apartment and slipped inside. If there was someone within, he'd teleport out before they ever saw him. But he felt only the cold emptiness of a place in which there had been no life for days.

Using a flashlight with its beam set on low, he checked both rooms. The furniture was still there, but from the looks of it, it might well have come with the apartment. There were no clothes in the wardrobe, no toiletries in the bathroom, and no food in the kitchen. More importantly, the apartment was clean.

Very, *very* clean.

The kind of clean that meant someone had been erased out of existence.

Gloria was dead.

His instincts told him someone—likely in the Council superstructure—had sent in a cleanup crew to ensure no trace remained of the woman who'd found herself in Xavier's church. But Judd wasn't going to give the priest that information until he was certain—because there was a slight chance Gloria had been rehabilitated instead.

A fate worse than death.

Deciding to work SnowDancer's Psy contacts when morning broke, he focused on the image of the bedroom he shared with his mate, and then . . . he was home. Dressed in a strawberry satin and white lace slip, Brenna lay curled up on his side of the futon. She always did that when he wasn't with her, as if she was holding him close even in sleep.

Taking off his clothes with a silent grace that came from a lifetime of training, he slipped in beside her, and then, bracing himself on one arm, leaned down to press a kiss to the silky warm curve of her neck.

She shivered, her body relaxing from its curled-up position as she turned to face him, her hands reaching out to press against his pectorals. "Judd." It was a sleepy murmur of welcome, her wolf apparent in the brilliant night-glow he glimpsed between her barely parted lids.

Claiming her lips with his own, he moved his hand down over her pretty little nightdress until he found skin. Then he indulged in a pleasure that seemed to get ever more piercing, ever more intense. Once, he hadn't been able to touch her without causing himself pain. Now, it only hurt when he didn't touch her.


**Though the day** dawned clear and bright, the sun promising a brilliant show, Indigo was in a snippy mood and she knew it well enough to keep it under control. It wasn't the fault of these poor teenagers milling in the White Zone that Drew was an idiot who'd changed everything between them with an imbecilic play for sex—then made the whole thing worse by refusing to face up to it.

Beating her snippiness into submission, she helped one of the juveniles tighten the straps of her small pack. "You looking forward to today, Silvia?"

The girl swallowed, flushing under the lush coffee of her skin, and her words, when they came out, were hesitant. "I'm not strong like you."

And *that*, Indigo thought, was even more of a problem than the control issues of the dominant males. "You listen to me," she said, cupping the girl's cheek, able to feel the soft down of youth against her callused palm, "we soldiers are the brawn, the muscle. It's the maternal females like you who are the heart of the pack. You're the glue that holds us together. Far as I'm concerned, you're the strongest part of SnowDancer."

Silvia blinked those long, silky lashes, leaning her cheek a little into Indigo's touch. "I . . . my mom said . . . but it's nice to hear it from you."

Smiling, Indigo hugged her, and they walked over to join the rest of the group. Twelve kids between the ages of thirteen and seventeen. All simply needing a little bit of extra attention to get them back on the right track. "Everyone ready?"

A sea of nods.

"I thought Drew was coming," said a slender young male with a thick mop of pale brown hair and a voice that was far too deep for his scrawny body. It'd be perfect when Brace grew into those shoulders, but right now, he tended to flush whenever he spoke up.

"He can catch up." Okay, so maybe she wasn't over the snippy. "Follow me."

She set a steady pace—not so easy that they got bored, not so hard that they couldn't keep up—taking them up into an unusual part of the mountains, one of such exquisite beauty it could make the heart stop, but an area even the pack rarely visited because it was more difficult to get to than so many other gorgeous spots. However, right now, it had the benefit of being almost entirely clear of snow, while comparable areas in the southern section of the Sierra remained packed with the white stuff.

They stopped for snacks around midmorning. No sign of Drew.

If he left her alone all weekend, she'd strip his hide. "Come on," she said, hoping her inner snarl didn't show. "We're not even halfway yet."

Pained groans, but she knew they were faking. She'd felt their exhilaration as they tested their bodies, as they loosened up enough to speak to her, ask her questions. So she upped the speed, knowing they could take it, that they'd be proud of it. But they were still exhausted when they walked over the edge of a hill and to the spot where she intended to break for lunch . . . to find the plateau set with a huge picnic blanket holding fruit, drinks, sandwiches, cake, and, of course, potato chips.

But it wasn't only food waiting for them.

Drew bent at the waist, a checkered tea towel folded dramatically over his arm. "Welcome to my kitchen."

Indigo clenched her stomach muscles against the shock of seeing him face-to-face after having mentally eviscerated him for most of the journey. The juveniles had no such qualms. Cheering, they descended upon the feast as if every single one of them hadn't gorged on trail bars and dried fruit a bare couple of hours ago.

Drew skirted the plundering horde and walked across to join her. "I set up a blanket for you over there. Thought you could do with a break."

Her wolf was more than suspicious of his solicitude after the recent awkwardness between them. Or maybe, she thought with a silent growl, this was all part of his "let's just pretend it never happened" policy. "This is why you abandoned me with twelve teenagers?" She folded her arms, refusing to give in to the urge to fix the wind-tousled mess of his hair. That was something she might have done before. When he'd been a trusted friend.

Reaching up, Drew flicked his ear. "Big ears."

Glancing over his shoulder, she saw their charges were involved in the food, but he had a point. So she didn't argue when he urged her to follow him down the slope a little and onto a small shelf of land out of sight and downwind of the others.

The picnic blanket waiting there was smaller, striped with blue and white, and lying in a dappled patch of sunlight. A collapsible picnic basket sat a little to the side, while the blanket itself was set with small platters holding plump berries, sliced chicken, fluffy bread, what looked like a fresh salad, and two bottles of water that sparkled in the sun.

Indigo's wolf liked the idea of food, but neither it nor she was about to let Drew off the hook. "I'm waiting for an answer."

"I knew you could handle the juveniles"—easy words with no apparent undertone—"and I figured I'd better run up here and check the trail in case of possible rock slides from the storm. Far as I know, no one's been up here since."

*Damn, she should've thought of that.* "You should've told me."

"I left a message on your phone."

Scowling, Indigo pulled her cell phone out of her pocket. *Double damn.* "I forgot to charge it." Still angry—though it was irrational and had nothing whatsoever to do with his actions today—she finally shrugged off her pack and took a seat on the blanket.

Drew sat in silence as she made herself a sandwich, then he made one for himself. The air up here was crisp, fresh, and somehow freeing. She felt her shoulders loosen up, her emotions turn mellow in spite of her vivid, almost uncomfortable awareness of the male wolf sitting on the other side of the picnic basket. When he reached for the basket, she was curious enough to glance over. "What else have you got?"

A smile that lit up his eyes to a blinding shade, making her suck in a startled breath. She wasn't obstinate without reason—she could admit Drew had a way about him. He'd always used it to make her smile before. But she wasn't ready to be charmed today.

Then he opened the bakery box in his hand to reveal a slice of New York cheesecake. "Since I ruined the experience of the other one." Putting it on the blanket between them, he placed several fresh berries on top and nudged it her way. "It's all for you."

Indigo's heart threatened to melt, but she held firm. Sure, he looked woebegone, but she'd known him far too long to fall for that. "Thanks." Taking the cheesecake, she picked up the fork and ate a bite, watching as Drew packed up the rest of the stuff and moved the basket so he could sidle up right next to her. "Watch it," she muttered.

"I'm sorry."

Startled, she glanced at him—to see that those always-laughing eyes had gone truly solemn, his expression intent. "About what?" Her wolf had to be certain. Neither part of her liked shades of gray.

"About the way I acted the other night." A sheepish smile. "You were right. I was high on adrenaline—I should've crashed instead of hitting on you."

Suspicion whispered through her veins. There was something he wasn't saying, she thought, but she couldn't quite figure out the loophole. "Why didn't you say this earlier?"

"I wanted to do it right—and you were too mad to listen."

Yes, she admitted, she had been. Her sense of betrayal had been—she could now admit—out of all proportion to what he'd actually done. Except that it had been *him*, a wolf she'd given her deepest trust.

He nudged her shoulder with his own when she stayed silent. "I hate that I'm worried about touching you now," he said. "And I know it's my fault." A pause. "Indy, come on. Do you know how early I had to get up to go get your cheesecake?" Big blue eyes that looked as guileless as a newborn pup's.

She knew half of it was an act—but her wolf liked his playfulness. She always had. And . . . he had apologized. Flat out. No reservations. Most dominant wolves—and Drew was categorically a dominant, for all that he fooled people into thinking otherwise—had trouble with the *s* word, even when they were utterly in the wrong. Maybe he hadn't been avoiding her because he was sulking, she decided; maybe he had actually been figuring out how to apologize. As a dominant herself, she understood exactly how hard it had to have been for him.

So she scooped up a bite of the cheesecake and lifted the fork to his mouth. He accepted it, a smile creasing his face. Then he nuzzled at her neck, and her wolf allowed it . . . welcomed it.

That was when Indigo realized she'd hated not being able to touch Drew, too.

**Andrew fisted** a hand on the blanket behind Indigo, drawing the rainstorm and steel scent of her into his lungs. His wolf was starved for it, rolled around in it as if it was drunk, unable to get enough. When she didn't push him away, he allowed himself another precious, excruciating second to indulge in the silken heat of her skin before raising his head.

She lifted another bite of cheesecake in his direction. Giving a huge sigh, he held out a hand. "No, no. I told you it was all for you."

A tug of her lips. "You're terrible, you know that." She put the fork to his lips.

He parted them, let her feed him, the small intimacy making his wolf want to sing in thrumming pleasure. "That's why you love me."

A shake of her head, but her lips curved upward, her eyes shimmering with laughter. "How did Riley ever put up with you when you were a child?"

"You know Riley. Nothing bothers him." Except Mercy, Andrew thought. His brother, the Wall, had fallen. And so would Andrew's smart, stubborn Indigo. "I'd do something stupid, he wouldn't yell, wouldn't snarl, he'd just dump me in the lake. Rinse and repeat until I got the point."

Indigo snickered, and it made his wolf go motionless, cock its head. The sound of her happiness . . . yeah, he'd do anything for it.

"Too bad you're too big to be dumped in the lake now."

Lying back on the blanket with his arms folded beneath his head, he stared up at the leaves outlined against the excruciating blue of the sky. It was a stunning beauty, but it couldn't hold his attention. Indigo's scent, her warmth so close, her hip brushing his, it scored him to the soul. "Oh, I dunno," he said, keeping it light because there was no way he wanted to spook her again, "he did it a few weeks ago."

He all but saw Indigo's wolf prick up its ears. Twisting her body, she leaned over to put the empty bakery box beside the picnic basket, then placed one hand on his chest, gave a little nudge. "Tell me."

Her touch locked the air in his throat, threatened to steal his words, his soul. Indigo nudged again when he didn't answer. "I'll find out anyway, you know."

Glad she'd misunderstood his silence, he made a face at her. "All I said was that he should shave."

Leaning down until her nose almost touched his, she narrowed her eyes, "Uh-huh. Which part of him did you suggest he shave?"

# CHAPTER 12

**He grinned,** his wolf delighted with her. "His head." When Indigo touched her nose to his, he dared raise one of his hands and play with strands of her hair, her ponytail having tumbled over her shoulder. "I might have hinted that he was turning old and gray. Oh, and maybe losing his hair anyway."

Indigo's body shook. "You know newly mated men are touchy about things like that." But her hand clenched on his T-shirt before she fell away and onto her back beside him, the sound of her laughter husky and open. "God, I wish I'd seen his face."

Andrew wanted nothing more than to raise himself on his elbow, reach down and stroke his hand over Indigo's face. He'd hold her with his fingers on her jaw as he took her smiling lips with his own, indulging once more in the taste he hadn't been able to get out of his mind since the night of the storm.

His body tensed, blood pumping hot and hard. Gritting his teeth, he bent one leg to hide the blunt evidence of his reaction, even as he said, "I couldn't believe he fell for it." His brother was in the prime of his life, one of the most powerful wolves in the pack. And he was assuredly in no danger of losing his hair.

"He's not going to think completely straight for a while," Indigo said, "but the mating dance is the worst part. Men go a little nuts during that time. I remember when Elias met Yuki. He turned into his evil twin, snarling at anyone who so much as looked her way."

Andrew couldn't imagine even-tempered Elias snarling at anyone. But as he himself knew, it was hard to be rational when your whole being was focused on a woman to the extent that the need to touch her skin, to draw the scent of her deep into your lungs, became a fever in your blood. "I think the natives are getting restless."

"Yeah, I hear them." Sitting up, she slapped him lightly on the chest. "I'll go help them clean up, pack up the leftovers for later."

"I'll take care of things here." Rising, he watched her walk away, a tall, strong woman with contentment humming through her stubborn bones—because he'd apologized, because she thought he'd turned the clock back to the way things had always been.

His hand fisted again, but not in anger. In determination.

**They made camp** late that afternoon. Since the weather was holding and the night sky promised to be beautiful beyond compare, Andrew suggested they lay their sleeping bags out on the ground. "It's not damp anymore," he said to Indigo, having tested the earth. "Doesn't look like it'll rain any tonight, either. And this area's only logged the odd snowfall the past few weeks, so we should be good on that score."

Indigo rolled her eyes. "You've clearly never been a teenage girl."

"Huh?" He looked out at the kids, who'd collapsed against trees or on the earth. "They're all good kids. And they're changelings." No matter what their place in the hierarchy, all wolves could survive in the forest with no amenities whatsoever.

Shaking her head, Indigo said, "I can't believe I'm having to explain this to the man who knows everyone and has probably had dinner with more people in the pack than me, Hawke, and Riley combined."

"Don't rub it in." He scowled at the teasing—though his wolf was spinning around in untrammeled joy that she was playing with him. "So?"

"Haven't you noticed the glances passing between male and female?" She raised an eyebrow, nudging his attention toward a certain pairing. "Sure, it's no big deal to be naked when you shift—but we're human, too. No teenage girl is comfortable with her body. *Especially* with a boy she's interested in looking on."

Andrew rubbed his jaw, aware he'd missed the signals passing between the kids because he'd been so focused on Indigo. "Huh. Cute."

"It might be. But there'll be no monkey business on my watch."

He grinned at her stern expression. "I bet you were confident about your body when you were a teen."

"You'd lose that bet." Snorting, she cupped her hands around her mouth. "Come on, boys and girls, get the tents up! Then we'll play a game."

"What's the prize?" was the cheeky response from Harley, who at sixteen was still fluctuating so wildly in his control—and resulting dominance—that no one knew where to put him in the hierarchy. Hawke was hoping that two days of concentrated time with the pack's dominants would decide the matter one way or another.

Indigo grinned. "An extra marshmallow in your hot chocolate—if you're lucky. Now snap to it."

Grumbling at her "slave driving," they began to put up their tents in pairs, as they would all be sharing. Indigo had worried about that with Drew, but now that they were back to normal, they'd do the same. It made her wolf happy. Like most SnowDancers, it preferred sleeping with Pack to a lonely bed. It was only the human half that chose privacy. But tonight with Drew, both sides would be satisfied.

Drew was already bending down to pull out the tent from

where it was attached to the bottom of his pack. "I can't believe it," he muttered, continuing their earlier conversation. "What did you have to worry about as a teenager?"

"Oh, please." She helped him spread the groundsheet on a level section of earth facing the other tents and hunted out the high-strength pegs as he unfolded the whisper-thin fabric of the tent itself. "I grew to my full height at fourteen." Five feet ten in her bare feet, Indigo loved her height. Now.

"But," she continued as they pegged down the edges, "I didn't have any curves. *None.* All I had were clown feet I kept tripping over, and a body that was all right angles. I felt like a giant in the land of little people. A flat-chested giant with elbows of doom."

Chuckling, Drew fed through one of the flexible struts that snapped the tent upright without the need for a central support pole. "I was short at fourteen. Really short."

Indigo thought back, tried to remember. But she'd been eighteen, and fourteen-year-old boys hadn't merited much attention. "That must've been tough."

"You have no idea." He watched as she fed through the second, cross-supporting strut. "Riley was already all manly, and I couldn't even see over the tops of my shoes." A mournful expression.

Laughing, she finished her task and opened the flaps so he could throw their packs inside. "Ah, well, we both grew into our bodies."

"In my case, I grew out of it," Drew corrected. "Shot up like a pine tree the summer between my fourteenth and fifteenth year. Unfortunately, I continued to lack any manliness whatsoever."

Reaching out, Indigo squeezed his upper arm, the skin of her fingertips a little rough from all the work she did combat training their young dominants. "Well, you bloomed nicely."

It took every ounce of control Andrew had to keep his tone light when all he wanted to do was to strip himself naked and have her stroke those capable hands over every straining inch of his body. Thank God his T-shirt covered the hard ridge of his cock as he took a seat beside her, his arms braced loosely on raised knees. "Thanks," he said when she looked to him for a response. "That's what Meadow Sanderson said when she divested me of my virginity."

"Meadow . . . hmm I don't remember her."

"Human," he said, recalling the lushly sensual girl who'd tied him up in knots over the course of a long, hazy summer. "She dumped me for the quarterback after she'd played my body like a banjo. So sad."

"I bet."

"I'm serious. I was heartbroken."

"For how long?"

"A whole week." An eternity in the life of a teenage boy. "Then I realized other girls had noticed my new manliness, too, and the rest, as they say, is history." Adoring girls had never been hard for him. He liked the way they smelled, the way their bodies curved, the way they laughed. But that blissful year, for the first time in his life, those girls had adored him back. "What about you?"

"I was the hunter, not the hunted," she said with a slow smile of remembrance. "I finally grew some breasts in my second-to-last year of high school—and decided I'd waited long enough, thank you very much."

He could see her in his mind—a tall, lusciously curved girl who'd made his head spin. It had been a general admiration at that stage—he'd thought she was hot, no doubt about it, but he'd been more focused on getting girls his own age to pay attention to him. "Who was the lucky guy?" Jealousy dug sharp little claws into his gut, but he shut that door tight almost before it opened.

Changelings were sensual creatures—touch was the cornerstone of how they related to each other. He would have never wished for Indigo to have spent her adult life without intimacy; it would've hurt her on the deepest level. But that was then. If she went to bed with another man now . . .

Andrew's wolf saw red.

"An Ecuadoran exchange student named Dominic." Indigo's voice cut through the haze, pulling him back into the present. "Dark, handsome, and with that accent—and the boy did know what he was doing." A laugh . . . but that husky tone was just a fraction "off." "Though I remember him scrambling backward when my claws sliced out."

Attuned to every tiny aspect of her, he paid close attention. "Was he human, too?"

"Changeling, and dominant, but I don't think he'd ever been with a female who was as dominant." A pause. "I don't think the experience made him want to repeat it."

"Stupid boy," Andrew said, too angry to be anything but blunt. "I hope you found someone with more balls for your next time."

Indigo's laugh was startled. "So to speak." Tension leaching from her expression, she nudged him with her shoulder. "Time for you to do your thing, hotshot. Make the tracks hard, but not impossible. It's all about building up their confidence."

"Yes ma'am." Getting up, he pulled off his sweatshirt and tee at the same time, throwing them inside the tent.

"Hey," Indigo said, looking up with a scowl, "I got the feeling you wanted to help the boys with their romantic interests."

Andrew followed her gaze . . . to see several pairs of female eyes on him. Teenage female eyes. "Shit." Ducking inside the tent, he finished stripping and shifted, hoping like hell his wolf would listen to reason when it came to the woman who put her hand on his ruff and whispered in his ear as soon as he stepped outside.

"No tricks."

Quivering inside with the urge to tumble her to the earth until she shifted, until she laughed and gave chase, he closed his teeth around her free hand. A gentle bite. "Okay," she said with a smile that almost shattered the wolf's control, "no tricks they can't handle. Go."


**Drew's fur slid** out from under Indigo's palm, the muscled weight of him fluid as he disappeared into the forest. She watched for him, but he was gone, a whisper in the early evening shadows. Turning back around to face her charges, she curled her fingers into her palm, disturbingly aware of how he'd felt, the heat and wild beauty of him.

"Simple rules," she told the teenagers once they'd shifted. "First one to find Drew wins. You can work in pairs, or you can go solo, but you have to decide now." She gave them a couple of minutes to make up their minds before continuing. "No booby traps, no blood. This is about tracking." Glancing around to make sure they all understood, she raised her arm, then dropped it in a sharp downward strike. "Go!"

As they shot out from around her like streaks of lightning, she followed on human feet. She could easily see—and scent—where Drew had gone, but the kids were moving slower, having seldom had the chance to work with someone of his skill. It made Indigo wonder if she could track him if he didn't want to be tracked.

Her wolf didn't like that thought—she was used to being able to run down anyone she chose except Hawke. Their alpha was all kinds of cunning when he didn't want to be found, but Drew was their tracker, born with an almost preternatural ability to zero in on rogue wolves. Lines marred her forehead as a new thought intruded. Was it possible Drew could locate Hawke even when their alpha preferred to be lost?

Catching a whiff of iron in the air, she changed direction to make sure no one had been injured. She found Silvia—a sharp branch had whipped across her muzzle. The girl was gone before Indigo could tell her that the damage was superficial. Indigo's wolf approved.

Burying the branch to ensure it wouldn't inadvertently lead the others this way, she carried on keeping watch over the hunters. True dark was hovering on the horizon when she heard a victorious howl on the cool evening wind.

*Brace.*

Nothing like wanting to impress a girl—in this case, Silvia—to nudge a male wolf into gear. Lifting her head, she joined in as the others in the group began to howl in response to Brace's triumph. The sound was . . . It touched the soul, the music haunting, starkly pure and yet so very earthy.

Home. Pack. Family.

Aware that Drew would herd everyone to camp, she lowered her head on the fading echo of the last note and jogged back herself—to find that Silvia had beaten her there. The girl's bruise looked worse in human form, but the maternal female wasn't worried. "I found something," she said with an almost puppyish eagerness. "Look." A round metal ball lay in the palm of her hand. It was rusted, and had clearly come off the worse against rocks, but was recognizable as a man-made object.

Indigo frowned. "Where did you find this?" SnowDancer was very strict about garbage. Nothing, but nothing, was allowed to pollute their lands.

Silvia described a location about a five-minute run east from where Indigo had last seen her. "It was stuck between two rocks on the edge of the stream. I think it must've been washed down."

That was Indigo's thought, too, and, given the network of tributaries that ran down through the mountains, it meant there was no way to trace the object's origin. "I don't think even Brenna will be able to figure out what this was meant to be." Because while she could see the remnants of a few wires inside, the metal orb was mostly hollow.

Silvia's face fell. Reaching out, Indigo squeezed the girl's rounded shoulder. "But you did good bringing it to me. Even if it is simply trash, we need to track down the guilty party and tell them to keep their junk off our land."

The others began to trickle in then, and she turned to put the sphere in the tent. Drew nudged his way inside while she was still packing it away. Shifting in a shower of sparks, he tugged at the clasps of his pack. "I'm going to go take a dip in the stream."

Indigo realized she was staring at the muscled slope of his back, her fingers uncurling as if in readiness to stroke. "Sure." Coloring at her own rudeness, she backed out of the tent. Thank God Drew had been too intent on pulling out a change of clothes to notice.

# CHAPTER 13

**Two hours after** the completion of the chase, and an hour after dinner, with their charges having collapsed in their tents, Andrew lay on top of his sleeping bag. He and Indigo had pinned up the flaps of their tent and placed their sleeping bags side by side facing outward. The position would allow them to drink in the night sky and keep watch at the same time.

Now, he waited for Indigo with taut anticipation in his gut.

Alone, they'd finally be alone—and within touching distance.

Indigo had gone down to the stream to bathe, and his wolf itched to prowl after her. She had the most beautiful body— all toned muscle and dangerous curves. He wanted to have the right to stroke those curves as he pleased, as pleased her. He wanted to have the right to watch her as she bathed, to caress her while she was sleek and wet. He just wanted.

Sucking in a breath as his cock hardened in response to his thoughts, he clenched the hands propped under his head, his gaze skyward. But no matter his teeth-gritting concentration, his body was still under no kind of control when he scented Indigo returning from her bath, all damp and fresh and lushly female. Damn. If she caught even a hint of his arousal, she'd put up that barrier of icy control between them before he could so much as blink.

It'd be almost impossible to get her to lower it a second time.

He flowed to his feet outside the tent, waiting only until she'd caught sight of him before hitching his thumb toward the forest, as if he was going to answer the call of nature. He faded into the solid bulk of the firs before she could do more than nod.

And then he ran.

**Lying between the** unzipped halves of her sleeping bag—to ensure a fast exit should she need to move—Indigo finally gave up waiting for Drew and closed her eyes in the shallow sleep she'd learned to utilize in her first year on the watch rotation. Drew, she thought with an exasperated smile, had probably been seduced by the cold, clear night into going for a run.

Her wolf pouted, if a wolf could be said to pout. She'd wanted to go running as well, but had forced herself to come back to the campsite . . . though it hadn't really taken much force, not when she knew Drew was waiting for her. Frowning, she shifted, uncomfortable with the direction of her thoughts, with the low hum of heat in her abdomen.

Her eyes snapped open as she identified the feeling. Lust. Desire. No doubt about it. When Drew had innocently shrugged off his T-shirt earlier, it hadn't only been the teenage girls who'd taken notice. Indigo had sucked in a pleased breath at the sight of those solid shoulders, those muscular arms, that gleaming, healthy skin with a shimmer of gold. Then had come the moment in the tent when she'd found herself drinking in the masculine beauty of his naked form.

The prickle of heat in her belly, across her breasts, was exacerbated by the fact that she'd tasted Drew's kiss, felt that strong body slippery and naked against her own. And now that Drew had let the genie out of the bottle, it refused to be put back in. It didn't even matter that she knew nothing good could come of even a fleeting sexual relationship.

She'd seen with her own eyes what happened when a dominant female chose a less dominant male, much less one who was four years younger. Pain. Hurt. Anger. Over and over again. A vicious cycle.

None of that mattered to her body.

It knew Drew's now—more, it knew that they had serious, combustible chemistry.

"It's just been a long time, that's all," she muttered to herself, but even as she said the words, she knew them for a lie. Yes, she was an adult changeling female. Yes, she ached for touch. But she'd always been able to control her needs.

The heat low in her abdomen curled even tighter, a heavy, waiting warmth.

Glaring at the sky, she was in no mood to catch Drew's scent tangled with the freshness of water. He'd obviously taken a dip in the stream after going running. He was, her mind supplied, likely naked—or at least half-naked. Determinedly shutting her eyes, she tried not to hear anything as he snuck in.

Except it was freaking impossible not to realize that he was throwing a sweaty pair of jeans in a corner and pulling on . . . something light, soft, something that brushed against his skin in a way she couldn't identify with her ears alone. "You woke me up."

He froze, and she knew he was looking at her, but she didn't open her eyes. Refused to give in to the temptation to see what exactly he was wearing. She wasn't some young female drunk on her own sexuality. She was a woman used to choosing her lovers with care—not being driven to it by the cravings of her body.

"You weren't really asleep," Drew said with a hint of a smile in his tone. "And I brought you a present."

She wasn't an acquisitive person, but neither was she dead. Blinking open her eyes at last, she couldn't resist taking a slow tour of his body as he knelt to get something from the pocket of his discarded jeans. Muscled shoulders in shadow, a back so beautiful it cried out to be stroked . . . and boxers. Plain black and—"Silk boxers while we're camping?"

A shrug that drew her attention to those shoulders again. "They were at the top of the clean laundry." Finding whatever it was that he'd brought her, he flipped onto his front on his sleeping bag and braced himself on one arm, holding out something in a closed fist with the other.

She stared, suspicious. "I don't smell anything." The scent of him—wild and earthy and a little rough—curled around her in an almost physical caress . . . until her wolf growled and nudged at the human half to press her lips to his skin, to satiate the touch-hunger that suddenly had her at breaking point.

Drew extended his fisted hand a little farther. "Come on, Ms. Grumpy, take it." A teasing smile that made her want to kiss it right off his lips . . . before she tumbled him to the ground and rubbed her body along the warm, muscled strength of his.

Swallowing the insane urge, she turned on her side and held out a hand. He placed a small, light object on her palm. "For your collection."

She jerked into a sitting position when she saw what it was, crossing her bare legs under her as she brought the small piece of flat rock to her eye. The fossil embedded within it was delicate—a tiny, beautifully preserved leaf. Heart thudding, she brought it even closer.

*Oooh, pretty. Perfect.*

When she turned to look at Drew's face as he lay on his back, arms crossed under his head, she saw a smug smile. He looked so pleased with himself that she couldn't help it—her own lips curved. "How did you know I collect fossils?"

"I see all and know all."

Scrunching up her nose at him, she cupped the precious fossil in her palm and bent to kiss him on the lips. It was meant to be a thank-you kiss, a little bit of affection between packmates who were close, nothing more. But when he froze under her, when her body turned into one big flame, she knew she'd made a mistake. A mistake that might burn them both to ash.

Wrenching back from the searing contact, she looked down at him, her chest heaving. He watched her with those clear blue eyes that gave away nothing—but his body told its own story. And she could no more stop herself from looking than she could stop the racing beat of her own heart. The flat plane of his abdomen was taut, the golden silk of his skin broken up only by the thin line of dark hair that disappeared into the waistband of his boxers. The black silk strained against the proud ridge of his erection.

So strong and beautiful and male—every part of her body warmed with pleasure at having him near. She wanted to reach over, stroke the hard demand of his cock, cup him with her palm, make him lose the control that had his tendons standing out in stark relief against his sk—

*Oh, God.*

She should've said something but couldn't make her throat unlock, her mouth open. Then Drew shot her a sharp, sheepish grin. "Hey, I can't help it if I'm male. Stupid biology." Turning over, he pillowed his head on one arm and went to sleep.

She blinked, not sure what had just happened. But five minutes later and his breathing was easy, even. Putting the precious fossil in the side pocket of her pack—after wrapping it in the soft fabric of an old tee—she finally lay back down and pulled the top flap of her sleeping bag over her uncomfortable body. Her nipples rubbed against the fabric of her T-shirt, taut and aching. Her panties suddenly felt far too constricting, and her wolf—she was pissed at being denied.

*Not Drew,* she told her wolf again. *I couldn't bear to hurt him.* And she would. Because a relationship between a dominant female and a lower-ranking dominant male was never going to end in anything but disaster.

**Andrew released his** fisted hand what felt like hours later, when he sensed Indigo drop off into real sleep at long last. Turning over carefully onto his back, conscious she'd wake to the slightest awareness of a threat, he allowed himself to run his gaze over the line of her body as she lay with her back to him. She'd kicked off the top of her sleeping bag and the long lines of her legs were bare below the white of her T-shirt, her skin smooth and oh-so-touchable.

Desire spiked again, but intertwined with it was an almost overwhelming tenderness. He wanted to curve his body around hers, wrap his arm over her waist, and tug her close. Just hold her. She might've let him earlier, but after that kiss . . . His gut went tight, his wolf pawing at the ground for another taste of her.

She'd wanted him. He'd seen the flare of shocked need in her eyes, glimpsed the hunger of the wolf. But as he'd already learned, when it came to Indigo, hunger alone would never be enough. A less stubborn man might've given up, but Andrew was playing for keeps.

She shivered a little.

Moving at once to pull across the top flap of her sleeping bag, he froze, close enough to feel the warmth of her body. What would she do if he snuggled into her? She might let it go, thinking he was doing it in his sleep—or she might kick his ass. The wickedness in him pricked its ears, game to take the risk.

Relaxing his body as much as possible, he spooned himself around her, stroking his arm over her waist. She woke the instant he touched her—but she didn't shove him away. Nuzzling his face into her hair, he let his eyes close. It was no longer pretense, not with her warm and luscious against him. Sleep began to whisper in his ear, and he decided to let it sweep him into dreams where Indigo didn't just let him hold her, but so much more.

**He had to** be asleep, Indigo thought, lying quiescent in the heat of Drew's embrace. There was no way he'd have done this if he'd been awake—not after the response she'd accidentally incited in both of them. Of course, he was also half demon, so he could be tormenting her to get some of his own back.

Still, when his fingers laced with her own, she relaxed. He

was blazingly hot against the mountain chill, Pack she trusted to the deepest core of her soul. Settling herself more comfortably against him, she drifted off to sleep, having no awareness that she'd be jackknifing to dangerous wakefulness less than an hour later.

# CHAPTER 14

**Miles away,** on the outskirts of a sleeping San Francisco, Judd took a seat beside Father Xavier Perez on the back steps of Xavier's church.

"I'm sorry, Xavier," he said, knowing the priest would prefer the truth at once. "Gloria is gone, murdered." He'd gotten the confirmation without having to tap his contacts. Brenna had hacked through a records database, found the death certificate. It had listed "sudden cardiac failure" as the cause of death, but her spotless apartment had told a different story.

Xavier let out a long, slow breath before dipping his head and murmuring a quiet, heartfelt prayer. Judd waited in silence until the other man raised his head. "She dared to reach for something beyond what was permitted," Xavier said. "And they killed her for it."

"Perhaps." He told Xavier something Drew had shared with him, having heard it from the Rat alpha. "There are rumors of other dead Psy in the city. Do you know anything about that?"

Xavier shook his head. "Our mutual friend may know more."

"Yes." So would another man. A man, Judd thought, that his outwardly careless younger brother-in-law called if not friend, then at least a friendly acquaintance. He'd ask Drew to follow up on the issue with that contact once he returned from the mountains.

Now, he listened to the insects going about their business in the back garden and waited.

The stir in the darkness came not long afterward.

Judd focused. "You're late tonight."

The Ghost leaned against an old oak tree, his face swathed in shadow as always. "I was delayed by an unexpected guest."

"Dead Psy in the city," Judd said, asking the most important question, "do you know anything about it?"

"No," the Ghost murmured. "I've been busy with other matters. What has occurred?"

Judd had an inkling about the nature of the Ghost's "other matters"—and if he was right, then the most dangerous rebel in the Net was about to become even more lethal. "I've got nothing but rumors at present."

"If I discover anything, I'll share it with you." The Ghost moved deeper into the shadows as the clouds parted to expose the moon's pearly light. "But San Francisco doesn't hold much interest for me at present."

Judd heard something in that statement, something that made his instincts snap to wakefulness. "What are you planning?"

"The three of us came together because we believe the Council is destroying the Psy race and taking the rest of the world along," the Ghost said. "The Councilors now have their knives out for each other. Any resulting war will devastate the Net, kill millions—Psy, human, and changeling."

Judd agreed . . . and he also understood. "You're planning to kill them all."

"If necessary," the Ghost said. "There can be no war if there is no Council."

And, Judd thought, it would leave the Net entirely in the Ghost's grasp.

# CHAPTER 15

*Metal. Intruder.*

Indigo was at full alert when her eyes snapped open. She felt Drew come to life at almost the same instant. Glancing at him, she saw his eyes had gone night-glow, the wolf at the forefront.

"Psy," he mouthed more than said.

She gave a decisive nod. Nothing else would account for that scent. It was as distinctive as blood on snow, and it cut against changeling senses with the jagged brutality of twisted metal. Not all Psy carried that metallic taint, and the current theory was that it clung only to those who had given in irrevocably to Silence . . . lost their soul to the emotionless chill of the PsyNet. Whatever the truth, there was no reason for it to be here, deep in the heart of SnowDancer territory.

Glancing at the kids—all asleep—Indigo made a snap decision. "Go."

Drew shifted and flowed away from the campsite as she walked to Harley's tent and reached in to squeeze his shoulder.

The boy woke at once. Putting a finger to her lips, Indigo bent down. "I need you to keep watch. Sound the alarm if you sense an intruder."

To his credit, the boy extricated himself from his tent without waking his tentmate, his eyes already watchful. "I'll use the wolf's call."

Confident he was up to the task, she shifted without bothering to strip off her T-shirt and streaked off after Drew. The metallic scent was strong, fresh, and not difficult to track, even if Drew hadn't gone ahead. Reaching the end of the trail, she found herself in a small moonlit glade bearing the faintest traces of boot prints.

Putting her nose to the earth, she attempted to find the intruders' exit route and came up blank. *Teleportation.* Which most likely meant the Council—or a Councilor, at least—was involved in this somewhere. Teleport-capable telekinetics were a scarce resource, and they were almost always pulled into the Council ranks, according to Judd. Frustrated, she looked up as Drew appeared from the other side of the glade, having apparently circled the area.

Coming over until their muzzles almost touched, he shook his head.

*Damn.*

She shifted. They needed to talk and better it be here than back at the campsite. It was no use scaring the kids when there was nothing to be done at this moment. "No hint of a trail?" She fisted her hand in his fur as she asked for confirmation of his nonverbal report, his coat incredibly soft beneath the protective roughness of the guard hairs.

Another shake of his head before he tugged away and shifted to crouch across from her, a sleekly muscled man with lake blue eyes that held the slightest night-glow edge—the wolf looking out from behind the human skin. "Tk's." His voice was low, deep, wolf.

"That's what I thought." Attempting to ignore the way that rough tone raised every tiny hair on her body, she spread her fingers on the stubby grass. "Why here?"

"Isolated—or it should've been." Drew angled his head in a way that had nothing to do with the human half of him.

"Maybe they were using it as a meeting place, realized we were up here, and poofed."

There was some merit to that, Indigo thought, her own wolf prowling inside her mind, its anger cold and rational. SnowDancer territory was unwelcoming to intruders, but by the same token, it was also so vast that if someone wanted to have a meeting away from watchful eyes, and could access the area without alerting the sentries, it was the perfect location. "We need to log this, get some extra patrols going up here in case they decide to return."

"We can do that back at camp." Drew shifted with those words, and for a moment she sat still and admired the beauty of the large silver wolf looking back at her with curious copper-colored eyes.

Raising a hand, she indulged herself as she wouldn't dare do while they were in human form, running her fingers through his fur in a long, slow caress. "You sure are a pretty wolf, Drew."

That got her an affectionate nip on the chin, a nuzzle into her neck. Feeling a smile creep across her face, she let him tumble her to the ground. The Psy were gone and, given the fact that their swift departure indicated they'd caught wind of the camp, unlikely to return tonight. A few more minutes wouldn't make any difference.

Staying in human form, she wrestled with Drew as he attempted to pin her, slipping out from underneath his paws and circling around to take him from behind. He was too fast for her, sliding out and away to leap on her. Laughing, she wiggled out from under his playful hold before shifting herself.

He pounced again, but she was already tumbling out of the way. Across from her, he crouched with his front feet forward, his back arched, a clear invitation to play. It was too tempting to resist. Jumping at him, she mock-attacked, growing low in her throat. He attacked back . . . but he was really just trying to get his teeth on her tail.

Laughing inwardly, she slipped and he almost got her . . . but she slammed her body against his, pushing him off balance. Then she went for *his* tail. Yipping, he danced out of the way, his eyes brimming with a joy that could come only from the heart of the wolf that lived within.

It was tempting to keep playing, but they couldn't leave their charges alone all night. Touching muzzles with him, she turned and led the way back to camp, where they pulled Harley off watch, then used Drew's cell phone to report their findings. Judd happened to be on the midnight-to-six shift at the den, and Indigo could see his gaze sharpen even on the tiny screen of the cell phone. "Did they leave anything behind?" the Psy male asked.

"Not that we could see," Indigo reported, very conscious of the living heat of Drew's body as he pressed up behind her—so he could look at the screen. "Silvia did find something metallic earlier today. It could've come from anywhere, however. There's a high chance it was washed down by the rivers."

"No harm in the techs having a look at it anyway." Judd made a note. "Threat assessment?"

"Low," Indigo said. "I don't see any reason to change our plans. Drew?"

"I'm with you. If they'd wanted to attack," he added, "their best chance would've been tonight while they had the element of surprise, and they didn't take it."

Judd nodded. "I'll organize some extra patrols in that area, starting from when you leave. Your presence there at the moment should act as a deterrent."

Indigo nodded. "Make sure you send up only experienced men and women. The Psy are too dangerous for the novices to handle."

"Agreed. Hawke will be joining you tomorrow, so you can discuss this further then."

Hanging up after a couple more words, Indigo frowned. "It takes some kind of balls to come into our territory knowing how tough we are on intruders." SnowDancer had a reputation for shooting first and asking questions of the corpses.

"That," Drew said, slipping his arms around her waist and tugging her against him, "or sheer arrogance."

Indigo didn't reply straightaway, her brain cells fried by the wave of flame that licked up her body. For a moment, she

considered turning her face to that of the beautiful wolf at
her back and letting the heat take over. It would be good—
that much was certain. He was big and gorgeous and playful
and gave every indication that he'd be a generous, affectionate
lover.

Tightening his arms around her, Drew propped his chin
on her shoulder. "With all the Psy stuff that's been happening
this past year, I want to think something sinister is going on,
but that feels like an overreaction to what was most likely a
simple territorial violation."

It was difficult to think past the pounding hunger of her
pulse. "Nothing's ever simple with the Psy," she said, turning
her head a little so she could feel his hair brushing against
her cheek.

He kissed her on the jaw, a quick, almost absentminded
caress. "True."

"But yes, there *is* a chance they were just using the location
as a safe meeting place." Unable to resist, she reached up to
touch his face. He pressed his beard-roughened jaw into her
palm, and as her wolf hummed in contentment inside her, she
remembered how much she'd missed this contact after they'd
had their blowup. If she seduced him—and it made her guilty
to even consider it—they'd be going right back there.

She treasured his friendship too much to risk it. Because
no matter what, sex would change everything, create a subtle
tension that nothing would ever erase. "We should get some
sleep," she said, not stopping to wonder why she was so certain she wouldn't be able to remain friends with Drew after
intimacy when she had perfectly cordial relationships with
her former lovers. "Early morning wakeup tomorrow."

Drew yawned and released her. The sudden chill caused
by the absence of his body heat made goose bumps rise over
her flesh.

"I want to talk to Hawke about Harley," Drew said, moving
to his own sleeping bag. "Kid's not really fluctuating as much
as everyone thinks—and from the looks of it, he's promising
to be a high-level dominant."

"I was wondering if you'd picked that up." She slipped
inside the unzipped halves of her sleeping bag.

Drew scowled at the raised bumps on her arm. "You're cold."

"I'll be fine." She was an adult wolf—cold wasn't something that really bothered her, even in human form. As for the emotional reasons behind the unexpected strength of her reaction—she wasn't going there.

"And Silvia," Drew murmured, his voice drowsy, "there's something about her."

"Hmm. She's a maternal dominant." The girl would be an anchor for the pack once she gained a little more confidence.

"G'night, Indy."

She thought about telling him not to use that nickname, but then he curled his body around hers, sliding one arm and leg under the top flap of her sleeping bag, and she decided to let it go for tonight . . . and allowed sleep to tug her under.

**Hawke turned up** at camp early the next morning—but he wasn't alone. "An*drew*," drawled the lissome young female he'd brought with him, "so this is where you've been hiding."

"Maria—" Drew's words of welcome were cut off when the petite but curvy woman jumped up and planted her plump, ruby red lips smack-bang on his, her legs wrapping around his waist as he caught her beneath the thighs.

Indigo narrowed her eyes at her alpha, unable to erase the image of Drew's fingers closing over Maria's taut flesh. "You brought me another camper?" Catty, she thought, that was catty.

A gleam in those pale eyes, but his tone was even as he said, "Maria's a soldier, as you very well know, and she's a capable one." Hawke looked over to where the kids were grinning and wolf-whistling at Drew and Maria. "I thought it'd be good experience for her to come up here, spend some time coaching the younger kids."

Drew was putting the girl on her feet now, having broken the kiss—though his hands remained on her tiny waist. Color burned hot and bright over his cheekbones, and Indigo wanted to believe it was embarrassment, not desire. Except that he was a healthy young male, and Maria of the big breasts, flashing dark eyes, and lush hips was giving him some hotly explicit signals, her hands splayed on his chest, all but openly petting.

Indigo felt her claws prick the insides of her skin just as Hawke put two fingers to his mouth and whistled. "Time to go hunting. I want everyone in wolf form."

Good, Indigo thought, because she was in the mood for blood. Preferably of the "sweet young thang" kind.

**Andrew wanted to** kill Hawke—slowly and with great pleasure. Of all the women to bring up here . . . "Why?" he muttered to his alpha when Maria detached herself at long last to go stash her pack, her hips swaying in invitation as she blew him a kiss over her shoulder.

Hawke's gaze was so innocent, Andrew knew it was pure bullshit. "I asked for a volunteer—she raised her hand."

"Uh-huh." Shoving his fingers through his hair, Andrew glared at the man he fully intended to strangle at the first opportunity.

"Maria's sweet, she's sexy, and she wants to bang your brains out." Hawke's grin was pure, amused wolf. "I don't see a problem here—especially since you obviously need to get banged."

His alpha knew exactly which buttons to press, but then so did Andrew. "Projecting, Hawke?"

Ice blue flared with something hotter, more brilliant, but Hawke didn't rise to the bait. "Smart-ass. Tell me about the problem last night."

Andrew laid it out, momentarily pushing aside the complication caused by Maria's entrance into his courtship of Indigo. "I went out and had another look this morning before you arrived. Nothing."

Frowning, Hawke stared out at the winter green of the forest. "We'll keep an eye on the situation, see what develops. Judd's heard nothing from his contacts that implies a Council operation, but we'll stay on alert."

"Cats?"

"I left a message for Lucas," he said, naming the leopard alpha. "Riaz and Elias are running things at the den today, so they'll contact us if the cats discover anything." Looking around, he took a deep breath of the chill morning air. "Let's enjoy this day—not often we get a chance like this." Reaching back to his nape, he pulled up his T-shirt, stripping it off as Andrew got rid of his own.

They'd both changed into wolf form by the time the kids ambled back. Maria, too, had shifted. She was a frisky little wolf, pretty and dainty, even in her animal form. Andrew thought she was sweet enough, but she wasn't the woman he wanted. That woman was an elegant, long-legged wolf with fur of a rich dark gray, and a distinctly haughty look in her golden eyes when she strolled up to stand beside Hawke.

He wanted to bite her.

Maria nipped his flank instead.

*I am so going to kill Hawke for this.*

# CHAPTER 16

**The juveniles were** exhausted that night, crawling into their sleeping bags as soon as darkness fell, but they'd dragged those bags outside, so they could sit and listen to the older members of the pack talk. A few had chosen to remain in wolf form, sitting curled up close to the laz-fire, a portable heating device that gave an excellent approximation of flames but with zero chance of creating a forest fire.

As Andrew watched from his spot on a log opposite Hawke and Indigo, *his* lieutenant—and yeah, he was discovering quick-fast that he was a possessive bastard—showed their alpha the little metal ball Silvia had discovered. Hawke played the object over his hand after sniffing at it to see if the wolf's nose could tell him anything. "We'll see what Bren and the other techs can do with this," he said. "I don't like anyone putting their shit on our land—Council or conglomerate."

Maria nudged Andrew with her elbow when Hawke and Indigo fell to discussing what adjustments they'd have to make to the watch patrols to free up soldiers for this area.

"Are you off shift next weekend?" she whispered, her breast soft and warm against his upper arm as she snuggled closer. "I have tickets to a new show. It's got really great reviews."

Andrew kept his arms hanging over his knees, his fingers loosely intertwined. "I thought you were seeing Kieran." He'd noticed—and been grateful—that she'd stopped throwing lures his way after hooking up with the boy.

A sniff, firelight glinting off the soft ebony of her curls as she ducked her head. "Yesterday's news."

Andrew's wolf stilled at the deep hurt he sensed beneath the blazing heat of her sensuality. "Come for a walk," he said, knowing she'd never open up within earshot of the others.

She agreed with alacrity. He wondered if Indigo even noticed their departure, she was so deep in conversation with Hawke—and that was one hell of a punch to the ego. But he kept that to himself as he led Maria away from the campsite and toward a more private spot, because if security was part of Indigo's mandate in the pack, this was part of his—looking after those who might not trust their pain to anyone else.

Maria slid her hand over his abdomen as soon as they hit the darkness of the trees, her goal the waistband of his jeans. "Soooooo . . ."

Fully in control, he gripped her wrist, squeezed. "Hush." Then, fingers locked around her wrist, he continued to lead them through the winter green firs.

Maria didn't resist either his hold or his order, and that was a clear indication that his hunch was right. Young predatory changeling females weren't at all shy about going after what they wanted, and Andrew had never before been able to discourage her so quickly. Bringing them to a flat glacial rock, he took a seat, tugging her up to sit beside him. "So, he broke your heart, huh?"

"Who?" She wrenched away her hand. "I thought you were bringing me out here to do something interesting, not talk about old rubbish."

*"Maria."* Reaching out, he did hug her then, rubbing his chin over the softness of those pretty curls. "Talk to me, sweetheart. You know you can."

Another sniff, this one distinctly wetter. "All the girls

warned me about him, but I didn't listen. I thought I could tame him. How stupid!"

Andrew cuddled her closer, until she was almost in his lap. "Tell me."

And she did, pouring out her heart. Kieran, for all his humanity—having been adopted into SnowDancer—was more of a wolf on the prowl than most, leaving a trail of broken hearts in his wake. Maria, Andrew thought, wasn't the first casualty, nor would she be the last. Her heart would heal, but he sympathized with the burning hurt of the fresh bruise—he knew better than most how badly the heart could ache when the one you wanted didn't want you back.

Indigo had been a warm, luscious presence beside him all night long, her legs tangled with his, smooth against his rougher skin, but he didn't make the mistake of thinking she'd changed her mind about his suitability as a lover. Still, she'd responded to him in a sexual way more than once since they'd hit the mountains, the scent of her desire a taunting perfume.

It had taken everything he had not to stroke his fingers up to cup her breast last night after she kissed him, to nuzzle his way down and lap up the warm, erotic scent at the juncture of her thighs, to pleasure her with his mouth and his hands, to adore her in the most rawly sexual of ways.

He'd almost snapped when he'd realized she was fighting against her own body's needs once again. Sometimes he wanted to shake Indigo, make her see sense. After the arousal he'd scented, he now knew he could seduce her by stoking up the embers of her passion until her wolf—sensual, tactile, with far fewer concerns than the human—pushed her into his arms.

But of course, it wasn't that simple.

Feeling Maria rub her damp cheek against his chest, he pulled his attention back to the present, running his hand over and along her back until she quieted down. "Kieran's an idiot," he murmured, continuing to pet her with the undemanding caresses of a packmate. "When you grow up a little more and become the woman you're going to be, he's going to kick himself. And you can rub his face in it."

Maria gave him a shaky smile, dark eyes near black even to his night vision. "You know how to stroke a woman's ego."

Using his thumbs, he wiped away the remnants of her tears. "It's easy with someone like you." Too bad he was stuck on a woman who might just drive them both to insanity with her refusal to even admit the possibility that there might be something between them.

**Indigo found herself** alone half an hour after Drew left with Maria clinging to him like kudzu. No guesses as to what the two of them were doing, though thankfully, they'd gone far enough out of range that she couldn't hear or scent their bodies. As for Hawke, he'd noticed that four of the juveniles weren't as exhausted as their peers and had rounded them up for an exploration of the night-swathed forest.

The eight Hawke had left behind were all lost in deep sleep, their faces—no matter the form they'd chosen—content. Only Indigo remained awake by the fire, her spine stiff, her wolf snarling inside her mind as she stared at the spot where Drew had disappeared into the dark, his arm curled around Maria's shapely form.

Her eyes shifted without conscious control, until she saw everything with the wolf's piercing night vision. Furious with her lack of control, she went to the tent—to be confronted by Drew's sleeping bag. He wasn't likely to come back here, and even if he did, she sure as hell did not intend to sleep next to a male who stank of another woman. Decision made, she rolled up his bag and put both it and his pack in a neat pile against a tree a small distance away, where he couldn't miss it.

Just being a good packmate, she told herself. It had nothing to do with the fact that an odd kind of anger was boiling through her system. She didn't want to sleep with Drew. Okay, yes, she did, but she wasn't going to do it, so she had no reason to be so savagely angry that he'd gone off with another female. There was nothing worse than a woman who played dog in the manger—it would be the worst kind of hypocrisy on her part.

Her mind snapshotted to an image of Drew's naked body as he dropped the towel the night of the storm, his muscled flesh inviting touch. Maria was probably in raptures— *Enough.*

Stripping off her clothes, she pulled on a large tee over her panties and slipped in between the unzipped halves of her sleeping bag. She'd ended up kicking off the top half last night, not needing it given the blazing heat of Drew's body. His heartbeat had been a slow, steady rhythm behind her, his breath warm against her temple. Sometime in the night, he'd spread his hand out over her abdomen and intertwined his legs with her own, the hairs on his thighs rubbing rough and sensuous against her skin. It hadn't only been comforting to sleep like two tangled pups, it had been . . . more.

Gritting her teeth against the heavy impression of memory, she closed her eyes. Sleep continued to evade her like the most frustrating prey . . . and she was wide awake when she scented two familiar forms coming back to camp. Her hand fisted and she set her jaw, determined *not* to take a deeper breath, to peel apart the scents in a search for the musky taste of sex.

"Looks like everyone's asleep." A feminine whisper.

A pause and though Indigo knew it was impossible, she could've sworn Drew's eyes were drilling into her skull. "You better get some rest, too."

Sounds, skin meeting. A kiss? "Good night, Drew. That was really nice . . . thank you."

*Nice?* Not exactly a ringing endorsement. She hoped that burned Drew's ego.

The next sounds were of Maria moving about, heading to her tent. Drew's heavier tread didn't follow. Instead, Indigo felt him go to his pack . . . and then more quiet, determined sounds—fabric being unrolled, boots being unlaced and dropped to the ground.

Unable to resist, she opened her eyes and twisted toward where she'd left his gear—to find him stripping off his T-shirt and throwing it on his pack in a way that shouted temper. His sleeping bag lay open beside him. She should've closed her eyes and gone back to sleep, but her wolf's edgy temper prodded her to get up and confront him. "What are you doing?" she asked in an almost subvocal tone, not wanting Maria to hear. The kids were too tired to wake.

Cool blue eyes met hers. "Going to sleep."

The cutting bite of his response took her aback for a second—she'd never really seen Drew angry before. "I thought you'd be sharing with Maria."

"Is that what you think of me?" he asked with a frost in his tone that made her want to wrap her arms around herself. "That I'd take advantage of a girl who's just had her heart broken?"

"I—what?" She was a good lieutenant, but she hadn't seen anything in Maria's behavior to betray that kind of hurt. "Who?"

"Doesn't matter. She'll be fine." His hands went to the top button of his jeans and he flicked it open. "Might as well shift," he muttered, not undoing the zipper. "Since it smells like rain, I don't think I'll be getting much sleep tonight if I stay in human form."

The way he said that, the way he looked at her, rubbed her temper raw. "Fine, I misread the situation." She folded her arms, curving her hands into fists. "You're welcome to—"

"No, thanks." He put his own hands on his hips, his chest a muscled plane only inches from her. "I think I prefer a little rain to being frozen out by Lieutenant Indigo Riviere for daring to ask her to step outside of her safe little worldview."

She saw red. "What's that supposed to mean?" It was sheer breath-stealing fury that kept her tone low.

"How about I ask a question instead?" Closing the distance between them until they stood toe to toe, the heat of his body a silent challenge, he said, "Why are you out here, sniping at me?"

"I do not 'snipe.'" Her wolf growled.

"Yeah, sure sounds like you're being snippy to me." And then the damn male did that thing he did—he kissed her. As if he had every right to just take her mouth with the wild heat of his, to cup the back of her head, to bite down on her lower lip and suck her upper one into his mouth.

Her toes curled, the rage in her bloodstream translating into pure wild heat as the touch-hungry wolf took control. She hadn't even realized she'd unfolded her arms until her palms met the hard wall of his chest. Hot. Strong. Beautiful. Overwhelmed by the sudden blaze of the sexual inferno, Indigo

wanted to push him to the ground, claim every solid male inch
with her mouth, her hands, and finally, her sex. The hunger
was a fever inside, a spiking, thudding pulse.

"Damn." Drew lifted his head, his chest heaving. "I can
scent Hawke and the others."

The words poured cold water on the flames of passion. She
realized she still had her hands on his body, the fingers of
one curved slightly into his flesh, as if she wanted to prick
at him with her claws—as if she was in heat. Shoving away,
she stumbled a little. "You lied," she said, taking out her own
stunned confusion on him. "All that bullshit about everything
being back to normal."

"So did you." His eyes gleamed, hard and bright. "You
want me, and if you'd stop fucking lying to yourself for one
second, you'd realize we could have something good."

Her wolf, no longer caught in the sexual inferno, snarled
at the challenge, at the arrogance of this male who thought
he could bring her to heel. "Don't kid yourself. Yeah, you
can kiss—but I need a little more in my man." Harsh, angry
words, torn from the part of her that hated how he'd made her
feel earlier when he'd gone off with Maria—so vulnerable, so
weak. She was never weak. She refused to allow it. "I might
play with boys, but I don't keep them."

Drew flinched, and she knew she'd drawn blood. Somehow, it didn't feel as good as it should have. But she couldn't
bring herself to take it back, too proud, too confused, too
fucking scared of what Drew was asking from her. She knew
how it would end. She'd *seen* how it would end. The hurt, the
pain, the constant effort to make herself *less* so that he would
feel better as a man.

It wasn't worth it. Not even if it hurt like a bitch to walk
away.

# CHAPTER 17

**Henry looked at** his man. "It can be done?"

"Yes." An unequivocal answer. "However, we'll have to be quick to get the rest of the operation in place now that they've detected us."

"I assume you have that under way." Henry had chosen this man because of his intelligence and dedication to Silence—and, unlike Shoshanna, he wasn't about to squander that resource by killing him simply because he happened to be strong enough to be a threat.

A nod. "Even if they somehow discover the first element, the second should give us what we need."

And the war to uphold Silence, Henry thought, would claim another victim.

# CHAPTER 18

**Andrew dumped his** pack in his room and began to tug off his clothes for the shower. The hike down from the campsite had been undemanding in spite of the rain that had fallen overnight, and, for the juveniles, fun. Most had abandoned their packs for later retrieval halfway down and shifted, gamboling in the pools of water like four-year-olds, their howls of pleasure singing to his soul.

But no matter his wolf's joy at being with his pack, the trip down had cut at him, made him bleed—because in spite of everything he'd told himself about charm, about courtship, he'd lost his temper the night before and it was still simmering. He'd been in no mood to play—and neither had Indigo.

They'd spoken to each other only when necessary and kept their distance the rest of the time. For Andrew, it had been partly self-preservation and partly because he didn't trust himself around her. The hunger to touch, to caress, to possess, was a constant craving in his gut by now. He was fully capable of going after her with the intent to claim rights he didn't have, rights she refused to give him, notwithstanding the addictive musk of her own desire.

Throwing the last of his clothing on the floor, he walked into the shower cubicle and tried to rub away the need, the fury that had him losing his mind. Of course it didn't disappear, but the time he spent under the deliberately cool spray did calm him down a fraction. He'd made a mistake in challenging Indigo that way—but he wasn't sorry. Because when it came down to it, he was a dominant same as her. He wasn't going to lie to her about that. But that didn't mean he wasn't also going to use his other skills to burn through the ice of her temper.

*I might play with boys, but I don't keep them.*

He clenched his jaw at the memory of her razor-sharp words, refusing to let them push him away. That was what she wanted—it would be the easy way out. And no matter how mad he was at her for what she'd said, he wasn't going to give her that out. No fucking way.

Switching off the shower, he got dressed, then scrawled something on a small piece of paper that he slipped under Indigo's door on his way down to the garage. He wasn't exactly fit company right now. Better he redirect his anger into something useful, like fixing one of the malfunctioning vehicles. Fact was, he was good with cars, but no expert—which meant he'd have to concentrate.

However, he'd barely reached the underground area that was home to all their vehicles when someone pulled him aside and whispered that he'd been hearing rumors to do with "purity." Freezing, Drew asked for further details, but the mechanic shrugged. "I think it's something nasty, but no one's sure quite what."

His anger tempered by the need to protect the pack, Andrew began to do what he did best—talk to people. Over the next few hours, he moved from group to group, eating lunch with the soldiers, playing chess with a few of the elders, hanging out in the infirmary and in the training rooms.

His gut was a knot at the start. The last traitor within the pack had almost killed SnowDancer, stabbing a knife straight into its heart. He wasn't sure they could bear it a second time.

The pack was too tight a unit, their loyalty to each other the bedrock on which they built their worlds. But what he found was something else, something unexpected.

"An e-mail," he said to Hawke later that day, after managing to get his hands on a copy at last. "Sent from an anonymous account but, from the content, it's connected to Pure Psy, that group all about maintaining Silence. No one knows where it originated—and a few of the people who received it had enough skill to attempt a backtrace. Nada."

Hawke held his hand out for the e-mail. Andrew passed it across, having already memorized the poison.

We invite our brothers and sisters in SnowDancer to help us achieve our aim of a world of absolute Purity. Surely you do not want your blood polluted with those of the other races—surely you do not want your pack weakened by humans.

Hawke threw down the piece of paper, his jaw a brutal line. "Do we have a problem?"

"No," Andrew was happy to say, his wolf's relief a powerful beat against his skin. "Everyone I ran into who'd had contact with the thing found it ugly and malicious and deleted it immediately. I got this copy from someone's recycle bin."

Hawke rubbed at his forehead. "Why the fuck didn't they e-mail it to me? I need to know about shit like this." When Andrew said nothing, his alpha sat back in his chair. "Yeah, yeah, that's why I have you."

Andrew gave him a wry smile. "Most people just didn't think it was that important—figured it was a nasty e-mail campaign by some crackpot group but nothing more." Relaxed now, but with a different tension thrumming in his blood, he nodded at the e-mail. "That was a miscalculation on the part of Pure Psy. Almost everyone in the pack has someone human in their family, and they've come to see the Lauren children as pups to protect." And wolves, changeling or feral, would give their lives to protect the young. "But I don't like the fact the sender seems to have targeted people lower down in the hierarchy."

"Means they've made enough of a study of us to get a handle on at least a little of how the pack functions." Hawke tapped a finger on his desk. "We need to figure out if they're trying to recruit outside the den as well."

"I've already got my team on it," Andrew told him. "So far, it looks like it was a concentrated e-mail blast to our people in this area."

"Good. The other thing we need to consider is whether they targeted other groups within the city's population. Something like this could generate serious friction."

"I'll put some feelers out, see if that's a possibility."

The wolf apparent in his gaze, Hawke picked up the e-mail again. "They're not going to get inside this pack," he said with cool finality. "But we need to know how strong they are in the PsyNet."

Andrew didn't need Hawke to explain why. Given the Psy race's influence on economics and politics, whatever happened inside the Net had the potential to affect them all. "I'm meeting Judd after this. I'll see what he can dig up. Last we heard, Pure Psy was mostly a splinter faction."

"Things change fast in that bloody hive mind." Lines marred his brow. "Maybe we should talk to the cop as well," Hawke said, referring to Nikita's new security chief.

"I'm on it," Andrew said, taking the e-mail and folding it into a square he could slide into the pocket of his jeans. "As an aside, Nikita can't exactly be popular with Pure Psy if she's got a human security chief."

That in itself, the fact of a human in a Councilor's domain, had to be one hell of a story. Andrew had heard bits and pieces of what had gone down with Max Shannon and the J-Psy who was his wife, but he'd been away in another area when most of it was taking place. However, he'd made it a point to get in touch with Max when he returned to the den, knowing the cop's position meant he'd be privy to some very useful information. Max, too, had seen the benefit of having a direct point of contact with SnowDancer.

"She's still a Councilor," Hawke said, his tone grim. "Be careful what intel you share."

"There's not much sharing going on right now." Andrew

knew true trust would take time. Hell, it had taken over a decade with the leopards. "We're feeling each other out."

Hawke's eyes gleamed with unexpected humor. "So, feel anything out with a certain lieutenant?"

Andrew didn't even bother to swear. He just got up and stabbed a finger in his alpha's direction. "No interference." He'd court, seduce, and tangle with Indigo his own way.

Hawke held up his hands, palms out, but the glint in his eye didn't disappear. "Is she playing with you?"

Andrew thought of the silence that had been her response to the note he'd slipped under her door. "Not yet. But she will." He wouldn't accept any other outcome.

**Coming in to** change for a session with the novice soldiers, Indigo couldn't keep from staring at the piece of paper sitting on her bedside table. It wasn't as if the words would've changed from this morning, but she picked it up, bringing it close to her face—as if that would make her understand it better.

*Have dinner with me tonight. —Drew*
*P.S. Don't you want to know?*

It was the last thing she'd have expected him to do after the bitterness of their fight. Because, all charm aside, Drew was a dominant predatory changeling male. He'd been in charge of the volatile San Diego sector until Hawke assigned him to his new position as a roaming liaison/spy across SnowDancer territory. And he was their tracker.

Men like that had tempers. They brooded and simmered. They did not extend olive branches . . . if that was what this was. Her eyes narrowed. Cunning, she thought; Drew wasn't only smart and strong, he had a whole streak of sneaky running right through him.

As to the P.S., she could've told herself she didn't understand, but that would've been disingenuous when the truth was beating her over the head with the subtlety of a hundred-pound hammer. A hammer wielded by an obstinate male with a wicked, wicked smile and a way of moving that made her want to sit back and simply admire.

It would be so easy to say yes, far easier than she could've ever imagined.

"But then what?" she whispered out loud, knowing that the disparity in their ages and—more crucially—positions in the hierarchy meant that any relationship would be a fleeting thing. It already tore her to shreds that they'd lost some of what had always been between them. No matter what, she'd never be able to touch Drew with the joyful familiarity of Pack again, never be able to sleep with her body tangled in his.

Frustrated and angry at him for doing this, for changing a relationship she hadn't known she relied on until it was yanked out from under her feet, she scrunched the piece of paper into a ball and threw it into the corner. But though it was out of sight, it refused to leave her mind.

**Having just had** an interesting discussion with Judd about Pure Psy, as well as about another matter his brother-in-law wanted him to pursue, Andrew stopped by Brenna's, knowing she had the day off. "So," he said, giving her his most winning smile, "what's for lunch?"

She laughed. "I got immune to that look around about when I turned five." But she hugged him before supplying him with a large piece of leftover lasagna, fruit, and even a slice of almond-orange cake.

He ate fast, kissing her on the forehead in thanks before using the privacy of her apartment to make a call to Nikita's security chief. Max was tied up all day today and tomorrow, so they set up a meeting for the morning of the day after.

"About the rumors Judd's heard?" Brenna asked after he hung up. "Possible dead Psy in the city?"

"Yep." Reviewing everything he had on his to-do list, Andrew realized he'd cleared it. Now it was time to pursue his personal prey—in a most unusual location. "See you later, baby sis."

"Hey," Brenna called out as he put his hand on the door-knob, "how's the charm offensive going?"

Andrew thought of how furious Indy was with him, thought, too, of her silence in response to his note. "I'm working on it." Leaving, he made his way through the corridors and to the White Zone. His target, the outdoor nursery, was tucked in one well-guarded corner of the designated safe area, and he wasn't more than a foot inside when he was accosted by a determined two-year-old.

"Up," she said, raising her arms imperiously.

Being the sucker that he was, he obliged, throwing her into the air. "Again!" she ordered when he caught her, the morning light blazing off the thick brown of her curls.

He obeyed. Four more times—to her squealing delight—before her chubby little arms hugged his neck. "Down." As he bent to put her on the ground, she smacked his lips with her own in a silent thank-you.

"So the charm works on two-year-olds, too?" A gentle comment from the woman who stood watch over the littlies as they played in the secure playground area—fenced off with stone walls to ensure no harm could come to the smallest of SnowDancers.

He rose to his full height. "The only one it doesn't seem to work on," he said, well aware that her acute gaze would see through any attempt at prevarication, "is your daughter."

Tarah Riviere's smile deepened, and there was such serenity in it that his own wolf turned calm, unwilling to disturb her with its chaotic emotions. "Your mate is a lucky man," he said without artifice. Such peace would never suit his own wild nature, but there was no denying the beauty and grace of it.

"Charming me won't do you any good with my daughter." Bending down, Tarah kissed a boo-boo, then sent the little boy toddling happily away.

Andrew shoved his hands into the pockets of his pants, rocking back on his heels. "I adore her," he said, figuring honesty would only help his case. "And if nothing else, she"—he couldn't say "wants me" to Indigo's mother—"is attracted to me, but I can't even get her to talk to me about it because I don't fit the image she has in her mind of the men she ought to date." His frustration punched through in spite of himself.

Tarah scowled. "No criticizing my baby."

"Sorry." Shoving his hands through his hair, he caught a pup in wolf form as the boy tried to make a daring escape, and tapped him gently on the muzzle before setting him back on the right path. "She's making me crazy." He remained hunkered on the ground, playing with the pup, who'd circled back to growl and bat at his hands with little paws.

Tarah's fingers touched his hair. "My Indigo is willful. Always has been, always will be." Affectionate words. "She knows what she wants."

"Well, she's wrong," he muttered, growling back at the pup when the little one tried a dominance display.

The pup froze.

Reaching out, Andrew picked him up, nipped him on one ear, and sent him on his way.

"Very well done," Tarah murmured. "The babies are always trying things like that. They need to know their boundaries at this age."

"It's the wolf," Andrew said, remaining where he was . . . because it was nice to have a mother's fingers playing through his hair. He only had a few precious memories of his own lieutenant mother, but he missed her—the way she'd pepper his face with kisses, the way she'd brush his hair, the way she'd smell after coming in from duty. Small moments, fleeting whispers, those were the things he remembered. "It needs the certainty of the hierarchy."

"That doesn't change with age." Sighing, she tugged a little at his hair, making him look up. "You don't fit the hierarchy, Andrew."

# CHAPTER 19

**Almost no one** called him Andrew. He felt like a little boy again. "That's not my fault."

"Oh?" An arch sound. "You knew exactly what you were doing from the instant you learned to walk. What that pup just tried? The Great Escape? Well, you succeeded nine times out of ten, and you did it by being so completely sweet and well behaved that no one thought to keep an eye on you." Another tug, a little harder. "Do you know how many times I had to go chasing after you?"

"Sorry?" Making a contrite face, he finally got to his feet, Tarah's hand sliding away to curl around his upper arm.

"No, you're not." A small laugh, but her eyes had turned solemn. "I like you, Andrew," she said, "and I like the way you sound when you speak about my girl."

Andrew touched the hand she had on his arm. "I'd do anything for her."

Tarah looked at him for long moments. "Your mama used to call you her 'loving baby.'"

"Yeah?" Andrew's throat grew thick. "What was Riley?"

"Her stubborn baby." Tarah smiled. "Brenna was her sunny baby."

"She had us pegged." Andrew couldn't hold Tarah's gaze anymore, his own misting over. Turning his head, he stared unseeing at the children.

Tarah didn't speak for long moments, but when she did, it wasn't about his mother. "Do you know my Evangeline?"

Glad for the change of subject, he said, "Sure." He had an impression of long black hair, deep gray eyes, and the slender body of a ballerina. "She used to play with Bren when they were young." The two girls had drifted apart as their interests diverged, but they still went to the occasional movie together when Evie was in the den. "She's away at college at the moment, isn't she?"

"Yes, but she'll be visiting in a couple of weeks." Squeezing his arm, she looked up. "Evie was a fragile child—spent weeks at a time in the hospital. She didn't really come into her own until she was about thirteen."

Knowing Indy as he did, Andrew immediately saw what Tarah was trying to tell him. Indigo, with her strength and her will, would've tried to take as much of the burden off her parents' shoulders as she could—but Tarah's expression said it was more than that. "Was Evie ever in danger of dying?"

"More than once." Solemn words. "And my Indigo, she loves her sister. It tore her apart each time Evangeline was taken to the hospital."

Out of that fire had been forged the steel of Indigo's nature. She loved her sister, her family, but she wouldn't easily allow anyone else close enough to create that depth of vulnerability in her heart. "Thank you, Tarah." Because he and Indy, it wasn't only about sex. They'd been locked together by the bonds of friendship long before he'd dared reach for her heart. And maybe, just maybe, she was running scared because somewhere deep within, she understood that he'd never be a lover who'd allow her to keep a safe emotional distance.

Tarah brushed a leaf that had fallen onto his arm with the absentminded touch of a mother. "I think you need to meet another member of our family, too."

He caught something hidden in that statement. "Who?"

"No," Tarah said after a thoughtful pause, releasing his arm. "Pass the first hurdle, then we'll talk about the second."

He wanted to pursue the oblique hint, but Tarah's tone made it clear she wouldn't be pushed. However, reaching up, she cupped his cheeks and, when he bent his head, brushed his hair off his face with a maternal hand. "You'll do, Andrew." A finger tapping on his nose. "Just don't drive my girl too crazy."

Andrew grinned, suddenly lighthearted. Indigo was very close to her mother; Tarah could've put a serious spanner in the works. Instead, she was looking at him with exasperated affection. "You know me too well, Tarah."

"Scamp." Shaking her head, she commandeered him to play with the pups.

Delighted with the whole world at that moment, with hope a blinding brilliance inside of him, he obeyed without protest.

**Indigo couldn't believe** she was considering Drew's invitation. Staring at the piece of paper she'd retrieved minutes after she'd crushed it and that had been taunting her since, she shoved it into her pants pocket for the umpteenth time. "Again," she said to the small group of novice soldiers she was putting through their paces in one of the less utilized gyms in the den.

They groaned but restarted the circuit. She watched, making note of weaknesses, strengths, things that needed to be corrected. Unfortunately, that still left her plenty of time to think about a certain wolf who was turning out to be mule stubborn beneath his playful exterior.

"Good group." Riaz's deep voice came from behind her.

She'd caught the dark woodsy scent of him, so she didn't startle. "Yes, they are—our best." At least one future lieutenant, most likely two.

"Is that Sienna Lauren?"

"Yep." The girl might be spending a lot of time with the DarkRiver leopards, but she was a SnowDancer soldier—and she never failed to put in the required hours in training, further honing the skills Indigo had all but beaten into her.

At the time they began, Sienna had been a belligerent seventeen-year-old determined to rely only on her psychic abilities. It had taken Indigo almost six months to break through that prickly exterior . . . and glimpse the ravaging fear within. Sienna Lauren was more afraid of her own power than she was of any real or imaginary monster.

"She's very, very good." Riaz walked to stand beside her, his arms loosely folded as he watched the group complete one section of the circuit and move on to the next. "I might have a go at the course myself—haven't had the chance to do this kind of thing for a while."

"This'll be too easy for you," she said, fully confident that he would've continued to further develop his skills during his absence from the den. "You should run the outdoor one."

A stirring of interest. "Is it the same as when I left?"

"A few changes but nothing drastic." Remembering something, she smiled and nudged him with her shoulder. "I think you still hold the record for running the old course."

"Yeah?" Obviously pleased, he gave her a lazy smile that turned his looks from handsome to devastating. "Do it with me?"

Woman and wolf both read the hidden invitation behind the obvious one, hesitated, then shoved forward. Because he was perfect. There would be no games of one-upmanship with Riaz, no drain on her emotions or her self-confidence as she worried about whether her dominance was hurting him, no having to catch herself before she did something that might dent his pride. "Sure. You free after this lot is done?"

He started to nod, then frowned. "No, I have a videoconference with some of my European contacts. Can we do it around four instead?"

"That'll work." Even as she spoke, Drew's note burned a hole in her pocket.

**Andrew had just** put down the phone after getting hold of the last of the small group of men and women under his direct command scattered throughout the pack—to warn them to keep an eye out for further attempts by Pure Psy—when his wolf caught the burgeoning wave of excitement in the den. It was an almost physical push against his fur—though he was in human form.

Poking his head out the door of his room, he hailed one of the soldiers heading down the corridor. "Eli, what's up?"

"Indigo and Riaz are running the outdoor course." Elias's words carried a hum of anticipation. "You know how fast she is, and he holds the record. No way to tell who'll win."

Andrew felt his spine knot with tension, a freezing chill spearing through his veins. "They starting now?" Somehow, his voice sounded normal, ordinary, when all he wanted to do was to hunt Indigo to ground and demand she fucking stop running from him. Because he knew exactly what was going through her head at this moment, knew exactly what her wolf would see in Riaz.

"Yeah. You coming?"

Andrew was already shutting his door behind him. "Wouldn't want to miss it." His wolf was beyond agitated, but he'd always been good at keeping his emotions off his face. His current work for Hawke had only refined that skill. As he exited the den with Elias and jogged out to the training ground, no one would've been able to tell that he was walking the sharpest of knife edges.

"You going to take bets?" Elias asked with a grin.

Since Andrew had been known to do just that on occasion when packmates challenged one another, he couldn't fault the question. "Not this time. Indigo might skin me." It was difficult to keep his voice light, to act as Elias expected him to act. He'd always known this courtship wasn't going to be easy, but he'd never expected Indy to kick him this hard in the guts.

Then they were on the edge of the run and the kick turned brutal. Indigo and Riaz stood side by side, both of them shoeless and clearly pumped. Indigo was wearing thin black exercise pants with white stripes down the sides, as was Riaz. The male lieutenant was shirtless, the tattoo on the back of his left shoulder striking against the naturally bronzed tone of his skin.

But it was Indigo who caught not only Andrew's but Elias's attention as well. "She's beautiful, isn't she?" It was a quiet comment.

The wolf bared its teeth inside Andrew. "You're mated."

"It's like appreciating a beautiful piece of art," Elias murmured. "Yuki would say the same if she was standing beside me."

Andrew understood what Elias meant. Dressed in those practical pants and a black tank that clung to her body like second skin, her hair pulled off her face in a tight ponytail, Indigo was beauty without ornamentation—strong, lethal beauty. And an instant later, she was beauty in motion as someone—Judd—set off the starter bell.

Indigo was liquid lightning as she scrambled up the massive first wall. Riaz, his body heavier, was slower in getting up. But he had the advantage in the next section, which was all about upper-body strength. They were neck and neck as they crawled under the rope-mesh maze, their bodies muddy when they shot out the other end—to run straight up a steep, steep climb where use of claws to ensure stability would get you disqualified.

Indigo slipped, fell back on the slick log, but managed to break her fall with her hands.

Andrew's wolf urged her to get up. She did.

And Riaz slid back down.

That was when Indigo turned to glance at her competitor. She was laughing, her wolf obviously exhilarated. Andrew's blood turned to ice. That look in her eyes, that joy . . . He swallowed, forced himself to watch as Riaz got back up the rise and joined Indigo in swinging over a water hazard before they clasped their hands over the bars of the "jungle gym" that had undone many a SnowDancer.

Created with interlocking pieces that were shifted around before each run, it was by nature unpredictable—and had more than its share of booby traps. Indigo set off one, swore as she was thrown to the ground and had to go back to the start of the confusion of metal. This time, she managed to swing herself on top of the whole thing and began to pick her way through with nimble sure-footedness. Riaz, who'd gotten ahead, turned the air blue as part of the metal structure gave away, almost dumping him on the earth.

He caught himself by flipping up his body, but the delay

had given Indigo time to close the gap, and they were moving beside each other once more as they dropped from the gym and shot through into the underground tubes that required both speed and strength. Riaz exited first, but Indigo was hot on his heels, and she was the faster runner. She flew past him on the last stretch of the curving run that brought them back to the start.

Laughing, she collapsed into a sitting position just over the finish line. "Too many baguettes, I think." She waved a finger at Riaz.

Riaz, his chest heaving, hands on his knees, grinned. "You've gotten faster since the last time I did this with you."

The shared history between the two of them didn't need to be stated; it was all the more painful for being so casually understood. Andrew watched as Riaz held out a hand, as Indigo took it and let her fellow lieutenant pull her to her feet. No hesitation, no worries about dominance—because they knew they were equals, were comfortable with that.

In a way Indigo might never be comfortable where Andrew was concerned.

As everyone clapped and congratulated both Riaz and Indigo—they'd run the course in an incredibly fast time—Andrew hung back, his eyes on Indigo's glowing face. No matter the mud on her cheek, the dirt that tangled her hair and streaked her clothing, she looked amazing. Stunning. And it wasn't Andrew who'd put that look on her face.

She turned right then, and her eyes locked with his.

A furious mix of anger and pain threatened to blind him, but he forced himself to walk forward, to keep his tone even as he said, "That was some run," directing his comment to both of them.

Riaz grinned, and his next words were good-natured. "She ran me to the fucking ground."

"You should do it with Judd next time," Indigo said, a tiny frown between her brows as she looked away from Andrew. "He can do weird things with his speed—and he never slips on the climb."

"Never?"

Indigo shook her head.

"Might have to take him on, then." Glancing at his watch, the male lieutenant met Indigo's eyes. "I'm starving. You want to grab dinner together after we shower?"

Time froze. Indigo glanced at Andrew for a fleeting second, and he saw her decision in her eyes before she turned to Riaz. "Yeah, that sounds good."

# CHAPTER 20

**Indigo looked up** after she accepted Riaz's offer, expecting to meet Drew's angry gaze, but he was gone, having melted into the crowd of packmates who'd come out to see her and Riaz run the course. Her stomach turned heavy, as if it was full of rocks—though she told herself she'd made the right decision.

Whatever it was that had blazed between her and Drew, it wouldn't have lasted—and more, it would've hurt them both in the process. Better to nip it in the bud, to focus on a relationship that had the possibility of going somewhere. Except that she found herself looking for Drew again, her wolf pacing this way and that.

There was no sign of him.

At that instant, she knew he wouldn't ever slip another note under her door. Because Andrew Liam Kincaid might be charming, he might laugh with ease and tease with smiling joy, but he was also a dominant male. He had pride in spades.

That pride would not allow him to approach her again when she'd openly—publicly—made another choice.

There would be no more presents of fossils or bribes of sweet desserts, no more ambushing kisses, no more challenges, no more Drew. The rocks in her gut turning to blocks of ice, she took a step toward the den, intent on following his fading scent.

"That was great!" A packmate slapped her on the back. "I knew you were fast, but that was something else."

There was no way to make a graceful exit, not with everyone around her—and she didn't know what she'd say to Drew if she caught up with him. Because her decision was the right one. It *was*.

**Having just watched** Riaz and Indigo drive off for their dinner, Andrew slung a light backpack over his shoulder and walked to Hawke's office. His alpha was marking something on the territorial map hung on one of the stone walls. "Drew," he said, shooting a penetrating look over his shoulder, "what is it?"

"I need tonight and tomorrow off." The words were forced out past the violent emotions still choking his throat.

Hawke frowned. "We're already going to be down a few people with Eli and Yuki taking Sakura to Disneyland tomorrow. Sing-Liu and D'Arn headed out an hour ago to visit her parents for a couple of days."

"One night, one day," Andrew repeated. It was all he trusted himself to say.

Hawke's pale blue eyes drilled into him, tiny lines flaring out at the corners. "Go," his alpha finally said. "And if you need Pack, don't be a dipshit and try to hack it alone. Call me."

Pack was One. Pack was family.

Andrew knew that, but right now, he wanted to be alone. It fucking hurt that Indigo had chosen someone else over him. But he'd have shrugged that off and continued to court her, to challenge Riaz for the right to her, if he hadn't seen that glowing expression on her face during the run, heard her laughter after it.

Riaz made her *happy*.

Really, truly happy, with none of the worry or anger that colored her relationship with Andrew.

And though the knowledge had his wolf clawing violently at the inside of his skin, Andrew would slit his own throat before he did anything to savage her happiness—as would inevitably happen if he saw her touch the other male. So he had to get out of here, find some way to gain control over the violence of his emotions, burn off the rage until he was in no danger of using his abilities as the pack's tracker to spill SnowDancer blood.

Most people tended to forget that the tracker was also trained to kill the rogues he tracked. Andrew never did. It was why he hadn't shifted, didn't intend to shift until he had a handle on himself—he didn't trust what he might do once he gave in to the much more primal mindset of the wolf.

Leaving Hawke's office without another word, he walked down the tunnels with his head bent, not inviting conversation.

He didn't count on Ben.

The five-year-old barreled around the corner and wrapped his baby-soft arms around Andrew's legs. "Drew!" A shining face lifted up to his, absolute trust in those dark, button brown eyes.

Andrew could no more squelch that joy than he could cut Indy out of his heart. "Mr. Ben." Bending, he picked the sweet-natured boy up and turned him upside down.

Ben's delighted laughter attracted the attention of passing packmates, made smiles break out on their faces. Andrew smiled, too, but his heart was too bruised to make it real. Turning Ben right side up, he settled the boy on his arm, his eyes on Ben's soft fleece pajamas. "Did you escape bedtime?" He began heading toward Ben's home.

A nod, one arm companionably around his neck. "You're taking me back."

"Yep."

A sigh, then he snuggled his head into the curve of Andrew's neck, sitting patiently until they reached the open doorway of his home. "Knock, knock," Andrew said. "I have an escapee to return."

Ben's mother walked out, shaking her head. "Slippery

little monkey. I thought you were in bed." Taking Ben, she sent Andrew a smile as bright and open as her son's. "Thanks for bringing my little man back."

Andrew nodded and was about to leave when Ben said, "Wait! I wanna give Drew something." Wiggling out of his mother's arms, he ran to the back of the apartment.

His mom went to say something when there was a cry from somewhere in the living area. "Oh, that's the baby," she said. "I better go pick her up."

Andrew stayed in the doorway as she did so. "How's Ben with her?"

"He plays with her for hours." Ava's cheeks dimpled with maternal pride as she glanced over her shoulder. "Such patience my Benny has, you wouldn't believe it."

Ben tumbled out of his room then, running as fast as his little legs would take him. When Andrew crouched in front of him, the boy handed over a tiny object. It was an action figure of a man in a blue jumpsuit sporting improbable muscles. "Thanks."

"It makes me happy when I play with it." Ben tapped him on the cheek with one baby-soft palm. "Don't be sad, Drew."

Andrew looked into those shining eyes and wondered who Ben was going to grow into. Whoever that man was, Andrew had a feeling the whole pack would be damned proud of him. "Yeah? Okay."

A smile full of sunshine.

"Come on, Benny," Ava called. "Let's get you to bed, my sweet boy."

Leaving with a wave, Andrew put the little action figure in a side pocket of his pack. Ben had seen. Hawke had seen. Andrew didn't want anyone else to see. So he made sure he wasn't stopped again as he headed out and away from this den where Indigo would return on the arm of another man. The rest of what might happen . . . he couldn't think about it without unleashing the wolf's tormented rage.

**Indigo sat across** from Riaz on the open patio of a rooftop restaurant you usually had to book weeks in advance, the glittering lights of the city spread out in shimmering ropes far below. And beyond that, the dark lap of the bay. It was a stunning view, and the man across from her was undeniably handsome, but she couldn't focus, her entire body tense as if for battle. As for her wolf—it was agitated, unable to sit still.

Riaz stirred across from her. "So?"

It was an effort to smile, to pretend everything was as it should be. "I'm impressed," she said, turning her gaze from the view to him. "How did you get reservations so fast?"

"I called in a favor. Wouldn't do to disappoint you." A slow smile that should've made her senses leap. "Did you notice how civilized I'm being?"

It was a reference to their past, when Riaz had been a wild, wild young male and she'd been coming into herself as a dominant female. "I almost don't recognize you." She tipped her wineglass toward him in a salute, though part of her missed the wild boy he'd been. He was almost too mature these days.

Riaz's smile deepened at her comment, but she thought she glimpsed something hidden behind it, a sharp echo of her own confusion. However, when he spoke, his voice was steady. "You ready to order?"

"You do it."

Riaz raised an eyebrow. "Testing how well I know you?"

"Maybe." She took a sip of the excellent wine and watched him over the top of her glass.

Amazing dark gold eyes, the eyes of a man who'd seen the world and knew exactly what he wanted. But since his return from Europe, those eyes were more often shuttered and introspective than laughing, and the only time she'd really seen him playful was when they'd done the run. Even when he'd been young, he'd been . . . intense.

Not that it mattered, she told herself. Play was for boys and children. Riaz was a strong male in the prime of his life. Both sides of her nature found him more than acceptable . . . except, the wolf thought wistfully, a little more playfulness would've been nice. After all, he was a wolf, too. Play was part of their life. Shouldn't he *want* to play with a female who attracted him?

As she listened, he placed their order. All perfect. Until he said, "No dessert. We'll go for coffee instead."

Her wolf sniffed. *No dessert?* Drew would've never made that mistake.

She caught that thought as soon as it rose, nipped it before it could take root. Drew wasn't only too young; he wasn't dominant enough to be able to handle her wolf, despite what he thought. And as she'd seen up close and personal, such an imbalanced relationship couldn't work—the emotional devastation would destroy them both, obliterating what friendship remained. There might even come a time when he'd look at her with barely concealed hate.

Shoving aside the painful images evoked by those thoughts, she turned her attention very deliberately to Riaz. "Tell me more about what you did while you were away."

The other lieutenant began to speak, his voice low, deep, smooth as caramel. As he spoke, she let herself truly look at him. His skin glowed a burnished brown in the light from the candles, his near black hair sparking with auburn highlights. The stunning blonde three tables over was giving him the eye when she thought Indigo wasn't watching, while the two gorgeous black women one table to the right didn't even try to hide their admiration.

Meeting Indigo's gaze, they gave her a discreet thumbs-up. Indigo smiled back at the friendly appreciation, returning her focus to Riaz's strong jawline, those beautifully shaped lips she'd once felt on her own. They'd been good as lovers, very good. But they'd parted as the best of friends. No broken hearts. No torn souls.

It made her wolf halt in its thoughts, consider.

Changeling wolves mated for life.

Her parents' relationship might not make sense to Indigo, but there wasn't a shred of doubt in her mind that they loved each other to the core of their beings. More, that they fit together like two pieces of a separated whole—as if without one, there would be no other.

She wanted that, she realized as she sat across from this incredible man who ticked all the right boxes, who'd make a good partner, but who would never be her heartbeat. She wanted the agony and the ecstasy, craved the ferocity of the bond that tied male to female in the most visceral way. Fear bloomed at the idea of the vulnerability that would accompany such a relationship, but it wasn't enough to overwhelm the hunger in her soul.

"Hey."

Blinking, she found Riaz watching her with a disconcertingly intent look. "Sorry," she said, her cheeks burning with cold heat. "My mind drifted away for a second."

Riaz didn't let her off the hook. "We've known each other too long to play games, Indigo." Lifting his wineglass, he took a sip of the golden liquid. "We know this isn't going to work—but we're trying to pretend that it will because it's easier, safer."

Hearing the echo of pain in his words, she reached out to touch his free hand—no matter what, he was her friend. He was Pack. "Who?"

"My mate."

Indigo's hand clenched on his. "You found her?"

"Too late." It was torn out of him, eyes gleaming amber in the flickering candlelight. "She's another man's wife, a good man." Raw hurt in those words. "Not touching her, not simply taking her, was the hardest thing I've ever done—but she would've despised herself for cheating."

So he'd walked away, Indigo thought, though it was clear doing so had savaged him. "I'm sorry, Riaz." She couldn't imagine the nightmare he was living, knowing his mate belonged to someone else. Predatory male changelings were possessive beyond belief—it had to be torture to know that another man had the right to touch his mate, to build a life with her.

"I wasn't playing games with you, Indigo," he said, turning his hand over so their fingers intertwined, his tone raw. "I thought—"

"I know," she interrupted with all the gentleness she had in her. Hurting and broken, he'd needed Pack, and she was someone he loved as a friend. It would've been instinct to turn to her, to try to find some kind of hope. "There's no need for apologies between us."

"It would've been so much easier if it was you." He gave a small smile, the pain in his eyes filmed over by the fist of control. "Drew's the one, isn't he?"

She went to tug back her hand but he held it. "Yes," she admitted. "It confuses me, confuses my wolf, what he makes me feel." Exhilaration and joy . . . and utter, utter terror. Because what if she was right? What if being with Drew would eventually mean a corrosive pain that would destroy them both, drop by slow drop?

Riaz leaned forward and lifted her fingers to his mouth, brushing a tender caress across her knuckles. "You know what I'm going to say." In his gaze, she saw a fierce want, a hunger that told her he'd give anything to have the right to court, to claim the woman who sang to his heart. The woman, Indigo thought with an insight born of her own turmoil, for whom he might just play.

"Take me home, Riaz." There was no use in pretending she wasn't aching to return to tangle with a wolf who shouldn't have made her feel this way. But he did. And she'd been a coward long enough.

It was time to come face-to-face with what might very well be her destiny.

# CHAPTER 21

**Indigo kicked off** her heels, shimmied out of her dress, and washed the makeup off her face. Brushing her hair out of its fancy knot and into her more usual ponytail, she pulled on some jeans, topped them with a sleek black turtleneck, stuffed her feet into boots . . . then took a deep breath.

Butterflies flitted here and there in her stomach, while her blood pumped jagged and erratic through her veins. Lifting her hands to her face, she rubbed. Her skin flushed hot, then cold, before the cycle repeated. "Stop stalling," she ordered herself and wrenched open the door.

The corridors were quiet, most of the den having bedded down for the night. Only those on night shift were up—they waved hello to her as she passed by. Waving back, she carried on. Drew's quarters were near the end of the passage, and she was raising a hand to knock when the soldier next door poked out his head. "Hey, Indigo. Thought I scented you. You looking for Drew?"

She nodded.

"He left a couple of hours ago," the other male told her.

"Do you know where he was going?"

"Had a backpack," was the response. "I figured he was heading out on one of his trips."

Her stomach dropped. Had he left? Had he finally given up and left? Her wolf went quiet, unsure, even as anger spiked. That wasn't how the game was played—the male didn't *leave*. He chased and he tangled and he fought. Except . . . she'd chosen someone else *in front of him*. She might as well have taken a buzz saw to his pride, the one vulnerable spot in a predatory changeling male's armor. "Thanks."

Nodding, the other soldier ducked back inside. Indigo forced herself to walk down the corridor and away from the quarters used by the single dominants in the pack. She didn't even realize she was heading for Hawke's office until she got there and found it empty. Frustration churned, but she turned back around and arrowed toward the training rooms. Their alpha slept very few hours a night, haunted by things that had marked him since childhood—and perhaps, right this moment, more than a little sexual frustration.

She tracked him down in the weight room, where he was sitting on a bench doing arm curls with free weights while reading what looked like stock-market reports on a transparent comm screen on the wall.

"There goes your image as all brawn, no brain," she said, turning her back to the reports.

Grunting, he put down the weight he'd been using. "Don't tell anyone. It's my secret weapon."

She passed him a towel when he nodded at where it was slung over another machine. Waiting until he'd wiped off his face and put down the towel, she took a seat on the bench opposite. It gave her a good view of his naked chest, and yes, gleaming with sweat and lightly furred with pale silver-gold, it was a damn nice view, the kind of view that would have made most women drool and beg for a chance to stroke him until he growled and took over.

"Ouch," Hawke muttered, but the wolf's laughter was apparent in his gaze. "Here I sit in all my glory, and she's comparing me to another man."

Blowing out a breath, Indigo fell back on the bench, staring up at the ceiling. "I don't know what I'm doing."

"The first step toward recovery is admitting that."

She showed him the middle finger of her left hand for that pithy statement. "Am I a stubborn fool?" As evidenced by the fact that she might just have driven away the only man who'd ever threatened to breach her defenses . . . who'd made her feel vulnerable enough that she'd struck out in self-protective panic.

"Your determination is part of what makes you a good lieutenant."

Sitting back up, she stared at him as he began to do curls again, the muscles of his upper arm bunching and flexing in all sorts of interesting ways. It was nice eye candy—but she still didn't want to bite. "Dominant female, equally dominant or more dominant male, that's the equation. That's how it always goes."

Ice blue eyes, shimmering with flickers of color from the screen opposite, met hers. "You already know that's not how it always works so why are you wasting time repeating the same argument? Just go find Drew and sort it out."

"It's annoying, you know, that habit you have of knowing everything."

"Good thing I'm bigger than you and you can't beat me to a pulp." Placing the weight on a rack, he got up and moved to an exercise mat. "Stand on my feet," he said, lying on his back.

"I'm wearing boots." But she walked over and pressed down with her palms on his raised knees as he did sit-up after sit-up without so much as his breathing altering. "You know about Adria."

Hawke curled his lip. "For a smart woman, you're being amazingly dense." When she glared, he deigned to explain himself. "You're not Adria, Indigo."

No, she thought, she wasn't. She'd never let a man treat her the way Martin treated Adria—had always treated her. Drew, by contrast . . . no, he wasn't Martin.

"Why are you still thinking?" Hawke asked, abdomen muscles crunching as he continued to exercise while they spoke. "You need to work this out face-to-face with Drew."

"Damn it, Hawke. I think I might've really messed up."
Tangling with each other, fighting with each other, that was
all fine. But she'd crossed a line when she'd brought a third
player into the equation—it had been done in that same self-
protective panic, but it had changed the equilibrium between
them in a sickening way.

"Yeah, I think you might have, too." Brutally honest words.
"But he's only got about three hours' head start, so you can
catch him if you leave now."

She looked down into his face as he stopped doing the
sit-ups to watch her with those eerily piercing eyes. "Will
he welcome me?"

"Nope." Flowing up into a standing position when she
released his knees, he picked up the remote to change the chan-
nel from stock reports to a roundup of the day's sports news.
"But you're not the giving-up type. Of course," he added as
she turned to leave, "that's your biggest weakness, too."

**Indigo tested the** straps of the pack on her back as she
stepped out of the den and into the cool night air. She could've
run up in wolf form, hunted to keep herself fed, but she was
already going to be plenty emotionally exposed when she
reached Drew. No use being naked on top of that.

Hawke had no idea which way Drew had gone, and the
rain-laced wind had made a mess of the scent trail, so she
was going to have to do this the hard way—using her tracking skills. Which would have been easier if the wind hadn't
decide to swirl up and merrily throw around the leaves, erasing any trace of Drew's passage.

Something rustled to her left just as she bent down to
check for more subtle evidence that might indicate a male
of his height and weight had passed this way. Jerking up her
head, she realized she'd been so deep in thought, she'd left her
flank unprotected. Of course, this was SnowDancer land, and
the man who walked out was a fellow lieutenant, but still . . .
"What're you doing lurking in the dark?"

Judd came to crouch beside her. "It's a natural gift." He
was dressed all in black, the quintessential assassin. He'd

given up his former career, but she knew he continued to be involved with the Psy—and more particularly, with the Ghost, the most dangerous Psy rebel of them all.

"Off to see your lethal buddy?"

Judd shook his head, dark brown hair gleaming black in the dark. "I'm not here to chat—I've got a meeting in an hour." Unspoken was the fact that the people he met with would be unlikely to wait. "Drew went in that direction." He pointed straight in front of him and up. "I tracked him for a while to make sure he wasn't doing anything stupid. Last I saw, he was at the Serpent Pass."

Indigo got to her feet as Judd rose. "Thanks." She tugged a little uncomfortably on a strap. "Why?"

Judd faded back into the darkness. "Because I was you, once."

As she shifted on her heel and began to trek to the Serpent Pass, Judd's words reverberated in her skull. The other lieutenant was Psy, had been an ice-cold bastard when he first joined the pack, as emotionless, as harsh as the rock faces in the Sierra Nevada.

She was changeling. Touch was her lifeblood, and she was tied to the pack by countless threads. There were no similarities between them.

Except . . .

A flicker of memory, of holding back tears after a bad fall because she didn't want to cry and give her parents something else to worry about. It had been instinct—she'd known they needed all their energy to care for Evie. Loving her sister as Indigo did, that choice, and the ones that came after, weren't anything she regretted—her independence and strength were qualities she was proud of.

There was nothing wrong with being steel, nothing wrong with being strong. It was expected with men. Just because she was a woman . . . But right when she was working up a good head of steam, she remembered who'd said the words that had begun this tumble of memories and thoughts.

If anyone knew about being ice, about being steel, it was Judd.

Her foot caught on a twisted root and she almost went

flying. "Shit." Steadying herself, she wrenched her focus firmly back to the present. The past and how it had shaped her could all come later. Much later.

Four hours after she began, in a rugged area lightly sprinkled with patches of snow, she caught the first hint of Drew's scent. Her instinct was to move at a faster clip, catch up to him as soon as possible, but she forced herself to slow down, consider what she was going to say when she reached him.

A blank.

"Great. Just great, Indigo," she muttered under her breath, unscrewing the water bottle she'd refilled at a spring a couple of hours earlier and gulping down half of it without pause. Thirst quenched, but mind no more forthcoming, she slid it back into its spot along the side of her pack and began to climb the jagged pathway in front of her. In truth, it wasn't really a path, more like a rock slide that had solidified over time and that the pack used as stairs when in wolf form.

It wasn't as straightforward in a human body. Her hands got banged up a little on the sharp edges, and she whacked her knees a couple of times, but she hardly noticed the small hurts as she crested the rise. Because Drew had stopped—on a small plateau bare of snow that would catch direct sunlight when the sun rose, though the area beyond it was thick with trees, their arms reaching into the clouds.

He'd set up a portable laz-fire and unrolled his sleeping bag on top of a groundsheet that would keep the damp from soaking in. It would've still been too cold for most humans— probably a lot of changelings, too. But she'd felt Drew's body against hers, knew he burned white-hot. Taking a deep breath, she made her way down to the campsite.

Above her, the night was a crystalline darkness, the stars as bright as shards of diamond; below her, only silence. Half-way down, she glimpsed Drew's pack lying against a tree not far from the fire, but there was no sign of the man she'd come to find. It was only when she was almost at the plateau that she heard the gurgle of water in the distance. Shrugging off her own pack along with her jacket, she left them by Drew's and followed that sound to what turned out to be a stream.

Swollen from the rains and melted snow, it crashed down into a natural pool formed by the long passage of water against rock, where it turned quiescent at last. The pool was black beyond the foam of the falling water, but she didn't need anything other than the starlight—her eyes went unerringly to the muscled body of the man cutting through the dark surface.

Scrambling down to the side of the pool, she saw the rock where Drew had abandoned his clothes. Sweat soaked her own clothes in spite of the chill air, and she looked longingly at the water. Drew hadn't noticed her yet, and when he did, she knew it wasn't going to be pretty. "Hell with it," she muttered and reached down to pull off her boots.

She'd just taken off her turtleneck and dumped it on the rest of the pile when Drew's head snapped up out of the water. Their eyes met and it felt as if the universe itself was holding its breath.

# CHAPTER 22

**Andrew would've thought** he was hallucinating, except that Indigo's scent surrounded him on every side, the air currents cruel and capricious. Staring at her standing there so proud and so beautiful—so goddamn beautiful—he had to fight with every ounce of his strength not to power through the water and pull her down so he could slick his hands over her breasts, claim her mouth with his own.

Continuing to hold his gaze, she reached up and released her hair from its ponytail. The dark mass rippled down her back, over her shoulders. She swept it away, baring the black curves of the bra that shaped her body. Even from this far away, he could tell it was no flimsy, lacy thing. No, it was functional, supported her . . . and cupped her with breathtaking intimacy.

He'd held her when she was naked, even kissed her when she was naked. But no moment had felt as intimate as this. As he watched, his body rock hard with a sudden, furious arousal that made him burn, she reached behind herself and unhooked her bra.

*No.*

He dove under, deep enough that there was nothing but silence, nothing but darkness, the water gliding over his body in a caress of liquid satin, cold and sweet. Emerging only when his lungs protested, he shoved the hair out of his eyes to see that the shoreline was empty, Indigo's clothes abandoned beside his.

A ripple of water against his side and he knew she was in the stone pool with him, her body as sleek and fast as that of a fur seal as she dove under and came up a few feet to his left. Body gleaming wet, she made her way to him, her movements slow and easy—as if she was afraid he'd disappear.

Her caution made him bare his teeth. "I'm not a fucking rabbit."

"No, you're a pissed-off male wolf," Indigo answered, her pulse hammering double time. "Rule of thumb there is to move slowly and try not to get your throat ripped out."

A low snarl vibrated in the sudden silence around them as the forest creatures froze. "I don't need my ego stroked, Indigo. You made your decision. It's done."

"Drew—"

"Why are you here?" Blunt words, with none of the charm she'd come to expect. "Were you worried that one of your chicks was in trouble?"

"You're not lettin—"

"Well, as you can see, I'm fine. So you can go back to the den with a clear conscience."

He'd cut through the water and was pulling himself out before she could stop him. Used to giving packmates privacy, she went to close her eyes, then thought, to hell with it, and kept them open. He was built gorgeously, all fluid lines and supple muscle that hid a ferocious power and strength.

He didn't look at her as he picked up his dirty clothes and left, but she knew he was aware she was watching. As he disappeared into the forest, she blew out a breath and, floating on her back, stared up at the jewel-strewn sky. "Well, that went well." No one answered her, the forest-denizens going about their business once more, uninterested in the fact that the rules she lived her life by were crumbling around her.

She didn't know how long she remained in the pool, but when shivers began to crawl over her skin, she finally hauled herself out . . . to find a clean T-shirt and towel placed where her dirty clothes had been. Her heart gave a little beat of hope. Toweling herself down as fast as possible in an attempt to rub heat into her skin, she pulled on the T-shirt.

*Earthy warmth and sunshine and laughter.*

It was Drew's T-shirt. Nuzzling her face into the shoulder, she inhaled deeply of his scent before wrapping the towel around her hair and making her way back to the campsite. The scent trail Drew had left behind led her up an easier path than the one she'd used to come down, and she reached the warm light of the laz-fire not long afterward.

Drew was lying on his back on top of his sleeping bag when she arrived, his arms folded behind his head, his body clad in faded jeans and nothing else. He'd made no effort to roll out her sleeping bag. In fact, even her dirty clothes had been packed away. The hint was as clear as a billboard sign.

Growling low in her throat, she ripped off the towel and dumped it on his pack. Then, driven by anger and the stubborn will that had created this mess in the first place, she walked over to straddle his fake-sleeping body. His eyes snapped open as her weight came down on his hips, her arms crossed over her chest.

She glimpsed a furious mix of raw hunger and pure rage in the blue of his eyes in the split second before he propped himself up on his elbows and said, "What? Riaz doesn't know what he's doing in bed?" in a voice harsh enough to strip paint.

"Is that an offer?" It was a sweet question as she shifted to cradle the powerful jut of his arousal between her thighs. He felt . . . Her stomach went all tight and twisty, her skin shimmering with a sudden, blinding heat that had nothing to do with the fire to her left.

His face was pure scowl when he responded. "I'm not looking to be the fucking booby prize, so no, it's not an offer."

Unfolding her arms, Indigo leaned down to brace herself with her palms flat on either side of his head. Drew fell back, his hands coming to close over her hips. "What are you doing?" Gritted out through clenched teeth.

Those hands, those fingers, they felt like brands on her skin, burning through the fabric of the tee to imprint her skin. "Trying to figure out why the hell I came all this way to get abused."

His fingers tightened. "Yeah, why did you?"

"Maybe because I wanted to do this." She nipped sharply at his full lower lip. "And this." Sucking his upper lip into her mouth, she released it with slow pleasure. "And this, too." Pushing her fingers into his damp hair, she swept her tongue inside his mouth in a brazen kiss that held nothing back.

A growl vibrated in his chest and it made her shiver. "That felt good," she said, breaking the kiss to gasp in a breath. "Do it again when I'm naked."

His hands slid down, then back up her thighs to close over her bare buttocks. "What are you doing, Indigo?"

But she stole the question with her mouth, raising one hand off the soft cushion of the sleeping bag to stroke against his cheek. The stubble of his unshaven jaw rasped over her palm, and she wanted to feel that same sensation on softer, far more delicate skin. Her thighs clenched around him, and he felt it, if his response was any indication.

Squeezing the flesh he'd palmed, he slid his hands down to her upper thighs, played his fingers along the highly sensitive inner faces just enough to make her gasp . . . then slid his hands right back to where they'd been. "Tease." She broke the kiss, looked down at him. And saw something that made her bury her face in his neck as she stretched out her legs until she lay on top of him, his hands still on her bare flesh, his erection rigid beneath her thigh, his chest rising and falling in a jagged rhythm.

Her own breathing wasn't exactly steady either, but she licked her lips, tried to talk. "This isn't a game." It came out soft, husky.

But Drew was a wolf, his ears predator-sharp. Shifting,

he rearranged her with possessive hands until she lay on her back, with him braced on one elbow above her. His damp hair was messy from her hands, tumbling over his forehead, making him appear even younger than he was.

Yet the firelight flickering over his eyes told a different story. There were shadows there, echoes of pain and sorrow, loss and hope. He'd lived, this wolf, fought and bled for the pack, and she had no right to devalue that simply because she had four years on him. "No games," she said again, daring to raise her hand to stroke his hair off his forehead.

"Then what?" he asked, allowing the touch, continuing to pin her with one leg thrown over her own, but still so coolly distant, still not the Drew she knew.

She ran her fingers down his cheek, along his jaw, stroking the heated silk of his shoulder. Her thighs clenched in silent, sensual response as the muscles flexed under her touch. "I'm willing to try."

"That's not good enough." Hard words, his jaw a brutal line.

Her wolf growled at the challenge. Drew stared back in unflinching demand. "I want to try," she said when he refused to break the deadlock. "I want you. But I don't know if my wolf will accept what it is you want from me."

It remained uncertain about a male who simply did not fit into what it considered the acceptable parameters for the mate it would take as its own—no matter how much he called to both woman and wolf. "I don't want to hurt you." What she didn't add was that she was terrified he'd hurt *her*, that he'd be unable to accept the truth of who she was. That would betray too big a vulnerability. But one thing she did have to say. "I don't want to make promises I may not be able to keep."

Lifting his hand, Drew took the one she had on his shoulder and pressed a kiss to her palm. Her heart twisted sharply inside her chest, and it might've made her panic if he hadn't shifted his leg at that moment—the rough caress of denim across her thighs made her hiss out a breath. *"Drew."*

No smile, but he released her hand and placed his own on her ribs just below the curve of her breasts.

"You let me worry about myself," he said into the charged silence. "But you have to be sure, Indigo." She opened her mouth to reply, but he pressed a finger to her lips, silencing her. "I let you walk away with Riaz because I thought he made you happy."

*Oh,* she thought, even as he continued with an unfamiliar ruthlessness in his tone, "I won't have the nobility to walk away a second time if you decide you prefer another man. I'll fight to the fucking bitter end and I won't care about the consequences. I'll take him, bloody him if I have to."

Her wolf flexed its claws inside her mind. "If I decide against you," she said, raising herself up on her elbows and tightening her stomach muscles against the impact of his thigh sliding between her legs, "I'll fight my own battles." She'd come to him because she'd fucked up, but that didn't mean she wasn't who she'd always been. "I don't need another man to do it for me."

"Good." He kissed her.

Hot.

Hard.

Exquisite.

"Just so we understand each other." A nip to her lower lip. Another to the curve of her neck and shoulder as he used his weight to press her down into the softness of the sleeping bag.

More than ready to dance with him, she wove her fingers through his hair. But he pulled away and was crouching on his feet several feet from her before she knew he'd gone. His eyes glinted night-glow in the darkness. "Run."

Adrenaline pumped through her. Shifting into the same position opposite him, she angled her head. "Feeling frisky?"

His eyes, gone that beautiful, strange, wolf copper, followed her every minute stir. *"Run."*

The tiny hairs on the back of her neck rose up, but it was a sign of anticipation, not fear. "You'll never catch me." It was a lazy taunt as she feigned right . . . then jumped over the fire in a leap no one but a changeling would ever make.

She heard him growl behind her, but she was already in the forest and doing everything she could to mess up her scent trail. She went through a shallow portion of the stream twice, doubled back, then retraced her steps before heading downwind. Cheeks pulsing with color, her heart thumping in her chest, she looked around.

Silence.

Too much silence.

He was close and the forest knew it.

Grinning, she messed up the trail some more, then found herself a hiding place on the other side of the stream—behind a bush hung with tiny red winter berries that were so inedible, even the birds passed them by. Looking over the top, she tracked the other side of the river using the wolf's night vision.

*There*.

He flowed out of the dark, a wolf in human form. She saw him scent the area around the stream and disappear back the way he'd come. What was he doing? She knew he wouldn't have fallen for that little trick—she wasn't *really* trying to lose him. They were playing. The fun was in the chase.

And Drew was cunning.

Realizing what he'd done, she spun around just in time to see him streak out of the trees behind her. Her chest filling with laughter, she managed to get on the other side of the bush as he came to crouch opposite her and said, "I found you," in a very wolfish tone.

She widened her eyes, looking beyond him. "Oh, no!"

Protectiveness built into his makeup, he turned to check on the threat . . . and she was gone, hopping across the rocks that forded the stream and up on the other side, her wolf laughing all the while.

**Andrew hadn't had** this much fun in . . . ever. Chasing after Indigo as she took off, he let her get ahead then circled around to wait in ambush behind a small tree. She scented him, stopped, but they'd passed through this area so many times, she had no way of knowing if he was actually there or if it was only his scent that lingered.

He saw her bite her lower lip and knew the instant she

decided to go for it. Snapping her back against his chest as she padded past his hiding spot, he nipped at the place in her neck that fascinated him and spun her free. He wanted to play some more.

She understood.

Throwing him a grin filled with pure delight, she pointed behind him. He turned, giving her a head start. He waited almost five minutes before beginning to look for her. She was hiding, not running this time. He couldn't feel the vibrations of her flight beneath the pads of his feet, and the forest creatures were chattering quietly once more, her willing accomplices in offering a cover of noise.

Prowling over the ground in a swift half run that was so fluid it would've appeared impossible to human eyes, he caught a hint of steel in the air, a hint of spring rainstorms . . . and was ready when she "attacked." Spinning while she was in midjump, he caught her against his chest, let her take him to the pine-needle-strewn earth in a tangle of limbs and hair. When she nipped at his jaw, he growled, but she laughed and repeated the provocation.

Pushing her hair off her face, he tugged her down until they were nose to nose, their wolves staring into each other's eyes. When he snapped his teeth at her, she snapped back. His smile spread until it felt as if it might crease his face forever. Their kiss was as wild as their chase, as playful as their game.

She wrapped her arms around him and didn't protest when he rose with her in his embrace, unwilling to do this on the cold earth, no matter that the pine needles provided a thick mattress. Bold and unashamed, she took his mouth with the passion of a woman who knew what she wanted . . . and the man she wanted it with. It was becoming impossible to have any kind of a rational thought, but he broke the kiss, put her on her feet by the fire. "Wait."

Stretching her arms above her head, she teased him with the promise of her body as he pulled her sleeping bag open, unzipped it, and laid it on top of his. There, he thought, that would be softer on her back. She jumped to crouch on it even as he finished, having used the discarded towel to clean off the bottoms of her feet. Her playful mood still apparent, she said, "You're wearing too many clothes," and reached for the button at the top of his fly.

# CHAPTER 23

**He didn't stop** her, though the sight, the touch of her fingers so close to his aching cock was torture. Button undone, she tugged him forward, pushed. He sprawled backward onto the sleeping bags, spreading his legs to give her room as she came to kneel in between. But she didn't lower his zipper.

No, she bent her head, and—continuing to hold the searing eye contact—pressed her lips to the very top of his groin, a bare centimeter above the pulsing thickness of his erection. Groaning, he clenched his hand in her hair and tugged her up. She came . . . to give him a bone-tingling kiss.

"I'm not the only one who's overdressed," he said against her lips.

"How remiss of me." Her smile was full of pure sensual temptation as she reached down and pulled the T-shirt he'd given her—the T-shirt that had covered her in his scent—off over the top of her head.

His mouth dried up, his brain cells scrambled like so much spaghetti.

Dear God but she was stunning, her breasts lush against the toned and sleekly muscular build of a woman who was a SnowDancer lieutenant. Her skin was lightly tanned, her nipples darker, the plane of her abdomen having the slightest curve that he had every intention of laving with his tongue before moving lower to nuzzle those dark curls that hid the moist, earthy scent of her desire. He'd part her delicate folds and stroke and lick and pet until she screamed his name.

As he watched, entranced, she shifted back to her position between his knees and began to tug at the tab of his zipper. He sucked in a breath, sucked in his abdomen, and hoped he wouldn't fucking embarrass himself. Lights flashed behind his closed eyelids as his erection sprang mercifully free, and he felt more than heard Indigo urge him to lift up his body so she could tug off his jeans.

Opening his eyes, he obeyed, and the jeans went flying somewhere to the side. Indigo put her hands on his thighs, her gaze on his erection. "I want to . . ." she began, but he reached down and pulled her up.

The damp heat of her stroked over his abdomen and he had to grit his teeth to keep from blowing like the Fourth of July. "I get to taste you first." He squeezed her hips. "Then I get to do it again."

She was straddling him, her knees on either side of his chest. When he urged her higher, her eyes went huge. "Like this?"

A chuckle broke its way through the sensual haze. "Don't tell me I've shocked the unshockable lieutenant."

"I should've expected you'd know all sorts of debauched things." But she obeyed him and shifted up . . . until all he had to do was hold her in place with his grip on her thighs, draw in the dark heat of her passion, and lap at what he'd been aching to taste.

**Indigo's spine arched** at the first touch, and she realized the damn wolf had her in a steely grip, would not allow her to wriggle away. The pleasure was excruciating. Her claws sliced out of her skin. She fought to pull them back in, failed.

"No more." She'd been hungry too long, and it only took a few wicked caresses to have her body riding a near-painful edge. *"Drew."*

He let her escape with one final lick. His eyes were pure wolf. "Next time," he said in a voice gone husky and deep and in no way human, "you're going to lie still until I've finished tasting you."

A growl rumbled in the back of her throat. "Am I?"

"Fair's fair."

Her wolf didn't understand his logic, its mind too torn with the hunger for the most intimate, most luscious, of skin privileges. "What?" Sliding down his body, she brushed herself against the velvet steel of his arousal.

Drew's abdomen was taut as rock under her palms, his cock even more rigid. "Because," he said in that gravelly, inhuman voice, "I'll lie here and let you do whatever you want, too."

Her wolf froze, looked at him, licked its lips. Big and gorgeous and dangerously aroused, he made her want to . . . The words wouldn't come, her body too hot, too needy. Ending the teasing play of her body against his, she said, "Now."

His hands tightened on her hips, and then he was flipping her so she lay beneath him, her legs spread wide to accommodate his bigger, heavier body. His skin shimmered with perspiration, and the tension in his muscles had turned them to steel. But though he nudged at her with the blunt head of his erection, the shaft pushing eagerly at the entrance to her body, he stopped long enough to give her a wet, openmouthed kiss that was all licks and little bites, tender and affectionate and sexy all at once.

And then, as her body arched up, he thrust into her in a single hard push.

Her scream fell into his mouth, her fingers clenching on his biceps.

Neither of them moved for the next few seconds. She could feel his heart pounding beneath her palms, and it echoed the frantic pace of her own. Realizing her claws were out just a tiny bit, just enough to blood him in the throes of passion, she went to pull them back.

He bit her lower jaw. "I like it."

Taking him at his word, she scratched lightly at him as she tried to get used to the feel of him inside her. Hard and thick and deliciously long, he stretched her to the limit, but they fit. Oh, they fit very, very nicely. "Guess," she managed to gasp out after several seconds, "the rumors weren't exaggerations."

He didn't answer, his entire body trembling with the effort it was obviously taking for him not to pound her into the earth.

"Drew," she whispered, nipping at his ear, "I'm not fragile."

Wolf-copper eyes met hers, nothing of humanity in them. "No, you're mine." Gripping her hip with one hand, he braced himself over her with the other, and then he rode her.

There was, Indigo thought as her senses exploded, no other word for it. It wasn't any kind of sophisticated mating—it was raw and hard and primal, the power of Drew's thrusts sending shock waves through her entire body. She'd have been shoved off the sleeping bags more than once if his grip hadn't pinned her to the earth, if she hadn't locked her legs around him and given in to the heat and strength and driving sexual hunger of him. She'd never had a lover as abandoned in her life, and she loved it. Adored it.

Adored him.

Clawing at his back, she lifted her hips to meet his strokes, but his rhythm was too fast, too aggressive, and her body was already tightening into an explosive bow. It didn't matter—it was impossible to halt the movements of her hips now, her flesh claiming and releasing his in an abandoned sexual rhythm that drove him impossibly deeper. Somewhere in between, she realized the fingers of his free hand were locked with hers as it lay palm up beside her head.

The tension built inside her. Tighter. Hotter. Agonizing. "Drew!" It was a scream as the pressure reached boiling point and exploded.

Her last thought was that Drew, too, had finally let go.

**She roused some** time later to find that he'd flipped them again, so that she lay sprawled on his chest. Her right hand remained entangled with his, while her left hand was curved around the back of his neck. She'd hooked one leg over his hip; the other lay stretched over one muscular male leg, the hairs on his skin deliciously abrasive against her sensitized flesh.

His own hand stroked up and down her back, a little rough, all perfect. "Wake up, Indy."

"Mmm." Shifting a fraction, she felt his renewed erection against the skin of her inner thigh. "Even changelings can't recover that fast." Her heart was still pumping from the ecstasy of the first ride. She was fairly sure the stars dancing in her vision had nothing to do with the ones in the sky.

He turned her onto her back, one of his arms cushioning her head. "See," he said, "this is what you get for choosing a younger lover." That cocky, teasing light was back in his eyes.

She hadn't realized how much she'd missed it, missed him.

Swinging her leg back over his hip, she pulled him down until he was braced on his elbows above her. "Is this where I have to lie still?"

"Yes." He pushed up her other leg so it was bent at the knee . . . and slid into her in a blunt thrust.

Her spine arched off the sleeping bag. "Drew!"

Freezing, he brushed her hair off her face. "You weren't ready?"

She heard the naked concern, saw the wolf flicker in his eyes. Stroking her arms around his chest, she nipped at his jaw. "Oh, I was ready—but a little warning might be nice."

A slow smile spread across his face, the wolf continuing to glow in his eyes, but amused now in the most sensual of ways. "No, I don't think so." Taking her mouth before she could snap at him for that adorably arrogant statement, he began to move in her.

She'd enjoyed the hell out of their first ride, expected hard, rough strokes again; he *was* a young (younger!) male and finesse wasn't exactly a strong point at that age. Except this was Drew—unpredictable, wild Drew. His strokes were long and slow and deep this time, and her claws were digging into his shoulders by the fourth, her body undulating beneath his.

He closed his teeth over her lower lip in playful reprimand. "You're not lying still." One hand cupped her breast, fingers tugging at the taut peak of her nipple.

Inhaling a gasping breath, she opened her eyes to fire a retort . . . and saw the wolf looking down at her. "Hello," she whispered.

His answer was to kiss her, his tongue pushing inside her mouth in audacious demand, his body strong and beautiful above her as he drove her stroke by slow stroke to another shimmering peak. This time, she held him as he shattered, his body going taut above her.

When he collapsed on top of her, she nuzzled him close, one leg wrapped around him, the other raised at the knee by his side. It felt sinfully luxurious to lie here so very, very sated with a man who made her body sing . . . and who apparently, she thought, licking her tongue over a few of the claw marks on his shoulders, had no trouble with the fact that she got more than a little wild during sex.

To be honest—her grin was wide and bright—it would be pretty much impossible to be too wild with a lover as unrestrained and as enthusiastic as Drew. Rubbing her cheek against the side of his head, she ran her fingers through his hair, massaging his nape.

Stirring a little, he relaxed even more heavily on top of her.

And with that much muscle, he *was* heavy. But she wasn't made of glass—and there was something to be said for being covered by the hot blanket of a sated male wolf. Smile curving her mouth, she tugged the top of the sleeping bag over him so he wouldn't freeze, and then she continued to pet him, this wolf who'd made every one of her preconceptions come crashing down around her ankles.

Now . . . now they'd see what the future held.

**They changed positions** when he muttered he was "squashing her" and moved to tuck her by his side, one hand spread across her abdomen. Curling her body into his, she went to sleep, well pleasured, warm, and certain the area was safe. Her wolf wasn't ready to give up full protection of her body, her self, to him—might never be ready to give that up to any man—but it was content enough with his skill and strength to close its eyes and let sleep sweep them both under.

She woke to find her nose snuggled into the crook of a male shoulder. There was no disorientation, no moment of wondering who he was—his scent was too familiar, too welcome. Allowing herself an uncharacteristic moment of laziness, she stroked her hand down his chest. He was asleep, his arms locked around her—no doubt about it, it was a possessive hold. She wasn't quite sure how she felt about that, but being with a dominant predatory changeling male required some adjustments.

*Adjustments.*

She thought of her aunt, Adria, thought, too, of the adjustments Adria made daily, and felt her muscles begin to lock. No, she whispered inside her mind, no. Hawke was right—she wasn't Adria. She'd kick Drew's ass out the door the instant he pulled shit like Martin pulled with Adria.

Not that she could imagine that kind of passive-aggressive behavior from Drew. For all his sneakiness, he wasn't subtle enough for that type of hostility, she thought with open affection. No, he was more likely to yell at her, and if that didn't work—now that they were intimate—strip her naked and try to win by drowning her in pleasure. Those kinds of dominance games, she understood and welcomed.

Cheered up by the realization, she pressed a kiss to the part of him closest to her mouth. He stirred but didn't rouse. Dropping another kiss on his skin, she pushed gently at him. He made a rumbling sound in his chest, the vibrations causing her nipples to tingle, pressed as they were against his muscular form, but he didn't let go. She bit him on the jaw. "I need to get up." When he still didn't move, she pushed harder.

Grumbling, he loosened his hold enough that she was able to wiggle free. He immediately sprawled over the space she'd vacated, his face on its side, hair all rumpled. She couldn't help it. She reached over and nuzzled a kiss into the warm curve of his neck. Another grumble. "Not a morning person," she said, nipping provokingly at his ear—that got her a sleepy snarl. "I never knew that." It was a half-wondering statement. She'd thought she'd known everything about him, but she hadn't known this.

Startled, she kissed him one more time before trying to

find a T-shirt. She finally located the one she'd been wearing the night before hanging over the limb of a tree branch. How it had gotten that far up, she had no idea. Standing on tiptoe, she'd just snagged it when she heard an appreciative wolf whistle.

# CHAPTER 24

**Smiling, she pulled** on the T-shirt and glanced over her shoulder. A drowsy-eyed male—a definite wolf—watched her with obvious sensual intent. "Indy." It was an invitation.

It was very, very tempting to go to him. So tempting that it made her wolf back off in sudden wariness. "Give me a second." Heading into the forest, she walked down to the stream to throw some water on her face, her fingers trembling as she thrust them through her hair. This, with Drew, it fit none of the parameters of what she knew. For a woman as used to exercising control over all aspects of her life as she was, it—

"I knew you'd be here doing this." A hand closing over the back of her neck, a kiss dropped on her parted lips before Drew bent down to throw some water onto his own face.

Dressed only in a pair of khaki cargo pants, he looked oh-so-touchable.

"Doing what?" Rising to her feet, she curled her fingers into her palms. This inexorable sensual pull she felt toward Drew, it unsettled her—more than unsettled her, if she was honest. She was used to holding the reins in her dealings with the opposite sex.

Shaking his head in a way that was distinctly wolfish, he curved one hand around her calf, looking up with those wonderful, changeable eyes. "Worrying about all the things that could go wrong. Enjoy the moment, Indy. Enjoy what we are—"

"If you think I can do that," she said with a wry smile, some of her tension dissipating, "you don't know me."

He squeezed her leg. "Yeah, that's why I decided to haul myself awake at this ungodly hour and come rescue you."

"It's at least a couple of hours past dawn." The forest was awash in the chatter of birds, the sky a pale azure with shimmering undertones of gold and pink that presaged a brilliant day.

Drew made a face, eyes on the play of sunlight dappling the water. "A couple of hours past dawn? Are you insane? Noon is when rational people wake up."

Laughing, she leaned lightly against him as he moved his hand over her leg in a lazy caress. "How do you function when you're on night watch or the early shift?"

"I function fine. I just prefer to lie in bed if at all possible."

"You sure you're a wolf?" she teased. "You sound like a big ole lazy cat to me."

He grumbled low in his throat. "I'd throw you in the pool for that, but I'm feeling too mellow after the way you worked me over last night."

"You're not the one with bruises on your back."

An unrepentant smile. "You don't have any—I checked already." Rising when she made as if to push him into the water, he slid his hands under her tee to cup her naked bottom. "Hey, Indy?"

Surprised by his oddly solemn tone, she looked up. "What is it?"

"How come you're avoiding touching me?"

She glanced down at her hands to see that she'd clenched them into fists again. Groaning, she pressed her forehead against his chest. "I'm sorry." He didn't deserve this.

A kiss on her temple, strong hands petting the globes they'd palmed. "Have you had enough after only one night?"

She almost fell for that mournful voice—but the fiend's eyes were dancing when she looked up. "Very funny."

He squeezed the flesh he'd been stroking. "Freak-out, huh? I told you, I kinda expected it."

Wrapping her arms around him, she nodded. "I'm not used to being this . . ." *Close to addiction.*

He dipped his head, met her gaze. "Does it help if I tell you I'm already a junkie? And that I intend to indulge as much as possible—and then do it some more? I can tie you to the bed if you like, so you can't touch."

Her wolf swiped a paw at him at the outrageous teasing. "I think it's you who needs to be tied up," she muttered darkly, but his complete ease with the hunger between them did go a long way toward making her more comfortable with the depth of her own need. "Come here."

"For what?" he asked, suspicion in every syllable.

Her wolf laughed. "For a good-morning kiss—I've decided to let you live."

His eyes gleamed. "Excellent idea." He'd slid down to his knees and pulled her sex to the voracious demand of his mouth before she could do more than gasp in a breath. Clenching her hand in his hair, she went to pull him back up . . . but then he did something with his tongue that made her toes curl, and she found herself spreading her legs to give him better access.

A pleased rumble against her, followed by pleasure upon pleasure.


**Later, after he'd** teased her to the point that she'd been driven to threats of murder, they took a dip and ate.

"Since we're both up at this ridiculous hour anyway," Drew grumbled afterward, "do you want to hike up to Wolf Point?"

Wolf Point, so named by the first wolves who'd settled in this region, offered a breathtaking view across the lakes that dotted the area. On a day like this, the sky up there would be an excruciating blue, the sun's rays bright and harsh. Her skin tingled in sensory pleasure. "Yes, let's."

"Take our packs so we can camp up there?"

At her nod, he began to roll up the sleeping bags while she

turned off and packed the laz-fire. "We should go back to the den tomorrow," she said as they finished.

"Yeah." Drew's gaze was serious. "We left Hawke short-handed. You think we should head back now?"

Mentally reviewing who was in the den and able to fill in, she shook her head. "I have my cell—he'd have called if he needed us." She wanted more time to explore this unexpected bond between her and Drew. Because there'd be no hiding it when they returned to the den, not with the intimacies they'd shared—and would continue to share. Wolf noses would sniff it out in about one second flat.

"Do you want to hide it?" Drew asked without warning.

Hearing the absolute neutrality of his voice, her spine went stiff. "What?"

"This. Us."

It startled her that he'd guessed the direction of her thoughts, but her answer was immediate. "No." She was unsure and confused, but she was no coward—not now that she'd made the decision to dance with him. More, she was proud of the male she'd chosen. Whatever happened, he was hers, and other women would do well to keep their paws off him. "I'll give you one phone call to warn your harem you're now off-limits."

A surprised expression . . . that segued into pleased arrogance. "No one'll dare come near me now that you've made a claim." A pause. "You're worried about the nosey parkers?"

"Maybe they'll have worked it out of their system with Riley and Mercy," she said in a burst of hope. "We're two wolves—no big deal."

Drew snorted, leaning over to pat her ass with casual proprietariness. "You're so cute when you're deluding yourself." Easily dodging her responding punch on the arm, he grabbed her pack and handed it to her. "They'll have a field day—the lieutenant who can drop a man in his tracks with nothing but the ice in her gaze, and . . . *Drew*?" He made a confused, disbelieving face.

Snorting, Indigo put her arms through the straps of her pack. "I've known you forever, and I still don't understand that thing you do."

A questioning look as he went to pick up his own pack.

"Making people think you're harmless." She clicked the support straps across her hips. "You didn't answer my question, Mr. Harmless."

"It's a gift." Pack on, he walked over to click the second support strap above the UC Berkeley emblem on her sweatshirt as she did the same for him.

"Thanks, Indy." A casual comment, but right then, the blue of his eyes hit her in the heart.

He could hurt her. Really hurt her. And they'd barely taken the first step into this unexpected relationship. "You're welcome," she said, fighting the wolf's wariness with the memory of how he'd teased her earlier by the stream.

*Taking care of her.*

Her wolf froze at the realization, and she had to consciously kick herself into gear as Drew turned to lead the way out of camp. She'd never have allowed him to care for her if he'd tried to do it straight out, but she'd been fooled by his playfulness into missing the protective drive beneath.

You'd think she'd know better by now, she thought with an inward shake of her head, but he continued to surprise her with that quicksilver mind. If she was being honest, his keen intelligence was one of the most attractive things about him— even if it did mean he had a way of catching her off guard. The thought made her frown, consider something else. "Drew?"

When he looked over, she said, "Is it because you're the pack's tracker? That you make such an effort to appear harmless?" It was a question she'd never thought to ask before— because he was so very good at making people forget what · he was.

Drew's hand tangled with her own, his expression solemn. "I didn't really think about it consciously when I was growing up," he said, "but as an adult, yeah, that's part of it. I'm wolf— I need to be a full part of the pack."

And, she understood, he couldn't be that if everyone was afraid of him.

Nodding, she let it go at that—this relationship was too new to push him to share such an intensely private aspect of himself. But Drew squeezed her hand. "It's okay, Indy. I don't mind talking about it. Hawke and Riley make me do it on a regular basis."

"They do?" She blinked.

"Uh-huh." A grin. "I think they want to make sure I'm not going to crack under the pressure."

It was then, looking into those amused eyes, that she realized the incredible depth of strength inside him. "It must be beyond hard to know that you could be called upon to track and execute a packmate at any time."

He didn't deny it. "The thing is, I was born with this uncanny ability to track my packmates, better than even Hawke's—so it was obvious what role I was meant to play in the pack. I had to either learn to deal with it or, once I was old enough to understand, give over the mantle so someone else could be trained."

Though she hadn't understood until today why he cultivated that air of irresponsibility, she'd known him far too long not to have seen beneath the surface years ago—and to the wolf who was one of the most trusted in the pack. "You never even thought about giving it up, did you?"

"When wolves go rogue"—quiet words, powerful words— "they do things they'd never have countenanced had they been thinking. They attempt to hunt, to slaughter their packmates, children included. If that happened to me, I'd want someone like me on my trail, someone who could find me before I did harm, and offer mercy."

Emotion a knot in her throat, Indigo stopped and reached up to cup his cheek. He rubbed against it. "Don't look that way, Indy." Fingers on her temple, tugging at a flyaway strand of her hair. "SnowDancer is a strong, coherent pack. You know that while I've tracked a lot of people, I've only had to execute one wolf once I found him—and I don't think he would've judged me for it."

"He was old," Indigo said, remembering the sorrow in the den at the elder's passing. "He had a disease of the mind that somehow evaded the health checks." But he'd lived a long and happy life before that, been a great-grandfather three times over. "No, he wouldn't have wanted to harm those he'd spent his life protecting."

Drew tugged at her hand, his touch warm and solid. "Come on."

As they walked hand in hand, she considered the titanic shift that had just occurred inside her when it came to this man. Always before, she'd simply not understood a large part of what made him who he was—but now she knew . . . now her wolf knew.

A glimpse of color, woman and wolf both stilling in wonder.

"Look up," she said to Drew, "very, very slowly."

When he obeyed, she said, "To your left a little. Do you see it?"

A long, slow exhale was her answer. "Beautiful."

The blue-gray bird sat proud and imperious on a snow-dusted branch, its claws providing a firm grip. "Northern goshawk?"

Drew hummed in agreement. "Has the eyebrow stripe, tail looks to be the right size—would love to see that beauty fly through the trees."

As they watched, the bird angled its head to tell her and Drew it saw them, but that they were beneath its notice. Laughing softly, she was startled when Drew brought their clasped hands to his mouth, dropped a kiss on her knuckles.

It was an affectionate act, a possessive one, too. Her wolf considered it alongside all else she'd gleaned about his nature. "Don't think I'm not noticing all your 'mine' gestures," she said to see what he'd do.

His lips were on hers an instant later, his free hand cupping her cheek as he made a thorough exploration of her mouth. "That was one, too."

Her lips twitched. Jerking up a hand before he could avoid it, she slashed a very careful line on his cheekbone. His wolf flared in his eyes in a blaze of wild copper before the human smiled, touched the small hurt. "It'll heal before we return to the den." A complaint.

"No, it won't." She almost couldn't believe she'd done that, marked him so openly—there'd be no end of ribbing from her packmates now. "And if it does, I'm sure all the claw marks on your back will do the job." Predatory changeling men were terrible exhibitionists when it came to flaunting their claim over a woman.

Satisfied by that, Drew moved back and they continued on their trek. "Look," he murmured almost half an hour later, pointing out a delicate white blossom where it peeked out from between two rocks.

She was about to draw his attention to a fossilized shell in one of the slabs of rock when he froze to predator stillness. Indigo went quiet with him, tilting up her chin in a silent question mark.

Eyes gone wolf-copper crashed into hers as he mouthed, "Psy."

# CHAPTER 25

**Indigo let her** own wolf rise to the surface, her senses expanding. A moment later, she caught it, the faintest whisper of scent, borne to them on cool mountain air currents. Touching Drew's hip, she caught his attention and tugged on the straps of her pack.

He nodded, and they helped each other remove their packs in silence. Stowing them in the hiding spot created by the gnarled roots of an ancient tree, they stripped; their wolves would be quieter, the pads of their feet made for the snow and leaf-strewn terrain of the rocky ground.

Her eye caught by the flexing muscle of Drew's back as he pulled off his clothing, she gave herself a fleeting second to drink in the sight. He was her lover, she thought, her claws beginning to slide out of her skin as she gave in to the shift—she had the right to watch him. And if there was a little possessiveness mixed in with her visual stroking . . . well, he'd chosen her. Now he'd have to deal.

It was her last thought before the shift took over.

Bone-deep pleasure spliced with electric pain as her body turned into a thousand sparks of light before re-forming into a new shape that was lower to the ground, the wolf's sense of smell so clear, so crisp, she could almost see the signs of the Psy trespassers as glittering metallic strands in the air.

Coming to her feet, she found that Drew, too, had completed his shift. He was bigger than her, but no less graceful, his ears pricked to catch the slightest sound. Nudging at her with his shoulder, he began to pad toward their prey. They went at a light trot until they were almost on top of the scent, and then, without speaking, they split to circle around the target.

Indigo crept up to the spot on her belly, not wanting to alert the Psy male at the center of the small clearing. She glimpsed Drew's silver fur appear between the dark trunks on the other side, but knew their target had no idea he'd been flanked. He was intent on whatever it was he was doing to the earth at his feet.

As she watched, he dusted off his hands and rose—as if he was waiting.

Given that SnowDancer security would've detected any unauthorized airborne or ground vehicle, that could only mean he'd telepathed for a telekinetic pickup. They had maybe a second or two to take this man down before the Tk arrived . . . but Indigo decided against it.

A little worm of worry wriggled into her mind as she wondered if Drew would follow her lead or go in himself. In any other operation, that wouldn't have been a question—as the most senior member of the pack in the area, she had automatic authority. But men—even the most intelligent—sometimes had a way of seeing things differently after they slept with a woman.

Even as the thought passed through her head, the Tk appeared in the circle. Thirty seconds after that, both Psy were gone, that grating metallic scent the only sign of their recent presence.

*Thirty seconds.* She made a mental note to check with Judd, but to her, that indicated the Tk had been one of the less powerful ones. Judd himself only needed to concentrate for a couple of seconds before teleporting, while he'd told her that the most powerful took literally no time at all.

Waiting a full ten minutes to ensure the Psy didn't intend to return, Indigo glided out of her hiding spot as Drew appeared out of his. He stayed in wolf form as she shifted; he'd be more lethal that way should the Psy reappear without warning. Releasing her claws, Indigo began to scrape away the dirt on top of whatever it was the Psy operative had buried. Her hand touched metal about thirty centimeters down.

Her senses didn't alert her to any explosives, but she waved Drew forward. "Do you scent anything dangerous?" He came, his paws silent on the leaf-strewn ground. Waiting until he shook his head, she reached in and kept digging until the earth was loose enough to allow her to see most of it. "It looks identical to that metal ball Silvia found." Except this one was clearly still in one piece. Gleaming steel once she brushed off the dirt, it appeared inert except for a red light blinking at the top.

Scent or no scent, instinct told her this augured danger, but she was no tech. "I don't think we should move it until we know what it is."

Drew, having come to stand by her shoulder, growled in agreement. Then, padding around to take a position opposite her, he shifted. It amazed her to watch him dissolve in a shimmer of multicolored sparks before re-forming into the muscled human male she knew so well. "We need a tech to do a full evaluation."

Indigo pushed the dirt back into the hole. "Just in case they come back to check."

"Good idea." Drew patted it down as the Psy operative had done, hiding all evidence of interference.

"I'll go get my cell." But when she did, she found she had no signal either at the spot where they'd stashed the packs or at the clearing itself. "Damn, the storm must've damaged the cell transmitter up here. I'll have to run to lower ground." The phone had worked fine at the campsite.

"I don't think there's any huge urgency," Drew said. "They'd have had no need to hide the object if it was meant to do something soon."

Indigo agreed. "Then one of us might as well head all the way back to the den. It'll be easier to lead the techs up here than try to direct them to the spot."

"You're faster," he said. "You do the run. I'll shift and stay in the trees."

Stashing the phone in the hollow of a fallen tree, Indigo shifted. Drew waited until she was in wolf form before stroking his hand down her back in a long, slow caress. "Be careful." A pause. "You belong to me now."

He was pushing. That's what predatory changeling men did—and it was something she could handle. Biting lightly at his arm in mock reproof, she streaked out from under his touch, his fingers trailing warm and heavy through her fur.

It was only when she was almost halfway down that she realized Drew hadn't even hesitated before stating that she was the faster runner. In spite of the fact that he'd followed her lead earlier, part of her had still been expecting some stupid male act, but again, he'd surprised h—

She yipped, having almost missed a jump.

Taking that as a sign, she pushed all human thought out of her mind and let her wolf take over. The den appeared out of the forest just as she was starting to tire from the intensity of the run, a welcome sight. Inside, she followed Hawke's scent to his quarters in the area set aside for unmated soldiers. As alpha, he could've commanded a far bigger space, but he had a room almost identical to Drew's. The sole difference was that he had another, slightly bigger, connected room— with an attached galley—where he could hold private, relaxed meetings with the senior members of the pack.

Scraping her paw on his door, she waited for him to open it. He did so almost at once. "Indigo," he said, his tone sharp. "I'll get you a T-shirt."

She nodded, grateful. Nudity with her alpha was no big deal, but she'd just come from Drew's arms—something Hawke had obviously scented—and it would feel odd to be naked in front of another man when things between her and Drew were so new, so fragile. Moving behind one of the armchairs in the front room, she shifted.

Hawke threw a large plain black tee to her on the heels

of the shift and she pulled it over her head as she rose to her feet. "We've got a situation," she said and laid out the facts. "Brenna's worked with Psy technology. She might be able to figure this thing out."

Hawke gave an immediate nod. "Dorian's here. He brought up something his mate wanted Bren to look at."

A year ago, Indigo would've been stunned at the idea of bringing a leopard into pack business, but now the leopards were, in a sense, Pack. Her wolf continued to find that odd, but even it accepted that the cats had proven their mettle, earned SnowDancer's trust. "Great," she said, knowing that though the DarkRiver sentinel was an architect by trade, he had both a keen interest in and experience with complex computronic systems. "The two of them together should be able to figure out what it is—and they can rope in Ashaya"—Dorian's mate—"if necessary."

Hawke was already making the calls. While he did so, she went into the well-stocked galley and made herself a huge sandwich to offset the calories used up during her high-speed run. She was chewing the final bite when Hawke walked in. "Dorian and Brenna will meet you out front in five. They'll have to come up in human form—with equipment to test the object."

"I figured." She gulped down a glass of milk fortified with a protein mix, then made a second—larger—sandwich, which she sealed in a lunch bag. "I'll grab one of the all-wheel drives." They'd still have to do the last part of the trek on foot, but they could always return to the vehicle for the heavier equipment if necessary.

Hawke's face was grim when she looked up. "I'm not letting the Psy poison our pack again, not with those e-mails about 'Purity' and not with this shit."

"We're stronger than we were before." They rarely spoke of the dark years when Hawke had been only a child, but those years had shaped so much of what SnowDancer was today. "And we're no longer alone."

Hawke didn't say anything.

Her energy levels back to full strength after the snack, she walked over to pat him affectionately on the cheek. "You and

Riley, no wonder you're best buds. You both hold things too tight, too close."

He didn't shake off her touch, their friendship old enough, deep enough, that such skin privileges were an accepted part of their relationship. "Look who's talking," he pointed out, tapping her on the nose.

Shrugging, she dropped her hand but didn't move away. "Takes one to know one."

"You going to tell me what's happening between you and Drew?"

"No." It was too new, too private, to expose to the light of day.

Hawke raised an eyebrow. "Word of advice—Drew and Riley are more similar than people realize."

Indigo thought of the way Drew pushed at her, the way he tried to steamroll in his own charming fashion. "You could've warned me earlier." It was a disgruntled statement.

"And miss all the fun?" A tug at a curling strand of her hair. "Now why would I do that?"

Scowling, she comforted herself with the thought that his time would come. Boy, would it come. "I better go put on some proper clothes for the drive." Borrowing a pair of his sweats—way too large for her frame—for the short walk to her quarters, she quickly shimmied into jeans and a long-sleeved sweatshirt for the drive back.

Even with that detour, she was the first person at the vehicle, Dorian and Brenna having stopped to assess and grab the necessary gear from SnowDancer's tech lab. After placing the cases in the back, Dorian took the front passenger seat while Brenna ducked into the back where she could fiddle with one of the scanners.

"Older model," she muttered. "It switched on okay, but I want to check that it's fully functional. Haven't had cause to use it for a while."

The drive passed by in a flow of technical dialogue between Dorian and Brenna, and they were soon stepping out for the final part of the journey—with only the essential gear. "Bren," Indigo said, picking up the sandwich she'd made from the dash, "can you stow this in your bag?"

"Sure."

Leading them to where she and Drew had left their packs, she stopped just long enough to pick out a sky blue T-shirt and jeans. Going commando, she thought with a hint of amusement, wouldn't be a problem for Drew. He was the least self-conscious male she knew, and that was saying something in a pack of wolves. "Alright. Let's go."

When they arrived, Drew padded out of the trees to greet them—it was clear from his relaxed state that the Psy hadn't returned.

Her wolf wanted to nuzzle at him, but she kept her tone professional. "Clothes," she said, placing them behind a tree.

As she returned to join the others, Drew brushed past her close enough that her fingertips stroked over his fur. Fighting the urge to follow him, to stroke him a little more, she came down on her haunches beside Bren and Dorian. "Any idea what it might be?"

Brenna tapped something on the little computer connected wirelessly to a device Dorian was running over the ground. "Nothing unusual about the metallic compound," she muttered. "Device is computronic without a doubt, and functional."

"It has to have a power source," Dorian said, putting down the scanner. "Battery of some kind."

Brenna brushed her bangs out of her eyes. "Time to dig, I think."

Indigo helped, and it took only a minute to unearth the metal ball. Instead of lifting it out, Brenna and Dorian put their heads together and muttered more technospeak. Having felt Drew come to stand at her shoulder, Indigo retrieved the sandwich from Brenna's bag and got to her feet. "Eat," she said, knowing he wouldn't have left the device unattended in order to hunt.

He ran his knuckles over her cheek. "Thanks."

As he took a big bite, she realized she'd forgotten to pick up his drink bottle. "Is there water nearby?"

"Yep, but it'll be faster to run down to the packs." He'd already demolished half the sandwich. "Be back soon."

Aware Brenna and Dorian had matters in hand, she walked

to the edges of the clearing after Drew left and began to do a detailed quadrant-by-quadrant search, just in case the Psy had left something else behind. Nothing in the immediate area. And more nothing in a radius of several meters from the site of the device. She was about to turn back when she caught Drew's scent on the breeze.

He found her a few seconds later. "Hey, Lieutenant." His mouth was on hers before she could do more than part her lips to respond.

She should've been used to the way he had of doing that, but she staggered back a little, gripping at his waist to keep herself upright. Not that it was necessary; his arms were already locked tight around her, his mouth exploring hers with a lazy sensuality that made her want to purr like a damn cat.

"This," she said on a breath, "is hardly the time."

Another kiss, one big hand moving down to shape her buttocks. "I'm behaving," he told her, all innocence. "I didn't do it in front of Dorian and Bren, did I?"

Her wolf laughing, she wiggled her arms out from around him and reached up to cup his face. Then she kissed the hell out of Andrew Liam Kincaid.

# CHAPTER 26

**Andrew was sure** he'd had a rational thought a minute or so ago, but it was a distant memory. The lieutenant was making his brains leak out his ears, her tongue a fast, sleek dart in his mouth, her teeth sharp little accents on his lips, her hands brands against his skin. Groaning, he gripped her hips and gave in.

His reward was a kiss so hot, it turned his jeans uncomfortably tight. Unable to keep his hands still, he stroked up over her sweatshirt to close his hand around one lush breast. Her nipple was already pebbled behind the soft fabric of her bra, and he played with it through the clothing, wanting to learn each and every facet of what drove her crazy.

The sound took time to filter into his consciousness, the voice recognizable. Dorian, calling Indigo's name. "Time to go back," he murmured against those lush lips that had turned him into a willing slave.

"If you're a very good boy," Indigo murmured in a sexy,

husky tone as she reached down to cup his straining cock for one electric second, "I might kiss you other places, too."

He bit back a very blue word as she withdrew her hand and stepped back. "How the hell am I supposed to go back and face my little sister if I have a raging hard-on?"

"Poor baby." Except her eyes were dancing with unfamiliar wickedness. "I'm sure you'll think of something." She walked away, her hips swiveling in a fashion that he knew was meant to shoot his already boiling temperature through the roof. Sexual frustration was a bitch, but his wolf smiled—because the lieutenant was playing with him again. And Indigo Riviere was a woman who played with very few.

Blowing out a breath, he gritted his teeth and counted to a thousand, somehow managing to get his body under control. "So, what did I miss?" he asked, rejoining the others where they crouched around the object.

"It's a transmitter," Dorian said, holding the steel orb in hand.

He met the leopard sentinel's surfer blue eyes. "You sound very sure."

But it was his sister who replied. "The tech is pretty common once you strip away the fancy exterior."

"Range isn't huge," Dorian added. "Maybe five hundred meters or so."

Brenna's eyes met Andrew's, a smile tugging at the corners of her mouth that augured trouble—but her words were practical. "We think it's meant to act as a locator beacon."

"Locator for what?" Indigo murmured. "This area is wilderness. Aside from the forest creatures, only wolves come—"

A pointed cough from Dorian.

"Wolves *and* leopards," Indigo said, shaking her head at the blond sentinel's smirk, "are the only ones who come up here." Lines formed between her brows. "The only ones who should. I wonder if the Psy we scented when we were with the juveniles were scouting for places to put these things."

"Would make sense," Brenna said. "You were a bit more east of here, but not that much lower down in terms of the elevation."

Dorian's hair flashed almost white in the harsh sunlight as he lowered his head to the device once more. "We can sweep the ground with high-strength scanners, but we have a logistical problem—den territory covers too wide an area." A glance at Brenna.

Andrew's sister nodded in confirmation. "We need to figure out some sort of specific region to search."

"How long would the batteries last in those things?" Indigo asked. "Best guess?"

"I'll confirm when we dismantle one, but three months would be the outer limits," Brenna said, looking at Dorian.

He nodded and added, "The transmitting function sucks juice. Three for safety, but I'd say two months would be a more realistic estimate."

Andrew saw where Indigo was going. "So we can probably eliminate all the areas where the snowpack has been pretty much solid for over two months." That would take care of a good chunk of their territory.

"Yes." Brenna's eyes sparked. "A telekinetic could have moved the snow, but one, it's a massive waste of power, and two, against all that white, any intruders would have stood out like sore thumbs to our satellite."

Indigo nodded. "I agree—we can safely eliminate the snowpack areas for now. We can also eliminate all those areas that get a high amount of traffic."

Andrew looked at his sister. "You got a piece of paper, Bren?"

"I think there's a pad in this bag . . ." Turning to rummage in it, she made a sound of success. "Here it is. And a pen."

"Thanks, baby sis." Grinning at the kiss she blew him, he flipped open the pad and sketched the basic outline of their territory. "Okay, so this is here." He made an X on the map. "The other one's useless as a marker since it could've come from anywhere, but how about this?" He drew a rough semicircle, using their current spot as the center of the arc.

Indigo looked over his shoulder. "The entire area's equidistant from the very edge of den territory." She took a moment to think about it, nodded. "We've got enough light that we can test the theory at least."

"We have two scanners," Brenna reminded them, "so we can go in both directions."

"Drew," Indigo said, her tone crisp as she slipped into full work mode, "you go with Bren. I'll work with Dorian."

He knew what she was doing—pairing each tech expert with someone who could keep an eye on security, but he found he didn't want her alone with the good-looking leopard male. Her eyes met his at that moment, and from the sudden frost in them, he knew she'd accurately read the hotly possessive urge. Gritting it back with sheer strength of will—and having to fight his wolf to do so—he turned to Brenna. "You need all the gear?"

"Just the scanner pack." She slid the little computer into a carry bag and swung it crosswise over her body, the scanner itself held in her hand. "Dorian, are you okay using the—"

"No problem, sweetheart." Setting the computer over his body the same way as Brenna, Dorian picked up the somewhat bulkier scanner. "It'll do the trick, but the range is shorter," he said to Indigo, "so we might cover less distance."

Brenna began to move out. Andrew followed, forcing himself to keep his attention on his sister and not on a woman who was quietly furious with him. Brenna didn't say anything until they were well out of earshot. "Judd told me."

Andrew grunted, not in the mood to be teased.

"She's a lieutenant, dumb-ass," Brenna muttered. "Going all he-man on her isn't exactly going to put you in her good book."

He blinked. "You have eyes in the back of your head now?"

A beatific smile. "I have experience with hardheaded men—though I never thought I'd be giving you this little talk. I always thought Riley was the one who'd have trouble. And he went and got himself happily mated to a sentinel."

Checking the area for threats and making the assessment that they were the only two out there, he allowed his attention to return to the subject of him and Indigo. "I couldn't help it," he muttered, feeling sulky and grumpy—though he'd have shown that to no one but the sister he'd watched over since she'd been but a babe. "My brain knew I was doing something stupid, but my hormones tell me to protect her—and right now, instinct is kicking reason's whiny ass."

Brenna shook her head, the late afternoon sun making the

fine strands of her hair shimmer like spun gold. "The easy fix is that you grovel and she forgives you . . ."

"But?" He nudged her shoulder with his, his wolf willing to listen to her even if she was younger and far less dominant.

"But this is who she is," Brenna murmured, her eyes troubled when she looked up. "You stood in front of a bullet for me, Drew." Her voice hitched. "That's who you are."

"Hey." He hugged her to him, kissing the top of her head. "I'm not going anywhere."

Holding on to him for a couple more seconds, Brenna stepped back and started scanning again. "What I'm saying is that you protect—do you think you can handle, *really* handle, being with a woman who not only doesn't need your protection, but for whom it would be an insult that you'd even offer?"

The words hit hard, cut deep. But the truth had nothing to do with his acceptance of Indigo's rank.

"I'm jealous," he admitted bluntly, to the one person with whom he could admit the vulnerability. "I know I don't fit the image she has in her mind of her perfect partner, and it rubs me the wrong way whenever she interacts with another male who does fit that image." A male who was probably far more acceptable to her wolf, for all that that wolf had accepted him on a certain level.

"Even though Dorian's mated and a leopard to boot?"

"Yeah. Stupid, huh?"

"We're all a little stupid when we're in love." Her machine beeped on the heels of her statement. "Hold up."

He waited patiently while she did a deeper scan.

"Nothing," she said after a minute. "It was set off by some metallic content in the rocks, I think."


**Dorian, Indigo thought,** moved like the cat he was. All fluid and graceful. She'd have pegged him for a leopard even if she hadn't known his changeling affiliation. Hamilton, the leopard she'd dated a couple of times a few months back, had moved with that same feline grace.

Sexy . . . except that it wasn't for Indigo.

Of course, in human form, Dorian was also ridiculously

attractive with his white-blond hair and eyes of electric blue. In the sharp mountain sunlight, his hair burned with pure white fire, drawing the eye. Hamilton, too, had made every female head turn when they'd gone out together in public.

Indigo had appreciated the visual impact—the same way she appreciated Hawke and Riaz. Her lungs had functioned just fine, her heart continuing to beat in a steady rhythm even when Hamilton kissed her. She'd allowed the caress, allowed him to slide his hand to her nape and hold her in place as he explored her mouth—because she'd wanted to know if there was any chance of chemistry. Nothing. Nada. Zilch.

In comparison, Drew only had to—

"Earth to Lieutenant Legs."

Indigo snapped her attention to Dorian. "You pick up something, Blondie?"

"Not sure." A feline smile that made her instincts prickle in warning even before he said, "Is that a love bite I see on your neck?"

She wasn't gullible enough to fall for that. "I know that's a great big bunch of baloney I see on your face."

The leopard male laughed, utterly unashamed of his blatant fishing as he returned his attention to the scanner. "I was trying for subtle."

"Uh-huh." Needing to burn off this restless energy, she looked at him. "Can you keep an eye around you while you scan?" He was one of the strongest cats in DarkRiver, and he trained in hand-to-hand combat with a former assassin—she was pretty sure there were very few things Dorian couldn't handle.

He gave her a curious look. "Sure. You going somewhere?"

"I want to do a bit of a scout around—might see evidence of places being dug up."

Dorian didn't tell her that was a crapshoot, simply nodded. "Hey, Indigo."

"What?"

"You can run," Dorian said in a neutral tone that did nothing to lessen the intensity of his expression, "but sooner or later, you run out of places to run to."

Already loping up the slight incline to her right, she didn't answer. But his words circled around and around in her head as she sliced through the cold mountain air. Was that what she was doing? Running? It made her wolf shake its head in violent rejection; she'd always stood her ground, taken the hits as they came. Dorian was talking out of his ass. He was a cat, so really, why was she surprised?

That kept her going for a few more minutes, until her practical nature pointed out that it wasn't the cat she was mad at. It was Drew. She'd seen that look, seen the way his hackles had risen when she'd given him the assignment. Though, to his credit, he'd kept his mouth shut. "Not too much credit, though," she muttered under her breath. Because the fact was, he was a dominant predatory changeling male. The words "possessive," "protective," and "annoying" were indelibly etched into his profile.

Just as independence, control, and stubbornness were etched into hers.

*There.*

She was almost fifty meters away in the time it took her to realize what she'd seen. Stopping, she circled back to the clearing that bore several patches of spring green grass that were starting to brown—where the blades had been crushed . . . as if by the tread of heavy boots. She could see nothing that indicated a device might've been buried there, but she didn't like the look of the place. Trusting her instincts, she marked the location in her mind, then ran back to get Dorian.

It took him less than ten seconds to find the transmitter. "Been here awhile," he said as they began to dig using their claws. "Grass has grown up over it."

"But these patches of crushed grass say the Psy returned recently, maybe to check up on it." Narrow eyed, she felt her claw tap the edge of the device. "There."

"Rusted a little, but otherwise in good condition," Dorian said after they unearthed it, "and identical to the other one we found." His gaze met hers. "What the hell are they planning?"


**They met back** at the starting point an hour later. Drew and Brenna had come up empty, but with the second device Indigo had found, they now had a better idea of how to structure the search radius.

"These objects can't go anywhere near the den," Indigo said. They'd spent too much time and effort hiding the exact location of the pack's true home to give it away so easily. "Can you deactivate them?"

Brenna conferred with Dorian, then nodded. "No problem. Like I said, they're fairly basic at the tech level. To be safe, I won't even take the components down, but do all the work up here—the one Silvia found was a husk, so we're safe on that front."

Drew rubbed at his jaw, his eyes narrowed. "I don't think we should deactivate them, not yet."

# CHAPTER 27

**When they all** looked at him, he put his hands on his hips, the glossy brown strands of his hair lifting in the early evening breeze. "If we switch off two in such close proximity, the Psy might come out to check—and we haven't got the numbers to cover them if a whole lot arrive at once."

Indigo's wolf was still irritated at him in spite of her acknowledgment that he almost certainly hadn't done what he had on purpose, but she could see the logic of his suggestion. "We should find as many of these things as possible before we start disabling them."

"If we put all the soldiers and trainees from both packs to searching," Dorian said, "we'll probably find the majority of the transmitters, but as soon as we start deactivating them en masse, the Psy will know they've been discovered."

"And we lose our chance to collar them." Indigo blew out a breath, frowned. "I think we take that hit; get these things off our land and worry about the why later." She pulled out the cell phone she'd retrieved earlier. "I need to discuss this with

Haw—Damn." She looked at Brenna. "The cell transmitter up here needs to be checked." That made her wonder—"Any chance these devices are affecting it?"

"I wouldn't think so," Brenna said. "But I'll oversee the maintenance myself to make sure."

"Probably just storm damage." Dorian was taking something out of his pocket as he spoke. "Satellite phone," he said, passing it over. "I thought you guys switched over."

"We did," Brenna said as Indigo stepped away to make the call. "But there was a problem with the batteries in the shipment. We're waiting for replacements."

Indigo returned to their side less than a minute later. "Bren," she said, "you and Dorian go down, gather up as many techs as you can. Hawke's already organizing the soldiers. Drew and I will stay up here, keep an eye on things."

"I'll leave the phone with you two," Dorian said.

Thanking the cat, Andrew borrowed it long enough to call Max and reschedule their meeting before handing it to Indigo. She took it and left to camp out at the second site—just in case their actions had alerted the Psy.

"Best-case scenario," Hawke said at daybreak the next morning when everyone converged at a central meeting point, "they take the hint and stay out of our territory." His voice shifted, turned wolf-rough. "But somehow, I doubt that'll happen."

Indigo nodded. "We need to extend our patrols even farther than we've already done. It might be an idea to ask units of men to spend a few days roaming the more far-flung areas in rotating shifts."

"Organize it," Hawke said before turning his attention to Riaz. "Can you pick up some of Indigo's normal duties?"

The male lieutenant gave a quick nod. "Has Judd got anything yet?"

Hawke's breath was white in the early morning chill. "This smells like Council, but he's confirmed the Council is no longer functioning as a cohesive unit so it could be any one of them."

That, Andrew thought, was very, very interesting. He'd have to bring it up with Max when he met with Nikita's security chief.

Hawke turned to Indigo. "Do we need to ask Riley and Mercy to cut short their trip?"

"I don't think it's that serious yet." Indigo's eyes were almost azure in the light up here, vivid against her golden tan. "We can handle it for the time being—some of the soldiers can pull a few extra shifts to cover."

Andrew leaned up against the trunk of a nearby pine, folding his arms to keep from reaching for Indigo and making his claim clear to the other dominants—especially Riaz. "They both need the break." His brother had been shattered when Mercy was injured just after they had mated. The couple had come through the trial with their bond even stronger but— "I don't think they've had much of a chance to honeymoon."

Hawke's lips curved upward. "I wonder if Riley considers his current situation a honeymoon or purgatory."

Everyone laughed, but the sound was muted, their instincts on alert for any sign of intruders. As soon as there was enough light, they split up into their assigned groups and headed out to comb for needles in haystacks.

**"We found ten** devices located on the northern edge of our territory," Andrew told Max over a beer that night in a dark little Chinatown tavern that served the best microbrew in the city. "We did a fairly comprehensive sweep along the other sides, but got nothing."

"Still, it's an enormous area," Max said, "and these devices sound small."

"Yeah." Watching the condensation run down the glass of his bottle, he met the cop's eyes. "But whatever they were up to, we've put a dent in their plans by increasing security across all the isolated sections."

"You have a theory?"

"A couple." He left it at that.

"I can confirm it's not Nikita," Max said, without waiting for Andrew to ask.

"How can you be certain?"

"No reason to hire me if she's got someone capable of organizing that kind of an operation." A shrug. "And, given the access she's handed me to Psy data, I don't think it's some kind of a massive double cross."

The only other Councilor in the area was Anthony Kyriakus, whose daughter, Faith, was mated to another Dark-River sentinel. The cats had already sent through word that Anthony wasn't involved. It wasn't like SnowDancer to accept anything on face value, but this time, Hawke had. Which said a hell of a lot about the SnowDancer-DarkRiver alliance.

"Did Nikita have anything else to say about this?" Andrew asked.

Max took a sip of his beer, making an appreciative noise at the back of his throat. "She paid attention when I told her, but something else is keeping her distracted."

"Want to share?" He drank some of his own beer.

Max leaned back against the maroon leather of the booth. "I didn't want to work for a Councilor, but now I do—and as long as she doesn't break the deal we've got going, I'm loyal."

Andrew didn't ask what the deal was. He could guess. "Fair enough." It would make his task harder, but at the same time, it solidified his wolf's respect for the cop. "But does it have anything to do with dead Psy in the city?"

Max tilted his beer bottle at Drew. "I wondered how long it would take for you lot to twig to that." Putting down the bottle, he braced his forearms on the table. "Four suspicious deaths, all psychic hits."

"Nothing in the media. You covering up for Nikita?"

Max's skin pulled tight over his jaw. "I'll allow that only because I would've come to the same conclusion six months ago." His anger was a cool flame in his eyes. "It's no cover-up. Enforcement's fully aware of the situation, just keeping its mouth shut for once."

Andrew heard the ring of truth in that. "Sorry, man. I had to ask."

"Yeah, well, don't do it again." The cop blew out a breath. "Look, we've warned the targeted group—low-Gradient

Psy—but we've done so quietly because there's a good chance the kills are politically motivated, meant to cause unrest in the civilian population."

"We've heard rumors of trouble in the Council ranks."

Max nodded. "Probability the murders are part of that is very high."

"Interesting." Andrew shared the e-mail Pure Psy had sent to SnowDancer wolves. "Connected, you think?"

"I'd bet on it." Max handed back the ugly e-mail. "I have to keep an open mind about the murders in case some other crazies were 'inspired' by Pure Psy, but my gut says Henry Scott and his fanatics are knee-deep in it."

"Gloria," Andrew said, watching the cop's face, "she was erased."

Lines flared out at the corners of the cop's slightly uptilted eyes. "You have very good intel. That was done without my knowledge; the other sites are being processed as they should be."

Andrew knew without asking that whoever had given the order for erasure wouldn't be doing so again. It made him very curious as to exactly what kind of a deal Nikita had struck with the cop that allowed him that much power, but he knew that wasn't a question Max would answer. So he asked another. "What's it like, working for a Councilor?"

"Half the time I'm rubbing my hands in insane glee at the information I have access to."

"And the other half?"

"I'm trying not to fucking murder someone myself—usually Nikita." Max's phone beeped on the heels of that comment. The cop glanced at the readout with a smile. "My wife wants me home for dinner."

Andrew didn't have to be psychic to sense the other man's unadulterated pleasure. Feeling bad tempered for no other reason than that Indigo was mad at him, he said, "Have you ever made her angry?" If the cop said that he and his wife lived in a state of constant connubial bliss, Andrew decided he'd have full cause to throw a punch.

Max raised an eyebrow. "Sure, I'm human." He slid the phone into the pocket of his suit pants and rose to his feet with a distinctly amused glint in his eye. "Making up is the fun part, in case you haven't figured that out yet."

**Indigo sank into** what she thought was a well-deserved bath late that night, having only now finished updating the other lieutenants as to the situation with the Psy incursions. Tomás had had further disturbing news to share—more dead Psy, this time on the edges of the state and left in public areas where they couldn't be missed.

Judd, having taken charge of keeping track of that situation earlier, had volunteered to continue to handle it, and Indigo was so grateful, she could've kissed him. She was tired from the search, her muscles tense, but mostly she had an itch and no one to scratch it. Hissing out a breath, she sank deeper into the hot water, damn glad she'd chosen one of the rooms with a bath rather than a shower. She'd just picked up the loofah to run it down her leg when she heard someone enter her apartment.

Very, very few people would've felt they had the right to waltz on in.

Then she caught the scent of wild, wicked male and the liquid heat between her legs had nothing to do with the bath. "How did the meeting go?" she asked as Drew appeared in the doorway, his eyes skating over the bubbles that covered her from neck to toe.

"Dead Psy might be connected to Pure Psy. Looks like they're collateral damage in a political showdown."

The Psy were the enemy, but today, she felt pity for those who had no choice but to remain in the PsyNet. "God, imagine having sociopathic bastards like that as your leadership."

"I'd rather not talk about the Council right now."

"Oh? What would you like to discuss?" She raised an arm out of the tub and began to run the loofah down it, wanting to torture him in revenge for her keening sexual frustration.

Closing the distance between them, he perched on the edge of the tub, dipping his fingers into the foam, his eyes on her face. "Indigo."

She looked up, raised an eyebrow.

And held his gaze as he shifted his hold so that one of his hands was on either side of the tub, enclosing her in a prison of steely male muscle. "I," he said quietly, "am a dominant male. You need to learn to deal with that."

His tone made her claws prick the insides of her skin, but she kept her own tone neutral. "I'm more than used to dealing with dominant males."

"Bull. Shit." Quiet. Intense. "You've had lovers, but never one whom you've let in enough that you actually had to deal with the implications."

"What makes you think you're about to break the pattern?"

Water sloshed over the edge and onto the tile floor as Drew got into the tub, jeans and all, and knelt to straddle her. In spite of her shock, she was ready for him when he cupped her face in his hands and swept his tongue into her mouth. She tasted an earthy masculine sensuality, a hint of beer—smooth and dark—and something that licked at her senses like fire. *Drew*. His tongue stroked and licked, while his hands kept her in place for his delectation, his teeth biting on her lower lip, teasing her upper one.

Heat uncurled in her abdomen, though she recognized exactly what he was doing. It was another display of possession. Her wolf bared its fangs at the idea, giving her enough strength of will to break the kiss, push at his shoulders with her claws. He refused to move, but he put his hands on the edge of the bath behind her.

She was sucking in a breath to speak when he simply bent his head and kissed her again. All hot and warm and sexy and demanding. Sex, she thought, wasn't going to solve anything . . . but then he slid one hand down to squeeze her breast and a surge of blinding passion eclipsed every other thought. Biting down on his lower lip, she tugged up his head with a hand fisted in his hair. "Take off the T-shirt."

To her surprise, he didn't argue, reaching down and pulling the half-sodden material over his head. It landed soundlessly on the fluffy bath mat as he threw it over the side. She was stroking her hands up his chest, delighting in the heated silk of his body, when he kissed her again—and this time, there was no buildup. No, he just continued on from where he'd left off, fondling her breast with a proprietary touch that made her want to moan and to bite him at the same time.

His free hand, he stroked down to press against her abdomen.

As she went to reach for his erection, he angled that hand down, spearing his fingers through her curls to—

She screamed into his mouth as he thrust two fingers inside her. "Damn it, Drew," she gasped, "that is not foreplay."

He bit at her neck, smoothing his other hand down her ribs, then back up to squeeze and caress her breasts, rubbing his thumb over one tightly furled nipple. "Yes, it is." Another kiss, another tangling of lips and teeth and tongue. "I can feel you all silky and luscious"—two fast thrusts that threw her shockingly close to orgasm—"and ready, so hot and ready."

Groaning, she reached down to struggle with his soaked jeans. The stupid button refused to come undone—and he refused to help, intent on driving her to madness—so she flicked out her claws and shredded the denim. Her hand met more sodden fabric, hiding the hot, throbbing ridge of his impressive arousal. "You decide to wear underwear today of all days," she muttered when he gave her a second to breathe.

Drew, she'd learned, liked to kiss. And she was becoming addicted to his brand of it.

"Touch me, Indy." A husky request against her mouth.

*Oh, God, that voice.*

She shivered in pure sensory pleasure. "I'm trying."

Squeezing and petting him through the fabric, she was gratified to feel his fingers lose their rhythm inside her body.

But he recovered fast, sliding his free hand up to clench in her hair so he could tug back her head and devour her mouth while his fingers began pumping harder, faster. Stars flickered at the corners of Indigo's vision, but she gritted her teeth and held on—she wanted the damn wolf inside her. Shredding the underwear—with considerable care, because she so did not want to damage him—she shoved at his chest with all her strength.

He broke the kiss, removing his fingers from her with a lingering stroke, and let her push him back until she could straddle him. That was all the control he gave her. An instant later, his hands were on her hips and his erection was nudging at her, and he was thrusting into her with blunt promise.

Crying out, Indigo gripped the edges of the bath, her breasts damp and gleaming above him as their bodies danced slick and hot beneath the water. The joining was a little rough, all raw. And then he closed his teeth over the delicate flesh of her breast and her body went taut in an explosion of pleasure, her muscles squeezing him tight as he crushed her to him and came with a hard, explosive grunt.

# CHAPTER 28

**Having received** a call from Drew after he spoke to Max, Judd made a call of his own. "The Council split," he said, "how bad is it?"

"Bad. The Scotts are determined to get rid of Nikita for one. She's made some provocative statements against Silence—and acted on them."

Judd considered what he knew of Councilor Nikita Duncan, wondered what was in this for her. "You can't kill them all," he said, remembering the Ghost's statement the last time they'd spoken.

"They are a disease, a virus that feeds upon our people."

"Have you considered how close you are to the Net?" Dark patches, dead patches, that was the information he had about the sprawling psychic network that fed the minds of millions of Psy on the planet—as if part of its psychic fabric was rotting away. "The degeneration could be affecting you."

"No," the Ghost said. "I am quite sane."

Judd wasn't certain the Ghost had ever been truly sane—no

one with that much power could be. But he'd always been logical. "The Council's collapse, with no new system in place, will destabilize the Net, kill hundreds of thousands of innocents."

"Do you think I have a heart?" the Ghost asked curiously. "To be affected by such a fact?"

Judd knew the Ghost was getting closer and closer to slipping over the edge—and he knew he couldn't let him. Not simply because of the rebel's lethal power, but because Judd considered him a friend. "One person," Judd said. "There must be one person who you do not want to die."

A long, long pause. "If there is?"

Judd's relief was crushing. "Consider that person each time you make a decision."

This time, the pause was longer, thicker, darker. "I will consider. For now."

# CHAPTER 29

**Indigo wasn't entirely** sure how they made it from the bath to the bed, but she surfaced to find herself warm, dry, and sprawled on her front on the bed, with an equally relaxed Andrew on his back beside her. Of course, one of his hands was on her butt, stroking in a way that said "mine" more strongly than words ever could.

Finding strength from somewhere, she poked him in the arm. "What was that?"

He squeezed the globe he was caressing. "Really excellent sex."

Her wolf growled, but it was all pretend. Drew had wrung the mean out of both of them. "You were trying to sex me into submission."

"Did it work?" A lazy grin as he turned to look at her. "I was just being me."

It was very close to what he'd said at the start. "I'm not going to suddenly accept all the dominance bullshit."

"Did I ask you to?" Blue eyes narrowing. "But if I'm learning how to deal with a lieutenant with a milewide streak of stubborn and a tendency to put up walls of ice, you better fucking learn to deal with a tracker who isn't about to let you walk all over him."

That made her roll her eyes. "The only steamroller I see around here is about six feet two and two-hundred-plus pounds of muscle."

Instead of adding fuel to the fire of his anger, that made his eyes turn warm. He shifted to throw one leg over her, petting her exposed body with an even more possessive hand. "You broke my heart when you said I didn't know about foreplay."

Her lips twitched. "Yes, you're terrible at sex. Terrible." That was why she was lying here with melted bones and an inner wolf who was so dozy, she was sprawled out in complete abandon.

"Hmm." A kiss pressed to her shoulder. "I guess I should work on that."

She was about to reply when he moved so that he was braced over her, supporting himself with one arm bent at the elbow, while he reached down to part her thighs with the other. The heat of his chest burned, and she sighed at the pleasure of having him so close. "If you tell me you're ready again after that, I'll have to call you a liar."

"Well, now, Lieutenant, I take that as a challenge."

She jerked as she felt the hard, silken heat of him nudging at her. "Drew . . ." Exhaustion forgotten, she raised her bottom a little, wanting him inside her. She loved the way he felt, loved the way he touched and stroked and petted.

"Uh-huh." Still teasing her with the barest touch of his cock, he kissed the back of her neck, the top of her spine, stroking a single maddening finger around the place that was damp and hot and ready for his penetration. "I need to regain my pride." More kisses down the line of her vertebrae, his hands gripping her hips. "Give you that foreplay."

She shivered as his unshaven chin brushed against her lower back, as his lips touched the dip of her spine, his tongue flicking out to wet the spot before he blew a hot breath on it. "Mmm." It was a sound of lazy pleasure as he shifted his body farther down the bed . . . and then he was gone.

Confused, she was about to turn when he gripped her ankles and tugged her until her hips were on the edge of the bed, her feet touching the floor. His hands moved again— to the backs of her thighs. Spreading them, he blew a breath against her. "What do you like, Indy? Licks"—quick, catlike flicks against her screamingly sensitive flesh—"nips"—the feel of teeth on her clitoris, her brain hazing over—"kisses?" Wet and hot and all consuming, his mouth claimed her, his tongue sliding into her in a teasing thrust before withdrawing.

She was trying to find air when he stopped, said, "So?"

"What?" she managed to gasp.

"You didn't tell me what you liked. I wouldn't want to get it wrong."

She could feel him laughing, the demon. "You have no idea who you're messing with."

He rubbed the roughness of his chin against the soft skin of her inner thighs, licking and nipping in a way that tormented without offering relief. "I think I like this kind of foreplay."

Indigo went to pull away, determined to grab him and ride him to exhaustion. But he felt the tenseness in her muscles and tightened his hold. Then his mouth delivered on the teasing. She hadn't thought he could wring more pleasure from her already sated flesh.

She was wrong.

He seduced her with that wicked, laughing mouth, licking and stroking and teasing until she was on the very edge.

When he pulled away this time, she arched her back, inviting his possession. His thighs met the backs of hers an instant later, his body entering hers in a tight, slow push. Biting back a cry at the intensity of the sensation, she clenched her fists on the sheets.

He pulled her up until she could brace herself with her palms flat on the bed. "Am I hurting you?"

"No." *Never.*

Then there was only the slick glide of flesh on flesh, heated, sensual murmurs, and the most searing pleasure.

* * *

**Indigo came to** wakefulness close to dawn, not the least surprised to find herself all but buried beneath heavy, warm male. Drew, she'd learned during the night, was a shameless bed hog—but he liked to keep her with him, so instead of being pushed off the bed, she was instead pulled under him, his thigh between hers, his hand on her breast, his face nuzzled into her neck.

She'd never had a lover attempt to claim her so totally. But, she thought, opening her heart a fraction, she could get used to this kind of affection. Because whatever he took, he gave back with staggering generosity.

Stroking her fingers into his hair, she thought over what he'd said. Because he wasn't just affection and laughter and play—as she'd understood for the first time on the mountain two days ago. He was the pack's tracker, with all that denoted. He was also a very, very strong dominant. He was absolutely right to demand that she learn to deal with him as he was learning to deal with her.

Her wolf growled, unhappy at the idea of bending for any man.

But was it really submitting, Indigo dared ask for the first time, if the man was bending toward you in return?

**Having been wide** awake since around three a.m., Hawke finished reading the latest draft of the proposed new building/land agreement in which SnowDancer was to be a silent partner and was about to push away from the desk when his phone beeped. Seeing the caller ID, he reined in his impatience. "Lucas, what is it?"

"We got hit with the Pure Psy e-mail last night," the DarkRiver alpha said, "and a couple of our juveniles came to me with stories of being approached in online chat rooms."

Hawke's wolf peeled back its lips at the boldness of the group. "Juveniles okay?"

"Just insulted," Lucas said, a thread of pride in his tone.

"I've got Dorian watching the chat rooms in case they try again. We might be able to get something out of it. I'll keep you updated."

Hanging up after a few more words, Hawke fired off a quick note to Drew with the new information, then strode to the door. He enjoyed being inside less than even most changelings, but this work was as important to the health of the pack as his more physical protection. So—his lieutenants by his side—he'd learned to do it well.

But, having cleared his desk, and with Indigo more than capable of holding the fort—and Riaz in charge of the security/search patrols in the mountains today—he surrendered to the wild hunger within and headed out for a run in wolf form. Several early risers among his pack saw him but none broke into his solitude. They all understood that, sometimes, a wolf needed to roam on its own.

However, he'd barely cleared the doorway when he caught a scent that instantly ruffled his fur the wrong way. She smelled like autumn fire and some rich, exotic spice. Far too potent a scent for someone so young, someone from whom he should keep his distance. Instead, he drew the spice-laced air into his lungs and ran at a ground-devouring lope that brought him to a small rise from where he could watch his prey.

Wearing a small pack and carrying what looked like a sleek holographic camera, she walked down the track that would eventually bring her to one of the midway areas in den territory, where he knew she'd parked the car she'd signed out of the garage for her trips to and from DarkRiver land. But it would still take her a couple of hours to reach that spot at her current pace.

When she stopped and raised her face to the dewy morning sunlight, releasing her breath in a long, slow exhale, he went motionless. Her unhidden joy at being in the stark, stunning beauty of the Sierra Nevada sang to him, and it was a dangerous pull. He should step back, should move in the opposite direction.

He should.

He turned and angled down through the trees until he appeared on the path beside her instead. Jerking back in surprise, Sienna stared at him with wide eyes. When he did nothing but wait for her, she continued on the trail, shooting him small looks filled with suspicion until it became clear he was intent only on keeping her company.

Then her stride relaxed, and they walked.

In silence.


It had been over a week since the day Andrew had ambushed Indigo in her bath, and he was feeling cautiously optimistic. The lieutenant wore his scent in her skin and, from what he could tell, wasn't worried about it. Aware how long it had taken his brother to gain the same concession from Mercy, Andrew allowed himself a little swagger—because that acceptance meant Indy's wolf was starting to get over its uncertainty when it came to him.

Of course, part of it likely had to do with the fact that the lieutenant was turning out to be as possessive as any male changeling. He wore her scent in his skin, too—along with more than a few marks. And he was very, very happy—no, *delighted*—with the whole state of affairs, he thought, grinning as he touched the love bite on his neck.

Their packmates, of course, found the whole situation highly entertaining, a welcome break from the constant vigilance of the security patrols in the mountains. The techs had found only three more transmitters after the main sweep, and it was looking like they might have unearthed most if not all of them, but SnowDancer wasn't about to lower its guard when the Council had dared invade the very heart of the pack's territory.

Of course, that didn't mean wolves stopped being wolves.

Andrew dealt with the ribbing with a grin and a shrug, while Indigo scowled. Neither response had any effect on the gossip—or the good-natured advice Andrew began receiving from the women in the pack.

"Give her her space," a dominant female advised him, "but not too much."

"Whatever you do, for God's sake don't treat her like a girl. She's a woman."

"Andrew, I love you, but you're the most sneaky, cunning wolf I've ever known—use it."

After several days of this, Andrew cornered one of the ladies. "Not that I'm not grateful," he said, "but why are you all being so helpful?"

That got him a chuckle, the touch of warm, capable hands on his face, and a smacking kiss. "Silly boy. She's ours and we love her—and we've all worried at how hard she rides herself on behalf of the pack. You make her happy."

The simple words were a revelation.

So he was ready to handle the next stage in their courtship when Indigo invited him to an official family event.

"Dinner with my parents at their place," she said casually, as if it wasn't a major deal. "Evie isn't back yet, but my aunt, Adria, and her lover, Martin, will also be there. They're flying in from near the Oregon border."

Having a vague memory of Tarah's sibling being much younger, he asked, "Are you close to Adria?"

"Yes." A smile. "She's nearer to my age than my mother's."

Instinct whispered that there was more at play here than a simple familial relationship, but he kept his silence. It would be far easier to get Indy to talk once he'd met her aunt, gained an idea of what it was that had caused Indigo's wolf to . . . almost shy away at the mention of her name.

As it was, he found himself surprised by the reality of Adria. The physical resemblance between the three women was startling; standing side by side, Tarah, Indigo, and Adria were almost mirror images of each other at different stages of life. But where Tarah was submissive, Adria was dominant. Where Tarah kissed him on the cheek in maternal affection, Adria gave him a narrow-eyed, assessing glare. And where he knew Tarah relied with open contentment on her mate, there was a real push-pull vibe going on between Adria and her lover, Martin.

Indigo, he realized at once, was far more like her aunt than her mother.

"So," Adria said after they shook hands, "you're the one."

He liked her—but then, he had a thing for cool-eyed, stubborn women. "I am."

Lines formed on her forehead, her eyebrows drawing together. "You're not what I expected."

He knew that wasn't a compliment. "I have a way of surprising people."

"Hmm." The wolf prowled behind eyes a shade lighter than Indigo's. "I've seen you in our sector, but we haven't spoken. Tell me about yourself."

As he obeyed the brusque order, his wolf more amused by her bristling protectiveness than anything else, he noticed something. Martin, while standing beside Adria, didn't join in the conversation. That, on its own, meant nothing—Riley had a way of standing silent as a sphinx beside Mercy. There was, however, never any doubt in people's minds that Riley was a hundred percent tuned in, not only to the conversation but to every tiny aspect of his mate's presence.

Something was disturbingly different here.

The stiffness of Adria's spine when her lover's shoulder brushed her own, the white lines around Martin's mouth, the way neither of them made eye contact with the other—the two were pissed at one another. Andrew took that in his stride. Being with a strong woman occasionally meant some fireworks. He couldn't imagine Indigo without her sass.

His wolf growling in agreement, he continued to talk with Adria until Tarah came over to catch up with her sister. Moving to where Indigo was standing against the wall finishing off an apple, he tugged on her ponytail. "What's with abandoning me to your aunt the inquisitor?"

She bumped her hip to his. "Don't say your smile didn't work?"

"Smart-ass." Reaching behind her, he patted that ass.

"Watch it."

"I intend to—later tonight."

Indigo threw him a quelling glance, but he caught the laughter behind it. "What did you think of my aunt?"

"She's like an older version of you," he said with complete honesty. "She's got her 'death stare' honed to perfection."

Holding her apple core in one hand, Indigo put her other one on his shoulder. "Give me a few years."

Deeply content at the thought of watching her grow further

into her skin, he stood beside her as the others spoke. It took him a little while to realize that in spite of his skill at reading the undercurrents in any given situation, he'd missed something here. Martin and Adria weren't pissed at each other—only one of them was angry.

Adria put her hand on Martin's arm . . . only to have it shaken off. Adria's face betrayed a stark heart pain in the terrible moment before she brought up her shields, cool and controlled once more.

Fighting the urge to punch Martin for putting that expression on the face of such a strong woman, Andrew thought back to the other little things he'd noticed, the way Martin had almost pointedly walked into the room first, saying, "Strongest should bring up the rear, right?"

At the time, Andrew had taken it as a joke between lovers, but now . . . "Who's more dominant?" he asked, feeling a chill whisper through his veins. "It's Adria, isn't it?"

# CHAPTER 30

**Indigo's body went** motionless beside him. "You know it is."

Andrew realized at once that he'd have to fight one hell of a battle to wipe the impression this toxic relationship had to have left on Indigo, but there was no time to follow up on the topic, because Abel walked in then, having been delayed at work—as training and resource coordinator for SnowDancer soldiers across the entire state.

First Abel kissed his mate. Then he tapped his cheek so his daughter could brace herself with one hand on his shoulder and kiss him. After that, he hugged Adria and shook Martin's hand. Then he walked over . . . and Andrew found himself being taken outside for a "little chat."

"I'll be blunt," Abel said as they stood in the crisp night air, drinks in hand, "Indigo's a grown woman who knows what she wants. She'll choose who she'll choose."

Since Abel paused for a response, Andrew said, "Yes, sir." Where his wolf had handled Adria fine, it was wary of Abel.

It wasn't a question of dominance, as Andrew outranked him, but of family.

Abel took a sip of his whiskey. "I've been asking about you."

Andrew waited.

"Women like you." A gleam in those deep gray eyes he'd bequeathed his younger daughter.

"You don't need to worry about my loyalty," Andrew said, wanting no mistakes or misunderstandings on that point. "Indigo's the only woman I want."

"I know that," Abel said to his surprise. "When we first met, I looked at Tarah the way you look at Indigo." A chuckle. "Still do, as a matter of fact."

Andrew relaxed.

Too soon.

"Just so you know," Abel said in that same warm tone, "you hurt her and I'll break every bone in your body. Twice."

**Having survived both** Abel and dinner, Andrew walked into the kitchen and went to stand at Tarah's shoulder while she cut the dessert cake into slices. "Tarah?"

Instead of answering, Tarah picked up a sliver of cake and turned to feed it to him. "So?"

He chewed, savored the burst of brandy and chocolate, swallowed. "Will you marry me?"

That got him a twinkling smile. "What is it you want to know, sweetheart?"

Utterly melted by her, he didn't bother to pretend he hadn't followed her in here with an ulterior motive. "Your sister is much younger than you."

"Our parents were very happily surprised when I was almost twenty."

Drew took a moment to think about that. Changelings were less fertile than humans or Psy, so while this kind of thing did happen, it was rare. "It must have been some celebration."

Having placed the cake on the tray, Tarah motioned for him to lift down the cups and saucers from an upper cupboard. "Oh, it was," she said as he obeyed. "Everyone thought

I'd be jealous, but I thought she was the cutest, most adorable thing I'd ever seen." A laugh husky with memory. "I used to steal her from my mother all the time and show her off like she was my own."

He chuckled, thinking back to how Riley had treated him and Brenna when they'd been younger. "Adria can't be much older than Indigo."

"I found my mate early"—a dazzling echo of memory—"and we had our beautiful Indigo soon afterward. Adria was only four at the time, so they grew up more as sisters than anything else."

Encouraged by her openness, he asked a question on a subject many would have said was none of his business. "How long has Adria been with Martin?"

"Ten years, on and off." Having arranged everything on the tray, Tarah went to pick it up.

He slid his hands past hers. "I'll get that."

Looking up, she stopped him with a hand on his upper arm. "You were a wonderful boy, Andrew. I'm so glad to know the man you've become."

Feeling the love in that touch, in those words, he asked the final, most important question. "How long has it been like that between them?"

"Since the start." Pain pinched her expression. "They love each other, but Martin's never quite been able to handle Adria's strength . . . and it breaks her heart each time he makes that clear."


**As Andrew lay** naked in bed and watched Indigo get ready to join him, he thought over the implications of what he'd learned tonight. He didn't have to be a shrink to see that Indigo's views on relationships had to have been shaped by the two closest to her.

Her parents' mating, while unsuitable to her own situation, fit the accepted parameters and was very, very successful. Adria, by contrast, had broken the mold, thrown in her lot with a less dominant man—and the results weren't exactly inspiring.

"Deep thoughts?" Indigo asked, brushing her hair in front of the vanity across from the bed.

He ran his eyes over the silky little boxers in a color that echoed her eyes that she'd paired with a thin black camisole, her hair a waterfall of shining ebony over her shoulders. "You're so beautiful, you make my heart stop."

Her hand froze in its smooth strokes and she stared at him across the length of the room. "Drew . . . you can't go around saying things like that."

"Why not?"

Putting the brush on the vanity, Indigo walked over to crawl onto the bed, straddling his body. "Because then it makes me adore you even more—and I'm not sure I can handle it." A teasing statement, but he heard the whisper of truth beneath. His lieutenant was afraid of the growing depth of the bonds between them.

He couldn't blame her. It had knocked him for six, too, when he'd first realized that she was it for him. Forever. "In that case—your eyes are funny and your teeth are crooked."

Her entire face sparkled. "Much better."

Letting the emotion in his heart translate into a slow smile, he stroked his hands up her thighs and under the edge of her camisole. "I have this fantasy."

"Really?" An arch comment. "Does it involve me naked?"

"How did you know?"

"You're not that hard to read, mister." She rubbed her body over the pulsing ridge of his erection. "Or should I say . . . your hardness is easy to read?"

He sucked in a breath, inhaling the lush, earthy warmth of her arousal. "Funny."

"I thought so." She stroked her palms down his chest, her claws pricking just enough to incite his wolf to snarling life. "I see someone's come out to play." Her own wolf in her eyes, she bent her head and ran her teeth over his nipple, her hair a thousand teasing fingers across his skin.

Fisting one hand in the silken mass, he clenched the other on the sheets. "Is that all you've got?"

A gleam of indigo blue between slitted lids, and then she rubbed her barely covered breasts oh-so-slowly against his chest, snaking her hand down to close over his erection in an openly possessive grip.

"Christ." It was gritted out between clenched teeth. When he went to grab her shoulders and pull her up, she tightened her hold, letting him feel her claws. Swearing, he dropped his hands. "Do your worst then, Lieutenant."

Stroking and squeezing the rigid length of his erection with warm, strong hands, she wiggled down over his thighs . . . lower. "Oh, I intend to." A hot, damp breath on the blunt tip of his cock, his body arching toward the warm wetness of her mouth.

"Patience." It was a laughing admonition as she rose back up, releasing him to press her palms against his thighs.

It took everything he had to keep himself in position, to let her play as she would. But he was still a predatory changeling male with a woman he considered his. "Top. Off." It came out husky, rough.

She flicked a finger at the strap of her camisole. "You mean this?"

Narrowing his eyes, he swiped up with a single precise claw.

Indigo jerked back, but not fast enough. Her mouth fell open as her camisole parted in two neat halves in front. "Hey!"

He traced the bared curves of her breasts with his eyes. "Oops."

Ripping off the camisole and throwing it to the side, Indigo prowled up his body, bracing herself with her palms on either side of his head. "You think you're so clever."

It was the most blinding pleasure to stroke his hands over her buttocks and lower back, to touch her as he would. "Yep." Nudging her down just enough, he gripped a nipple between his teeth. When she thrust her hand into his hair, he released it before sucking it back in and tugging hard.

She shivered against him. "More." It was an order and a demand in one.

Andrew smiled and bestowed the same caress on her neglected breast, bringing up a hand to fondle her with a proprietary pleasure he'd never bothered to hide.

"You," she murmured against his mouth as she pulled

away, "have a way of taking over in bed, but I have intentions of my own today."

Dropping his head back on the pillows, he watched without breathing as she finger-walked her way down his chest and back to the raging hardness of his cock. This time, her fingers circled him with purpose, and there was no warning; one minute she was straddling him, the next, she'd shimmied down to take him into the wet heat of her mouth.

"Fuck!" It was torn out of him as pleasure short-circuited his senses. Reaching down, he thrust one hand into her hair.

When she pulled away, teasing him to madness, he nudged her forward. She let him feel her teeth. He growled. Laughter in the eyes that met his. And he knew he was sunk.

Groaning, he took everything she had to give, and he gloried in it. *Mine,* he thought as she laved pleasure upon pleasure, as she gave the wolf within her control, *you're mine.*

**Indigo brought Drew** to the edge again and again, backing off a split second before he would've lost control. Her own need was at a keening pitch when she gave one final lick, got rid of her boxers, and straddled him once more.

His wolf was in his eyes, in the claws he'd dug into the bed, shredding the sheets. "I'd apologize," he growled, following her gaze, "but I don't think you deserve it."

Even now, with hunger a voracious beast between them, he could make her smile. "In that case . . . maybe I'll just do this for a while." Lifting herself, she brushed her core against the tip of his cock.

It was meant to be a teasing punishment.

It drove her wild.

Drew's hands clamped on her hips. "Down!" He pulled.

Sliding onto him in a hard rush, she cried out at the almost painful fullness. His hands flexed on her, and she realized he hadn't sheathed his claws. That was alright. Hers were pricking into his chest as she braced herself.

"Indy?" A word so hoarse, she knew it had been a struggle for him to get it out.

Sucking in a breath, she squeezed her inner muscles, saw

his eyes roll back in his head, and still his hands stayed her hips, keeping her from moving. "I'm okay," she said, knowing his protective streak had risen to the fore with her cry. "You're just a little more . . . significant in this position."

A tug of his lips, a playful arrogance that made her want to tease and delight him in equal measures. Stroking away his hands, she clasped them with her own, and then she rode her wolf. The slick glide of flesh against flesh, the rich musk of their combined scents, the blazing fire of the heat in her belly, it all added to the exotic, erotic dance. But the most powerful sensation of all was seeing Drew's eyes flicker from blue to copper and back again as both wolf and man surrendered to the inferno between them.

As he took her with him.

# CHAPTER 31

**Henry picked up** a transmitter similar to the ones he'd had his men place in SnowDancer territory. A pity they had been discovered; they would've offered him a small tactical advantage in the future—but it was nothing close to game over. Blinded by the weakness of their animal natures, the wolves hadn't yet found the other pieces of technology.

By the time they did, it would be too late.

# CHAPTER 32

**Midmorning the next** day, Andrew walked into Hawke's office just as his alpha finished a conversation with Judd via comm screen. Nodding to his brother-in-law before the screen blanked, he glanced at Hawke. "Where's Judd?"

"Somewhere in South America."

The answer wouldn't have made sense to most people, given that Judd had been in the den until only a couple of hours ago. Only a limited few knew the man was a very powerful telekinetic. Not a true teleporter, but well able to teleport long distances.

"Still nothing to confirm why the transmitters were there?" he asked, grabbing a seat.

"Four possibilities." Hawke raised a finger, his anger banked but no less lethal for it. "To act as locator beacons for teleportation or airborne vehicles"—a second finger—"a test to see how quickly we'd detect that type of intrusion"—a third finger—"or as markers on where to place explosives."

Andrew blew out a breath. "Trying to cause a massive rock slide?"

Hawke gave a nod, tapping the scrawled diagram in front of him. "You blow this section, you not only cut off a chunk of our land, any invading army has far less distance to cover to get to the heart of den territory."

"You said four possibilities. What's the fourth?"

"We found these so fast, you'd think we were meant to find them."

"Decoys." Andrew frowned. "But to what purpose?"

"That's part of what Judd's hoping to run down. He's hearing whispers that say this might be linked to Pure Psy. I've also sent the techs back up to scan for anything else that shouldn't be there." Shoving his hands through his hair, Hawke clenched his jaw. "Whatever the truth, instinct tells me things are going to come to a violent head sooner rather than later."

"If Judd does connect the transmitters categorically to Pure Psy," Andrew said, slotting in the other pieces in his mind, "and we add the e-mails to the mix, then I'm certain the packs haven't been targeted in isolation, but as part of a campaign against the city as a whole."

The wolf looked out of Hawke's eyes when he turned to Andrew. "You found something else."

"Teijan called me this morning. His people have noticed a steady stream of Psy slipping into the city and setting up house. Some of them don't appear to have jobs."

Hawke's jaw tightened. "Trouble?"

"Not according to what I got from Max after I spoke to Teijan. Seems like word's gotten out that Nikita has accepted a flawed Psy in her administration." Max's wife, Sophia, was still in the Net. And she was no longer Silent.

Hawke thought about the cold-eyed woman who'd disowned her own daughter and knew there had to be something in the stance for Nikita. Either that, or the Councilor was simply waiting for a chance to turn on the poor souls who looked to her for hope. "Are they making waves?"

"Max has an eye on them and says most are only trying to find sanctuary."

"But it's going to shift the balance of the city." And Hawke's first priority was the safety of his pack. "I'll talk to Lucas, make sure our own people have the situation under surveillance."

Drew played a pen over his fingers. "The fact that San Francisco is becoming ground zero for Psy who are breaking Silence . . . well, it explains the dead Psy in the city and on the edges of the state, doesn't it?"

"Poor buggers got caught up in the crossfire between two Council factions." Picking up a small ball from the corner of his desk, Hawke threw it against the wall, catching it as it rebounded. "You think we've been hit by the crossfire, too."

Drew nodded. "Judd's intel is that Henry Scott is out to get rid of Nikita, and we already know Henry controls Pure Psy. And San Francisco might be a changeling city, but it's also Nikita's power base."

"Psychological warfare," Hawke murmured. "He wants the city in turmoil to undermine Nikita—and . . ." Hawke caught the ball as it rebounded again, held it. "What better way to do that than by inciting the humans and changelings against each other?"

"That's what worries me," Drew said. "But I think we'd have heard—sensed—if that kind of ugliness was simmering."

Hawke threw the ball, bouncing it so that it rebounded toward Drew. "What's the date?"

Catching the ball, Andrew glanced at his watch and gave the ball to Hawke. "Why?"

"The Cherry Blossom Festival in Japantown."

"It's on right now." He immediately realized what his alpha wanted him to do. "Cats will have a much better chance of getting information from the population down there." DarkRiver held the city, and they had held it long enough and well enough that they were a trusted part of its fabric. Snow-Dancer, by comparison, evoked a wary caution—which was how they wanted it.

"Work with them," Hawke said, "but I want you down there as well."

"Don't trust the cats even now?"

Hawke shrugged. "It's not about trust. It's about Pack."

Andrew understood. Hawke's job was to protect Snow-Dancer. No matter the blood bond between SnowDancer and DarkRiver, he would never place the lives of his people in their hands alone.

**Indigo wasn't exactly** pleased to be pulled off her—considerable—duties to come "play girlfriend," as Drew had put it. "If you needed a decoy," she muttered as they meandered through the bustling stalls that lined the street, offering goodies of every variety, "why didn't you pick one of your harem?"

Tugging her close with the arm he had around her shoulders, he nipped at the tip of her nose. "Because," he said with a grin when she glared, "you would've cut me to pieces with that ice glare of yours"—his hand slid down her back—"after you kicked my bleeding, whimpering ass out of your bed. And I really like your mattress."

*She would not laugh.* "There'll be some whimpering going on very soon if you don't stop petting my ass in public."

He stroked his hand even lower and, cupping her face with his free hand, took her mouth in a laughing kiss that simply melted any temper out of her. God, she thought, she'd have to watch him. He could charm himself out of any situation—and make her a co-conspirator.

When he broke the kiss, he didn't pull away, but rubbed his nose affectionately against hers. "Think of it as a date."

At that moment, for the first time in forever, Indigo decided what the hell. It was a beautiful, sunshiny day in San Francisco; she was with a gorgeous, sexy man who couldn't keep his hands off her; and, given their underhanded tactics to date, the group of Psy behind the current attempts to brew up trouble weren't about to come in guns blazing anytime soon. "In that case," she said, sliding her arm around his waist, "you have to buy me an ice cream."

It was only as they began walking again that she realized how much attention they'd drawn despite the crowd. She glimpsed more than one smile directed their way, along with the odd wink. Her wolf sighed, but even it had to admit it was delighted by Drew's sense of play.

Just then, as Drew went to grab their ice creams, Indigo found herself being waved over by a tiny Japanese lady seated at a small stall. Intrigued, she went. When the yukata-clad lady urged her forward with a wrinkled little hand, Indigo bent across the trays of sweet *mochi* on the table until she could hear the woman over the buzz of the festival crowd.

"That one," the elderly lady said in a soft but robust voice, "trouble."

Indigo grinned. "Absolutely."

Laughing out loud, the woman picked up a mochi from the table. "Does my heart good to see a man who's not afraid of a strong woman." Putting the treat in Indigo's hand, she waved away her offer of payment and told her to get back to her "trouble."

Smiling her thanks, Indigo sank her teeth into the sticky rice concoction to discover that the center was liquid chocolate. "Mmm." Licking the syrup off her lips, she looked up to see Andrew in front of her, his eyes very much on her mouth.

"Share," he said, in a husky voice.

Deliberately misunderstanding—because it was, she'd realized over the past few weeks, fun to tease him—she put the uneaten half of the mochi in his mouth. When he scowled, she grabbed her ice cream—mango swirl—and took a lick. "What did you get?"

Drew's fingers tangled with her own as he swallowed the tidbit in his mouth and said, "Chocolate, rum raisin, and tutti-frutti."

Freezing, Indigo stared at his triple cone. "Doesn't that taste weird?"

"No. Try." It was a relaxed gesture, but as she tasted his mix of flavors, their eyes met and suddenly the moment seemed far from lighthearted.

. . . *a man who's not afraid of a strong woman.*

The elderly lady's words whispered through her mind as she pulled back, as she squeezed her fingers around his and they started walking again through the mingled scents of sugar and ice, and later, through seafood stalls redolent with hints of the most delicate sashimi. Farther down, in the area set aside for arts and crafts, she picked up scents as distant as cured wood and cherry blossoms in gloriously full bloom.

The day seemed even brighter than before—and for the first time, the hope in her heart outweighed the fear. Because that elder had been right. While Drew challenged her, attempted to take over in his own charming way, and beyond a doubt liked being in control, he'd never—no matter what—denigrated her strength or made her feel less feminine because of who and what she was. In fact, he'd made it clear in countless ways that her capable, independent nature was part of the attraction.

"Come here," she murmured, her heart feeling fragile and yet hugely powerful as she dared consider that this unorthodox—and utterly wonderful—relationship might just work after all.

When he dipped his head, she kissed him. "How do you like mango swirl?" she murmured against those lips she knew so very well.

"I think I need a second taste."

**Andrew could've spent** the whole day playing with Indigo, but aware of how important it was that they get a feel for the emotional health of the city, he worked the people they met, keeping his questions light, his comments innocuous. And piece by piece, word by word, he began to get fragments of information.

Indigo remained uncharacteristically silent.

"You okay?" he asked when they stopped to look at the parade.

"I've never seen you do this kind of work before," she said, looking up at him. "You're very good."

Pride unfurled its wings inside him, and his wolf strutted.

An hour later, when they ran into a DarkRiver couple they both knew—Emmett and Ria—they ducked out of the rush of the crowds to grab seats at a wrought-iron table outside a small café. Drinks ordered, Andrew asked the couple if they'd noticed anything, aware that all of DarkRiver's senior people would've been briefed on the possible situation.

Emmett nodded to his mate, a small, curvy brunette with eyes uptilted just enough to speak of ancestry from Asia. "Ria's family is in Chinatown, and they've been worried about some of what they've been hearing from their customers."

Ria picked up the thread of the conversation so smoothly, it was obvious the two had been mated long enough to learn each other's rhythms. "There are whispers around the city about 'Purity,'" she said, making a face as she shifted her body to lean against her mate. "Some group is trying to get humans to believe they'd be better off with 'untainted' blood."

Beside her, Emmett played with strands of his mate's hair. "If they want to cause division, they're barking up the wrong tree." He curved one hand around Ria's neck, fingers stroking gently. "This city and its people are loyal to DarkRiver; we've helped them when the Psy wouldn't, and enough times that that loyalty is set in stone."

Andrew took a drink, his wolf fascinated by the couple's interaction. It wasn't hard to guess why—he was just a little bit jealous. Not because he couldn't touch Indigo, but because they hadn't yet reached that depth of intimacy. No, that kind of love took years to settle, to grow and form.

And Indy hadn't yet committed fully to him. In spite of everything they'd become to each other, he knew her wolf continued to see him as a younger male first, and everything else second. He wasn't an impatient man, but neither was he a saint. At times like this, when he saw what they could have, that subtle distance threatened to get to him.

"That's pretty much what I picked up today," he said, forcing his attention to the matter at hand when he realized everyone was waiting for him to respond. "People are disturbed, but more at the idea of Purity than because they subscribe to it."

Indigo put down her smoothie. "There are going to be pockets of malcontents. Nothing we can do about that except monitor the situation."

"Yep," Emmett agreed, his body angled toward his mate in a way that Andrew didn't think the other man was even aware of. "But my take? We don't have to worry about the population in general."

Andrew agreed. "By the way," he said, figuring it'd be silly not to mention it since he'd guessed, "congratulations."

Ria glowed. "I didn't realize changelings outside the pack would know."

"Most won't." Indigo's tone was dry even as she reached out to squeeze Ria's hand. "But Drew's made a lifelong study of the female form."

Emmett laughed and nuzzled a kiss to his mate's temple. "Tell them what Lucas said when he found out."

"You know I'm Luc's admin assistant, right?" At their nods, Ria continued, "When he realized I was pregnant, he yelled at me."

Andrew blinked. "Seriously?" The cats adored kids as much as the SnowDancers did. He couldn't imagine the leopard alpha not being pleased about the event.

"Uh-huh. He asked me what the hell he was supposed to do when I went on maternity leave." Ria waited for a beat before delivering the punch line. "Then he told me to put my feet up and wouldn't even let me pick up a stapler until I threatened to bash his head in with it."

Indigo burst out laughing. "How many times has she threatened you since you found out?" she asked Emmett.

"Only twenty or so." Emmett gave a slow smile as he answered, and Ria jumped a little.

*"Emmett."*

Andrew saw Indigo bite back a grin as the other woman's cheeks colored. "You'll have to excuse Emmett," Ria said in a laughter-choked voice, "he's absolutely uncivilized. Can't take him out in publi—*Emmett!*"

Andrew dipped his head toward Indigo. "What do you think he's doing under the table?" he whispered in her ear, even as he slid his own hand up her thigh.

"Don't get ideas, hotshot." But her wolf flickered a shimmering gold in her eyes.

And later that night, when they lay entwined in bed, her eyes turned night-glow on him, and he knew that he danced with the wolf and the woman both. It wasn't quite everything, but it was close enough to soothe his own wolf.

# CHAPTER 33

**Having just sent** through an update to the other lieutenants on the situation in the city and in den territory, Indigo was heading to her office to read the report Riaz had filed after his shift when Brace came crashing into the den. He was scratched and bloody, his T-shirt ripped. Seeing Indigo, he began talking. It was obvious he was one step away from total panic. "Silvia fell down a cliff. I tried to catch her but I couldn't grab her in time. I couldn't—"

Indigo put her hands on those lanky shoulders, made him meet her eyes. "Where?" It was a question imbued with her innate dominance.

Giving her the location in a fast gallop, he heaved out another breath. "She wouldn't respond when I called down. Indigo, she wouldn't—"

"Focus, Brace." She squeezed his shoulders, anchoring him with the touch of Pack. "How far down is she and how accessible is the area?"

"Um"—she could see him attempting to clear the cobwebs from his mind—"you'll need ropes, climbing gear. I tried to go down but it's almost a sheer rock face. She's trapped on a ledge so far down you can hardly see her."

"I'll organize the rescue," she said and, knowing he'd function far better if he had a concrete task, added, "Your job is to track down Lara and bring her to the site. Understood?"

A sharp nod, his wolf appreciating the direct order. "I'll find her."

Making calls on her cell phone as Brace left, Indigo gathered the soldiers that she knew were in the den and available, updating Hawke on the situation as well.

He was driving away from the den but turned back at her call. "I'll meet you at the site," he said in a terse voice.

Drew, Sing-Liu, and Tai took only minutes to answer her summons. They met at one of the pack's supply lockers and, working at rapid speed, picked up the ropes, climbing gear, and other equipment they'd need to winch up Silvia's injured form.

No one even discussed the possibility of her being dead. She was Pack. She'd be brought back, no matter what. "Let's go," Indigo said, and it was the first words any of them had spoken since she'd shared the details of the accident. Now they ran together, the location being impossible to reach by even the most rugged of vehicles.

Every second that passed brought Silvia closer to death, so they pushed and made it in under half the usual time. Dropping the gear she'd carried in a pile a little ways back from the cliff edge, Indigo belly-crawled to the part that had crumbled until she could peer over it. Her eyesight was changeling keen, but Brace had been right. She could only just see the pale blue of Silvia's jeans, the red of her cardigan as she lay crumpled on a ledge at least a hundred meters down, one hand outflung. Her legs appeared to be twisted under her body in a way that they simply shouldn't have been.

Aware of Drew crawling up beside her, she turned her head. "What do you think?" She'd done more than one climb with him, knew he was highly skilled.

"One of us will have to rappel down," he said and glanced over his shoulder, pointing to a sturdy pine. "We can use that tree to rig up the main anchor, set up a belay line for backup."

Indigo agreed. Waiting until they'd both drawn back from the edge, she nodded at Sing-Liu to bring her the harness. "I'll—"

Drew put a hand on her arm. "That's one hell of a dangerous cliff face. I'll go—I've got more experience."

That first sentence irritated her, but she shrugged it off to focus on the practical reason why she was the better choice for the descent. "If something goes wrong, it'll be easier for the people up here to handle someone of my weight than yours."

"Not with Tai's strength added to yours and Sing-Liu's—and if Silvia needs to be stabilized, I've had more medical training than you."

Indigo had forgotten about the modules he'd done with Lara. Added to the fact that he was the more experienced climber, it tipped the scales in favor of his descent. She was about to say so when he shook his head and said, "We can't waste time arguing, Indy. Sing-Liu, give me the harness."

It was a slap that made her head ring. "I'm the lieutenant," she reminded him with ice in her tone. "I give the commands." Hell, she thought even as the words spilled out, she'd deal with his actions later. Right now, Silvia needed them. "Here's what—"

Drew got in her face before she could finish. "You might be the lieutenant," he bit out, "but I'm a senior member of the pack, and you've got no cause to fucking ignore my opinion just because you insist on seeing me as a less dominant young male to the exclusion of all else."

Indigo was damned if she was going to have this fight in public. Grabbing the harness, she slammed it onto his chest. "Gear up."

He began to do so, moving at high speed, but his temper continued to flash. "If we weren't sleeping together," he muttered, "you would've listened to me from the word go, instead of trying to go in half-assed because you think you have something to prove."

Indigo's hold on her own temper snapped, a snarl burning its way out of her throat even as her claws sliced out. That was when Hawke appeared out of the trees. "Enough." It was a snapped order. "Drew, check your harness. Indigo, do you need to take a walk?"

Only a lifetime of control allowed her to rein back the wolf, to say, "I'm fine. I'll organize things on this end." As she spoke, she realized Lara and Brace had also arrived. The fact that they'd witnessed Hawke slapping her down further increased her icy rage, but she kept it in ruthless check.

Drew didn't say a word as he double-checked everything and slipped a listening device in his ear while Sing-Liu clipped a mike to the collar of his tee. "I'm ready."

"So are we." Indigo had set up the anchor using the tree as a base, but she and the others would manually control the backup; they couldn't be too careful with two lives at stake. "Go."

Hooking himself up, Drew disappeared over the edge of the cliff, and Indigo's heart slammed bruisingly hard against her ribs for a long, still instant. Then the rope went taut and she knew he'd started to rappel down.

**Having made the** descent faster than would've been safe for most, Andrew crouched down beside his fallen packmate, doing a visual check for injuries after he'd ensured her airway was clear and felt for a pulse. "Broken leg, broken ribs, it looks like," he said into the mike, "severe bruising, a bad gash on the back of her head." He could feel her blood, wet and sticky. "She's unconscious, but breathing."

Lara asked him to assess the breaks more closely. "Do you think you can move her onto a stretcher for us to haul up?"

Andrew shifted his body carefully on the narrow ledge so he could get a better angle at Silvia's back. "I'm worried about her spine, Lara. The way she's twisted . . . there could be damage if I move her." In spite of the huge technological advances of the late twenty-first century, spinal injuries continued to be problematic. Most could be healed, but the recovery process was brutal.

Lara's voice faded a fraction, as if she was speaking to someone else. "I need to go down."

"I'll come back up, guide you down," Andrew said, because even a controlled rappel down this cliff face could prove dangerous for the inexperienced. "I see some footholds. I should be able to climb up unassisted."

"We've got you if you slip." Indigo's voice in his ear, calm and steady.

"Thanks." It took him considerably longer to clear the cliff face than it had to come down. His muscles were screaming by the time he reached the top, but it was a burn he could live with.

Lara was ready to go when he arrived. As the healer took a deep breath and prepared to descend with him all but glued to her, Andrew fought the urge to search for Indigo's gaze—that particular fight could come later—and stepped back over the edge of the cliff.

**It took an** hour for Lara to heal Silvia enough for the girl to be safely winched up, another quarter of an hour for Lara to ascend, with Andrew climbing behind her. In the chaos of stripping Lara of her harness and coiling the ropes, he didn't see Indigo leave, though he assumed she was helping carry the injured girl to the infirmary.

Just as well, he thought, teeth gritted. Putting his rope on the ground, he was coiling Lara's when Hawke returned. "Jesus Christ, Drew," his alpha muttered, gathering up the other abandoned gear. "I thought you were good with women."

Andrew dumped the rope and turned on the other wolf. "I was right. She wasn't using resources properly."

Hawke didn't growl back, simply raised an eyebrow. "That's not what I said."

Blowing out a breath, Andrew turned to stare out over the jagged mountainous vista. So fucking beautiful—and so incredibly lethal when the mood took it. The description, he thought, fit his lieutenant to a T. "Then what?"

"You're telling me you're still pissed at Indigo?"

Swiveling on his heel, he scowled at his alpha. "Of course I am."

Hawke shook his head, sleek strands of silver-gold whipping across his face in a sudden wind. Pushing them back, he said, "Then maybe you need to go cool off so your brain can function."

Andrew bent down and restarted coiling the second rope, his arms scratched and dirty. But he had no patience for the task. Throwing the whole lot onto the ground, he stood up again. "She was taking too long to come to a decision."

"From what I can tell, it took her maybe fifteen seconds, and it's her job to weigh up the risks and consider all options in any given situation," Hawke said, continuing to stack the gear. "If she didn't think with that kind of calm, you wouldn't have headed out here with every piece of equipment you needed."

Andrew stared at his alpha's back, knowing he was missing something. "What aren't you saying?"

Hawke shrugged. "You could've gotten exactly what you wanted with no problems if you'd gone about it the right way."

"I'm not going to dance with her on things like this." Everything else, but not this. "I've told her she needs to learn to treat me as what I am."

"Yeah, because you're doing such a good job of doing the same with her." The sarcasm was a razor across his face.

"I—" He paused, felt a chill creep up his spine. "Shit, shit, *shit!*"

Hawke didn't say a word until Andrew had gotten himself back under control.

"I overrode her in front of the others." The reality of what he'd done slammed into him like a body blow. "I forced you to pull rank on her in front of subordinates." And her pride, Jesus, her pride.

Hawke nodded, lines carved around his mouth. "You should've taken her aside, discussed your climbing skill and medical training. Hell, she acted reasonably even after you let your cock control your brain."

"But I kept pushing until she almost lost control." Control was everything to Indigo, an essential part of how she saw herself. "Fuck." Shoving his hands through his hair, he picked up one of the ropes Hawke had coiled, and put it over his arm as Hawke took the other.

"I'll send Tai back for the rest of the stuff," his alpha said as they began to walk. "She's not going to forgive you easily for this. To be quite blunt, I don't blame her. Anyone tried that with me, we'd be wiping up blood now."

Andrew remembered how much it had hurt Indigo to witness her aunt's poisonous relationship, knew exactly the courage it had taken for her to trust in this relationship with him. And still he'd fucked up. "I blew it." Maybe she'd been having trouble lowering her final barriers, but she'd taken a thousand small steps toward it. This mess was all on him.

Hawke snorted. "Forget about blowing it. You nuked it."

**Silvia safely in** Lara's hands—and thankfully stable—Indigo sat on the edge of her bed. Her hair was damp from her shower, her palms bearing the slightest of rope burns. But she didn't feel any of that. All she felt was a crushing sense of humiliation . . . and hurt. Drew had pushed her, challenging her in front of less dominant members of the pack, until her wolf lashed out, going against every rule she lived by.

God, Hawke had rebuked her in public.

Red fire flamed across her cheeks, but while the embarrassment burned, it wasn't as important in the scheme of things. Everyone lost their temper sometimes. Sing-Liu, Tai, Lara, hell, even Hawke, none of them would think less of her.

It was Drew who'd stabbed a knife right into her heart. It was one thing for them to tangle with each other in private, but . . . "Enough." Picking up a comb, she began to run it through her hair. What was done was done. She'd apologize to Hawke for letting her temper get the better of her, pick up her duties, and carry on.

As for Drew . . . Her heart twisted. Professional, she told herself, she'd be professional. That was the only way to deal with this. Anything else and it would hurt too—

Her head snapped toward her door as she caught the whisper of a very familiar scent. The knock came several seconds later. For a moment, she debated answering it, but then her wolf raised its head in steely pride and nudged her on. Glancing down, she checked that the belt of her knee-length terry-cloth robe was secure and padded to the door.

"Yes?" she said to the man on the other side, having pasted an expression of professional disinterest on her face, though the hand hidden behind the folds of her robe was fisted so tight she was cutting half-moon circles in her palm.

Drew took one look at her and muttered something harsh under his breath. "What do I do?"

He looked so lost, so vulnerable that she blinked, taken aback, but only for an instant. "There's nothing to do. Hawke sorted us out on-site—and for what it's worth, I apologize for bringing my temper into the situation." The words were sincere, though her heart was a cold rock in her chest. "That was neither the time nor the place."

Drew's eyes shifted to that brilliant, wild copper. "Don't do this to us, Indy. Don't shut me out."

Her hand clenched on the door, but she kept her composure, aware of packmates walking by in the corridor outside. "Was there anything in particular you wanted?"

"I messed up." Blunt words, unexpected and raw. "I'm sorry."

Her resolve wavered, the strength of the bond between them pushing at her to open the door, to invite him in. But— "What you did, it was a dominance challenge." She held up a hand when he would've interrupted. "You can't help it." He was a dominant, one hell of a strong one. "It'll keep happening, and I can't afford to let it."

"Indigo, you—"

"No, Drew. For the health of the pack, the hierarchy *must* be explicit." They were too strong, too wild at heart to accept anything else. "If we continue being lovers . . . you won't be able to stop yourself from challenging me again." As a predatory changeling male, Drew could no more have stopped himself from doing what he had than she could've stopped her instinctive antagonistic response.

Drew didn't immediately respond, but there was a set to

his jaw that she recognized all too well. Then he said, "So that's it? You won't even try?"

Her wolf peeled back its lips, all hope of a rational discussion going down the proverbial drain. "What the hell do you think I've been doing all this time?"

# CHAPTER 34

**Drew pressed his** palms against the edges of the door frame, blocking out the outside world. "But when push comes to shove, you're choosing the easy out."

Gritting her teeth, Indigo stared straight into those eyes of wolf copper. "I'm choosing the good of the pack. It's what a lieutenant does."

Drew bent until his breath whispered over her lips, a sweet, hot, angry caress. "Yeah? Well, since you know predatory changeling men so well, you know exactly what I'm going to do next."

She shoved a hand against his chest. "Touch me and I'll slice you to shreds."

Instead of continuing on his set path as any other male she knew would've done, he gave her a faint smile she didn't trust an inch . . . and pushed off the door. "Until next we meet, Lieutenant."

He was gone a second later.

Indigo stood there stupefied until a passing packmate called out a hello. Muttering back a response, she closed her door. Her wolf shook its head, attempting to figure out what had just happened. It had no idea, but it did know Drew was up to something.

She fisted her hands. Whatever it was, she'd handle it. Because no matter how much he pulled at her, no matter how deeply interwoven he was in her heart, she'd taken an oath to protect the pack when she became a lieutenant, and it was time to uphold it. That was what drove her.

*Liar.*

Steeling her spine, she tried to ignore that voice, but it wouldn't shut up. Because it wasn't only about the pack. It was about her. Her pride . . . and her heart. He'd hurt her. She'd made herself vulnerable, opened up her heart . . . and he'd hurt her.

**Andrew managed to** keep himself under control only by sheer force of will as he walked away.

"Dominance challenge, my ass," he muttered under his breath as he stalked to his room. He had no desire to fight for a higher rank in the hierarchy. He was *exactly* where he needed to be. So he'd lost his temper—everybody lost their temper now and then. The situation had been highly stressful. Was it any wonder he'd spoken before he'd thought?

He was so involved in his internal monologue that it took a packmate three tries to get his attention. When Andrew finally looked up, the woman said, "Er, Drew? You can't go to the nursery looking like you want to shred someone with your claws and then eat the bloody, dismembered pieces."

"Nursery?" Shaking his head, he looked around. "Shit." He turned on his heel, throwing a "thanks" over his shoulder.

But the interruption had reset his mind. Getting angry, he realized, would achieve nothing. Yes, Indigo was being stubborn in refusing to talk this through with him, but what he'd done . . . yeah, okay, she was right to be pissed.

And hurt, his conscience whispered, remembering the pain he'd glimpsed in the shadowed violet of her gaze. He'd hurt her, and it made him feel like shit. He wanted to stalk to her apartment, bully his way in, and argue with her until the ice cracked enough that he could hold her close and convince her to listen. But of course, he thought with another flare of temper, she wouldn't fight with him like every other dominant female he knew did with her man when she was mad or hurting. No, Indigo had to go all dignified and silent, her emotions rigidly contained.

"Fine," he muttered, pushing through his door, "then I'll just make it so fucking difficult for her to ignore me that she'll *have* to fight with me."

**Indigo found the** first rose the next morning—in the locker she used to store her gear when training indoors. It was a deep, deep red. Scarlet, she thought, that was the right word. And it smelled like heaven. But beneath the lush floral bouquet lay the scent of male—wild and playful.

Heat uncurled in her abdomen, but she doused it with cold reason. This wasn't some lover's tiff that could be smoothed over with a rose and an apology. This went to the heart of who they were, the choices they had to make.

Dropping the rose back inside the locker, she closed the door and went out to whip her current group of eighteen-year-olds into some kind of fighting shape. "All right, boys and girls, I want two reps of the set we practiced last time. Go!"

By the time the session was over, more than one student was close to crawling, yet Indigo's own energy level remained high, her senses on alert for any hint of Drew's presence. But he didn't come to her. Which, she thought, ignoring the growling of her wolf, was exactly right. Maybe the rose had been nothing but a good-bye.

A chill slithered through her veins, and when she wrenched open her locker again, she was well on the way to hating roses. Stupid, she thought, she was being stupid, acting like one of those ninnies who didn't know her own mind. The decision was made. End of stor—

Blooms tumbled out all over her. Soft and fragrant and exquisite.

"What the—" Staring, startled, she realized her locker was stuffed to the brim with roses.

Red, red roses.

Behind her, Sing-Liu whistled as she closed up her own locker. "Now that's what I call an apology. Man's got style."

"You can have them." Indigo scowled, scooping out the roses and putting them on the bench between the lockers. "Here."

Sing-Liu took one perfect bloom and stuck it behind her ear, the color shockingly bright against the shimmering jet of her hair. "Hey, come on," the soldier said with a small smile, "I know he was an ass, but he should get some credit for creativity. Most men just snarl and growl and try to sex their lovers into a good mood." A sensual smile. "Not that I mind being sexed until my toes curl. You should try it."

Indigo snarled at the soldier. "Don't you have somewhere to be?"

"I guess I do." Lips still curved in that provocative smile, the small, lean human woman who was more lethal than a large number of the wolves in the den, disappeared around the corner.

Locker cleared, Indigo shut the door and turned to leave.

Her feet hesitated.

She stared at the dark red spill of roses, felt the vulnerable heart of her soften. But she built fences around that softening as soon as it occurred. If she accepted this apology, if she allowed their relationship to progress again, then what she'd said would come to pass. Drew *would* attempt to dominate her wolf in unacceptable ways again, *would* force her to the point where her wolf would strike out. Over and over and over again.

Such a relationship would destroy them both, until the love that bound them was twisted and broken. Adria and Martin almost hated each other now. Not enough to separate, but any remaining love was tainted and pitted. Indigo didn't know why they continued to stay together—they never laughed with each other, and there was so much dead air between them that Indigo's wolf was hurt by the piercing silence.

She wouldn't allow that to happen to her and Drew.

Her hand reached out, touched the petals of a rose. Snapping it back before the velvety softness could seduce her into dropping her guard, she stalked down the corridor. No one stopped her, though there were a few interested glances thrown her way. In no mood to gossip, she slammed into her room . . . and came to a complete halt.

The damn wolf had drowned the room in silver-foiled chocolate kisses.

Thousands of them.

She growled.

And then she opened the closet door.


**The treats started** showing up the next day. A bowl of decadent champagne-soaked berries on the desk of her small office, passion fruit cheesecake with white chocolate swirls mysteriously in her fridge, crystallized fruit in the pocket of her jacket. And always, always kisses. Chocolate kisses. Everywhere she turned.

By contrast, she never saw Drew, though she caught his scent every place she went. His shadowy presence served to ratchet up her frustration, even as it fed her ever-growing hunger for him. She'd thought distance would lessen the need. Instead, it only seemed to be making it stronger—until the ache was a constant pulse in her body, and she was starting to look for those damn chocolate kisses.

"I swear," she muttered under her breath as another packmate grinned at her as she strode to a meeting with Hawke, "I'm going to wring his neck." Because the demon had gotten the pack on his side now.

"He just lost his temper, Indigo," Yuki had said to her a couple of nights ago. "Can happen to anyone."

"If you don't give him a chance," Jem had offered, all the way from Los Angeles—knowing everything, thanks to the pack rumor mill—"how will he ever learn?"

"*Mi amigo* is hurting," Tomás had said not much later, all long face and soulful dark eyes that she didn't trust an inch. "How can you be so cruel to someone who adores you so much?"

"Cut him a break," Lara had said only yesterday. "He looks so depressed it's breaking my heart."

"Depressed, my foot," Indigo muttered. She knew him far too well. He was using that charm of his to fool everyo—"Damn." Realizing she'd forgotten the little notepad on which she'd jotted down a few things she needed to discuss with Hawke, she turned on her heel and headed back to her room.

The grins should've warned her, but she just figured on another rose. And maybe her heart skipped a beat at the thought, but she was determined not to give in to this relentless pursuit. Andrew Liam Kincaid was not going to wear her down.

Then she came within sight of her door. And froze.

It was a soft toy. A wolf, to be precise. A wolf with lush silver fur and blue, blue eyes. It was carrying an envelope in its mouth.

Glancing around the suspiciously empty corridor—hah!—her packmates were likely stacked up five deep around the corner—she stared down at the furry thing. She should ignore it.

Opening her door, she walked inside and picked up the notepad, sticking it in a pocket. But as she went to walk back out, the wolf looked so adorably sweet that she couldn't leave it abandoned in the corridor. Growling, she picked up the toy and brought it inside, shutting the door behind her.

Now that she had the cuddly thing in her hand, she couldn't stop from reaching for the envelope. Holding the toy by her side, she slit open the flap and withdrew a card embossed with a rose that someone had embellished with hand-drawn thorns—big ones. "Cute," she said, her wolf flexing its claws inside her mind.

Opening the flap, she found herself looking at fine handwriting that couldn't be Drew's. Written in gold ink, it was an invitation to dinner that night at one of San Francisco's swankiest restaurants, for the occasion of . . . Indigo blinked, read the line again.

. . . *for the occasion of Andrew Kincaid's good-bye party.*

Indigo narrowed her eyes, her wolf motionless with suspicion. What was he up to now? Because no way did she believe that he was giving up. Predatory changeling men didn't have the word "surrender" in their vocabularies.

Or maybe, part of her whispered, she just didn't want to believe that. Because if he gave up, then this was it. Over and done with. Forever. Her wolf would never in a million years accept a quitter.

"Argh!" she said, shaking her head. He'd done it again, got her thinking as if they were still courting. When, in spite of his persistence, they were *not*. But, she thought, glaring at the thorny rose, she would be accepting the invitation.

It was time she and Drew had this out face-to-face.

# CHAPTER 35

**Andrew gave** a sigh of relief when the pack rumor mill informed him that Indigo had taken the toy inside, and not only that, she'd looked pissed. "Good," he said to Brenna as he sat bothering her while she tried to work. Putting his feet up on the table opposite him, he leaned his back against the console next to his sister's.

She glanced up from where she was doing something on the touch screen. "Good? You're happy because the strongest, most lethal woman in the den wants to turn you into a shish kebab?"

"She does the ice thing," he said to his sister, his wolf growling at the mere thought of it. "I hate the ice thing."

Brenna paused, threw him a startled glance. "Yeah, me, too." Stopping in her task for a second, she rubbed the bridge of her nose. "Judd can't get away with the ice thing anymore."

Andrew remembered how cold the Psy male had been before his mating to Brenna. "How'd you manage that?" Maybe he could learn something.

"Nothing I'd like to share with my brother," Brenna said with a saucy smile.

"Brat."

"Thank you."

Her smirk made his wolf laugh. "How're you doing with Judd still away?"

"He came back a few nights ago." She scowled. "I swore I'd strip his hide if he did it again. Teleporting that far really wipes him out, even if he does it in stages. He was all but unconscious for hours."

Andrew knew without asking that Judd had left as quietly as he'd arrived. The Psy male had sent them dispatches from various South American countries where he was following the scent of a Pure Psy operation. He was now certain that the group, with Henry's backing, was behind the transmitters on SnowDancer land.

"You know," Andrew said, turning his mind away from that situation for now, "that you can come to me for anything while he's away, right?"

"As if I'd have to," she muttered, "when somebody in the pack would rat me out to you the instant I even vaguely looked like I might be in trouble." But she leaned over and brushed a kiss on his jaw before beginning to work on the screen again, erasing and redrawing points of what appeared to be parts of a complex computronic design.

"Is that your teleportation machine?" The FAST project was, he knew, her most important long-term undertaking. If she could one day invent a way to send anyone—not just Tks—place to place with such speed, it would change the world.

"Uh-huh." Tiny frown lines between her brows. "Now that you've got the lieutenant's attention," she said, returning to their earlier subject, "what're you planning on doing next?"

"Never you mind." Shooting her a smug look when she gave a disgruntled scowl, he swung his legs off the table. "I need to go have a comm-conference with my team, make sure there's nothing that needs to be brought to Hawke's attention around the territory."

"You can use the room through there," Brenna said,

pointing to her right. "No one's booked it for now." A pause, laughing eyes looking up at him. "And it'll let you hide from Indigo until you're ready to spring the ambush."

Leaning down, Andrew kissed the top of his sister's head. "I love you." It was a smiling statement, but no less true for it.

"I love you, too," Brenna said, "even if you are driving Indigo so insane, she's starting to snap at everyone in the den. Did you really steal her phone and record your voice howling her name as the ringtone?"

"Maybe." Deeply satisfied by the current state of affairs, Andrew strolled into the conference room, shut the door, and initiated the calls. He trusted Bren, but other techs could come in at any moment, and the information his team gathered was quite often sensitive. Having brought them all into the call, he sat back and listened, making notes as necessary.

Thankfully, things were very steady at present, partly as a result of Riley and Mercy's mating. A strong mated couple wasn't essential at the top of the hierarchy, but it did help steady the pack as a whole. "What about that group of old ones?" he asked one of the women on his team. "The ones you were worried were stewing over something?"

"I've come to the conclusion that they're just being grumpy old men."

Laughter, then a few more snippets of information before they wrapped up the meeting early and Andrew snuck through the corridors to update Hawke on some of the smaller matters. His alpha liked to keep his finger on the pulse of his pack.

"We're in good shape," Hawke said after Andrew finished, neither of them having elected to sit for the short briefing. "Except for these games the Psy are playing."

"Pure Psy seems to have accepted defeat in its proselytizing efforts at least," Andrew said, having monitored the situation. "No new reports within the pack or in the city."

"And we've had no more detected incursions onto our land." Hawke folded his arms, staring at the territorial map on the wall. "But something tells me that's not over yet."

"No," Andrew agreed, "there was too much planning there for them to give up their aim—whatever it is—so easily."

"We might, at some stage, have to give Councilor Henry

Scott a little warning tap to let him know he's not welcome here."

Since SnowDancer, together with DarkRiver, had already taken down one Councilor, Andrew knew that "warning tap" was a real possibility. "Are you thinking sometime soon?"

"No. We need more intel on the bastard. He's smart." Turning from the map, Hawke raised an eyebrow. "As of right now, you're off shift for the next forty-eight hours. Go play your favorite game."

Feeling the hum of anticipation in his belly, Andrew gave his alpha an innocent smile. "I have no idea what you mean."

Hawke pointed a finger at him. "I want my calm, collected lieutenant back by the end of the week, or I'm packing you in a box and shipping you to fucking Siberia."

Andrew grinned. "I hear it's nice there this time of year."

**Indigo knew she** looked good in the strapless little black dress that came to midthigh and skimmed over her body like a lover's caress. Feet encased in three-inch heels, hair cascading down to the dip of her spine, and lips plump and red, she intended to make Andrew Kincaid's eyes pop out in revenge for the relentless pressure she was under to "forgive him." It didn't matter how many times she explained that it wasn't about forgiveness, but about the health of the pack; no one listened.

She'd had enough.

Several men waiting at the bar went stock-still as she entered the restaurant. "Andrew Kincaid," she said to the hostess, ignoring everyone else.

The petite brunette checked her sleek computronic organizer. "This way, Ms. Riviere."

Indigo narrowed her eyes, but said nothing as she followed the woman through the carpeted center of the restaurant and up the small flight of stairs at the back. She heard several men suck in a breath as she passed, while one audibly moaned, "Oh, God, *those* are what I call legs," but none of it eased her temper.

Instead of showing her to a table on the upper level, the

hostess took her to the door of a small private room. "I hope you enjoy your meal, Ms. Riviere," the woman said, opening the door and waiting for Indigo to enter.

"Thank you." She heard the door close behind her, but her eyes were on the man who stood beside the table dressed in a tuxedo that turned him from gorgeous and deliciously sexy to devastatingly handsome—but with the wicked still in his eye.

"Wow." He ran his eyes down her body, back up, then down again. Slowly. Very, very slowly.

Every inch of her skin felt hypersensitive by the time those playful blue eyes met hers again. "I'm officially slayed," he said, placing a hand on his heart.

She would not smile. "I thought this was a party."

"Of two." Pulling out her chair, he inclined his head. "Won't you take a seat, Indigo?"

It felt strange to hear him use her full name. But deciding to take him up on his offer since the whole point of tonight was to talk to him face-to-face, she closed the distance between them and, placing her purse on the table, sat down. He eased the chair in behind her, his arms on either side of her body. "You smell . . ." A long, slow breath, as if he was savoring the scent of her.

She didn't reply, overwhelmed by the sensory impact of him. The warmth of his body lapped against her skin even as the wild male scent of him wrapped around her like an invisible caress. She almost expected him to bend his head and kiss her nape, so much so that her body tightened in anticipation, but he released his hold on the arms of the chair and moved around to sit across from her.

"You still carry my scent in your skin."

She closed her hands hard on the chair arms to get herself under control. "It'll fade." Pain and an untamed, unnamed emotion flared within her even as she spoke.

"I've got you in my skin, too," he said in a tone that she couldn't read, before pushing a code on the little touch pad sitting to the side. "I hope you don't mind, but I placed an order for both of us earlier. I wanted to be able to talk to you without interruptions."

Unsure how to read his behavior, she said, "That's fine,"

and watched as the door opened to admit an attendant dressed in a smart black suit. Rolling in the serving cart, the slender man placed it quietly by the side of the table. "You're certain you do not wish for me to stay, sir?"

"No, we'll manage."

The man left with a nod to both Drew and Indigo.

Rising, Drew lifted off a cover to place a plate of delicacies in front of her. "I thought you'd like a choice of starters."

Starting to feel an odd prickling at the back of her neck—as if she'd walked unawares into a trap—Indigo nonetheless picked up an artwork of a pastry and popped it into her mouth as he retrieved his own plate. The flavors exploded on her tongue in a burst of sweetness and spice. "Delicious."

Drew's smile was sharp, satisfied . . . and something else, something she couldn't quite put her finger on but that made her wolf growl in warning as he murmured, "Good."

Deciding to take the bull by the horns, she allowed him to pour the wine before saying, "So, what's this about?"

"I'm leaving the pack."

Her heart skipped a beat before she narrowed her eyes. "Uh-huh."

He gave her a crooked smile. "No joke. I spoke to Winter-Fire in North Dakota. They're willing to welcome me into the fold."

WinterFire was a strong, but much, much smaller pack. "And what will you do in WinterFire?" She wasn't buying it, not for an instant.

"Same thing I do here."

"You'll be bored out of your skull." The breadth of their territory suited his skills particularly well.

Drew shrugged. "I'm willing to take that risk."

Rolling her eyes, she leaned forward and saw his gaze dip to her cleavage. He didn't even bother to pretend he wasn't checking her out as she said, "Cut the crap, Drew. What're you really up to?" Her breasts suddenly felt too tight, too confined, her skin hot and aching.

Putting down his glass, Drew lifted his gaze to hers. "I'm serious, Indigo." Solemn words.

For the first time, she felt a hint of uncertainty. "Are you insane? We can't afford to lose one of the strongest males in the pack! Not to mention our tracker!"

"I want you," he said with a blunt honesty that made her mind spin. "And you want me."

Since her entire body was aflame at his proximity—to the point where he had to be able to scent her arousal—she could hardly deny that. "I'm not following your logic."

"Far as I can see," he murmured, stroking her flushed breasts with his gaze, "only two things are keeping us apart. The first is the fact that you don't think our union would be good for the health of the pack."

"Removing yourself from the pack won't exactly help the situation."

"Yes," he said, his tone intent, "it will. You won't have to worry about confusion when it comes to the hierarchy—and WinterFire is happy for me to continue to work with Snow-Dancer as necessary."

Hearing the rational argument, she felt her wolf's claws dig into her skin, not in anger, but in a strange, wild panic. "You've thought this out."

A muscle pulled taut in his jaw. "Yeah, I have. Because I'm not walking away from us, Indigo. I don't care how hard I have to fight you."

She curled her hand into a fist under the table. "You said two things. What's the second?"

"Your mule-headedness."

Scrunching up her napkin, she threw it at him. "*My* mule-headedness? I'm not the one who refuses to accept that we're over!"

Having caught the napkin without effort, Drew put it down on the table. "Is that what you really want, Indy?"

"Of course! I don't go around saying things I don't mean."

He got up, walking around and behind her while she remained in place—courtesy of her "mule-headedness." Putting his hands on the arms of her chair, he leaned down until his lips brushed her ear. "Liar."

"Drew, I'm in no mood—"

Kisses on her neck, slow, wet, coaxing. "I can put you in

the mood." Teeth, little nips and bites that made her entire body clench.

"Stop it." She put her hands on his but didn't push him away, too starved for skin-to-skin contact with him. God, but he'd addicted her to him. The realization terrified her, but not enough to break the connection. "We're talking about your foolhardy idea to leave the pack."

"Decision's made." Another kiss.

Claws threatening to release, she pushed back her chair and rose to face him. He watched her without blinking. "Where's the zipper on your dress?"

Indigo lifted a shaking finger, pointed. "You are not leaving SnowDancer."

"Decision's not yours to make." Cool words, dominance shimmering beneath the surface.

# CHAPTER 36

**Moving out from** behind the chair, she glared at him, one hand on the chair back, the other on her hip. "You're being an idiot."

"No, I'm being smart." Taking a step toward her, he put his hand on the back of her neck and hauled her forward to meet his lips.

She was so shocked by the hard, fast move—though why, she didn't know—she didn't put up her defenses in time. Her hands flew to grip his waist, and she found herself not only giving him full access, but taking liberties of her own, her tongue tangling deliciously with his. He tasted of sin and temptation and all kinds of wicked. And her body, her body was starved for him.

When he moved both hands up to cup her face, she shivered and felt another barrier crumble. Because where the kiss ravaged, took, and demanded, his hold was almost unbearably tender. "You're a stubborn fool," she muttered against his mouth. "But I can't seem to stop adoring you."

He froze, his expression showing a sudden, unexpected vulnerability. "Don't play with me like that, Indy."

This time, she kissed him, wrapping her arms around his neck and shoving one hand into the rich silk of his hair to pull his mouth down to hers. "You are not leaving SnowDancer." She bit him hard on his lower lip. "You do and we're done."

Slits of blue gleamed beneath lowered lashes. "I thought we were already done."

"I changed my mind." Fact was, she hadn't stopped thinking about him since the instant she'd told him they were over—and though she'd never in a million years admit it, it would've destroyed her if he had taken her at her word and backed off. That wasn't how dominant wolves courted, and somewhat to her surprise, she found she'd still been tangling with him on that level. "Would you like to argue, or would you like to go home and tear each other's clothes off?"

The curve of his lips against hers. "I never really liked North Dakota anyway."

Hearing the wolf's laughter in that, she looked up, felt her eyes widen, her own wolf sitting up in shocked disbelief. "You played me!" No one had ever fooled either woman or wolf to this extent.

He nibbled on her ear. "I was serious about leaving, but I was hoping you wouldn't let me." A look so guileless she knew it was the wolf attempting to appear innocent.

Leaving, her foot, she thought. He'd had no intention whatsoever of doing that.

For some reason, his wickedness made her own wolf shake its head and grin. "Just for that," she said, nipping at his chin, able to feel the eager thrust of his erection against her abdomen, "I'm going to make you finish treating me to dinner." Her thighs tightened with anticipation, her skin shimmering with a touch-hunger only Drew could satisfy.

Taking her lips in a sweet, hot kiss, he slid his hand to her bottom, squeezed. "You're on, Lieutenant."

The starters and the mains passed by relatively smoothly— if Indigo disregarded the fact that Drew was eating *her* up with his eyes—but then they got to dessert. "Oh," she all but purred as she saw what he'd ordered.

A miniature triple-chocolate baked cheesecake with lime sorbet on the side.

When he put the plate in front of himself and crooked a finger, her wolf bared its teeth but decided to play along . . . and torture him a little. Walking over, she put one hand on the back of his neck and slid her fingers into his hair as she settled herself on his lap. "Oh, my," she murmured, flicking her tongue over her lower lip, "what is that I feel beneath me?"

Drew's laugh was pained. "Witch." Dipping the spoon into the sorbet, he brought it to her lips.

Holding her. Claiming her.

As the cool silver touched her lips, her eyes locked with his . . . and all laughter leached away. He waited, patient. "I can see your wolf," he said to her.

Her wolf saw him, too. And it decided that this male who confused, puzzled, amused, delighted, and pleasured them in equal measures was a worthy opponent. Parting her lips, she let him slip the spoon inside. "Mmm." It was a throaty sound of bliss as she savored the crisp taste of lime, tart and sweet at the same time.

Drew's hand spread on her lower back as he returned to scoop up a piece of cheesecake. When he put it to her lips this time, she opened without hesitation, holding his gaze the entire time, knowing her own had gone wolf on him. Then the chocolate flavors burst to life on her tongue and she decided that Drew Kincaid had earned the mind-blowing sex she was going to give him tonight.

Leaning down, she shared the taste of the cheesecake with him in the most intimate of ways. "Good, isn't it?" She stroked her tongue lazily against his as his hand clenched on her hip.

The spoon clattered onto the plate, and Drew's hand was suddenly between her thighs, cupping her with shocking, raw intimacy. *"Drew."*

He shuddered. "You're so wet, so ready." The sound of something tearing, and then black lace was fluttering to the floor. "Straddle me."

"I—we can't—what if—"

He was already maneuvering her body into position, his

hands pushing up her dress to the edge of her butt. "No one will come in. I initiated the lock after the meal was delivered."

Indigo shivered as he moved his hands up to cup her buttocks. "We can't have sex in a restaurant." She was scandalized at the idea.

"Take me out, Indy." Kisses on her neck, hot, passionate, earthy.

She could no more stop her hands from smoothing down his clothed chest to the buckle of his belt than she could stop her body from rubbing sensuously against his. Managing to undo the belt in spite of her suddenly clumsy fingers, she unbuttoned the top button of his pants before giving in to temptation and placing fingers over him. He sucked in a breath and seemed to freeze against her. "Zipper, Indy." The hoarse need in his voice further incited her own hunger as she lowered the zipper, her fingers brushing against the warm, stiff ridge of his arousal.

"What do you have against underwear?" Not that she was complaining. Not when he was so hard and beautiful in her hand. Thick and silky and pulsing with lust. For her. Only for her. Possessiveness made her stroke him slow and easy, taking her time, placing her mark.

He bit her nipple through the dress—a short, sharp warning. "Underwear is overrated." In her hands, he pulsed hotter, and suddenly she couldn't wait any longer.

Changing position a fraction, she brought them into perfect sync. Feeling him push into her was . . . Shuddering, she clenched her hands in his hair and let him ease her down on that beautiful cock. "Mine." She nipped his ear. "Touch any other woman and I'll cut it off."

He tapped her lightly on the bottom. "Touch any other man and I'll tie you naked to the bed and keep you that way until you realize the error of your ways."

She smiled against his mouth. "Just so we're clear."

"Crystal." And then he was sliding hilt-deep into her, and she couldn't contain her cry of delight.

Drew caught it with his mouth, moving up his hands to pull down the top of her dress until her breasts popped free of

their confines. Murmuring rough, sexual words of appreciation and pleasure, he licked and kissed and petted as he let
her set the pace. Bracing herself with her feet on the rungs of
his chair, her hands on his jacket-covered shoulders, she went
slow and easy . . . for the first few strokes. But it had been too
long. She'd missed him too much.

So when he dropped his hands back down to her hips and
urged her to pick up the pace, she made no argument. Instead,
she fused her mouth with his as he set a far more punishing
rhythm, rocking them both to an orgasm that had been days
in the making.

**"I cannot believe** you talked me into sex in a public place,"
Indigo said later that night as they strolled down the corridor
to the hotel room they'd decided to take in the city. They
needed to spend some time alone, apart from everyone.
Things had changed, and they both needed time to accept and
assess.

Drew stroked his hand over her bottom in that possessive
way of his as he opened the door and ushered her inside. "As
I keep telling you, there are advantages to dating a younger
man."

She felt her lips twitch. "I'm beginning to see that." It was
a lighthearted comment, but there was an element of truth in
it. Drew's sexuality was wild, open, exuberant. Of course, she
thought, most of that was simply who he was. Age made little
difference. He'd probably be ambushing her with kisses well
into his eighth decade.

Wasn't that a thought . . . that they might make it, be
together that long.

About to kick off her heels now that they were in the privacy of the room, she was halted by Drew's hands on her hips.
"Keep them on?" It was a husky request, his body strong and
hard behind hers.

Reaching back with her arms, she wrapped them around
his neck. "The zipper is hidden along the side."

Andrew stroked his hand down Indigo's side, curving
his fingers over her breast and smoothing them over her hip

before stroking back up to find the cleverly hidden tag. One pull and the black material began to part in a sensuous whisper. She was naked beneath the dress, the remains of her panties stuffed in one of his pockets.

His wolf grinned as it remembered the way she'd glared at him when he'd teased her by suggesting they leave it behind to shock the waiter. "I like this dress," he murmured. The zipper was almost to her hip now and the dress was all but falling off her body.

"That's because it allows you easy access." Giving a little shimmer that was unalterably feminine, she dropped her arms from around his neck as the dress fell off her body. Stepping out of it, she nudged it delicately to the side.

He didn't say anything—because his brain seemed to have deserted him. Still wearing those spiked heels, and unashamedly naked otherwise, she was a fantasy come to life, strong and sexy and so pettable that he couldn't keep his hands from roaming. When she shivered and leaned back into him, his wolf growled with pride. *Mine,* he thought, *she's mine.*

Sliding his hands up her rib cage to cup her breasts, he teased her nipples before caressing her with a slightly rougher touch. She made a low, throaty sound of pleasure but pulled away. As he watched, she walked to the bed and climbed on to lie on her front facing him. Bracing herself up on her elbows, she bent her knees up and crossed her ankles, those sexy heels in the air. "Strip." It was a sensual order.

But more, Andrew realized with a leap of joy in his soul, it was an invitation to play. And the lieutenant rarely initiated their play.

"Your wish. My command." Bowing with a theatrical flourish, he shrugged off his jacket and hung it carefully on a chair before moving his fingers to the bow tie at his throat. The strip of black fabric took bare seconds to slip out from around his neck, but he spent several more placing it over the jacket with care.

Only then did he move his fingers to his cuff links, aware of Indigo watching his every move, the perfume of her desire scenting the air in a rich musk that made his cock throb. Cuff links in hand, he walked to place them on the dresser, then returned to stand in front of her and began to unbutton his shirt. Halfway down, he said, "Shoes first, don't you think?"

Her nod was slow, her eyes on the strip of skin revealed by the open sides of his shirt. Masculine pride shot warmth through every part of him as he got rid of his shoes and socks.

"Faster," she commanded, every inch the imperious female, when he rose back to his full height.

He obeyed, tugging his shirt out from his pants and beginning to undo the remaining buttons even as he used his gaze to caress the lush curves of her breasts, the sleek length of her legs, the sexy dip of her spine.

"An . . . *drew* . . ." Indigo drawled out his name and only then did he realize he'd finished with the buttons.

Too delighted in the moment to care how much of his emotions he was exposing, he shrugged off the shirt and threw it carelessly on the chair. "Shouldn't there be some whipped cream and oil at this point?"

Bright indigo-colored eyes met his. "I'll make a note of that for next time." The words were a sultry promise. "You planning to take off your pants anytime soon?"

"Depends," Andrew said, stepping closer to the bed as he began to undo his belt. "Are you planning to use and abuse my poor body like you did at the restaurant?"

"That was nothing." Flowing up into a kneeling position on the end of the bed, she tugged off his belt and threw it to the floor. "You'll be whimpering by the time I'm through with you."

"Yeah? We'll see." He stepped out of reach and unzipped his pants, turning to give her his back. "Close your eyes."

"Why?"

"I'm shy."

Something hit him in the back, and he realized she'd thrown one of the small cushions piled up beside the pillows on the bed. "Demon."

His wolf smiled at the way she said that—with open, sensual affection. Not saying anything in response, he pulled off his pants and threw them to the side.

Indigo sighed at the sheer gorgeous perfection of the man

in front of her. "Come here so I can take merciless advantage of you." His body was all smooth golden skin and toned muscle, his butt just made for her teeth.

When he turned, his fingers circling his erection, she felt her own body grow impossibly more ready for him. Looking into his eyes, she saw pure blue flame . . . and something else. A deep, inexorable possessiveness. Her wolf didn't snarl, not this time. Because whatever the future held, she'd claimed him as hers, too. This was the trade-off, and if she was honest with herself, she didn't mind belonging to someone who was happy to belong to her.

"On your back," he said in a voice gone rough with desire.

She slid up the bed until she lay half braced on the pillows, her legs bent, her knees together. "I thought I was the one taking advantage."

Releasing the rigid length of his erection, he got on the bed and put one hand on each of her knees. "Later." Spreading her thighs with open sexual intent, he slid his hands down to the exquisitely sensitive skin of her inner thighs.

Her body arched up in shameless welcome.

Shifting closer, he thrust in. The blunt penetration was exactly what she craved. Moaning at the shock wave of pleasure, she wrapped her legs around his waist, pushed her fingers into his hair. When his gaze met hers, she saw eyes of wild copper looking back at her. *Wolf.* Tugging down his head, she nipped at his lower lip before sucking it into her mouth.

He growled against her, and then he began to move.

Hard and fast, until she had to brace her hands against the headboard to keep from being pounded right into the wood. But, oh, it felt gooood. Meeting him thrust for thrust, she felt one of his big hands close over her breast, squeezing and petting with a proprietariness she'd never allowed anyone else. And the kisses . . . he sucked and licked and nipped at her mouth, her neck, throughout, making her feel unbearably cherished even as he sexed her brains out.

# CHAPTER 37

**Afterward, she lay** crushed under hard male muscle, almost certain her heart would regain a normal rhythm sometime in the next century. Curving one hand around the back of Drew's neck as he lay slumped over her, his chest rising and falling in gasping breaths, she nuzzled at the side of his face. "I do believe I've just been royally tumbled."

His lips curved against her. "Tumbled?"

"It seems like the right word. I feel like the country maid who got her skirts thrown up over her head."

"Next time."

Biting lightly at his ear, she rubbed the now bare heel of one foot over his buttocks, enjoying having him all to herself.

For a while, they just lay there, soaking in each other's scents. When Drew did move, it was only so he could spoon her body with his. "Indy?"

Catching the oddly solemn note in his voice, she ran her hand over the arm she was using as a pillow. "What is it?"

"I'm sorry." It was a stark statement. "I shouldn't have

done what I did in front of the others. I won't do it again, no matter how hard I have to fight my wolf."

She didn't brush off the apology this time. Because it was important. Not simply what he'd said—but that he'd said it after she'd already come back to him. "You were right about something, too," she said, opening herself up in a way she'd never done for any other man. "You might be younger, but you *are* very much a dominant male. I'm sorry if I made you feel—"

"Hush." A kiss on her neck. "We're good."

God, he was so generous, he'd spoil her terribly if she let him. "No," she said, "let me finish. This mule-headed woman might not say it again."

A husky chuckle, but he didn't interrupt her this time.

"In spite of what I told myself, I've been burying my head in the sand about you," she said with brutal honesty, "because it was easier to deal with this thing between us if I stripped you down to just the younger, less dominant male." So long as he was that, she could justify maintaining a subtle emotional distance under the masquerade of caution. "I won't be doing that again. I'm going to learn to deal with you exactly as you are." And that man, she thought, was more than a match for her wolf.

He ran a hand over her hip, the touch warm and affectionate. "You know this means I get a free pass on certain actions that are likely to drive you insane." Light words, and yet there was a grain of truth in them.

Stroking his arm, able to feel the caress of the crisp hairs beneath her palm, she said, "No free pass. I'll get mad. I might even yell."

He hugged her closer to him. "That I can take. Hell, I like arguing with you." A kiss on the curve of her shoulder. "But I won't let you put up those walls of ice between us again, Indy. Fair warning."

"What do you mean 'let me'?" she asked in a tone that she knew was disgruntled. "You call bombarding me with roses, kisses, and adorable soft toys 'letting me'? I'm not even going to mention my cell phone or the closet."

A chuckle. "Yes—now imagine how much worse I can get."

Unable to resist smiling, she shook her head. "You'll probably come up against the ice walls again in the future," she said, knowing herself. "But you have full permission to do your worst."

His laughter was warm and open. "Snuggle closer to me."

"I can't get any closer." But she pressed deeper into him, her wolf still sprawled out in abandon inside of her from their recent loving. Andrew Kincaid, she thought sleepily as Drew continued to run his hand over her hip, his breath steady against her hair, had some serious moves.

He also had an endless supply of energy.

She woke in darkness to his nibbling kiss along the line of her neck, his fingers playing between her thighs. Melting, she pulled his head down for a kiss. When he lifted up her leg and slid into her, it made her nerve endings sizzle with delight.

It was a lazy loving this time, Drew rocking her to a long, deep orgasm before coming in a pulse of heat inside her.

**Andrew knew he** had a smug arrogance to his step when he walked back into the den with Indigo by his side, but he couldn't help it. He was so damn happy, the joy bubbled through his veins. Even when Indigo gave him a scowling look that said "behave," all he wanted to do was grin and shout to the world that she was *his*.

And he was keeping her, mating dance or no mating dance.

"What're you doing today, Lieutenant?" he asked after they'd gotten changed.

"I'm going to check up on Silvia."

Andrew had looked in on the girl the previous day, happy to see that she was conscious and well on the road to recovery. "I'll come with you. Lara's certain now that she won't have any long-term injuries."

"Damn lucky, given the height she fell from." Wrapping an arm around his waist, she said, "Did the cats' little healers have anything to do with it?"

Andrew shook his head, curving his own arm around her shoulders. The "little healers" were two very gifted children—whose talents DarkRiver had only divulged to a tight group in SnowDancer because the kids often came to play with their friends in the den, and the wolves needed to know to keep them away from the infirmary. "Everyone's in agreement that those two need their childhood," he said. "I think the cats have decided to put them off-limits until they turn eighteen."

"Good. Pups need to be pups."

"And," Andrew added, "might be, the kids can't heal all physical injuries. Lara and the DarkRiver healer are starting to think their gift may be linked directly to traumatic brain injuries."

"Makes sense," Indigo murmured, "since the Psy are so cerebral."

Andrew nodded in agreement as they neared the infirmary. "There goes Brace." The boy was heading in the other direction.

"I hear he's been skipping classes to go sit with Silvia."

"Boy's got it bad. Teachers are letting it slide for the moment since he's normally such a good student." Smiling at the way she walked close enough to him that their bodies occasionally brushed, much as courting wolves walked in the wild, he drew in the scent of her skin—which now carried his own so deep and true, there'd be no more talk of it fading.


**Indigo shot him** a warning glance when they headed out of the infirmary after visiting Silvia. "We're doing the outside run with the novices today. Riaz is helping me."

His wolf snarled, but Andrew wasn't stupid. She was waiting to see what he'd do. Maybe it would've been better to pretend he didn't still want Riaz's blood, but he wasn't about to lie to the woman he wanted by his side forever. Showing her his teeth, he said, "Then I'll make sure I'm not in the vicinity."

Indigo paused in the corridor. "You're going to behave?"

"Maybe." He let his wolf rise to the surface. "We both know who and what I am. Therefore, we both also know I don't think too straight when another male is near the woman I consider mine. So I can't promise you completely rational behavior, but since you let me tumble you so thoroughly, I will try."

Indigo's lips twitched a little. "Awful man." Gripping the lapels of his white shirt, she tugged him down for a kiss.

A passing packmate whistled at them and was ignored.

"Try hard." She let him feel the prick of her claws before she let go. "What're you doing today?"

"I had a message on my phone to see Hawke when I returned to the den, so he's probably got a job for me."

Frown lines marred Indigo's brow. "When are you supposed to head back out again to do your rounds of our territory?"

"A couple of weeks." He hated the idea of being away from her for that long. Especially since they were finally really, truly bonding. Because, though strong, that bond wasn't yet set in stone. "I might be able to rework things, come back to the den on a more regular basis."

Indigo's gaze was dark when she looked at him. "What you do, it's important, Drew. Don't shortchange the pack because—"

"Shh." He kissed her this time. "You make me happy. A happy Andrew is a more productive Andrew."

Indigo rolled her eyes. "When was the last time you lost an argument?"

He pretended to think about it. Then, leaning down, he whispered in her ear, "A few hours ago when you refused to stop the car and crawl into the backseat with me."

**Not long afterward,** Andrew stared at his alpha as they stood looking down over a beautiful green valley. "Huh."

Hawke raised an eyebrow. "Not quite the reaction I was hoping for."

"Just a little unexpected, that's all." He took a moment to think about the proposal. "Why me?"

"Adam likes you," Hawke said, naming the leader of the WindHaven falcons as he leaned against a large fir, his hair almost pure silver in this light. But it wasn't a silver that shouted of age—no, it was the silver of precious metals, unique and startling. Especially given the other man's wolf-pale eyes. "You okay with taking it on?"

Looking away from his alpha, Andrew paced to the edge of

the cliff. "Sure. I mean, I've got no problem acting as liaison with the falcons, but won't Adam be talking to you directly on most matters?"

"The big things, yes," Hawke said. "But, as with Dark-River, there are going to be matters that don't need an alpha's attention, but do need to be looked at by someone senior."

Andrew nodded. As alpha, Hawke had a thousand things on his plate. Delegation of some responsibility was key not only to his own sanity, but to ensuring the health of his pack; that many strong wolves with nothing to do would be a recipe for disaster. "Why not ask one of the lieutenants?"

"They've all got heavy responsibilities already . . . and we both know you could be a lieutenant if you wanted to be."

Andrew shook his head. "I couldn't do what I do if I was." He needed to be seen as approachable by even their weakest and least confident, not someone who was automatically identified as part of the pack's power structure.

"It would make your relationship with Indigo easier," Hawke said, and Andrew knew it was a question.

"No, it wouldn't. The basic issues would remain." His age, the fact of her higher dominance. "Out of curiosity—when did I hit your radar as a possible lieutenant?"

"I always knew you had it in you," Hawke said, surprising him. "That's why I originally had you stationed as the sector leader in San Diego, and you more than delivered. Your work over the past ten months has only been the icing on the cake. But I'm ruthless when it comes to the pack. You were useful to me exactly where you were."

"You, ruthless?" Andrew put a hand on his chest, feigning a heart attack.

Hawke's grin was sharp. "Adam says the liaison on their side will be Jacques."

"I met him. He's okay." A little quiet, but after growing up with Riley, Andrew could deal with that fine. You just had to poke at the quiet ones until they spoke up. "Who're the cats using as their liaison?" Because Andrew would have to work with him or her.

"Nathan," Hawke said, naming the most senior of Dark-River's sentinels.

"We should probably set up a meeting to nut out some basics." Pushing his hands into the pockets of his jeans, he rocked back on his heels. "I'll try and hook us all up for a quick comm-conference when I get back to the den."

Hawke nodded and pushed off the tree. "I'm going to run up to the northern edge, see how things are going."

"Any further indications of Psy interference?"

"No. And the techs have found no other buried objects of any kind." Deep grooves appeared on either side of Hawke's mouth. "But Judd called with some information last night. He's heard whispers that suggest Henry Scott wanted—still wants—our land to use as a staging post for an armed take-over of the entire city."

"Wouldn't they be too far, physically speaking?" Andrew asked.

"Yes, but evidence indicates they have several teleport-capable telekinetics in their group."

Andrew thought about it. "Yeah, that could have worked." SnowDancer land was remote enough that any invading army wouldn't be immediately noted from the city. "Especially if they're considering surgical strikes, rather than a full assault."

"You really need to start sitting in on the lieutenant meetings," Hawke said. "Since intel is your job."

Andrew nodded. When he'd first taken on this position, it had only been about keeping a finger on the pulse of the pack, but the network he'd constructed now meant information of all kinds flowed through to him. "I'll have Indy give me a heads-up before the next one."

"Good." Hawke reached down to pet a wild wolf that appeared out of the trees. "Judd found something else, too—looks like Pure Psy has commandeered a remote mountain village to use as its gathering place for arms and supplies, and as a training ground."

"What's he recommend?"

"Leaving the operation in place. He says he can keep an eye on them—and it's better to know where the vipers are hiding." Hawke's face was without mercy when he looked up. "That way, we can hit them hard if the Scotts do move to strike against the city, disabling a large part of their strength at a critical time."

**Dismissing the group** of her people that she'd brought outside for a meeting on how best to cover—in the long term—the wider patrol area necessitated by the Psy incursions, Indigo picked up a bracelet that had slipped off someone's wrist and was about to head back up to the den herself when she caught an unexpected—but not unknown—scent on the wind. Her wolf was already crouching to leap in welcome when Matthias walked into the clearing. Giving a whoop, she flew into his arms, wrapping her legs around his hips.

Not many men could've stood firm against the impact of her welcome, but since Matthias was built like a tank, he just caught her, giving her one of those small, quiet smiles that had fooled many a woman into thinking him shy. Half an hour after that and most of those women had probably found themselves sprawled naked under him.

"What're you doing here?" she asked after giving him an affectionate kiss.

Eyes as dark as mountain skies at midnight met hers as he squeezed the arm he had around her hips. "I've been hearing some mighty surprising rumors about you, darling."

"Is that right?" Arching an eyebrow, she unhooked herself from his body and took enough of a step back that she could look up into his face.

Matthias wasn't only built like a tank, he was taller than every other male in the pack, coming to something like six feet six. All of which would've made him a threatening-looking package but for that amazing face; a haunting mixture of Spain, the Far East, and the warm dark of his mother's homeland of Tanzania, it had a way of making people forget just how lethal he could be.

But Indigo had known him too long to be bamboozled—and right now, she was very aware of the teasing light in those eyes of liquid night. "And what exactly," she drawled, "have you been hearing?"

"Something about you setting up house with Riley's baby brother."

She knew it was a deliberate dig, meant to get her to give up information, so she plastered an innocent expression on her face. "Really? How interesting." The hairs on the back of her neck rose at that moment, and she suddenly realized she could scent another male getting ever closer.

"Yeah," Matthias said even as she was turning on her heel, "so I thought I better come on over and make sure you hadn't forgotten who you belonged to."

A growl of rage filled the air an instant before Drew's body slammed out of the forest and into Matthias's, taking the male lieutenant down to the ground.

# CHAPTER 38

**"Fuck," Indigo muttered** as Matthias retaliated instinctively, one of those massive fists clocking Drew in the ribs.

Shaking off the blow as if he hadn't even felt it, Drew slammed a punch into Matthias's face, snapping it back. Matthias snarled and shoved Drew off his chest. Except Drew didn't budge, crunching another fist into the other man's jaw. This time, Matthias responded with a similar hit.

Indigo, having watched for a gap, jumped in between the two men as they flowed to their feet. *"Stop!"*

Drew's eyes were wolf-copper when she looked up at him, and they were focused on Matthias. Who was doing a good job of imitating a wolf in human form. "Get out of my way, Indigo," the big lieutenant snarled.

Drew's body vibrated against her palm. "Don't give her orders!" Reaching as if to pull her behind him, Drew sucked in a breath when she elbowed him sharply in the stomach at the same time that she kicked Matthias in the knee. He was too big to go down, but it did snap his attention to her.

"Enough," she said, speaking to both of them. "Matthias, I need you to go to the den."

"Why the fuc—" Matthias froze, blinked, and suddenly he was human again. "Aw, shit."

Indigo stared at him. "What?" She'd expected to have to deal with his considerable sleeping volcano of a temper . . . except that it looked like he was going to apologize. *"What?"*

Matthias continued to look at Drew. "I was only kidding, man, you know that. I'd never have said it if I'd known."

Drew was still growling low in his throat, his eyes that strange, fascinating copper. They tracked Matthias with unrelenting focus as the other man began to back off toward the den, rubbing at his bruised jaw with one hand.

"Matthias," Indigo snapped. "What—"

Drew gripped the back of her neck, his mouth suddenly at her ear. "Don't *talk* to him."

Snarling, she was about to turn her own temper on him when the pieces fell into place with dizzying suddenness. Yes, Drew was dominant. Yes, Drew had a temper—one he was usually very good at hiding. But Drew was also very, very smart. He'd never have come out at a bigger, stronger opponent the way he had unless he'd been driven by something other than logic and reason.

Barely aware of Matthias disappearing into the trees, she put her hand on Drew's chest. "Andrew," she said in a calm, rational tone, "let me go or I'll make spaghetti out of your insides."

His hand still around her nape, he bent his head until his eyes were staring into hers—dominant, primitive, and devoid of civilized thought. It didn't surprise her in the least when he growled and sank his teeth into the tender curve where her neck met her shoulder.

Hissing out a breath, she clenched one hand in his hair. Rational obviously was not going to work. In any other situation, her wolf would have gone for blood. But this wasn't any other situation. This wasn't any other man.

He'd bent for her more than once.

So today, she bent for him.

Letting her body soften in welcome, she held his head

against her while she shoved her free hand under his T-shirt to lie on the heated skin of his back. *Skin privileges.* He didn't change position for several seconds. When she didn't move either, except to stroke her hand over his back, he finally released the grip he had on her with his teeth, laving his tongue over the small hurt even as his arms came around her in a much gentler—though no less possessive—hold.

His lips on her neck, over her cheek, on her lips.

She groaned as he demanded she open her mouth, and gave in. Hard and hot and deep, the kiss could have only one conclusion. She didn't stop him when he ripped away her T-shirt to expose the sports bra she wore underneath, cried out when he broke the kiss to take her right nipple into his mouth through the soft fabric, his hand covering the mound of her neglected breast, fondling and teasing.

He'd never stopped growling low in his throat, but now that growl became more a quiet rumble than a roar. She was ready when he pushed her down to the earth, ready when he lifted his head and kissed her again, ready when his hand stroked and petted her body with rough promise.

What she wasn't ready for was for him to raise his head and give her a dazed look. "Indy?"

She closed her hands over the taut muscle silk of his shoulders. "It's okay," she said, tugging him back down.

But he resisted, shaking his head as he knelt to straddle her body. A blink, and when he looked at her again, his eyes were the blue of Sierra lakes in sunshine once more. "I hurt you." He touched the bite mark with careful fingers.

She pushed herself up on her elbows, unable to go any farther—he'd trapped her lower body with his own. "Yeah, well, I've clawed you more than a few times during sex and you don't seem to mind."

"That's different." A thunderous scowl.

Once, her response would've been anger . . . but being with Drew had changed something in her, taught her that laughter could be as powerful as fury. "Because it's okay for you to be a show-off but not me?"

Putting his hands palms down on either side of her, he glowered. "A male doesn't hurt his mate."

And there it was. The reason her gorgeous, generous, laughing lover had turned into a crazed beast without warning.

The words seemed to penetrate his mind at the same moment. "We're in the mating dance."

They stared at each other for several long minutes. Then Drew began to smile, his eyes shifting from blue to copper and back again. "We're in the mating dance."

Falling back onto the earth, she poked him in the chest. "Don't look so satisfied. Just because we're in the dance doesn't mean my wolf will accept the mating itself." Exhilaration raced through her, along with a healthy dose of panic.

**Andrew, able to** think again now that the red haze of jealous rage was no longer clouding his judgment, looked down into those stunning eyes, saw the wolf prowling beyond, and knew he'd have to walk carefully. He'd courted her, played with her, and won her. But now the stakes had changed again, become much, much higher. Because there was no "out" once wolves mated—it was for life.

"Yeah?" he murmured, changing position so that his legs tangled with hers, though he kept his upper body braced on his forearms. "Then maybe I'll just have to seduce your wolf into it."

She stroked her hands across his shoulders to curve over his nape. "Why didn't you know?" she asked, her hold possessive in a way that made his own wolf sing. "The male always knows when the dance begins."

"That's why I headed out to see you—I felt it kick in without warning." It had been a shock to his system, a joy he'd never expected, and he hadn't even thought about not sharing it with Indigo, whatever the consequences. "Then I reached here and heard what Matthias was saying and smelled your scent mixed with his and . . ."

"Kaboom," Indigo completed with a laugh. "Well, now we know one thing—Matthias *can* be taken down if you hit him hard enough."

Andrew's wolf growled in pride. "I was feeling no pain.

I can't actually remember most of it—ouch!" he cried as Indigo poked gently at his side.

She winced. "Sorry. Let me look."

Bracing his weight on his opposite side, he allowed her to tug up his T-shirt. Angling her head, she winced again. "I think he probably broke your ribs. The bruise is already forming."

"Worth it," he said, nuzzling his nose against hers as she petted the hurt spot with a tender touch. "When are you going to mate with me?"

She nipped his jaw. "When you convince me it's worth my while."

Dipping his head into her neck, he kissed the bite mark and hid his smile against her skin.

Because she hadn't pulled back, hadn't pulled away. He'd been half-terrified that she would, that all they'd achieved would be buried under her wolf's savage refusal to surrender to that depth of vulnerability. Instead, that wolf had looked out of her eyes with pure challenge a moment ago. Catch me, it had said, catch me and maybe I'll be yours.

**Dressing for work** the next day—and given that she wouldn't be doing any physical training—Indigo pulled on a pair of jeans that fit her like a second skin and sat easily on her hips, her favorite boots, and a black tee with a respectable scoop neck. When she pulled her hair off her face and into her usual ponytail, the bite mark on the lower curve of her neck stood out like a beacon.

Smiling, she finished getting ready, throwing on a hip-length leather-synth jacket as a final touch. She was about to head out when she hesitated. She wasn't bothered by the mark—her wolf actually approved of the aggressive way Drew had reacted to what he'd read as a threat to his claim over his mate. But Drew was still beating himself up over it. Every time he saw the mark, he got a black look on his face.

She could cover it up . . . but her wolf rejected the idea. This was who she was, and if the man who wanted to be her mate didn't know that by now, well, she'd have to beat him over the head with the truth until he got it.

Scowling at the thought, she wrenched open her door and stalked out.

The first packmate who came upon her stared at the mark until she had to growl at him. Raising his hands, he walked off . . . but not before she'd caught the startled look on his face. She saw that same look everywhere, until it began to make her skin itch. Yeah, she could understand a bit of surprise, but usually it'd have been teamed with catcalls and teasing suggestions for revenge.

Today, nothing.

She cornered Hawke in his room before he'd even had his first cup of coffee, his jeans hanging perilously low on lean hips. When he blinked drowsily at her, she pushed past him, folded her arms, and started to rant about the over-the-top reaction. "He didn't hurt me, so I don't know why they're—"

Shaking his head as if snapping himself awake, Hawke pressed a finger to her lips. "The mark is very precise," he said, his eyes on the flesh of her neck. "No rips, no tears. Means you didn't struggle."

"So?" she asked, knowing she sounded belligerent but too annoyed to care.

"So you're Indigo," Hawke murmured. "For you to have allowed this means something, and the pack understands that."

Scowling because she still didn't think it was a big deal, she unfolded her arms and said, "As long as they don't hassle Drew about it."

A look in his eyes she didn't trust—it was too sneaky. "I wouldn't worry about Drew." A pause. "I'd worry about how he's planning to win the mating dance."

"Hmph." Indigo knew Drew very well by now. She was ready for his tricks. Raising her hand, she straightened Hawke's thick hair with the familiarity of a long and deep friendship. "You need to go have sex."

Hawke blinked, then stared at her. *"What?"*

She rolled her eyes. "I can sense your wolf straining at the reins, almost feel its hunger. It's going to become obvious to the less dominant wolves sooner rather than later." Ignoring the fact that he was growling low in his throat, she stepped closer. "And because you're alpha, your craziness will affect the rest of the pack."

She was right; Hawke knew she was right. That didn't mean he wanted to listen to her. "There's the door. Use it."

Blowing out a breath, she turned and headed away. "She hasn't slept with him, you know."

Hawke froze, his eyes on his lieutenant's retreating back.

Indigo put her hand on the knob and shot him a look over her shoulder. "A woman can tell," she said, answering his unasked question. "Don't leave it too late, Hawke, or you might just lose her."

# CHAPTER 39

**Nikita met Anthony's** eyes as they sat at the Tahoe cabin again, having agreed on physical meetings as much as possible. Words spoken on the PsyNet had too high a risk of being heard by other ears. "Henry's army is getting bigger day by day."

"There are enough people in the population disturbed by the problems in the Net that he has a wide pool to choose from."

"Yes." The Psy race had become used to the illusion of safety provided by Silence, would continue to cling to it as long as they possibly could—even when it was clear the illusion was slowly turning dark, rotting away until the Net was riddled with sickness.

"We have the strength to hold the Scotts off for a period of time, but neither of us is a military powerhouse," Anthony pointed out with perfect calm. "We need to consider our options."

"I have strong support in the city's population base,"

Nikita said, "and that strength will continue to grow." Henry had made a critical mistake in the murders. In truth, there were very, very few "perfect" Psy in the Net, and now they all knew, thanks to Nikita's careful whispers, that Henry found them dispensable. "The populace has reacted unfavorably to his attempts at intimidating them away from this region."

"And Kaleb?" Anthony asked. "There is a high chance he'll seize control of the Arrows."

One Arrow was worth dozens of ordinary soldiers, but— "Asking Kaleb for assistance has to be a last-case scenario." Because it was highly likely he'd walk in and capture the city himself. "There is one more option." If they took it, it would shift the balance of power in the world forever.

# CHAPTER 40

**Two days after** the beginning of the mating dance, Indigo found herself standing on a ridge along the northern edge of their territory thanks to a report from Judd. The other lieutenant had somehow managed to "listen in" on a meeting between two high-level people in Pure Psy, and had come out with a disturbing account of their confidence in being able to take SnowDancer whenever they chose.

"There's something else on the land that we haven't found," he'd said in his last message, "something they're certain will give them an insurmountable tactical advantage."

Hawke had immediately prioritized the task, placing Indigo in charge.

"We've swept this area, and other outlying areas, several times since the transmitters were originally discovered," Indigo now said to Riaz and Elias, both of whom stood with her, "and got nothing. So what are we missing?" Even now, the techs spread out below them like an army of ants, but she could tell they were discouraged.

"Chance the Psy penetrated deeper into regions we haven't checked?" Riaz asked.

Elias was the one who answered. "Ask me, zero percent. We're too unpredictable in those areas. An adult wolf could decide to go for a run at any time, night or day."

"I agree with Eli. The isolated sections are the only parts where they would've been sure of having an uninterrupted stretch of time." Letting her wolf rise to the surface, its vision more acute, Indigo focused in the distance—to see a heavily muscled wolf with fur the rich color of silver-birch bark loping up toward her. Her lips curved.

"Do we need to disappear?" Elias asked with a cough that struck her as suspicious.

When Indigo raised an eyebrow at him, he winked. "Drew's style of courtship seems to involve pulling you into as many shadowy corners as he can."

Riaz snickered.

She decided to handle the ribbing with grace. "Didn't you once get caught butt naked with Yuki?" she asked Elias. "Weren't you covered in chocolate sauce at the time?"

"Shuddup." Elias folded his arms. "And for your information, it was honey."

Riaz was doubled over by now, and though his hilarity was partly at her expense, Indigo's wolf was glad to see him, if not happy, then at least able to find some joy. Turning to watch as Drew crested the final hill to circle around and stand beside her, she stroked her fingers over that proud head.

Having recovered from his fit of laughter, Riaz pointed to a small valley to the west. "They could've hidden something there. We haven't paid much attention to that area because it's so flood prone."

Indigo, her wolf rubbing contentedly inside her skin as Drew leaned his weight against her, nodded. "The four of us are free right now. We can borrow a couple of scanners and go have a preliminary look." But when she glanced down into Drew's copper gaze, she saw disagreement. "What?"

He looked up.

"Are you rolling your eyes?" Her wolf was miffed.

A long sigh, and then he looked up again. Pointedly.

Indigo followed his gaze. "Eli, Riaz, am I blind?"

"No." Riaz's deep voice. "I see sky and tree branches same as you."

"I think I spotted a squirrel," Elias put in.

This time, they all turned to look at Drew.

If a wolf could be said to look exasperated, he did.

About to ask him to shift and explain himself, she saw his head snap toward the sky, his gaze following something.

A goshawk, its wings spread in a wash of blue-gray and white as it swept down to grab its hapless prey in powerful claws before rising.

Into the sky.

"Up," Indigo breathed. "We're creatures of the earth—we rarely look *up*."

Drew gave a short bark to indicate she'd got it. Going to her knees beside this wolf who was able to see the world through so many different lenses, she clenched her fingers in the fur at the ruff of his neck. "I'll get the techs to scanning, but I need you to find me some cats." The leopards were much more arboreal than SnowDancers, could search in a way the wolves couldn't. "You know who'll be good at this."

He hesitated, glancing at Riaz.

She rubbed her cheek against his fur, conscious the mating dance had to be playing havoc with his instincts. "I'll be waiting for you."

Though it was clear the wolf was in no way pleased, he went. Rising to her feet, she glanced at a silent Riaz. He shook his head. "Damn, but his control must be good."

Seeing the large silver wolf disappear from sight, she realized Riaz was absolutely right. At that same moment, she understood that Drew had followed her request for one reason only—because he'd promised her he'd never again do anything that would lead anyone to question her rank.

Comprehending as it did the compulsions of the mating dance, her wolf was staggered by the fact that he'd remembered his promise even now.

One more barrier fell.

\* \* \*

**Bringing in the** cats turned out to be a wise decision. Drew had rounded up several of the nimble, curious, and energetic juveniles and young adults. Among them, Kit—who was as gorgeous in leopard form as he was in human.

However, it wasn't Sienna's maybe-boyfriend who found it, but a sleek little leopard named Grey. "Mercy's youngest brother," Indigo said to Riaz as Grey ran over and, having got their attention, led them back to a gnarled old tree.

It took him one lunge and two seconds to scale it.

Releasing her claws, Indigo followed a little more slowly. Once in the lee of the branches, she watched as Grey jumped up to a higher branch and pointed a paw to the one below. Balancing carefully, she walked over to the spot he'd indicated. For an instant, she saw nothing—and then she did. "Shit." The camouflage was brilliant, the piece of technology blending so well into the leaves that she was astounded Grey had spotted it.

Looking down, she saw Drew had followed her scent. "Bren," she said.

He left at once to track down his sister, who'd come up to help sweep the area. When Brenna saw the device, she hissed out a breath. "It's a camera," she said, removing the battery at once. "Short-range transmission capacity—more than enough if you had a receiver just beyond the edge of our territory."

Indigo's blood ran cold, but she had no time to worry about the devastating impact the surveillance could've had. Not right now. "Grey," she said, jumping onto the ground beside Mercy's brother, "can you explain to the others how you found it?"

He nodded, eyes a crystal clear blue-green amid the gold and black of his fur.

"Do it."

With the cats helping—more arriving as word spread— and the techs climbing through the trees as best they could, they found fifteen more cameras in the area by nightfall, along with one larger object that Brenna determined acted as a signal booster.

"No way to know how far they're spread out," Indigo reported to Hawke that night. "It's going to take a long time to sweep the entire compromised section—and while it remains a low-probability target, we should check the snowpack areas, too. I've already rejigged our schedules, but we're going to continue to need the cats' help."

White lines bracketed her alpha's mouth, but his words were calm. "I'll talk to Lucas." He met her gaze. "They were watching our sentries, learning our patterns."

That was Indigo's take as well. "Judd's intel was on the money. No one goes to this much trouble unless they're planning to launch a major offensive." Though, she'd been thinking . . . "If I were a Councilor who wanted to take Snow-Dancer, I'd go after you first." The pack had one weakness and perhaps, just perhaps, Henry Scott had figured it out.

Hawke's eyes were chips of ice by now. "Riley, you, or Cooper could step into the breach."

"Yes, but we'd be constantly challenged. It would take us months to fend off the challengers, and it'd leave the pack in disarray." No one challenged Hawke because he'd proven himself, been bathed in blood for the pack.

"Even if I am a target," he said, "this kind of planning goes beyond that."

"Yes. They undeniably want what we hold."

"They'll have to kill every last SnowDancer to get it."

**Exhausted by the** events of the day, Indigo should've gone to her room and crashed in readiness for the next day's exertions. But Drew was waiting for her when she turned the corner, his eyes solemn but his words light. "Massage and a slice of white chocolate gâteau with fresh cherries?"

Which was how she found herself naked in his bed not much later.

Head on his chest, she stroked him as they spoke. "I don't want the pack to go through what we did all those years ago," she murmured. "I can't forget the blood, the loss."

Drew ran his hand down her back. "I was younger, but I

remember parts of it. My parents were lost in the first wave of trouble, only a couple of years earlier."

Hugging him tight, she took a moment to appreciate just how very good it felt to lie with him, to discuss their day. She couldn't imagine being this comfortable with anyone else. "Drew?"

"Hmm?"

"Thank you for getting the cats." For following her orders no matter the possessive drive that had to be pushing him close to insanity these days.

"That's okay." He rubbed the back of her neck. "I've decided to kill Riaz later, when you're not watching."

Sitting up, she looked into his eyes. "I want you to know something."

"So serious." He brushed strands of hair off her face. "Tell me."

"If I *am* ever talking out of my ass, I fully expect you to call me on it."

"Don't worry about that, Lieutenant." He tapped her bottom. "I'll never let things slide." A more sober look. "But any arguing we do on pack issues won't be in front of others."

She knew that would be hard on him, predatory changeling male that he was. But the past weeks had shown her the staggering depth of his will. He'd bite his tongue until it bled, but he would *never* again diminish her in public—and would certainly never fail to back her up when she needed it, like Martin so often did with Adria.

And that, she decided with absolute finality, would be the last time she ever compared her man to her aunt's. Because Drew was a thousand times the man, the wolf, that Martin was. "I thought there was cake," she said, tracing his lip with her fingertip.

He nipped at her. "I would never lie to you about cake."

Nibbling at that pretty mouth, she said, "Yeah?"

He groaned. "In the cooler. But—"

Laughing, she pushed off him. "Let me replenish my energy first. You boy toys are exhausting."

"Toys?" he growled.

She winked at him as she jumped off the bed. "I, of course, am only interested in my own personal boy toy."

"That's better," he said, stealing a kiss as he got out, too, and walked—gloriously nude—to the cooler.

"Have you no shame?" She tried her best to sound scandalized, difficult when the only thing she wanted to do was lick him all over.

"Nope."

Not as ready to eat naked, she went to Drew's dresser to pull out a T-shirt. "Since somebody tore mine." Her glare had no effect on the gorgeous man who was currently chugging down milk straight from the carton.

Wiping his mouth, he put down the milk and crooked a finger. "Come 'ere."

"I don't know that I—" Hand on a T-shirt, she frowned. "What's this?"

Drew was suddenly beside her, trying to shut the drawer. "Don't worry about it. It's just—"

But she'd already pulled out the raggedy soft toy. It was a bear, probably once a plush brown but now sadly bedraggled, most of its fur gone, one eye missing, and the ears nibbled half-off. Definitely in rough shape, but not uncared for, she realized, noticing the neat stitches that had mended the tears.

Aware Drew had gone silent beside her, she glanced up. And for the first time in her life, she saw a mask on Drew's face. It hit her like a punch to the gut.

# CHAPTER 41

"I'm sorry," she said, certain she'd hurt him in some terrible way. "I didn't mean to—"

Drew's hand slipped behind her neck to tug her to his chest. "Shh." The warmth had returned to his voice, the tone husky. "I just wasn't ready."

"It's okay." She stroked his back with her free hand, the bear between them. "We'll put it back until you are." It hurt her to know that he was hurting. Really hurt her.

Drew nuzzled at her neck. "No, I think Platypus is probably tired of being in that drawer."

She blinked. "You have a bear named Platypus?"

A grin as he took the bear from her and ran his hands affectionately over the chewed-off ears. "Hey, I was a kid. How was I supposed to know what a platypus was?" Walking to the bed, he sat down, tugging the sheet across just enough to cover the most distracting part of him. "Come, sit."

Pulling on the T-shirt, she went to sit beside him, her legs curled under her. Still uncertain what she'd inadvertently done, she put one hand on his shoulder, pressing her body a little against his. "He was yours?"

"When I was small."

She saw him swallow, remembered how young he'd been when he'd lost both parents. Her own throat grew choked. "You were a feral little thing, weren't you?" she said past the knot of emotion, tugging at the bear's abbreviated ears.

Drew gave a small laugh, and the tightness in her chest relaxed. Her wolf didn't like seeing him in distress.

"My mom gave Platty to me." He brought the bear up to his nose, drew in a long breath. "Sometimes, I think I can scent her perfume if I try hard enough."

A tear threatened to streak its way down Indigo's cheek, but she blinked it back, knowing Drew needed her to listen today. "You've taken good care of him."

"You know we were fostered in the pack," he said quietly. "Our foster parents were good, really good to all three of us. They'd brought up their own kids, understood exactly what we needed."

"But they weren't your parents." Indigo understood, knew that his foster parents—who'd both gone roaming around the world a few years ago—would've understood as well.

Drew surprised her by laughing. "I don't think Riley would've allowed them to take over." A sharp grin, full of affection. "He was the one we instinctively looked toward, as the oldest, and he never let us down. We loved our foster parents for the home they gave us, but we bonded the strongest with each other."

"That makes me better understand the way Riley treats the two of you." Especially with Brenna, the other lieutenant was severely overprotective—more like a father than a brother. He was less so with Drew, but there was still a hint of it in his dealings with his brother.

"Yeah." Holding Platypus in one hand, Drew put his other one on her thigh, his fingers stroking with an affection that she'd long understood was as natural to him as breathing. "You know, part of the way he is, is because of the fact that he all but brought us up, but—"

"—part of it is just Riley," Indigo completed. "I remember

him as a kid, you know. So intense, so focused. If you needed to get something done in the kid circles, you went to either Hawke or Riley. Hawke to lead the trouble, and Riley to make sure we didn't get caught."

Drew squeezed her thigh. "I kept Platypus with me all through my childhood," he said, then gave a self-conscious shrug. "When I turned into a teenager, I hid him in the cupboard, but I used to take him out at night sometimes and talk to him."

Shifting her hold, she hugged him around the shoulders, putting her face cheek-first against his back. "It was like being with your mom again."

"Yeah." Drew stroked the bear's ragged ears once more. "Riley and Brenna don't know I still have him."

Her wolf understood what he was telling her, accepted the gift. "I think he'd look good on top of the dresser," she murmured, pressing a kiss to his nape. "Don't you?"

Drew thought about it for a long second before lifting her hand up to his lips and rising to place Platypus in pride of place on the polished wood of his dresser. There was a vulnerability to him she could almost touch—and she knew he was embarrassed by it. Yet still he'd shared so much of his heart. It humbled her, his courage.

And it pushed her to the precipice of accepting the mating bond.

Her remaining hesitation had nothing to do with his youth or dominance. It was far more visceral. Her wolf adored Drew now, but used to control, to protecting itself, it was uneasy at the idea of the total, absolute surrender signified by the mating bond. Yet in spite of that, it found itself compelled to the edge by Drew's open commitment, by the fearless way he grabbed onto life . . . onto love.


**Andrew could almost** taste the mating bond the next morning as he worked beside Indigo to clear the northern edge of their territory of surveillance devices. It was serious work—but he was a wolf. "Hey, Indy," he said around midmorning, feeling a little raw after the previous night. But because it had been his mate who'd seen him so very vulnerable, he was able to deal.

"No more kisses," she warned with a scowl that he knew was all pretend. "People are placing bets now on how long till you ambush me again."

"It's good for morale."

Indigo shot him a narrow-eyed look. "You're right. Sneak."

"Fringe benefit," he said. "I just like kissing you." In front of people. So everyone would know she was his. "But this time I wanted to tell you that you have something in your hair."

Reaching up, she stroked over and stopped at her hair tie. "What the—" A chocolate kiss sat in her hand.

He waited for her reaction.

Holding his gaze, she peeled away the silver wrapper and closed her lips over it in a way designed to make a certain part of his anatomy throb. "Delicious." Licking her lips, she pointed south. "Time to work."

He worked, but by the time Indigo left to return to the den to take one of her classes—they couldn't afford to be slack on that, especially now—he'd kissed her on the lips five more times and showered her with several hidden candy kisses.

A few were found by gleeful packmates, who solemnly delivered them to Indigo . . . who just as solemnly accepted each offering. His wolf was pleased with this day's work.

Tai came up to him after Indigo left. "Teach me," he demanded.

"What?"

"Courtship. Because, from the smile on Indigo's face, you're really good at it."

Andrew thought of last night, of the power of the emotions that had passed between them. She'd opened her arms to him when he'd returned to the bed, and he'd felt her wolf's presence in every atom of her being as they lay intertwined. It had been a stunning intimacy, but—"She hasn't accepted the mating yet." You could never, ever be certain of a dominant female's choice until that moment.

"I know I'm only a novice, but I think that's because female wolves like to run their men ragged." A scowl. "And because she's having too much fun playing with you."

Andrew was still thinking over Tai's words as he entered his room that night, having spent all day with the search team. They'd discovered only one other camera, but they weren't going to let up. The bloody things were so small and cunningly camouflaged that they could be easily overlooked.

Frowning, he stopped on the way to the shower.

There was something wrong with the room, but he couldn't put a finger on it. Shucking his clothes, he washed, then walked out. He still couldn't figure out what was different . . . until he went to grab a pair of sweatpants from the dresser.

A laugh escaped him.

Platypus had been given an eye patch embroidered with a skull and crossbones.

Picking up the little note under the bear's paw, he saw Indigo's scrawl: *I think he looks rather dashing, don't you? Come sleep with me when you get back.*

That was exactly what he did. "When are you going to mate with me?" he asked her in the midnight hours, as he slid into the melting heat of her body.

Her eyes, gone wolf-gold, gleamed in the darkness at him. "We're considering it."

His own wolf bit back a grin of triumph, even as his heart expanded. "I'm going to sleep with you every night."

"You sound very certain." An edge of dominance.

"Oh, I am." Instead of snarling at her, he kissed her slow and easy. "You'd miss me if I wasn't here."

Her body arched up as he stopped his strokes. "Drew." It was a warning.

But he was bigger and heavier, so he pinned her to the sheets. "Admit it." Kisses on her lips, nibbles on her jaw, licks on the line of her throat. "Say it."

She twisted her body and almost managed to put him on his back. Laughing, he pinned her again. "Hey, you nearly broke a very important part of my anatomy in half." Unable to resist the slick heat of her, he began to move again, deep and hard.

Indigo fractured under him moments later, and he wasn't far behind. He realized she hadn't said what he'd asked her to, hadn't admitted that vulnerability, and that worried him, because for the mating bond to snap into place, she had to open her soul to him.

No shields, no walls, no protections.

Still, he thought, cuddling her close, she *was* without a doubt taking an active part in the mating dance, and that was a very good sign. Patience, he counseled his wolf, just a little more patience.

# CHAPTER 42

**Councilor Henry Scott** looked at the man he'd put in charge of the SnowDancer operation. "You assured me they wouldn't uncover the surveillance."

"They shouldn't have, but at the current pace, they'll have the entire area cleared within a week, two at most."

Henry shook his head. "We can't rely on having that length of time. We need to act now." While they still maintained something of an element of surprise.

"I have a team ready to go. When would you like us to mobilize?"

"Tomorrow. Focus on the primary target."

"It'll be done."

"Wait." Henry flicked up a second image. "Send a couple of your men to remove him, too." There was no point in waiting, not when a dual assassination would have a much stronger impact.

# CHAPTER 43

**Early the next** morning, her heart smiling at the way she'd woken to find Drew sprawled all over her—and the bed— Indigo sat beside Joshua on the pebbled shore of the lake nearest the den.

The search for the cameras was ongoing in the mountains, with different men and women being rotated in each day, but she and Hawke had both agreed she needed to continue to work with their young. They didn't want to lose all the progress they'd made to date.

"So?" she asked the boy beside her, examining his expression, his posture, for any hint that he continued to have problems with his wolf.

A quick smile. "I'm doing better. Hawke's been keeping an eye on me, too."

"Good." Indigo's wolf looked out at the boy, made a judgment. "Your wolf is still very near the surface."

"Yeah, but Hawke said it's like that for some of us."

"He should know." Hawke's own wolf was difficult to spot,

because his eyes never changed color—which, of course, was an answer in itself. "But he can control it. Has he been teaching you to handle your wolf when it gets pushy?"

Joshua nodded. "The things you've been teaching me—about focus and discipline—that's helping as well. I think I'm coming to an understanding with my wolf."

That made Indigo relax, because the boy was talking of his wolf as a partner, not a combatant. "I hear you're seeing Molly," she said, having made a few discreet inquiries after Drew hinted at it this morning.

Joshua's eyes went wide right before a hot flush burned across his cheekbones. "Jesus, Indigo, do you have spies everywhere?"

"Yep." Laughing at his embarrassment, she reached out to ruffle his hair. "She's good for you, puppy. And too good for you."

He bore the affection in silence but shot her a pleased look. "I know, but I'm keeping her anyway." Such a smug expression, she couldn't decide whether to laugh or growl. "She's much more mature than I am," he said bluntly, "so calm and easy with her wolf."

Surprised at his insight, she looked at him. "That doesn't bother you?"

"No." His shoulders were relaxed, his lips curved. "My wolf wants to please hers so much, it behaves . . . and I think we're both learning and becoming better from it."

It was such an astute comment that Indigo was silent for a while. Because she, too, understood about learning from another wolf.

"So," Joshua said into the silence, "are you and Drew going to mate?"

Indigo's wolf flexed its claws. "Why exactly," she said, looking at the boy who was very much her subordinate, "do you feel you have the right to ask me that question?"

Joshua winced at her tone. "Um, never mind. I'll just go get a clue now."

Her wolf resheathed its claws. "Don't forget your session tomorrow."

"I won't." A pause as he got to his feet. "And Indigo . . . thanks."

Indigo sat there staring at the water long after he left. *Mate*. She knew Drew was it for her, but the idea of taking that final step . . . it made her breath catch in her throat, her wolf pace from side to side within her mind.

"Indigo!"

Startled, she looked up to see Mercy scrambling down the bank. Dressed in a white peasant blouse embroidered with red roses around the deep neckline and faded jeans, the Dark-River sentinel's freckles glowed against her creamy skin. Her red hair, in contrast, appeared lighter, shot with strands of blonde.

"When did you get back?" Indigo cried, rising to her feet and grabbing Mercy in a hug as the other woman reached the edge of the lake. Odd as it was, Mercy had somehow become one of her closest friends—and even odder, the feeling seemed to be mutual. They were both the lone high-ranking female dominants in a group of men in this area, and it was damn nice to have someone to talk to who understood the unique issues they had to face.

Drawing back from the hug, Mercy said, "Just now. Riley's talking with Drew and Hawke, but I caught your scent and decided to follow you down here."

"Want to sit?"

Nodding, Mercy took a seat on the pebbles beside her, her gaze on the tranquil surface of the lake. "It's good to be home."

Indigo shot her a glance. "Do you think of SnowDancer territory as home, too?"

"Anywhere Riley is," Mercy said simply. "We stopped in at my parents', too, on the way up. Oh, and the DarkRiver building—Dorian would've never forgiven me otherwise."

Indigo laughed and asked a question she'd always wondered about. "Why did you and Dorian never . . . you know?"

"God, it would've been like sleeping with one of my brothers." Mercy shuddered. "But hey, I'm not the one with all the hot news. You and Drew, huh? Riley told me he scented the mating dance."

Indigo blew out a breath, tried to keep her words light in

spite of the chaos of emotion within her. "I don't know how it happened. He just sort of snuck up on me."

Mercy patted her on the shoulder. "He's got sneaky down pat. But"—a pause—"there's a damn powerful heart in there, Indigo."

"I know." Swallowing, she glanced at Mercy's suddenly solemn face. "I'm afraid, Mercy," she said, admitting the truth to perhaps the only person who'd truly understand.

Mercy didn't give her platitudes. Hooking her arms around her raised knees, she nodded. "It's terrifying," she said with frank honesty, "when you find yourself facing the one man who you know could cut through your defenses and lay you bare. Our animals don't like that, don't even like the idea of it."

"That scared part of me wants to snarl at him until he decides I'm not worth the effort," Indigo admitted. "But I know he'd never leave—and that makes me want to take his face in my hands and kiss the hell out of him."

Mercy snorted. "That sounds like the kind of response Drew would provoke." A pause, then the leopard sentinel said, "I don't know if I should point this out, but . . . you do realize he's not at full strength yet."

Indigo whipped her head around so fast she got whiplash. "What?"

"Riley told me that Drew has gained in strength, in dominance, every year since he reached adulthood, and he shows no signs of stopping."

Indigo *had* known that, vaguely—but she'd never really thought about the implications. "He could end up more dominant than me." Her wolf sat stunned.

"Yep." Mercy played with a pebble. "That bother you?"

Indigo opened her mouth to respond, closed it, thought about what she felt. "I'm no stranger to dealing with dominant men—and Drew's plenty dominant now." She'd learn and grow, as he would. "We'll work out our own balance."

"So you trust him, trust your relationship"—Mercy's hair lifted in the breeze as she turned to look at Indigo—"but something's still holding you back."

"It's nothing concrete, just . . ." Indigo squeezed her arms around her knees. "It feels like standing on the edge of a cliff, knowing all it'd take is one step to change everything forever." Terror and excitement and a wild, wild hunger churned within her.

"The thing is," Mercy said, "it's so amazing when you give in and fall. If you can fight the panic, if you can fight your animal's instinctive need to protect you against that kind of vulnerability, the prize is something—" She shook her head, a catch in her voice. "He's my forever."

Indigo felt her own eyes burn at the simple truth in that statement. It was as well that she heard male voices that instant. Riley, Drew, and Hawke all appeared out of the forest a moment later and began to make their way down the incline.

Drew was laughing at something Riley had said, his face tilted toward his brother. It was an ordinary moment, on an ordinary day. He was simply being Drew, with his easy smile and his way of teasing that had his brother scowling and Hawke grinning. And she felt the most insane urge to rise up, press her lips to that jaw, and mark him.

*Mine,* her wolf murmured for the first time, *he's mine.*

**Having left Indigo** soon after his brother and Mercy's arrival, to go up and spend several hours in the search area—while Indy briefed the honeymooners—Andrew returned home just as daylight was fading to find Brenna haunting the entrance. "What's up, baby sis?" Hugging her, he pressed a kiss to her forehead.

She squeezed him tight. "I got a message from Judd to say he was back in the city and heading up."

Moving aside, he stood with her by the entrance. "He too wiped out to do his 'thing'?"

Brenna nodded, leaning close enough to rest her cheek against his arm. "He found out some really disturbing stuff."

Having seen Judd's earlier reports, Andrew could well believe that. "I'll wait with you."

Brenna threw him a teasing look. "Go on, you're all but salivating to get your paws on Indigo."

"Hey, I resent that remark." Leaning over to tug at her hair, he felt the wind shift to bring him a familiar scent. "Isn't that—"

But Brenna was already gone, running out toward the scent that announced her mate was nearby. His wolf was happy for its sibling, but it wanted its own mate.

**Brenna felt the** rumble of the vehicle getting closer and guessed that Judd had picked up one of the cars the pack kept in the city. But she didn't stop running toward him, knowing he'd sense her approach. And he did. The vehicle pulled off to the side of the track as she came around the corner, and her mate stepped out.

"Judd!" She flew into his arms, locking her own around his neck, her face buried in the warmth of his skin. Her wolf batted at his scent, delighted and drunk on the pleasure of his presence. Woman and wolf, they'd both missed him until they couldn't breathe, though the mating bond had made things easier.

When he kissed the curve of her neck, his arms steel bands around her, she smiled and echoed the caress before pulling back enough that she could look at his face. "Baby, you look exhausted," she said, noting the deep shadows under his eyes, the gaunt lines of his face. "Are you close to flaming out?" The last time he'd looked this bad, he'd been kicked into unconsciousness soon afterward, his power reserves wiped out.

"Yes," Judd said, ducking his head as if he expected a severe talking-to.

"You need rest." She'd yell at him later for not taking better care of himself. "Get back in the car and let me drive us home."

"Bossy."

She frowned at him when he refused to release her. "Someone has to be or you'll run yourself into the ground." Then, unable to resist, she cupped his face in her hands, his unshaven jaw rasping against her palms, and kissed him . . . and kissed him. Phantom fingers stroked intimately between her legs in time to the thrust of his tongue in her mouth and she gasped. "Stop that," she said. "You're running on empty as it is."

He used his telekinesis to caress her once more before the sensation faded. "Unfortunately, you're right. I can feel my brain shutting down."

That decided it. She bullied her much bigger and stronger mate into the car and took them home. He insisted on a shower, but she made sure it was a quick one, pulling back the sheets so he could fall facedown on the futon after doing a haphazard job of drying himself. Picking up the towel he'd dropped on the floor, she rubbed it over his hair as he turned his face sideways on the pillow, his strong body sprawled naked across the bedding.

Her own body shimmered with flame at the temptation of him, and she couldn't resist running the towel slowly over the sweep of his back and lower, patting him dry with loving motions. "Sleep," she murmured, kissing the soft skin behind his ear. "I've got plans for you when you wake."

"Stay." It was an almost soundless request as sleep sucked him under, but she had no intention of doing anything else. Shucking off her clothes after putting away the towel, she crawled into bed beside her mate. Though he was lost in deepest sleep by then, he reached out and hauled her against the heat of his body.

For the first time since he'd left the den, she closed her eyes and fell into true, deep sleep.


**Andrew had managed** to corner Indigo in her office and was demanding a kiss in exchange for the little fossil he'd picked up for her when her cell phone started beeping in what he knew as the emergency code. He stood back as she took the call.

"What is it?" he asked after she hung up.

"Signs of Psy incursion in an entirely different location from where we've got most of our people," Indigo said, leaving the office at a jog. "Equipment, scent of explosives."

"Can we redirect our soldiers to that area?" he asked as he went with her to find Hawke.

She shook her head, told him the position of the site. "The

terrain means we have a better chance of reaching it faster from here." They walked into a small training room to find Hawke sparring hand to hand with a sweating Harley.

Dismissing the boy when he saw Indigo, Hawke came to join them. His wolf was in his voice by the time Indigo finished speaking, but his orders were cool, intelligent. "Prep a team. We won't let them push us into responding half-assed, but neither are we going to sit back while they play games."

"It's a trap," Indigo said, voicing what Andrew was thinking. "No question about it. They probably chose that location because they still have cameras there. They'll be able to confirm if you're with us before they strike."

"Are you asking me to stay behind?" A soft question.

Andrew stepped up beside Indigo. "They can't assassinate you if you're not there."

"How do you think the pack will take the knowledge that I sat here safe while my people walked into danger?"

*Shit.* Andrew looked at Indigo, saw the same realization on her face. Hawke's lack of participation would do as much damage as his being hurt.

After that, it took only twenty minutes to put together a team. Indigo, Andrew, D'Arn, Riaz, and six other soldiers would go with Hawke, while Riley would organize a team to protect the den just in case. "Where's Judd?" Riley asked.

"Down," Indigo answered, "but that's as well. We can't risk exposing him—not unless it's absolutely necessary." As far as the rest of the world—especially the PsyNet—was concerned, the entire Lauren family was long dead.

Riley gave a swift nod. "I've let Mercy know what's happening. She'll get the word out to the cats that there might be trouble in the city, too."

Grabbing high-powered weapons, they streamed out of the den and toward the area that looked to be the focal point of activity. The three SnowDancer sentries who'd detected the intrusion were already in position.

But the Psy had learned from their earlier mistakes when coming up against keen changeling senses. They teleported in just as the changeling group began to crest a rise at least a ten-minute walk from the site of the reported incursion.

The black-garbed men were shooting with high-impact projectile weapons as they appeared, the bullets designed to hit hard and splinter inside the body, ensuring the shrapnel would ricochet within walls of flesh, causing severe organ damage.

The SnowDancer group was directly in the line of fire.

# CHAPTER 44

"Down!" Hawke's call came as he twisted out of the way of a bullet, slamming D'Arn out of the way of another.

No one was hit in the first volley as they used bursts of changeling speed to find cover, but Andrew felt a hard punch across his mind an instant later. His natural mental shield protected him from brain damage, but his ears rang—and he knew the shield wouldn't protect him if the Psy paused long enough to concentrate the blast of telepathic power.

Which meant the changelings couldn't allow them time to focus.

Leaving the sharpshooting to the marksmen in the group, Andrew circled out and around the Psy in the early evening gloom, sensing more than seeing two other SnowDancers melt away into the forest to do likewise. The Psy spun around, attempting to pick them off in the trees. But this was wolf territory, and Andrew didn't even need to look to see where he was going.

Not bothering to strip, he shifted into wolf form. And

waited. When the Psy who'd trained his gun on the trees finally decided he'd killed what awaited within and turned, Andrew made his move, streaking out to sink his teeth into the man's throat. He'd ripped out that throat and was gone before the Psy's colleague noticed how far his partner had ventured from the tight formation of the attacking group. Even when they did notice the fallen male, a lone man turned to protect their flank.

Something was wrong. Very wrong.

And it didn't have to do with the fact that they were unmistakably only interested in Hawke—even to the extent of leaving themselves open to enemy fire. A moment later, he heard gunshots from the other side. Somehow, in spite of the security beyond, the Psy had flanked them, pinning the SnowDancers.

The human half of Andrew might've sworn, but the wolf thought only in terms of turning the tables on this threat. Running to a better position, he saw Hawke, Riaz, and D'Arn standing back-to-back, holding off the Psy with well-placed bullets from weapons of their own. Indigo was gone, as were Elias, Sing-Liu, and a couple of others, and he knew Hawke had spun them off to deal with the group approaching from the other side.

The two other wolves who'd shifted had stayed behind, and Andrew saw one of them dart out and take down another Psy soldier when the man lowered his guard. A shot rang out and the wolf disappeared back into the trees, but the Psy male was already dead or dying, his throat so much meat.

Good. One less enemy to worry about.

As Andrew shimmied forward on his belly, having crept up behind another Psy attacker, he scented D'Arn's nose start to run. The mental assaults were beginning to get through. Seeing that his prey had moved far enough away from the main group to be vulnerable, Andrew bunched his muscles, ready to take him out. But then he noticed the man in the center. He was shooting, but only enough to cover himself, most of his attention seeming to be on *looking* at Hawke . . . as if he was sending through a visual transmission.

Andrew realized what was about to happen a fraction of

a second before another Psy teleported in directly in front
of his alpha. Even Hawke's superhuman speed couldn't have
avoided a bullet at that range. But Andrew had jumped toward
Hawke in the split second between realization and the appearance of the assassin.

The bullet felt like a fucking anvil thrust into his abdomen, bloodying his fur and sending him crashing into Hawke
and the others. His alpha went down, but didn't stay in place,
rolling with Andrew to take up a more secure position behind
a tree, Riaz and D'Arn doing the same on the other side.
"Stay with me, Drew," Hawke ordered, putting pressure on
Andrew's gushing wound. "If you die, Indigo will fucking
skin me."

Andrew, his body starting to shut down, kept his eyes open
long enough to see the Psy fall. They'd left themselves too
open in focusing on their charge toward Hawke and now had
no cover. Riaz took down two, D'Arn another. Two of the Psy
managed to teleport out. That left three. Keeping pressure on
Andrew's wound with his knee, Hawke steadied his arms and
took aim. He shot the closest Psy operative in the kneecaps.
As the target collapsed, Hawke took aim at the man next to
the fallen Psy, his mouth grim, blood streaking his chest from
Andrew's wounds.

But before Hawke could shoot, the second man turned his
gun on his colleague and drilled a bullet through the injured
male's skull. Hawke's bullet took him out a second later. The
last man fell to a shot from Riaz.

Silence.

*Indigo,* Andrew thought as his chest spasmed, as blood
began to pour out of his mouth, *where was Indigo?*

A rush of scent an instant later, of windstorms cut by steel.

His soul sighed in peace. His eyes closed.


**Indigo felt her** heart stop. "No, no!" Falling beside the
severely injured wolf, she replaced Hawke's hands with her
own.

"Judd," Hawke said, his gaze icy with control. "He can fix—"

"He wasn't just sleeping when we left—he was unconscious,"

Indigo said, throwing Hawke her new sat phone. "See if he's awake."

Hawke made the call, and she knew from his bleak expression that Judd remained unconscious. His powers to use telekinesis on the cell level, literally putting shattered bodies back together, would take time to regenerate after his recent trip.

Time Drew didn't have.

"Lara," Indigo said, determined not to lose this wolf who'd chased, charmed, and played his way into her heart. "We need to get him to Lara."

Hawke didn't bother to tell her that Drew was too badly injured, that they'd never be able to get him down to the den in time. He simply slipped his arms beneath the heavy body of the wolf and said, "Hold him here."

*Hold him here.*

Her wolf didn't hesitate. It dropped even its innermost barriers, and Indigo's heart, her soul went wide open. For an instant, nothing happened, and she wanted to keen in agony. It wasn't fair. He was hers! A mate could hold her other half to life, could *will* him to live.

Then untrammeled power slammed into her with such force that she went to her knees, her mind crashing with pain that wasn't hers as the mating bond snapped into place. "I've got him," she said, holding on to Drew's fading spirit with steely hands. "I've got you, Drew. Don't you dare make me fall in love with you and then leave. I'll hunt you down in the afterlife if I have to."

Hawke was already moving. And, somehow, she was walking beside him.

Riaz, she belatedly realized, had one muscular arm around her waist, was almost carrying her. "You just hold him," the lieutenant whispered in her ear, his voice harsh. "Hold him, Indigo."

She'd have nodded, but she didn't have the energy. It was taking everything she had to keep pushing her will, her anger, her fear, into the mating bond. She wasn't Psy, couldn't see the bond. But she could feel it, could almost touch it. And she knew when it flickered. So she poured more of her energy, her strength into it. She refused to allow herself to think of anything but success.

Of course it would work. Of course Drew would awaken to torment her again. Of course he wouldn't leave her. *Please, Drew.* She didn't know if she said the words out loud, but she knew when Lara ran out of the trees close to the den, her healer's heart having felt the tug of hurt.

"Drew," the healer said with pain shattering her voice before her expression turned practical, her shoulders going stiff. "Put him down. I'll see if I can heal some of the damage here."

That was the last thing Indigo was aware of hearing, her mind encasing her in a dark good-night. But she held on to Drew even then. He was hers. She would not let him go.

**Lara glanced at** Indigo even as she placed her hands over Drew's injury and fed her healing power into him. "God, she's stubborn. I'm going to have to kiss her after she wakes. She held him. She's still holding him."

Hawke glanced at Indigo's unconscious body and then at Drew. He said nothing, knowing Lara was well aware she could pull Pack energy from his body. It was something every healer could do, but only when it came to her own pack, her own alpha. He felt it when she began to pull, opened himself up to give more and more. He'd give the last drop of his blood for his pack.

Except this time, he wasn't sure if it would be enough to save two lives. Because if they lost Andrew, Indigo would go with him, stubbornly holding on to the very end. "Lara?"

"He's stable enough to move," the healer said, lines of strain flaring at the corners of her eyes. "But there's so much damage. The bullet shards ripped through most of his major organs."

Hawke said nothing as he carried Drew, with Riaz at his heels with Indigo. He simply concentrated on gathering strength from his blood bond with his lieutenants. It flowed in from Riley, from Riaz, from all of them across the state, strong and pure and given freely. He even felt Judd's cool energy as the Psy male responded in spite of his unconscious state. "We can't lose them, Lara."

Andrew was one of the "heart" pieces of the pack, those wolves who connected them all to each other in a way that was difficult to explain, but integral to the functioning of a healthy pack. Losing him would cut that heart wide open, leave them all bleeding . . . and losing Indigo would crush what hope remained. She was one of SnowDancer's strongest support pillars, the woman everyone—even Hawke—went to for advice.

"We won't," Lara said as they reached the infirmary, and she began to work, using both her healing gifts and her skill as a medical practitioner. Her assistant, Lucy, chased out everyone except Hawke, who stayed with one hand on Lara's shoulder to ease her access to the Pack energy inside him— and of course Indigo, who had woken long enough to collapse into a chair at the top of the bed, her hand on Drew's head.

It took hours.

Indigo came to consciousness again toward the end. He met her namesake eyes, saw that they were devoid of tears. He understood. Now was not the time to cry. Now was the time to fight. Finally, deep in the early hours of morning, he felt Lara stop drawing from him, from his lieutenants.

Her normally tan-brown skin holding a tinge of gray, she nodded at Indigo. "Tell him to stay in wolf form for the time being."

Indigo didn't argue, just said the words, and Hawke knew she'd be sending the force of her command down the mating bond as well. "Don't you dare shift until I say it's okay." Her voice was taut, her will absolute. "Lara?"

"I think I got the major damage," the healer said, her body trembling from the exertion.

Hawke tugged Lara to the warmth of his body. "He finally got Indigo to accept the mating bond," he said. "Do you really think the damn stubborn wolf will give that up?"

That made Lara's lips curve a little and she rested against him as Lucy started to clean up. But she only allowed herself a short break. "I don't think we should move him, but we need to change this sheet. I have just about enough energy left for that."

"Hold on." Releasing her after a small squeeze, he moved around to slide his arms under the body of the large silver wolf as Indigo did the same for his head. "Lucy?"

The trainee nurse, her eyes red with unshed tears, nodded. "Ready."

As they lifted, she whipped out the bloodied sheet and slipped in a new one, with Lara helping from the other side. It only took a few seconds, and Drew didn't stir once.

# CHAPTER 45

**Shoshanna put down** the incident report. "Your unit failed."

"Yes." The only positive news was that the highly intelligent man who'd organized the operation had made it out alive. "We won't get another chance. They're continuing to dismantle the surveillance and they've further strengthened their security."

"You should have hit the wolf alpha in the city."

Henry wondered if his wife thought she was in charge of their "partnership" again. But he said nothing on that point. Let Shoshanna lull herself into a false sense of superiority. It would, in the end, make her easier to kill. "Such an operation would not have fit in with our long-range plan."

As that plan included taking the city and its resources as cleanly as possible, Shoshanna had to agree with her husband. "The others?"

"My men were ordered to eliminate the DarkRiver alpha, but as our surveillance efforts were focused on the wolves, they could not get to him. It appears he spends most of his time away from the city at present."

"Protecting his unborn child," Shoshanna said. "A child that should not exist."

"Be that as it may, we've tipped our hand and they are now all on high alert." Henry's head gleamed mahogany dark under the lights as he rose to his feet. "It may be time to change the long-range plan."

Shoshanna wasn't Henry's wife except in the legal sense, but she'd worked with him long enough to comprehend his meaning. "You want to sacrifice San Francisco."

Henry turned from the window. "It will cause economic chaos on a mass scale, but that can be managed once we remove the roots of the trouble."

Shoshanna considered their options. An all-out war would have a serious impact on the world, including on the businesses that had backed the Scotts to date, but by the same token, a clean strike would eliminate ninety percent of the problem. "How strong is your army?"

"Give me two more months."

And then, Shoshanna thought, San Francisco would burn.

# CHAPTER 46

**Indigo sat in** the curve of her father's arm on the edge of the White Zone forty-eight hours after the shooting. She hadn't wanted to leave Drew even for an instant, but Lara had pulled in Hawke, and her alpha had ordered Indigo to take a break or he'd carry her out.

"I'd decided on him," she told her father. "My wolf had decided on him, but he didn't know." There had been too many people around before he went up for his security shift, and she'd wanted it to be a special, private moment. "I was going to tell him when he got home, but—"

Her father stroked a big hand over her hair, slow and easy. "Do you think he didn't know when the bond snapped into place?"

"I just keep thinking if I'd accepted the bond earlier, I could've—"

"You held him," her father said, his voice stern. "That's all a mate can do in that situation. You did it. You're still doing it."

"Drew's in my heart. So deep," she said, "until the thought of losing him feels like razors cutting across my soul."

"It's who we are, pumpkin."

She knew the childhood nickname was meant to make her smile. Nothing could. But she accepted the comfort of his hold. "All this time, this was what I was so scared of—of loving someone this much and losing them."

Abel brushed her hair off her face. "You were always going to love with all your soul, sweetheart. You're built that way."

"So is he," she whispered. "There's so much love in him, Dad." The mating bond showed her a depth of feeling, of heart, even greater than she'd imagined. He was someone special, Andrew Liam Kincaid, and he was hers. "I wish you could see him as I do."

"That would be against the laws of nature," Abel said in a somber tone. "I have to be able to kick his ass if necessary—therefore, I must see him as the filthy bastard who dared hurt my daughter by getting himself shot."

"Are you threatening my mortally wounded mate?"

Her father pressed a kiss to her temple. "I'll hold off until he's healthy."

About to respond, she caught a gentle scent as familiar to her as her own. "Evie's here."

"Of course she is."

Her sister's embrace almost brought moisture to Indigo's eyes, but she swallowed back the tears. She would not cry. To do so would be a surrender. And she refused to give Drew up.

**Having just spent** an hour beside Drew's motionless form, Hawke pressed his palms to the wall outside the infirmary, wanting to do some damage, find his revenge, but knowing that even if he was able to get his hands around Councilor Henry Scott's neck this instant, it wouldn't help Drew.

Logic didn't matter to his wolf. It was enraged and—

A scent. Rich and exotic. Sandpaper across his skin.

He stayed still, hoping like hell she'd pass by.

But she stopped and to his shock, put a hesitant hand on his back. "Is he . . . ?"

He didn't turn, knowing that if he looked at her right now, he might do things that could never be taken back. "He's stable, but otherwise, no change."

Her fingernails scraped against his T-shirt as she curled her hand into a fist. "He'll be okay, though, won't he?"

She was asking him for reassurance, and had it been any other member of the pack, he would've turned and taken them into his arms. But this was Sienna Lauren, and he couldn't trust himself around her. "He's strong." When her hand dropped from his back, he felt the loss like a knife wound. "Lara's hopeful—and your uncle's worked on him, too, helped repair some of the microscopic damage." But the bullet fragments had caused so much harm that even Judd couldn't be sure he'd found every lethal cut and nick.

Sienna nodded and he just caught the movement with his peripheral vision. As he watched, she went to the door of the infirmary and slipped in. Only then did he push off the wall, his muscles taut as iron.

It was agonizingly tempting to give in to his wolf, to run until the violent emotions within him were exhausted to silence, but he was alpha. And there was work to be done. One of the most important things was ensuring that every single surveillance device within the entirety of den territory had been found and destroyed. SnowDancer, in concert with DarkRiver, had already launched an all-out search, but there was still a chance of overlooking one or two.

"Do you have anyone who can help us be certain the land is clear?" Hawke asked Lucas on the phone a few minutes later, thinking about the Psy members of the leopard pack.

Lucas didn't. But he made a discreet inquiry, which led him to ask Hawke an odd question. "The devices you've found all have metallic components?"

Hawke checked with Brenna. "Yeah, there's at least a little metal in some form or another in every single one of these things."

"Give me a few minutes."

When Lucas called back, it was with an offer of assistance from one hell of an unexpected source. Devraj Santos, director of the Shine Foundation and one of the Forgotten—

descendants of those Psy who'd dropped out of the Net before Silence—had volunteered his services.

"How is he going to find them?" Hawke asked, his wolf unwilling to put its faith in a man he hadn't ever met. "And what does the metal have to do with it?"

The leopard alpha sounded annoyed when he answered. "He won't say, but I trust him. The Forgotten hate the Council even more than we do."

That much was true, and it made him consider Santos's offer. "What does he want in exchange?" Hawke knew of Shine, knew Santos wielded considerable power. No man kept that many people safe from the Council's assassins by doing good deeds for free.

"We're already linked to Shine," Lucas said. "He wants some kind of relationship with SnowDancer."

"No alliance." Hawke didn't ally with anyone he didn't know inside out. "But we'll owe him one if he can deliver." A favor from SnowDancer was worth a hell of a lot.

Dev Santos agreed to the deal.

It took the Shine director a week of eighteen-hour days— the man located the cameras unerringly even in the blackest darkness and across immense distances—to clear their entire territory.

Hawke decided to up the favor count to Santos's benefit.

"I occasionally need to 'disappear' people when the Council gets too interested in them," the man said afterward. "Can't think of any place better than in a pack of wolves. You're so secretive, I had to sign my name in blood in triplicate before being allowed to set foot on your land."

"No promises," Hawke said, "but contact me when you need a disappearance and we'll talk." There were hundreds of places across the state controlled by wolves where a man or woman could vanish and not be found. And Dev Santos's people had Psy genes; as the man himself had shown, those genes could prove very useful.

Devraj Santos held out a hand.

Hawke's wolf decided they could deal with the man. They shook.

# CHAPTER 47

**Indigo touched her** lips to Drew's. They were soft, warm, as if he was simply resting. He'd shifted into human form spontaneously earlier that morning, and they were all hoping that meant he was about to break through the comalike sleep that had held him in thrall. She hated seeing him so quiet, so still.

Drew was never quiet. He was energy and life and mischief.

"Indigo?" Lara asked. "You okay?"

"Yes." *No.* "What's this?" she asked, distracting the healer by gesturing at something on Drew's bedside table.

"What?"

She held up a small yellow action figure, complete with fangs and claws.

"Ben." Lara smiled. "He keeps sneaking in here and leaving his soldiers to 'guard' Drew."

"See, Drew," Indigo said as Lara left to check on Silvia, who was well on the way to recovery, "you have to wake up now. What's Ben going to play with if he gives you all his soldiers?"

She was brushing Drew's hair off his face when she caught Riley's scent. The other lieutenant came in and took his brother's hand. "How is he?"

Riley always asked her, not Lara. Because he was mated. And he'd almost lost his mate once. "Strong," Indigo said, "so strong that when I fall asleep, I swear he's curled up around me." Sometimes she woke feeling as if she'd been rubbing her face against thick, lustrous fur the shade of silver-birch bark. It comforted her in sleep . . . and caused incredible desolation when she woke.

Meeting her gaze in silent understanding, Riley leaned down to whisper something in Drew's ear before leaving several minutes later. Brenna had already been by that morning and would likely return again within the hour.

Lara touched Indigo's shoulder some time afterward. "Come have a cup of coffee."

Indigo shook her head.

"Fine, then I'm pulling rank," Lara said in a steely voice. "You will get up right now, sit your ass down at my desk, and eat what I put in front of you."

Startled, Indigo stared at Lara. "You can only pull rank when a pack member is in danger of harming herself." In that situation, Lara outranked even Hawke.

Lara poked Indigo in the ribs. "When was the last time you ate?" She didn't wait for a response. "If you don't do this voluntarily, I'll call Hawke and Riaz and have them hog-tie you to a chair. Then I'll spoon-feed you, and after that, I'll pump you full of narcotics so that you get at least eight solid hours of rest."

Indigo's wolf wanted to snarl, but it loved the pack healer too much. "You play mean, Lara." Bending down, she pressed her lips to Drew's. "I'll be back after I satisfy General Lara." It was hard to pull herself away, harder still to stuff food down her gullet.

It took her ten minutes—because Lara refused to let her go until she'd finished every bite. "Drew, sweetie, I have some bad news," Lara said, after Indigo returned to his side. "Your mate's lost twenty pounds and looks like a fish stick. You're going to find yourself mated to a skeleton if you don't open those baby blues."

Indigo scowled, but her response was lost in a rush of noise as Riley, Brenna, and Judd all returned, along with Hawke and a couple of the teenagers who'd gone up into the mountains with her and Drew. Too many people—but this was how they healed.

By touch. By Pack.

Hawke asked Lara for an update, and the healer began to speak, but Indigo was focused only on Drew . . . and her wolf caught it the instant his breathing changed.

Then she heard the sweetest sound of all.

"Where's Indy?" It was a groggy question.


**A whirl of** sounds and scents crashed against Andrew's senses. He felt Lara's warm hands on his face, his chest, heard his sister's cry of welcome, saw Hawke's distinctive hair glint in the light, but—

*There she was.*

"Hey." Memories tumbled into him, pain and anguish . . . and the incredible power of someone holding him to life.

*His mate.*

She didn't say a word, just pushed past Lara to crawl into bed beside him, her face buried in his neck. His heart almost stopped. She'd done it in front of everyone, his strong, private, incredibly proud mate. And then he didn't care, because he could feel damp heat against his skin. "Out," he snapped.

Everyone left.

"Indy, please don't cry." He couldn't stand it. Indigo was tough to her bones; he'd never seen her cry. "Please, baby, please."

Her hand clenched on his shoulder, her tears heartbreakingly silent.

He stroked one hand into her hair, a little lost, but determined to give his mate what she needed. "I promise not to get shot again. Twice in one lifetime should be enough to fulfill anyone's quota." He kissed the parts of her face he could see, her ear, the corner of her eye. "Baby, you have to stop."

His wolf was going insane inside him, scratching and clawing in distress. Giving in to the animal—and ignoring the sharp aches and twinges of his body—he shifted to take her mouth in a kiss that was a passionate mix of apology, possession, and sheer tenderness. When he finally allowed her to breathe, her eyes glittered up at him, a bright, brilliant indigo.

Unable to bear the sight of the tear trails that marked her cheeks, he kissed them off. "I'm sorry," he said against her lips.

"You should be." A husky reprimand, his Indigo coming back to sparking life. "If you make me go through that again"—her fingers clenching in his hair, holding him close—"so help me, God, I'm going to kick your ass three ways to Sunday."

He bent his head and let her tell him off, hiding the wolf's smile against her neck. Because her hands were stroking over his body even as she spoke, her legs locked around him. Sighing because he was home, he closed his eyes and gave in to the demands of his bruised and battered body.

**Indigo knew the** instant Drew fell asleep, sprawled over her in a big, gorgeous spread of muscled male flesh. Feeling her throat thicken again at the thought of how close she'd come to losing him, she pressed a kiss to his temple and forced herself to unhook her legs from around him, afraid she'd put pressure on his wounds.

"Is it safe to come in?" It was a whisper from the doorway.

Indigo nodded at Lara. "He's out."

Lara tiptoed in—though Indigo had a feeling Drew was well and truly down for the count—and ran her hands over his body. "He's fine." Relieved words. "His body's healing the remaining damage at its own pace, and I'm going to let it. It'll ensure he rests."

"I'll make sure he does exactly as you order." Indigo's hands tightened in Drew's hair. "God, but he's got me good." It was a heart-shuddering jolt, the rush of emotion she'd finally allowed herself to feel now that he was safe.

Lara hitched herself up to sit on the bed. "We're all jealous, you know, all the unmated women." A smile full of the wolf's laughter. "Not only is he a strong, younger male who'll probably drive you ragged in bed—"

Indigo's glare had no effect.

"—he adores the ground you walk on." The healer placed one hand on the back of Drew's shoulder in gentle affection. "I'd cut off my right arm to have a man look at me the way Drew looks at you."

"Sorry, he's mine." The sudden, violent need to hold him close, to quench her thirst for him, had her scowling at Lara's hand.

The healer lifted it off with a grin. "How are you going to get out from under him?"

Indigo tried to shift Drew off a fraction. He grumbled in his sleep and shoved a hand under her T-shirt to cup her breast as he snuggled his face deeper into her neck. Looking up to see Lara trying not to burst out laughing, Indigo felt her own lips twitch. "Maybe you should lock the door on your way out."

The healer did just that . . . and Indigo decided she'd earned some time off. Hooking one leg carefully over Drew's uninjured side, she put her arms around the heavy heat of him and let sleep sweep her under.

**Indigo left Drew** to brief Hawke on an unexpected message Drew discovered on his phone when he rose again and was able to check his messages. As a result, she found herself at a highly secure and private location three days later, about to take part in a meeting none of them could've dreamed up, even in their wildest, most insane dreams.

Hawke sat on one side of the table, Riley to his left and a heavily pregnant Sascha Duncan to his right, with her mate, Lucas, next to her. Indigo, DarkRiver sentinels Nathan and Dorian, and a still-healing but stubborn Drew, held up the wall at their back, while Riaz was standing watch outside the meeting room with Mercy by his side.

Across from them sat Councilors Nikita Duncan and Anthony Kyriakus. Nikita had Max Shannon to her right, with Max's wife, Sophia, sitting beside him; while Anthony had a tall, brown-eyed, brown-skinned young man next to him. Tanique Gray was apparently Anthony's son and Faith's half brother, and, from the looks of things, he had chosen to ally himself with his father in adulthood.

Indigo's job was to protect her alpha, and to that aim, she kept her eyes resolutely on the threat posed by the Councilors. She had, she thought, never brushed against so cold a personality as that of Nikita Duncan. Even Anthony Kyriakus, for all his power, didn't ruffle her wolf's fur as badly.

"I suppose someone needs to speak first," Sascha said, her voice the only sound in the silence.

Nikita Duncan gave a single short nod to acknowledge her daughter's words. But it was Lucas who spoke next. "We all know why we're here. This territory belongs—in some part or another—to all of us."

Nikita looked straight at the DarkRiver alpha. "That territory is now under threat."

Indigo could sense Hawke exercising savage control to rein in his instinctive and feral dislike of the Councilors. The Council had almost destroyed SnowDancer once, and none of them would ever trust its members again.

"You"—Nikita glanced from Hawke to Lucas—"were both targeted, because your deaths would've sent your packs into at least temporary disarray."

Neither alpha said anything, though they'd figured out that much for themselves.

"Take down SnowDancer and DarkRiver," Anthony added, his tone measured, calm, "and you crack the city's defenses."

Indigo wasn't fooled by his outwardly mild demeanor. According to SnowDancer's research, the reclusive Councilor had access to a network of F-Psy stronger than any other. Anthony Kyriakus knew more secrets than anyone else in this room, and she was quite certain the Councilor didn't hesitate to use those secrets to leverage power when necessary.

Riley broke his silence to say, "Our information is that the Council is at war." The statement was a test. Judd had already confirmed the rumors. Now, Indigo waited to see what Nikita would say.

Sascha's mother didn't even blink as she answered. "Henry, Shoshanna, and possibly Tatiana have decided that Silence must hold at all costs. They seek to eliminate anyone who goes against that rhetoric."

Riley spoke again, his tone so calm, you'd think they were discussing the watch rotation. "Why share that when the Council prefers to keep its secrets?"

"The reason they're focusing on this city, this state," Anthony responded, "is because both Nikita and I call it home, as do the two most powerful changeling packs in the country. Given all that—take this city, and they take the country."

True, Indigo thought. Because even if Anthony or Nikita survived an attack, Henry and the others, having proven their strength on this battleground, would continue to claim city after city, state after state.

"Why target us at all?" Hawke asked, and Indigo knew his wolf was weighing all the options with cold, hard focus. Part of what made Hawke such a good alpha was that no matter how savage his emotions, both man and wolf never stopped thinking. "What makes them think we'd care one way or another about an internal Psy war?"

Sascha was the one who spoke, her gaze locked to her mother's. "Because of me, because of Faith." Quiet words from a woman who'd once been viciously rejected by the Councilor in front of her. "DarkRiver's emotional connection to us, the pack's inability to sit by and let our parents die, will have been factored into their calculations."

"It's more than that," Max said as Drew shifted his position a fraction, placing his weight on his other foot.

Indigo moved her body a tiny increment to the left to support him if necessary. A pulse of love came down the mating bond, an affectionate caress that "tasted" of Drew. It was still new, that intimate connection, but it was already so much a part of her life that she couldn't imagine how she'd existed without it.

Wrapping her mate's love around herself, she watched Nikita shoot her security chief a cool glance, but the human male shook his head, a grim line to his jaw. "They need all the information," he said to Nikita. "Otherwise, Hawke will be more than happy to throw us to"—a wry grin—"the wolves."

Nikita took several seconds to reply. "It appears Mr. Shannon is correct. They are targeting all of us because I am seen as too liberal in my business dealings with you." Another pause, and then she met her daughter's eyes. "And because I no longer support the Protocol."

Quiet, so quiet Indigo could hear the heartbeat of every person in the room.

Even that of the child in Sascha's womb.

# CHAPTER 48

**They'd all heard** the rumors, seen the Psy coming into the city, but for Nikita to admit it . . .

"What are you saying, Mother?" Sascha asked at last. "Are you advocating the fall of Silence?"

"Silence cannot fall with such quickness," Nikita retorted, "not without immense devastation. But it is starting to crumble at the edges—and I have never stayed on a sinking ship in my life. I'm unlikely to start now."

Sascha moved a little in her chair, one hand on the hard mound of her belly. "No, you've always known how to ride the tides."

"You haven't mentioned Ming or Kaleb," Lucas pointed out, massaging his mate's lower back unobtrusively as he spoke.

Nikita turned her eyes to the DarkRiver alpha. "Kaleb is highly unpredictable and may, in the end, double-cross everyone, but he doesn't stay on sinking ships, either. Ming is having issues of his own and is more concerned with that than taking over this or any territory."

"Henry and Shoshanna are the strongest advocates of Silence proceeding as it has for the past century," Anthony added. "They want to increase the involuntary reconditionings, force those who are fractured to submit—or face total rehabilitation."

Max's wife, Sophia, spoke for the first time. "By refusing to sign my rehabilitation warrant, Nikita sent a signal that she was no longer toeing the party line. It has left her . . . unpopular."

"If the packs step back in a public fashion," Sascha said, to Indigo's surprise, "make it clear we're not allied with you, what will happen?"

Tension gripped the room.

"They may leave you alone," Anthony said, "come after Nikita and me in force."

"But I wouldn't bet on it," Max added, pushing back strands of his jet-black hair. "From what Sophie here tells me, far as the PsyNet is concerned, this area is *already* seen to be functioning as a cohesive unit. There's a hell of a lot more cross-pollination than in any other sector."

Indigo thought of the connections that tied the people in this room to each other and knew Max Shannon was right. There was also the fact that both packs had proven themselves a threat to even the most powerful Psy. No matter what, the other Councilors would not leave them in peace.

Nikita spoke into the quiet, her words directed at her daughter. "That is a decision your emotional nature would never allow you to make," she said with icy practicality, "so why did you ask the question?"

"I have a child to protect now, Mother." Soft, powerful words. "Priorities change."

Nikita said nothing, and Indigo's wolf wanted to claw at her. Because that wolf understood only family, knew that its own mother would never look at her child with such coldness.

"But," Sascha said, "it doesn't matter how we try to distance ourselves. Max is right—we're all connected now.

We all call this region home. They can't attack one without affecting the other."

That, Andrew thought, leaning a little on his mate as his body began to protest at being forced upright for this long, was the crux of it all.

*The enemy of my enemy is my friend.*

Andrew wouldn't go that far, but he could almost see Hawke calculating the possible options before saying, "We'd be more apt to take you seriously if you gave us information we could actually use." It was a challenge.

"Henry and Shoshanna are assembling an army," Anthony said, meeting Hawke's gaze. "They've got a few Arrows on their side, along with all those who believe in Purity."

"They lost people when they came after Hawke"—Riley's steady voice again—"and at least one of them was a teleport-capable telekinetic."

"A scarce resource," Anthony agreed. "It may prove a setback to their plans—but a small one. As Tks have one of the most dangerous abilities, they tend to most strongly embrace the Protocol."

Giving the Scotts a powerful pool of assassins.

"Ming and Kaleb may assist us when the Scotts strike," Nikita added. "But only if that assistance serves their own interests."

"Some assistance," Hawke said, "we don't need."

Andrew agreed. Ming LeBon, by all accounts, was a sociopath masquerading as a Councilor. Kaleb Krychek was harder to pin down, which might simply mean he was better at hiding his crimes—because according to the intel Andrew had unearthed, Kaleb Krychek had been mentored by the same sadistic killer who'd not only tortured Brenna, but killed a number of other young changeling women.

"Yes," Nikita said, "so any defensive measures we take will have to be based on our own resources. I have a not insignificant pool of strong telepaths under my direct command, but the primary asset I bring to the table is my considerable economic strength. I am already in the process of strangling some of the Scotts' finances."

Anthony, it went without saying, brought his foreseers to the table.

"Have you considered a preemptive strike?" Hawke asked, and Andrew recalled the "warning tap" they'd discussed not long ago.

Anthony nodded. "However, they have a strong advantage on home ground. The opposite is true here."

A long, silent pause broken by Hawke. "Another meeting. One week."

"Very well." Anthony inclined his head, the threads of silver at his temples catching the light. "There is one more thing you should know. Every strong F-Psy in the NightStar Group has made at least one spontaneous nonbusiness prediction over the past month, a highly unusual event."

"What did they see?" Lucas asked.

"Blood and death and fire. Over and over, with no alternate futures logged. Whatever we decide at the next meeting, I do not believe any of us will escape the coming holocaust."

**Drew patted Indigo's** butt as she lay sprawled over him later that night. "I think I'm dead." He squeezed her toned flesh with blatant possessiveness. "And this is my idea of heaven."

Well aware she had to keep a watch on those sneaky steamroller tactics of his, Indigo gave a halfhearted growl, but she was too sated to work up any real outrage.

"I like seeing you this way." He petted her ass again before beginning to draw designs on her lower back with a desultory finger. "All pleasured and warm and mine."

Possessive demon. But she was the same, so she couldn't complain. Yawning, she snuggled closer, her eyes heavy lidded. His body was hot and muscled under her touch, his heartbeat still a little erratic, and his scent . . .

Her wolf rolled into a happy little ball, but she dragged up the willpower to say, "I thought Lara ordered you to rest." He'd literally ambushed her as she walked in the door, his mouth on hers and his body inside hers before she could corral her brain cells into objecting.

He kissed her again. "I decided pouncing on you sounded like more fun."

Smiling against his mouth, she stroked her hand over his ribs. "That was some meeting, huh?"

"Especially that last comment by Anthony." Shifting to accommodate Indigo when she tangled her legs with his, Andrew played his fingers through her hair. "Cats say Faith confirmed the prediction." And Faith NightStar was the strongest foreseer in or out of the PsyNet.

Indigo circled a finger over his chest. "Whatever happens, we'll handle it. SnowDancer hasn't survived this long to fall to the Councilors' megalomania." Another lazy circle. "I couldn't read Hawke—guess we'll find out what he thinks at the lieutenant meeting tomorrow."

"I kept expecting him to get up and tear out someone's jugular today."

Indigo laughed. "You sound so disappointed."

"He's acting reasonable. It's vaguely terrifying."

This time, Indigo's laughter was long and deep. Shifting onto her back, she untangled their legs and looped her arms around his neck as he rose over her. "You're terrible, you know that?"

"That's why you love me." Rubbing his nose against hers, he felt his wolf stretch out inside him in naked pleasure.

She nipped at his chin, dropped a kiss onto his lips. "Yeah. The day you begin behaving, I'll know I have an impostor on my hands." Playing her fingers into his hair, she swung a leg over his hip. "I've been thinking about what we're going to do with the traveling you have to do for your position in the pack."

"My team's got things under control for now," Drew said, his eyes such a clear blue that she felt bathed in sunlight.

"But they need you." Pride was a fierce beat inside of her, for this wolf who was smart enough, strong enough, to reach their most vulnerable. "With Riaz here, in the den, I can come on a lot of the trips with you."

Drew blinked, his lashes long and beautiful. "If Riley is Hawke's right arm, you're his left. He needs you here. Especially now."

"I've spoken to him." She pulled him down against her, enjoying the all over contact. Such exquisite skin privileges.

"We won't be gone for months at a time; you've got your network set up now."

"That's true. But I'm still going to need to make a lot of short trips—especially to San Diego. Seb is damn strong," he said of his replacement in that sector, "but he's younger than me."

"We can play those times by ear," Indigo said, knowing she'd miss him when he was away, but also knowing the mating bond would ensure she was never lonely.

A long, quiet pause. Then, "Indy?"

Hearing the edge in his tone, she nuzzled a kiss against his neck. "What is it?"

"You were put in a situation where you had to accept the mating bond," Drew said, shadows whispering over the clarity of his gaze when she looked up. "Do you regret it?"

She knew exactly how much it had to have cost him to ask that. "The only thing I regret is not being able to end the mating dance as I planned."

A spark in the blue. "You had a plan?"

"Uh-huh."

"Tell." Fingers dancing over her abdomen, threatening to tickle.

"Well," she said, brushing her lips against his ear, "it involved tying you naked to my bed, having my wicked way with you in revenge for all your crazy-making tactics . . . and then telling you that you belong to me. Forever. No outs. No givebacks."

Drew thrust his hand into her hair, his gaze gone that startling wolf-copper. "Tell me now."

She did. And then, because she was in a good mood and she adored him and he'd taught her about opening her heart, she whispered more love words in his ear, until he broke every single one of Lara's rules and drove them both to heaven a second time around.

Turn the page for a special preview
of Nalini Singh's next Guild Hunter Novel

# Archangel's Consort

Coming February 2011 from
Berkley Sensation!

**Swathed in the** silken shadows of deepest night, New York was the same . . . and altered beyond compare. Once, Elena had watched angels take flight from the light-filled column of the Tower as she sat in front of the distant window of her cherished apartment. Now, she was one of those angels, perched high atop a balcony that had no railing, nothing to prevent a deadly fall.

Except, of course, she would no longer fall.

Her wings were stronger now. She was stronger.

Flaring out those wings, she took a deep breath of the air of home. A fusion of scents—spice and smoke, human and vampire, earthy and sophisticated—hit her with the wild fever of a welcoming rainstorm. Her chest, tight for so long, relaxed, and she stretched her wings out to their greatest width. It was time to explore this familiar place that had become a foreign land, this home that was suddenly new again.

Diving down from the balcony, she swept across Manhattan on air currents kissed by the cool bite of spring. The bright green season had thawed the snows that had kept the city in thrall this winter, and now held court, summer not even a peach-colored blush on the horizon. This was the time of rebirth, of blooming things and baby birds, bright and young and fragile even in the frenetic rush of a city that never slept.

*Home. She was home.*

Letting the air currents sweep her where they would above the diamond-studded lights of the city, she tested her wings, tested her strength.

Stronger.

But still weak. An immortal barely Made.

One whose heart remained painfully mortal.

So it was no surprise when she found herself trying to hover outside the plate-glass window of her apartment. She didn't yet have the skill to execute the maneuver, and she kept dropping, then having to pull herself back up with fast wing beats. Still, she saw enough in those fleeting glimpses to know that while the once-shattered glass had been flawlessly repaired, the rooms were empty.

There wasn't even a bloodstain on the carpet to mark the spot where she'd spilled Raphael's blood, where she'd tried to staunch the crimson river until her fingers were the same murderous shade.

*Elena.*

The scent of the wind and the rain, fresh and wild, around her, inside her, and then strong hands on her hips as Raphael held her effortlessly in position so she could look through the window, her hands flat on the glass.

Emptiness.

No sign remained of the home she'd created piece by precious piece.

"You must teach me the hovering," she said, forcing herself to speak past the knot of loss. It was just a place. Just things. "It'll be a very good way to spy on potential targets."

"I intend to teach you many things." Tugging her back against his body, her wings trapped in between, the Archangel of New York pressed his lips to the tip of her ear. "You are full of sorrow."

It was instinct to lie, to protect herself, but they'd gone

beyond that, she and her archangel. "I guess I somehow expected my apartment to still be here. Sara didn't say anything when she sent me my things." And her best friend had never lied to her.

"It was as you left it when Sara visited," Raphael said, drawing back enough that she could flare out her wings and angle her body into the air currents once again. *Come, I have something to show you.*

The words were in her mind, along with the wind and the rain. She didn't order him to get out—because she knew he wasn't in it. This, the way she could sense him so deeply, speak to him with such ease, was part of whatever it was that tied them to each other . . . that taut, twisting emotion that ripped away old scars and created new vulnerabilities in a whip of fire across the soul.

But as she watched him fly through the lush black of the sky high over the glittering city, her archangel with his wings of white-gold and eyes of endless, relentless blue, she wasn't sorry. She didn't want to turn back the clock, didn't want to return to a life in which she'd never been held in the arms of an archangel, never felt her heart tear open and reform into something stronger, capable of such furies of emotion that it scared her at times. *Where are you taking me, Archangel?*

*Patience, Guild Hunter.*

She smiled, her grief at the loss of her apartment buried under a wave of amusement. No matter how many times he decreed that her loyalty was now to the angels and not to the Hunters Guild, he kept betraying how he saw her—as a hunter, as a warrior. Shooting down below him, she dove and then rose through the biting freshness of the air with hard, strong wing beats. Her back and shoulder muscles protested the acrobatics, but she was having too much fun to worry— she'd pay for it in a few hours, no doubt about it, but for now, she felt free and protected in the dark.

"Do you think anyone is watching?" she asked, breathless from the exertion, once they were side by side once more.

"Perhaps. But the darkness will conceal your identity for the moment."

Tomorrow, she knew, when light broke, the circus would

begin. An angel-Made . . . Even the oldest of vampires and the angels themselves found her a curiosity. She had no doubts about how the human population would react. "Can't you do your scary thing and make them keep their distance?" However, even as she spoke, she knew it wasn't the reaction of the general population that worried her.

Her father . . . No. She wouldn't think about Jeffrey. Not tonight.

As she forced away thoughts of the man who had repudiated her when she'd been barely eighteen, Raphael swept out over the Hudson, dropping so hard and fast that she yelped before she could catch herself. The Archangel of New York was one hell of a flier—he skimmed along the water until he could've trailed his fingers in its rushing cold, before pulling himself up in a steep ascent. Showing off.

For her.

It made her heart lighten, her lips curve.

Dipping down to join him at a lower altitude, she watched the night winds whip that sleek ebony hair across his face, as if they could not resist touching him.

*It will do no good.*

"What?" Fascinated by the almost cruel beauty of him, this male she dared call her lover, she'd forgotten what she'd asked him.

*For me to scare them away—you are not a woman to stay in seclusion.*

"Damn. You're right." Feeling her shoulder muscles begin to pull in ominous warning, she winced. "I think I need to set down soon." Her body had been damaged in the fight against Lijuan. Not much, and the injuries had healed, but the enforced rest period meant she'd lost some of the muscle she'd built up prior to the fight that had turned Beijing into a crater, its voice the silent cry of the dead.

*We're almost home.*

Concentrating on keeping herself heading in a straight line, she realized he'd shifted position so she was effectively riding his wake—meaning she no longer had to make as much effort to hold herself aloft. Pride had her scrunching her face into a scowl, but contrasting with that was a deep warmth that came from knowing she was important, more than important, to Raphael.

And then she saw it, the sprawling mansion that was Raphael's cliff-top home on the other side of the river. Though the land backed up against the Hudson, the place was hidden from casual view by a thick verge of trees. However, they were coming at it from above, and from there it looked like a jewel set in the velvet darkness, warm golden light in every window—turning into pulses of color where it hit the clean lines of the stained glass on one side of the building. The rose bushes weren't visible from this angle, but she knew they were there, their leaves lush and glossy against the elegant white of the house, hundreds of buds ready to bloom in a profusion of color as the weather grew warmer.

She followed Raphael down as he landed in the yard, the light from the stained glass turning his wings into a kaleidoscope of wild blue, crystalline green, and ruby red. *You could've landed on one of the balconies,* she said, too focused on ensuring a good landing to speak the words aloud.

Raphael didn't disagree, waiting until she was on the ground beside him to say, "I could have." Reaching out as she folded away her wings, he gripped her gently at the curve where her neck flowed into her shoulder, his fingers pressing into the sensitive inner seam of her right wing. "But then your lips would not have been so very close to mine."

Her toes curled as he tugged her forward, pleasure blooming in her stomach. "Not here," she murmured, voice husky. "I don't want to shock Jeeves."

Raphael kissed away her words with an unhurried thoroughness that had her forgetting all about his butler, her body warming with a slow, luscious sense of anticipation. *Raphael.*

*You tremble, Elena. You are tired.*

*Never too tired for your touch.* It terrified her how addicted she'd become to him. The only thing that made it bearable was that his hunger, too, was a raw, near-violent craving.

A lick of storm ran up against her senses before he drew back with a hotly sexual promise. *Later.* A slow, intimate stroke along the upper curve of her wing. *I would take my time with you.* His lips parted, his spoken words far less incendiary. "Montgomery will like having you for his mistress, Elena."

She licked her lips, tried to breathe—and heard the rapid tattoo of her heart against her ribs. Yeah, the archangel knew how to kiss. "Why?" she finally managed to say, falling into step beside him as he walked to the door.

"You're likely to get dirty and destroy your clothes on a regular basis." Raphael's humor was dry, his voice an exquisite caress in the night. "It is the same reason he likes it when Illium occasionally stays here. You both give him plenty to do."

She made a face at him, but her lips kicked up at the corners. "Is Illium coming to join us?" The blue-winged angel was part of Raphael's Seven, the vampires and angels who had given their loyalty to the Archangel of New York—even to the extent of placing his life before their own. Illium was the only one of the Seven who saw her human heart not as a weakness, but as a gift. And in him, she saw a kind of innocence that had been lost in the other immortals.

The door opened at that moment to expose the beaming face of Raphael's butler. "Sire," he said in a plummy English accent she was certain could turn cold and intimidating on command. "It is good to have you home."

"Montgomery." Raphael placed a hand on the vampire's shoulder as he passed.

Elena smiled at the butler, delighted by him all over again. "Hello."

"Mistress."

She blinked. "Elena," she said firmly. "I'm no one's mistress but my own." And for all that he chose to work in the service of an archangel, Montgomery was a strong vampire, hundreds of years old.

The butler's spine went stiff as a board, his eyes shooting to Raphael—who gave a languid smile. "You must not shock Montgomery so, Elena." Reaching out to take her hand, he tugged her to his side. "Perhaps you will allow him to call you Guild Hunter?"

Elena looked up, certain the archangel was laughing. But his expression was clear, his lips set with their familiar sensual grace. "Um, yes, okay." She nodded at Montgomery, then felt compelled to ask, "Will that do?"

"Of course, Guild Hunter." He gave a small bow and waved his hand. "I was not sure if you would wish a meal, Sire, but I have sent a small tray up to your rooms."

"That will be all for tonight, Montgomery."

As the butler whispered away, Elena looked with growing suspicion at a large Chinese vase in one corner of the hall, opposite the stained glass wall beside the door. It was decorated with a pattern of sunflowers that seemed oddly familiar. Letting go of Raphael's hand, she stepped closer . . . closer. Her eyes went wide. "This is mine!" Given as a gift by an angel in China after Elena completed a particularly dangerous hunt, one that had taken her into the bowels of the Shanghai underworld.

Raphael touched his fingers to the small of her back, a searing brand. "All of your things are here." He waited until she looked up before saying, "They were moved to this house for safekeeping until your return."

"However," he continued when she remained silent, her throat a knot of emotion, "it seems Montgomery could not help himself when it came to this vase. I'm afraid he has a weakness for beautiful things and has been known to relocate an item if he feels its beauty is not being properly appreciated. Once, he 'relocated' an ancient sculpture from the home of another archangel."

Elena stared down the corridor where the butler had disappeared in refined silence. "I don't believe you. He's too prim and proper." It was easier to say that, to focus on the humor, than to accept the tightness in her heart, the feelings locking up her throat.

"You would be surprised." Touching her lower back again, he nudged her down the hall and up a flight of stairs. "Come, you can look at your things in the morning."

She dragged her feet at the top of the staircase. "No."

Raphael measured her expression with those eyes no mortal would ever possess, a silent visual reminder that he had

never been human, would never be anything close to mortal.
"Such will." Leading her to a room that flowed off what she
knew to be the master bedroom, he opened the door.

Everything from her apartment lay neatly stacked, slipcov-
ers over the furnishings, her knickknacks in boxes.

She froze on the doorstep, uncertain how she felt—relief
and anger and joy all battled for space inside of her. She'd
known she could never go back to the apartment that had been
her haven, and more, a furious rebuttal against her father's
abandonment. The place wasn't built for a being with wings—
but the loss had hurt. So much.

Now . . . "Why?"

His hand closed around her nape with no attempt to hide
the possession inherent in the act. "You are mine, Elena. If
you choose to sleep in another bed, I will simply pick you up
and bring you home."

Arrogant words. But he was an archangel. And she'd made
a claim of her own. "As long as you remember that goes both
ways."

*Acknowledged, Guild Hunter.* A kiss pressed to the curve
of her shoulder, his fingers tightening on her nape just a fraction. *Come to bed.*

Arousal kicked her hard, her body knowing full well what
pleasure awaited her at those strong, lethal hands. "So we can
talk knives and sheaths?"

Sensual male laughter, another kiss, the caress of teeth.
But he released his hold, watching in silence as she stepped
into the room and ran her fingers over the delicately embroidered comforter on the bed that had been her own, before
she moved to explore the vanity with its store of pretty glass
bottles and brushes set tidily inside a small box. She felt like
a child, wanting to reassure herself that everything was there,
the need visceral enough to hurt.

As she gave in to that emotional hunger, her mind dis-
gorged images of another homecoming, of the shock and
humiliation that had burned her throat when she'd found her
things piled up like so much garbage on the street. Nothing
would ever erase that hurt, the pain of the knowledge that that

was exactly what she was to her father, but tonight, Raphael had crushed the memory under the weight of a far more powerful act.

She had no illusions about her archangel, knew he'd done it in part precisely for the reason he'd given her—so she wouldn't be tempted to treat her apartment as a bolt-hole. But had that been his sole motivation, he could as easily have sent her stuff to the dump. Instead, every single piece had been carefully packed and moved here. Some of it had been exposed to the elements when her window shattered that night, and yet now looked pristine, speaking of meticulous restoration.

Heart aching at the wonder of being so cherished, she said, "We can go now." She'd come back later, decide what to do with everything. "Raphael—thank you."

The brush of his wing against her own, a silent tenderness as they entered the master suite. No one else ever saw this part of him, she thought, eyes on her archangel as he moved closer to the bed and began to strip without flicking on the lights. His shirt fell off his body, revealing that magnificent chest she'd kissed her way across more than once. And suddenly, the overwhelming weight of her emotions was gone, buried under an avalanche of gut-wrenching need.

Raphael looked up at that moment, his gaze glittering with an earthy hunger that said he'd sensed her arousal. Deciding to save the talking for later, she was raising her fingers to tug off her own top when rain—no, *hail*—hit the windows in staccato bullets that made her jump. She'd have ignored it, except the hard little pellets of ice kept smashing into the glass over and over again. "Must be a storm." Dropping her hands, she walked to the one of the windows after glancing over to ensure the French doors to the balcony were secure.

Lighting flashed in vicious spikes in front of her as savage winds began to pound the house with unremitting fury, the hail turning to torrential rain between one blink and the next. "I've never seen it come in this hard, this fast."

Raphael walked to stand beside her, his naked upper body patterned with the image of the raindrops against the window.

She looked up when he didn't say anything, saw the shadows that had turned his gaze turbulent in an unexpected reflection of the storm. "What is it? What am I not seeing?" Because that look in his eyes . . .

"What do you know of recent weather patterns across the world?"

Elena traced a raindrop with her gaze as it tunneled across the glass. "I caught a weather update while we were at the Tower. The reporter said a tsunami had just hit the east coast of New Zealand, and that the floods in India are getting worse." Sri Lanka and the Maldives had apparently already been evacuated, but they were starting to run out of places to put people.

"Earthquakes have been rocking Elijah's territory," Raphael told her, speaking of the South American archangel, "and he fears that at least one major volcano is about to erupt. That is not all. Michaela tells me most of Europe is shuddering in the grip of an unseasonal ice storm so vicious, it threatens to kill thousands."

Elena's shoulder muscles went stiff at the mention of the most beautiful—and most venomous—of archangels. "The Middle East, at least," she said, forcing herself to relax, "seems to have escaped major catastrophe from what I saw on the news."

"Yes. Favashi is helping Neha deal with the disasters in her region."

The Archangel of Persia and the Archangel of India, Elena knew, had worked together previously. And now, when Neha hated almost everyone else in the Cadre, she seemed to be able to tolerate Favashi—perhaps because the other archangel was so much younger. "It means something, doesn't it?" she said, turning to place her hand on the wild heat of Raphael's chest, the shadowy raindrops whispering over her skin. "All this extreme weather."

"There is a legend," Raphael murmured, his wings flaring out as he tugged her into the curve of his body—as if he would protect her. "That mountains will shake and rivers overflow, while ice creeps across the world and fields drown in rain." He looked down at her, his eyes that impossible, inhuman chrome blue. "All this will come to pass . . . when an Ancient awakens."

The chill in his tone raised every hair on her body.

THE NEW BOOK IN THE GUILD HUNTER SERIES
FROM *NEW YORK TIMES* BESTSELLING AUTHOR

# NALINI SINGH

# ARCHANGEL'S KISS

Waking from a yearlong coma, vampire hunter Elena
Deveraux finds herself thrust into a darkly seductive
new life alongside her stunningly dangerous lover, the
archangel Raphael.

But another archangel has been waiting for Elena to
wake. Ancient and without conscience, Lijuan's power
lies with the reawakening of the dead—and she has
prepared the most perfect and most vicious of wel-
comes for Elena . . .

M642T0110

The New Psy-Changeling Novel from
*New York Times* Bestselling Author

## NALINI SINGH

# Bonds of Justice

Max Shannon is a good cop, one of the best in New York Enforcement. Born with a natural shield that protects him against Psy mental invasions, he knows he has little chance of advancement within the Psy-dominated power structure. The last case he expects to be assigned to is that of a murderer targeting a Psy Councilor's closest advisors. And the last woman he expects to compel him in the most sensual of ways is a Psy on the verge of a catastrophic mental fracture.

penguin.com

Book seven in the *New York Times* bestselling
Psy-Changeling series from

## NALINI SINGH

# Blaze of Memory

Dev Santos finds a woman with amnesia—all she can
remember is that she's dangerous. Stripped of her memories by a shadowy oppressor and programmed to kill,
Katya's only hope for sanity is Dev. But how can he trust
her when he could very well be her next target?

penguin.com

## Penguin Group (USA) Online

*What will you be reading tomorrow?*

Patricia Cornwell, Nora Roberts, Catherine Coulter,
Ken Follett, John Sandford, Clive Cussler,
Tom Clancy, Laurell K. Hamilton, Charlaine Harris,
J. R. Ward, W.E.B. Griffin, William Gibson,
Robin Cook, Brian Jacques, Stephen King,
Dean Koontz, Eric Jerome Dickey, Terry McMillan,
Sue Monk Kidd, Amy Tan, Jayne Ann Krentz,
Daniel Silva, Kate Jacobs...

You'll find them all at
**penguin.com**

*Read excerpts and newsletters,*
*find tour schedules and reading group guides,*
*and enter contests.*

Subscribe to Penguin Group (USA) newsletters
and get an exclusive inside look
at exciting new titles and the authors you love
long before everyone else does.

PENGUIN GROUP (USA)
penguin.com